THE GIRL IN THE PAINTING

ALSO BY TEA COOPER

The Cartographer's Secret

The Woman in the Green Dress

The Naturalist's Daughter

The Horse Thief

The House on Boundary Street

The Currency Lass

The Cedar Cutter

Lily's Leap

Matilda's Freedom

Forgotten Fragrance

THE GIRL IN THE PAINTING

TEA COOPER

THOMAS NELSON
Since 1798

The Girl in the Painting

Copyright © 2021 Tea Cooper

Original edition published in Australia in 2020 by Tea Cooper

Published in Nashville, Tennessee, by Thomas Nelson. Thomas Nelson is a registered trademark of HarperCollins Christian Publishing, Inc.

Thomas Nelson titles may be purchased in bulk for educational, business, fundraising, or sales promotional use. For information, please email SpecialMarkets@ThomasNelson.com.

Library of Congress Cataloging-in-Publication Data

Names: Cooper, Tea, author.
Title: The girl in the painting / Tea Cooper.
Description: Nashville, Tennessee : Thomas Nelson, [2021] | "Original edition of this book published in Australia in 2019 by Tea Cooper" | Summary: "Ranging from the gritty reality of the Australian goldfields to the grand institutions of Sydney, the bucolic English countryside to the charm of Maitland Town, this compelling historical mystery in the company of an eccentric and original heroine is rich with atmosphere and detail"-- Provided by publisher.
Identifiers: LCCN 2020037282 (print) | LCCN 2020037283 (ebook) | ISBN 9780785240334 (paperback) | ISBN 9780785240341 (epub) | ISBN 9780785240358
Classification: LCC PR9619.4.C659 G57 2021 (print) | LCC PR9619.4.C659 (ebook) | DDC 823/.92--dc23
LC record available at https://lccn.loc.gov/2020037282
LC ebook record available at https://lccn.loc.gov/2020037283

Printed in the United States of America
21 22 23 24 25 LSC 5 4 3 2 1

Charles—this is as much your book as it is mine.
Thank you.

ONE

MAITLAND TOWN, AUSTRALIA, 1906

The bell rang late. Not until after 7:18. This didn't bode well.

Jane scrambled out of bed, clambered into her Sunday best, and wrangled her hateful lisle stockings up above her knees. Sister Mary Ann wasn't one for patience. *"Before breakfast,"* she'd said.

"What're you galloping around for—you're not going to miss out. It's Sunday. Wine and wafers first." Lydia Lie-All-You-Like Lewis rolled over and buried her head under her pillow.

"She wants me downstairs." Leaving her unmade bed, Jane clattered down the twenty-nine timber stairs to where Sister Mary Ann stood waiting, her black habit flapping like a bedraggled crow.

For the first time in her memory Jane had a clear conscience, although she'd known from the moment the bell rang the day wouldn't go well. Three minutes and twenty-four seconds could make all the difference.

Sister Mary Ann stood beneath the wall clock waiting. She gestured to the bottle-green door across the landing. "Don't speak until you're spoken to and mind your manners."

Encouraged by a hefty shove between her shoulder blades, Jane catapulted into the room.

A man sat at the desk, head bent, studying a piece of paper. Did

"Don't speak until you're spoken to and mind your manners" mean Jane shouldn't move? She hadn't a clue. Wouldn't it be good manners to invite a girl in, especially after you'd demanded her presence before Communion?

The man lifted his head, and eyes, deep and dark, drilled into her. "Come in! Come in! Don't be hanging around like a hoverfly." The Irish brogue came as a bit of a surprise. He didn't sound anywhere near as fierce as he looked.

Jane ran her tongue over her lips and tried to speak, but nothing wanted to come out. Not a single word. Jane was never stuck for words. Not ever. At least not that she could remember. The thick carpet cushioned her feet as she took a step into the room and closed the door behind her.

"Sit down." He pointed across the desk to the chair opposite, his unsettling gaze fixed on her. If she sat down she'd be lucky to be able to see over the top of the desk.

Without raising her eyes from the tips of her boots, she mumbled, "I'll stand."

"Very well, Jane."

Good grief! He knew her name. Who was he?

"The name's Michael, Michael Quinn."

Michael Quinn! She'd seen that name, seen it on the big polished board in the hallway along with the names of all the governors and other important people in town. He was nothing like she imagined. The creases around his eyes made it look like he did a lot of smiling, and his voice held more than an echo of Ireland, a bit like Mrs. O'Rourke in the laundry but deeper, richer. He stood and held out a hand about four times the size of hers.

She gave her palm a surreptitious swipe and took it. "I'm Jane." He knew that; he'd called her by name. "Pleased to meet you."

"Please sit down." He inclined his head toward the chair and fidgeted his hand.

Oh no! She loosened her fingers, let her hand drop from his, then perched on the edge of the chair.

Once he'd stopped rubbing his squashed fingers, he interlaced them under his clipped beard. It was strange: he had black hair but a beard the gray of the old pots in the scullery.

"Now, Jane, how old are you?"

Not so bad a start, she could manage that. "I've been here for nine years, three months, one hour, and twenty-three minutes. Maybe twenty-seven, the breakfast bell was close to three and a half minutes late." And in all that time, no one had claimed her. "See, that's how long ago I was dropped off on the doorstep, in the dead of night." Three thousand, three hundred and seventy-eight days ago. "November the first. It was a Sunday. I was two weeks old." Not that she could remember. Sister Mary Ann had told her in the end, after a deal of prodding and poking, though how she knew was anyone's guess.

Jane always dreamed that one day Florence Nightingale would glide through the dormitory door, light in hand, and spirit her away, the child of her heart she'd been forced to relinquish while she went off saving people.

"So you've been here ever since?"

"Yes, sir." Why was he asking her these questions? Sister Mary Ann could've answered them. She'd got everything about every one of the foundlings written in that big leather book of hers, the one with the brass key that she kept dangling from the chain around her waist, same as the one to the cupboard under the stairs.

"And you have no idea who your mother or father may be?"

Her heart gave a little leap. Was he going to tell her Miss Nightingale had come to claim her? Rubbish. That wasn't going to happen. Not to her. She wasn't going to get a new family either. Last time someone had tried they'd sent her back, claimed she talked too much. They'd taken Emmaline instead. It was because of her name. She knew it was. Jane, plain Jane. Couldn't Sister Mary Ann have done any better?

"Jane?"

And Piper, what kind of a surname was that? She had no intention of taking up the bagpipes. Nasty, squealing things made from sheep's innards fiddled with by men in skirts.

"Your mother or father? You've no idea?"

"No, sir. None at all." She sat up a little straighter.

"Your aptitude with numbers must have come from somewhere."

Aptitude. What was that? Was it good or bad? "I don't know nothing about my aptitude, sir."

"My mistake. Let me try again." He picked up the sheaf of papers from the desk and flicked through them. The sun glinted on the stained glass window behind him. So many delicious shapes and such perfect symmetry: six diamonds, four rhombi, sixty-two perfect small green squares, an equal number of rectangles . . .

"Jane!"

The patterns blurred. "Yes, sir."

Mr. Quinn tapped the top paper. "When you completed this evaluation, who were you sitting next to?"

It wasn't an evaluation. It was a test, plain and simple, like they did at the end of every year so Sister Mary Ann could tell who'd done their lessons right and could go to the next class. "Emmaline, sir. I always sit . . . no, sat—she's gone now, gone to her new family—next to Emmaline. She comes before me in the alphabet see, sir."

Jane never could understand that, why there was no one whose name began with *F, G, H,* or *I.* Whatever happened to all the Florences,

Glorias, Harriets, and Irises? Maybe they didn't give names like that to girls dumped on the doorsteps of orphanages.

The frown lines on Mr. Quinn's forehead wriggled up and down as he flicked through the papers. "Can't be that. Who sits on the other side?"

"No one, sir. Sister Mary Ann makes me sit next to the wall, says I'd talk the hind leg off a donkey, so it's the safest place." She clamped her hand over her mouth. Not the right thing to say, not at all. Not in polite company, and sure as eggs Mr. Quinn was polite company, with his neatly folded cravat and high-winged collar. He made an impolite snort and his lips curled, a smile perhaps.

"Is this work all your own?"

Now he thought she was a hoaxer! "I'm no cheat, sir." She clamped her back teeth. Not a good thing. She mustn't get angry, not like she did when those people had taken her home for tea. That hadn't ended well—it had for Emmaline, though.

"I'm not suggesting you are, Jane. I am trying to discover if this is all your own work. You haven't made a single error. I've never seen a set of results like these. You should be very proud of yourself."

Next thing she was standing, leaning across the desk. There it was in black and white: 100 percent. "Ha! I thought it was easy." She'd told Sister Mary Ann and got her knuckles rapped for her trouble. "Sister Mary Ann says pride comes before a fall."

"Well, you haven't fallen. No one else has achieved such a remarkable score. Not even in the senior class. Congratulations!"

She sat back down on the chair and gave Mr. Quinn her biggest smile. "I like numbers, sir. See, they don't lie, sir. Not like people. There's only right or wrong, no in-betweens."

"An excellent summary. You and my sister would get along just fine. Perhaps you'd like to meet her, come to tea."

5

His sister! No! It wouldn't be fine. "Oh. No, thank you, sir. I'm not good at tea. See, I spill things and I can't keep me mouth shut. I talk too much. I can't help it. I have all these ideas rushing around in my head and they fall out, like Wallaman Falls."

"Wallaman Falls?"

"The highest permanent single-drop waterfall in Australia. Almost a thousand feet." Surely he knew that. "It's in Queensland."

He made that funny snorting sound again so Jane sat on her hands and shut her mouth.

"There are four scholarships available at the girls' school here in Maitland, and my sister and I would like to offer you one."

"I'm already at school, here at the orphanage. I've got two more years, then I start me apprenticeship so I can find a job." Get away, begin her real life, away from the nuns and their flapping black robes and plaster faces.

"I understand, but what we are proposing is sending you to St. Joseph's Girls School to complete your education. After that you'd be able to find worthwhile employment, perhaps as a governess or even a teacher at the school."

The thought didn't fill her with a huge rush of excitement, although it sounded better than working in the laundry and the piles of mending she never got through. Sewing buttons was fine, she'd worked that out, four nice little symmetrical holes, but she detested darning!

"So what do you think of that idea?" Mr. Quinn's eyes twinkled at her from the other side of the desk.

"I don't want to be a governess or a teacher. I wouldn't be any good at that."

That made him frown. She'd done it again, spoken her mind. He'd offered her an escape and she'd as good as spat in his eye.

"You're young yet."

"I'll be ten in eight months, twelve days, twenty-two hours, and . . ."—she glanced at the clock on the mantelpiece—"and twenty-three minutes." Providing Sister Mary Ann had told her the truth. "All the girls begin their apprenticeships when they're twelve."

"Jane, this isn't going to be an apprenticeship. This'll be all about furthering your education—history, geography, literature, the classics."

"What about arithmetic? That's what I like, but there ain't no apprenticeships for arithmetic."

He grabbed at his chin and gave his beard a scratch; it made a rasping sound, a bit like the antechinus in the roof above the dormitory. "There are jobs that involve arithmetic."

A jolt ran right up her spine and made her scalp prickle. Lice or excitement? She wasn't sure. What jobs? Working in a bank maybe, counting other people's money. Nobody would give her a job like that, not after the muddle about Bertha's sixpence. Jane hadn't taken it; she'd found it on the floor and didn't know who it belonged to. She'd handed it over the minute Sister Mary Ann had told her it had gone missing. "What sort of jobs?"

"I mentioned my sister. Do you remember?"

"Yes, you said we could have tea." She slumped back in the chair. Would it be rude to ask again about jobs that involved arithmetic?

"My sister is the accountant for our business."

"Accountant?" It wasn't often people used words she didn't know, but he'd come up with two. *Aptitude* and now *accountant*. Strange that both should start with the first letter of the alphabet. What was an accountant? Sister Mary Ann often said "on no account." Perhaps he meant she'd put her foot in it. Lost this scholarship before she'd even discovered what it was about.

"An accountant is a person whose job it is to keep or inspect financial records."

"Like a bookkeeper, you mean?" Now, that wouldn't be a bad idea. But she'd never seen a girl who kept the books. The well-named Mr. Noseworthy, who was about a hundred and came once a month to sit in Sister Mary Ann's cubbyhole and made it smell of sweat and ink, called himself a bookkeeper.

"Not the same, however some of their duties do overlap. You'd need to have an excellent grasp of bookkeeping before you could call yourself an accountant. An accountant's job is broader; they analyze figures and offer business and financial advice."

Offer advice? Who'd take the advice of a girl like her, a foundling?

"I think it would be a good idea if you talked with my sister."

The tinkle of the bell on his desk brought Jane up short. Two seconds later Sister Mary Ann stuck her bulbous nose around the door; odds on she'd been listening to every word. "Come along, Jane. We can't be wasting anymore of Mr. Quinn's time."

"On the contrary, Sister Mary Ann, Jane and I have been having a delightful discussion, which we wish to continue tomorrow afternoon at my home. Would you be so good as to ensure she is delivered to the house at 4:00 p.m. sharp? I shall escort her back here afterward."

"Yes, sir." Sister Mary Ann performed a series of head bobs that she must have learned from the apostlebirds in the park over the road.

"Off you go, Jane. Elizabeth and I will look forward to seeing you tomorrow afternoon."

Jane opened her mouth but no words seemed to want to come out.

"You have heard of my sister, I'm sure." Good grief! Of course she had.

Everyone knew Miss Elizabeth Quinn.

TWO

Ó'Cuinn. Michael." The clerk studied the sheath of papers in his hand, then spat toward the rail. The globule missed, landing with a plop on the deck. "Where's your sister?"

A small hand crept into Michael's palm and his sister turned her face up, leaned against his legs.

The mismatched group of people—men, women, children—standing behind him pushed closer, impatient to present their papers and secure a berth.

"Get a move on. Answer the question."

He stared up at the mast, his mind in turmoil. The crowd behind him rumbled. "She's here."

The clerk scribbled a series of unintelligible marks on their papers and glared down. "Got you down for the single men's accommodation." He flicked his thumb over his shoulder, down into the bowels of the ship. "No berth for her down there. Says here she's in the family accommodation with Nuala Ó'Cuinn."

"That's me aunty. She died six months ago. I told them in the office." A bloke behind him gave a shove, releasing the festering coil of anger deep in Michael's gut. "We've been on the manifest for almost

9

a year, down for family accommodation." He stabbed at the papers. "Says so right there. You sort it out. You're the one pushing your weight around, keeping everyone waiting."

"Remarks like that ain't going to get you anything special. No single men in family accommodation. How old are you?"

"Fifteen."

"Over fourteen. Too old for family accommodation."

Michael drew in a slow breath. Jesus, Mary, and Joseph! What was a man supposed to do? It couldn't be the first time a brother and sister had immigrated to Australia.

A stout woman who barely reached his shoulder pushed forward. "I'll take the little angel with me."

Michael reached down and hitched the mop-headed little bundle of bones up against his shoulder.

"Who are you?" The clerk rolled his eyes and leaned on his elbow.

"Mrs. Cameron. Mrs. William Cameron. Full fare-paying passenger." She thrust her ticket at the clerk and smiled down at Michael's sister. "You're a pretty little thing, ain't you, with them big blue eyes and lovely curls. Lucky you didn't get your brother's black looks."

What was a man to do? The woman looked kindly enough.

"I'll get her settled with me. Be good to have some company. What's your name, poppet?"

"Elizabeth. Her name's Elizabeth."

She buried her worried little face in his neck and gave a snotty sniff.

Michael set her down and hefted the bag, the one he'd packed with care when the immigration office had handed out the clothes. Two dresses and a bonnet for Sunday best, new boots and stockings. "One moment." He squatted down, felt along the back. It was there, tucked in the back as he remembered. The rag doll Mam had made from scraps; he'd saved it for this very moment. Grief snatched at the back of his throat. He pulled the doll out. Gave it a shake. "I've got something for you. Mam made it."

For a moment Elizabeth didn't respond; she just looked at him with those ancient eyes. Then her mouth formed a little circle of surprise. She reached out her hands and clutched the doll tight to her chest.

"What will you be calling her?" Mrs. Cameron bent down and smoothed the doll's woolen hair.

She hesitated for a moment, opened her mouth, and as clear as a bell said, "Lizzie."

"Aye. That's a pretty name. Is that what your mam calls you?"

She turned her wide, watchful eyes to Michael and nodded.

"Come along. We'll go and get matters sorted. You bring Lizzie and we'll see your brother once we're settled."

Without a word, she tucked the doll beneath her chin and slipped her hand into Mrs. Cameron's, and they disappeared into the crowd.

The two men behind him hoisted their trunks onto their shoulders and peeled off in the direction of the lower decks. It was as much as he could do to put one foot in front of the other. His heart bled, everything around him a distant blur of noise and disharmony. For a long time he'd begrudged Mam and Da's decision to leave him and Lizzie behind with Aunty Nuala and take advantage of the free passage for married couples without children. This was supposed to be the first day of their new life. The life Mam and Da had planned, scrimped, and saved for.

The pathetic queue of humanity shuffled forward as their names were crossed off yet another list, papers checked again before they were allocated a spot. "Last one on the left."

Michael eased his way between the cramped bunks and threw the bag down, the stench of sweat and bilge water turning his gut. They hadn't even left the river yet. He never thought he'd be seasick, hadn't been when they'd crossed from Dublin to Liverpool. Air, he needed fresh air. He slipped back onto the deck.

The clouds had darkened and a biting wind swept across the river. It matched his mood. He doubted he'd ever be warm again. He leaned over the rail, squinted into the distance trying to pick out the ravaged spire of the workhouse chapel.

Someone behind jostled him. He straightened up, felt a tug at the back of his jacket. Unbelievable. They'd no patience. Let a man alone to grieve.

He whipped around, intent on delivering a mouthful, then felt a nudge against the back of his knees. "What are you doing here?" He darted a glance around and squatted down. "Darlin', you can't be staying with me."

Her face crumpled into a ferocious frown and her bottom lip quivered. He scooped her up and she burrowed into his chest. "I can't change anything, darlin'. The ship's sailing."

He nudged her forward through the stinking, cloying crush. Where was Mrs. Cameron? She said she'd take care of her. He set her down and she wedged herself between his boots, eyes pleading.

The ship juddered and groaned in the river current as the steam-tug came alongside. Before he could release the swell of frustration building in his chest, a series of scuffles broke out, then a splash as a body hit the water.

"What's going on?" He turned to the bloke standing next to him at the rail.

"Stowaways. They'll take 'em ashore while they can. On the pilot boat, along with the officials."

Six men, hardly more than boys, hands manacled, bumped along the deck.

"Stowaways?"

"Trying to get themselves a free passage, or worse, paid their money to the wrong person, to the runners. If they got aboard and managed not to show themselves for three or four days, the captain ain't going to turn the boat around."

"Hadn't occurred to me." Michael's gut churned, then lightened. Their papers were in order.

"Heard tell of a lass who hid herself in a box. All well and good, but she hadn't taken mind of the lack of air. Found her body amongst the cargo when they docked. Gruesome sight, that would be."

Michael watched as the motley band of stowaways were prodded and pushed down the rope ladder into the row boats. Not bound for the colonies but for Canning Half Tide Dock, then Walton Gaol. His stomach gave another lurch. It was fine. They'd passed the check.

Michael stepped to one side and crouched down. "Look at me, darlin'."

She gazed up at him, big blue eyes, trust shimmering bright. A wan smile tugged at the corner of her lips, tugged at his heart, more like.

"We'll forget all about the workhouse. Can you do that?"

She nodded her head and rested against his leg, her smallness and vulnerability killing him.

"Look, darlin', trust me. I'm taking you home. Mam and Da will be waiting for us. Until then I'll look after you."

Tears welled.

Biting back his frustration, he drew in a breath. "Pretend it's a game. You know how to play a game?"

Curls bouncing, she brightened.

Consumed by the need to do right by her, he squatted down on his haunches and drew her close. "You're safe with me." He held her tight as the ropes tethering the ship slipped into the water, leaving behind his heart and all he held dear.

THREE

MAITLAND TOWN, 1906

Still glowing from the scrubbing Sister Mary Ann had administered, Jane stood quaking on the doorstep of the Quinns' Church Street house and rang the bell. Noisier than a fire engine, it filled the entire street. She whipped around in case anyone came running.

No one did, so she turned back to the door. It opened to reveal a red-faced girl done up like a leg of lamb in the butcher's shop, her frilly little cap and ruffled apron so white it made Jane squint. "Better come in. And none of your nonsense. Think you're some kind of clever sticks, I'll bet."

Lucy Smith! So that's what had happened to her. The Quinns must make a habit of choosing girls from the orphanage. Well, Mr. Quinn could forget it. She wasn't going to prance around in a get-up like that; besides, she'd be no good at it. All that bobbing and curtsying.

Before Jane had time to respond to Lucy's smart remark, Mr. Quinn's booming voice echoed down the long hallway. "Right on time. Good girl. Off you go, Lucy."

With her nose twitching, Lucy scurried off, leaving Jane in the doorway with no idea what to do next.

"Come along, come and meet Elizabeth."

Mr. Quinn beckoned and Jane tiptoed along the patterned carpet runner down the hallway, hands clasped tightly. Some sort of paper covered the walls on either side of her, painted with what looked like flannel flowers. There had to be at least five hundred and twelve flowers in the space between the front door and the spot where Mr. Quinn stood.

At his invitation she stepped over the threshold and into a fairy tale.

Miss Elizabeth Quinn sat on a small rose-patterned sofa next to the window, looking like some kind of an angel with the sun behind her, hair the color of roasted chestnuts, loose curls swept back from her face. And her eyes! She had the brightest blue eyes, almost violet, putting Jane in mind of a doll she and Emmaline had seen in Owen and Beckett's shop window last Christmas, all porcelain skin and shiny blue. Emmaline reckoned the doll's eyes opened and closed.

"My name is Elizabeth. Elizabeth Quinn. I'm Michael's sister." She patted the cushion next to her on the sofa. It was the palest of pinks, like the inside of a real rose.

"How d'you do, miss." She tried to do one of those curtsy things, but her stocking started to slither. Did Miss Quinn truly want Jane to sit next to her?

"Come and sit by me. We girls must stick together. Michael, you sit opposite us." She picked up a small bell from the table next to her and gave it a shake.

Two seconds later Lucy Smith returned, bobbing in the doorway like a foraging duck. "Yes, ma'am?" She shot Jane a disparaging look.

Not to be outdone, Jane stuck her nose in the air, crossed the room, and plonked herself down on the pink sofa, her hands neatly folded like Miss Quinn's. Lucy's eyes narrowed. That'd teach her.

"We'd like tea now, if you wouldn't mind, and some of Bessie's delicious macaroons."

Lucy dawdled for a moment, looking for all the world as though she'd like to stick her tongue out, then gave a huff and flounced from the room, banging the door behind her.

"Now, Jane." Miss Quinn turned sideways and smiled right into her eyes.

Jane caught Mr. Quinn smiling too. They were up to something, and she had no idea what.

"Michael's been telling me about your skill with figures. He thinks your acumen should be fostered."

Acumen? What was an acumen? Another *A* word. She hadn't had time to look up *aptitude* and *accountant* yet, and now she had to remember *acumen*.

"As I expect you know, we own the auction house in the main street."

The auction house! No, she didn't. Sister Mary Ann had given Jane a long lecture before she left, saying Mr. and Miss Quinn were important benefactors. Come to think of it, she wasn't too sure what a benefactor was either. Did they own the orphanage? No, that was the Benevolent Society.

"Many of the people we employ here at home and at the auction house started life at the orphanage."

Jane couldn't sit quiet any longer. "I'm almost old enough to go to work."

"We'd like to offer you the opportunity to extend your education."

Extend it? How could an education be extended? At twelve she'd have to find a job; everyone knew that. Out into the cottages and off to work. Only Sister Mary Ann's treasures escaped that fate.

"Come along, Elizabeth, stop picking your words. Tell Jane what she needs to know and let's see if she agrees."

"I was simply trying to break the idea gently. It's all well and good for you with your blunt, no-nonsense approach . . ."

"I like blunt, no nonsense." Jane slapped her hand over her mouth, making Mr. Quinn's big laugh echo around the room.

At the exact same moment the door swung open and there stood Lucy Smith. If she'd been gawking before, her eyes now looked as if they were about to bounce across the room.

"I'm sorry to disturb. I've brought tea." She said it in such a hoity-toity voice it would have made Sister Mary Ann right proud.

"Thank you, put the tray down here." Miss Quinn pointed to the table in front of the sofa. "That will be all."

The cups rattled as the tray hit the table, and Lucy shot back out through the door as though she had a Chinese firecracker up her bum.

"Now, where were we?"

"Blunt. No nonsense." Mr. Quinn gave another snort and pulled out a big red handkerchief from his pocket and wiped at his eyes.

"Ah yes." Miss Quinn held the pot up high, and a stream of perfumed tea filled the cups, cups so thin you could see the light through them, and they were covered with roses the same color as the cushions underneath her. Jane smoothed the sofa with her fingers, then snatched her hand back.

"Michael and I would like to sponsor you to attend St. Joseph's Girls School here in Maitland. We feel your aptitude . . ."

There was that word again. She must look it up.

". . . for numbers is remarkable and should be fostered. After you've completed the education program, there are evening courses in accounting, bookkeeping, typing, and shorthand you could attend. Women need more in life than a husband."

Well, Jane certainly didn't want a husband. "Why me?"

Miss Quinn reached out and laid her fingers on Jane's arm. "Neither Michael nor I have any children and we'd like to help you, become your benefactors, and when you have completed your education we'd like to offer you a position in our business."

"But I can't. I'm going to leave the orphanage and get meself a job, find somewhere to live. I can't be going to school and evening classes."

"Elizabeth has that covered, too, Jane. Be patient a little longer."

"Bessie, our cook, has decided not to live in anymore now that her daughter's had twins and needs some help. She'll come in daily. I'm proposing you take Bessie's room. It's on the attic floor, a little bigger than Lucy's, so there'd be room for a desk, which you'll need because you'll have plenty of studying to do."

"You'd do all this for nothing?"

"It wouldn't be for nothing. While you're at school you'd be able to help me in the afternoons and at weekends with the accounts, learn about the business. Now, how does that sound? Would you be interested?"

Interested, yes, maybe if she could get her head around it all. Not adopted like Emmaline and some of the other girls, and truth be told, she wasn't even sure she wanted to be. Bertha Brightman had come back with dreadful tales of whiskery old men and wandering hands. She shot a look at Mr. Quinn. He couldn't be described as whiskery or even very old, and he smelt nice, of some sort of hair oil, something sweet like caramel and a hint of tobacco.

"Are you all right, Jane?" Miss Quinn's cool hand covered hers. "I realize this is a lot to take in."

"Mmm. Yes. But I still don't get it. Why me?"

Mr. Quinn pushed to his feet and came and stood next to the sofa. Jane hadn't realized he was so tall.

"I don't think you understand, Jane. You have a gift. A gift that should be fostered."

He'd gotten her a present? "What gift?"

"Your ability, your aptitude with numbers."

"What is this aptitude thing I've got?" Perhaps they were telling her gently she had some dreadful disease. Like consumption or something. Betty Brown had consumption. She'd ended up in the infirmary and they'd never seen her again.

Mr. Quinn boomed out that laugh again. "I'm sorry. We've made an assumption. I've been following your progress for some time now. Your mathematic results indicate that you are gifted, have a talent for numbers. That gift should be fostered."

"Not ignored because you're a girl," added Miss Quinn. "Why, there are girls attending Sydney University, studying mathematics. Have you heard of Fanny Hunt?"

Jane raked through her memory. She couldn't place anyone called Fanny Hunt at the orphanage, but maybe she'd been there while Jane was in the nursery. Stuck in one of those dreadful cots day in and day out with nothing to do but make patterns with the bars and watch the slant of the sun through the high windows. No, Fanny Hunt didn't sound familiar.

"She was the first woman to graduate from Sydney University. She gained a bachelor of science. I see no reason why you couldn't do the same one day. So, would you like to come and live here, Jane?" Miss Quinn's bright eyes stared into her own with such kindness.

Roses and sunshine or flapping robes and plaster saints. Not much of a decision.

FOUR

There were days when Michael hardly remembered the past as he paced the deck of the ship, reveling in fresh air, freedom, and the promise of the future. As luck would have it, he and Elizabeth had the strongest of stomachs. When everyone else lay below decks heaving and moaning, they'd braved the swell around the Bay of Biscay and basked in the fierce ride.

As the weeks slipped into summer and the ship into warmer waters, the horror of Liverpool, Aunty Nuala's passing, and the workhouse faded.

"She's a bonnie lass." Mrs. Cameron kept Elizabeth close to her side, as she had ever since she'd snuck away from her that first day.

"Aye, she is that, me little darlin'." Michael passed his hand across the top of Elizabeth's soft hair. The fresh air and regular meals had filled out her cheeks and brought a glow to her pale skin. He'd make sure she'd never be wanting again.

"Not long now. Your mam will be happy to have her little one back, albeit not much of a bairn now. They grow quick. She'll be waiting on the dock, her arms wide. A son's a son 'til he takes a wife, but a daughter's a daughter for the rest of your life."

And that was the one thing that worried him as the ship made its way between the two ominous cliff faces standing sentinel to the harbor. He hadn't heard from Mam and Da for nigh on twelve months.

From the water, Sydney didn't look like much. A small, ugly town, surrounded by barren sandy coves, the trees—short and stunted—clinging to the rocks. None of the green of Ireland. The blinding sun had leached the color from all but the sky and water. All about them smaller boats glided over the smooth, calm surface of the water—steamers, lighters plying their trade, and the bigger ships disgorging their cargo of immigrants and gold seekers.

The quay swarmed with life beneath the shadows of the tall warehouses; behind them a craggy, crowded ridge was packed with precariously perched buildings that threatened to topple into the busy harbor.

It took hours to dock, the wind and the waves taking them backward and forward. After close to five months aboard ship, Michael yearned for dry land under his feet and the chance to hand family decisions over to Da.

A pilot and an official-looking chap came on board, spoke with the captain and the surgeon, peered through mounds of paperwork, then muttered. There'd not been much illness aboard apart from bouts of seasickness and three cases of measles. Some of the hands reckoned they'd be up for a stint in quarantine, but there hadn't been any other outbreaks.

Michael patted the papers in his breast pocket. If all else failed he had the address the immigration bloke had given him.

"Not long now." Mrs. Cameron pressed a piece of paper into his hands.

He looked down at it and frowned.

"You can read, can't you?"

Of course he could read; he had the hedge school and his mam to thank for that.

CAMERON VICTUALLERS

"You be hanging on to that, and if something strange comes to pass, you come and see me. No hanging about. No ridiculous pride. I want to make sure this little angel is well cared for." She lifted Elizabeth into her arms and planted a firm kiss on her cheek. "I'll miss you, my little poppet." Mrs. Cameron lowered Elizabeth to the deck and sailed down the gangplank, one of the first to leave the ship.

While Michael and Elizabeth waited their turn, his eyes scanned the dockside crowd, searching for Mam and Da, but the crush of bodies and upturned faces made it all a blur.

It wasn't until the crew finished bringing the trunks and baggage up from the hold that they were finally given a nod, and with nothing but their one bag he and Elizabeth stepped ashore.

Some were grasped in long-awaited hugs and greetings; others wandered aimlessly, almost as lost as they'd looked in Liverpool. The crowds swirled and massed around them among the ropes, bollards, and bales and the stink of horse manure, sweat, and rotting vegetables, but there was no shriek of pleasure, no warm, enfolding arms.

"Michael Ó'Cuinn."

He turned, heart in his mouth.

A tall, redheaded Scotsman with a drinker's nose grinned at him. "I'm William Cameron, Bill to me mates. The wife's brokenhearted, says if you want to leave the girl with us while you sort yourself out, she'd be more than happy to oblige."

At the very moment he opened his mouth to decline, a passing cart overloaded with bales thumped his shoulder and Elizabeth's hand slipped from his. He grabbed at her coat and hauled her to safety seconds before she disappeared beneath the wheels.

"Mind Lizzie. She's scared." Elizabeth tucked her doll back under her chin.

"Aye, me darlin', we're all a bit scared. I'll be thanking you . . ." Before Michael finished, Mrs. Cameron bumbled up.

"You've found him, I see." She held out her arms to Elizabeth, who slid into her embrace, Lizzie clutched tight against her chest. "Let me take her, make it easier. You can sort yourself out, and you know where to find us."

"Aye, I do."

"Off you go, boy. You find your mam and da. Afterward come back and collect her."

A little piece of his heart flew to Elizabeth as she gave a jaunty wave over Mrs. Cameron's shoulder, then he pulled down his jacket and set off across the quay through the seething crowds.

Once the confusion and chaos settled to a tolerable level, he stopped at a barrow selling a range of fruit and vegetables that as good as made him weep.

"What'll it be, sir? Oranges, lemons? Straight off the ship, are you? These'll set you up a treat." He handed Michael a slice of juiciness that he thrust into his mouth, the taste and smell taking him back, back to that night in the chapel. His gorge rose and he spat the remains into the gutter.

"You'll learn to like them. Came out on the *Earl Canning*, did you?"

"Aye. I'm looking for the assisted immigration offices in Kent Street."

"Go along the street over there for a couple of hundred yards.

You'll find Windmill Street, turn right, and go up the hill. You'll see Kent Street. Lord Nelson's on the corner. Sure you wouldn't like an orange? Only a penny."

Michael shook his head. "Not right now." He needed every one of the pennies he'd tied in his handkerchief and tucked beneath his shirt until he knew what was what.

Ignoring all the other quayside vendors, he ploughed on until he found himself on Windmill Street. A mixture of stone and timber buildings lined the way—inns, shops, and offices, and every so often the entrance to a dark alleyway or courtyard.

Half an hour and one missed turn later, he stood in front of a window proclaiming itself to be the office of the assisted immigration scheme. He pushed open the door.

"How may I help you?"

Michael scooped off his cap and squinted at the voice, waiting for his eyes to adjust after the bright sunshine.

"Arrived on the *Earl Canning* this morning, did you?"

He must have had the fact painted across his forehead in large letters. "Aye."

"There'll be a talk for new arrivals tonight at six o'clock. Help you find your feet. Come to pay your dues, have you?"

"Dues?"

"The remainder of your passage. What's your name?"

"Michael, Michael Ó'Cuinn."

The clerk's head came up with a snap. "Ah! I have something here for you." He rummaged in the desk drawer and brought out a folded piece of paper and handed it to him. *M Quinn* was scrawled across the front.

"This ain't for me."

"It is, lad. Came hand delivered straight from your father."

"Me name's not Quinn. It's Ó'Cuinn."

The clerk winked. "One and the same. Ó'Cuinn's too much of a mouthful for folks around here. Open your letter and be thankful your dues are paid."

Michael's hand shook as his heart soared. He unfolded the piece of paper.

THE DIGGERS REST, HILL END

Nothing more. "Where's Hill End?"

"Off in search of gold, are you? You and the rest of the world."

"No, off to find me da. It says here Hill End, a place called the Diggers Rest."

"Yep. Hill End district. That's where you'll find him. Hasn't done the run of late."

"The run?"

"Quarterly run via Bathurst to Sydney. Set himself up real well, employs a bloke now to drive the dray, since your mam passed."

The world tipped and Michael reached for the desk. "Me mam passed?" How could that be?

"Sit yourself down, lad. I'm sorry. You didn't know." Hands settled on his shoulders, eased him down. "Take a moment."

Michael knuckled a rogue tear from the corner of his eye. "What happened?"

"Not real sure. Heard it from one of your da's drivers. I remember your mam, good-looker." The clerk's face turned ruddy. "Beggin' your pardon. They took off for Hill End soon after they arrived. Your da made a go of it. Didn't waste time chasing gold, just had that first lucky strike within a couple of months of arriving. Then bought the bullock dray and set himself up carting goods back and forth to

Sydney. Deposited the money in, regular as clockwork every quarter for your ticket."

Michael slammed his fist on the desk, anger easier to show than the sorrow swelling in his chest. "Is me da all right?"

"Last I heard. Note came last quarter."

Maybe the note wasn't for him. Maybe it was a mistake. His mam wouldn't leave without saying goodbye, dropping a kiss on his brow, cupping his cheek, same as she had before she'd climbed aboard the ship.

"How far's this Hill End place?"

"Couple of hundred miles, west." He waved his hand behind him in a generous arc. "I'll give you a chit to draw rations for the long haul over the mountains; another three days'll see you to Bathurst. You'll pick up a ride from there. Come by tomorrow early. Once the drivers know you're Quinn's lad, they'll be happy to take you on, big strappin' lad like you, give them a hand over the mountain passes."

Michael staggered to his feet, his head swirling. He'd clung to the vision of Mam and Da standing on the dock welcoming him with open arms for so long, and now this. "How well do you know me da?"

"A bit. Nice little cartage business he's got going for himself, though, as I said, haven't seen him for a while."

"But he left the note last quarter?" Mary and Joseph, he couldn't get his head around it.

"Nah, it wasn't your da, 'twas one of the Celestials."

"Celestials?"

"Chinese. Lots of them out that way."

He didn't need to know about Chinamen; he needed to get a move on. "I've got to go and see about Elizabeth, me little sister."

"Your sister?" The clerk ran a grubby finger across the papers. "I'd forgotten about her." He threw a sheepish look, cleared his throat, and opened the desk drawer. "I'm to give you this." He handed over a pouch. "Something to tide you over. Your da sent it. But Hill End's no place to be taking a child, specially not a girl. It's tough out there. A man's world." He shrugged his shoulders.

Aye, it was. And Michael wasn't yet a man, though he'd been making the decisions for far too long, since Mam and Da left. Wasn't sure if he wanted to do it anymore. Wasn't sure if he'd made the right call.

"I'll have the ride sorted tomorrow," the clerk promised.

Michael dragged the piece of paper Mrs. Cameron had given him. "Can you tell me where I'll find Cameron Victuallers."

"Cameron Victuallers?" The clerk sat up a little straighter, eyed him with a tad more respect. "Not too hard. Thriving business. Out of here, turn right, take the next on the left down the hill, and you'll see the Metropolitan. Turn left and follow the road. Place you're looking for is on the left, couple of doors down from the Fortune of War."

"Ta." He held out his hand.

The clerk tipped his head and winked. "See you this evening. Meeting for new arrivals is at six sharp."

Once he was outside, Michael turned his face up to the sun, let out a long breath, and shrugged out of his jacket. A man could fry in the heat.

And nothing, nothing was as he'd expected. From here on in he'd never believe a word 'til he saw for himself.

Hoisting his bag onto his shoulder, he set off down the hill back through the chaos, the barking dogs, frolicking women, and drunken sailors.

It didn't take him long to find the warehouse with "Cameron Victuallers" emblazoned above the wide doors. Before he'd had a chance to look around, Bill Cameron, stripped to his singlet, brawny muscles bulging, appeared. "Ah! There you are. Everything sorted?"

Michael dropped his bag down inside the door and followed Mr. Cameron through a greasy-aired warehouse packed with mountains of canvas bales marked for London. They climbed up a flight of narrow stairs and stepped into a cozy room.

Mrs. Cameron smiled up at him from the chair beside the open window, a cup of tea in hand. "Sit yourself down and tell me how it went."

Michael drew in a deep breath and collapsed onto a chair. "It's not as simple as I thought." He pulled off his hat and scratched at his sweat-soaked hair. He'd no idea where he was going other than the name of the place. Hill End—it sounded like the road to Hades. "The immigration bloke seems to think me mam's dead." He swallowed the threatening sob. He'd not be believing it. "Me da's in some place called Hill End."

"Michael, Michael!" Elizabeth flew into the room, her doll tucked under one arm and an apple on a stick clutched in her other hand. "Toffee apple." She thrust the sticky mess into his face and grinned a gap-toothed smile.

"Come here, me little poppet." Mrs. Cameron stretched out her arms. Elizabeth hesitated for a moment, then nestled at her feet.

Mrs. Cameron caressed her halo of curls. "She cannae go out there. Not one this bonny." Her eyes narrowed. "Not without her mam."

He lifted his finger to his lips. No point in telling Elizabeth something she'd not understand.

"The good Lord's not seen fit to grant me children." She smoothed Elizabeth's hair back from her sticky cheeks. "Leave her here with me and go and find your da. She'll be safe and sound until you're ready. Goldfields are no place for a little girl. Since we sighted land I've been hearing nothing but terrible tales of dirt, heat, vicious animals, bushrangers, and sickness."

The thought of leaving Elizabeth made his stomach sink. Perhaps it was the best solution. The immigration bloke had said the same, and Elizabeth had taken to Mrs. Cameron.

"Some say Sydney Town's hard. Set foot outside and you've got dirt like you've never seen before, and heat that'd suck you dry."

Bill Cameron threw in his five-pennyworth from the doorway. "Never mind the bloody animals, the bushrangers, and the Chinamen."

Michael had to find out what happened to Mam, had to find Da. "I can't ask you to look after her. I can't pay for her board." Maybe a bit, the pound Da sent. He'd not much else except a couple of pennies.

"Bill's doing all right for himself. He's got his own business, the boat, and the warehouse. Give us what you can and leave Elizabeth here. If you don't like what you see out there, you come back. We'll see you right."

FIVE

MAITLAND TOWN, 1912

Jane couldn't believe how quickly her life had changed in the last six years. She'd moved into the attic bedroom just a week after she'd had tea with Michael and Elizabeth, and found a brand-new school uniform hanging in the wardrobe, straw boater and all. Not only that, but new shoes, two new skirts, and three blouses.

Once she'd finished at St. Joseph's there were classes at the School of Arts and Maitland Technical College, and her life had followed the same pattern. When she finished classes she'd walk home for lunch and spend the afternoon working with Elizabeth on the accounts. Not just those of the auction house and the other Quinn businesses, but many of the local charities and ventures Elizabeth and Michael supported.

Jane discovered there was a whole lot more to arithmetic than she thought. But most fascinating of all was Elizabeth's abacus. Why didn't everyone use one? It made everything so much faster.

Today, however, was not an accounts day. She had a day off because she was going to Sydney. On the train with Michael and Elizabeth!

She clattered down the stairs and into the kitchen. Bessie had a bowl of porridge waiting for her. She'd hated porridge at the orphanage; now it was one of her favorites. Cream made all the difference, and the knob of butter Bessie always sat in the middle, but best of all was the brown sugar, forming a lovely crust on the top.

"Got a big day ahead of you, I hear." Bessie plonked a glass of milk down on the table, all creamy and frothy on the top. "Take your hat off while you're eating."

"I've never been on a train before and I've never been to Sydney. We are going to the National Art Gallery of New South Wales." She swallowed the last mouthful of delicious porridge. "It is a temple to art. I'm very interested in the proportions of the building." The last spoonful of oatmeal disappeared. "Then tomorrow I have a philosophy class with Professor Watling at the School of Arts. I'm giving a talk. The last one before the Christmas holidays."

"Oh, are you now. You'd be good at that. What would you be talking about?"

"Fibonacci."

"Fibon—who?"

"Fibonacci. He was an Italian mathematician, although that wasn't his real name. He lived in the twelfth century. He introduced the Fibonacci sequence, the Golden Mean." And it made sense of everything. Patterns never lied.

"I suppose now you'll be heading off to Victoria to them there goldfields."

"Not that kind of gold. The Golden Mean is represented everywhere in nature. In the coil of a seashell, the seeds of a sunflower. Leaves, branches, and petals can all grow in spirals."

"And, you'll be telling me next, in those stinkin' rabbit paws, rotten shells, dried plants, and all them numbers."

"One, one, two, three, five, eight, thirteen."

"I thought you were good at numbers and counting. They ain't right. Even I know that."

"It's a sequence. You simply add the previous two numbers to create the next." Jane sketched a spiral with her index finger. "The Golden Mean. It explains the perfect shape of nature."

"Nature, is it? That would account for the fact your room is full to the gunnels with desiccated rubbish, making it stink worse than the compost heap. I'm planning on sending Lucy in there to clean up today."

Jane shot to her feet and grabbed Bessie's floury hand. "Oh no. Please don't. I promise I'll clean it up as soon as I get home." She couldn't have Lucy in there messing with her belongings. She'd never find anything again.

"The floor is covered with pieces of paper. Why can't you use a bin like any normal person?"

"Because they're not rubbish. I might need them."

"Just as well you're tucked away in the attic, not in one of the guest rooms. Don't see why you can't use a notebook like any sane person."

Jane slipped her hand into her pocket and ran her fingers over the beautiful leather-bound notebook Elizabeth had given her last Christmas. The trouble was she always tore the pages out, either to pin them to the wall or keep in her pocket where she could check them easily, whenever she had a spare moment.

"Pull your stockings up and tie that hair back. You look like a tramp."

"I'll clean my room up when I get back. Tomorrow."

"That will be a little difficult, won't it? You're off to the School of Arts with Mr. Fibon Archie."

"I'll do it after supper."

"Then you'll be banging and crashing in there all night and Lucy'll be complaining in the morning that she couldn't get any sleep."

If Lucy hadn't kicked up such a fuss and managed to wheedle her way into the other attic room, it wouldn't be an issue. Besides, she did nothing but sleep. Said she needed eight hours a night. What a lot of poppycock. Jane hardly ever slept more than two hours at a time. Her eyes would flash open and her mind would whir and she'd be out of bed and at her desk.

"I'll be quiet. I promise. Please, please don't let Lucy into my room." She clasped her hands together and schooled her face into the most beseeching expression she could manage.

"Stop your nonsense. Let me look at you."

Jane gave a small pirouette and hoped she'd got her outfit right— her navy skirt, just the right length; her boots, which she'd polished until her arm wanted to drop off, peeping out; gloves; and her straw boater trimmed with one of her navy hair ribbons.

"Perfect," said Bessie. "Just right for a day in the city. Mr. Michael's waiting for you in the sitting room, and don't forget to say goodbye to Miss Elizabeth."

"Isn't she coming?" The brightness of the morning dimmed a little. Jane had thought the three of them would be going. "Why not?"

"Better ask her." Bessie shrugged her shoulders and turned back to her scones. "Off you go."

Jane found Elizabeth at her desk in the sitting room, writing letters. Michael was standing and gazing out of the window, tapping his cane against the skirting board.

"Good morning, Aunt Elizabeth, Uncle Michael." Despite everything they had done for her, she still wasn't quite sure where she fit in. Neither servant nor family, she fluctuated between the two. Sometimes on the outside looking in and sometimes more intimate than she ever hoped to be in their strangely compelling home on Church Street.

They insisted she call them aunt and uncle, and who was she to complain? Besides, it made her feel more like family.

Elizabeth lifted her head and smiled. "All ready?"

"Please tell me you're coming too."

She offered a wry smile. "I have a mound of correspondence to attend to and a meeting this afternoon. Sydney's not my favorite place, and I'm not overfond of train travel. Too many memories . . ."

Michael rested his hand on Elizabeth's shoulder. "That was over forty years ago, although I know you couldn't get out of the place fast enough."

"Don't blame me! You were running from the law and couldn't wait to whisk me away."

Jane's head came up with a snap. Aunt Elizabeth as a headstrong young girl? Michael in trouble with the law? This information didn't fit the pattern. He was such an affable man, and Elizabeth . . . She always went along with Michael's plans.

"All ready, are we?" Michael crooked his elbow and invited Jane to walk with him. "We need to leave now so we'll make the eight o'clock train."

———≈———

Steam swirled and churned along the platform. A shrill whistle sounded and the giant wheels gave a mighty heave and picked up speed. The compartment rattled and banged and strained from left to right, then settled into a steady movement, the wheels *clickety-clacking* on the tracks.

For the first half of the journey Jane stared out of the window, content calculating the differentials in the speeds compared to the varying gradients. Then she yanked down the window, almost falling out as they crossed the Brooklyn Bridge, trying to estimate the deformation under load at the center of each span. Her reward was nothing but an eye full of sooty smoke.

An hour later Jane's patience had come to an end. "Are we almost there?"

"Not much longer. We're approaching Redfern."

"Is that where we get off?"

"No, we'll continue to Central Station and then take a cab down College Street and through the park. It'll save us a walk."

Jane pulled the scrunched piece of paper from her pocket and smoothed it out. It had taken an age for the authorities to decide on the exact design of the building for the new gallery, and the description in the *Maitland Mercury* sounded quite fascinating. She ran her finger down the smudged ink.

Classical Greek lines, interior divided into four halls, each one hundred by thirty feet with pillared archways.

"We're here."

The train ground to a halt, and Michael opened the door and descended to a platform stretching forever. Jane pulled on her gloves, stepped down, and lost her balance. She landed with a wrenched ankle, Michael's hand steadying her.

"I wasn't looking where I was going. How long do you think the platform is?" She spread out her hand and held her palm flat. Four palms equaled a foot, and six a cubit. She took a long step, catching her foot in the hem of her skirt. If a pace equaled two cubits, an average man's height would be twenty-two palms.

"Oh, Jane, I have absolutely no idea." Michael gave a chuckle. "There's more to life than calculations, you know."

Nothing that particularly interested her—although it was the description of the new gallery that had caught her attention, that and the chance to visit Sydney. The possibility of the proportions of the building conforming to the Golden Mean had fascinated her ever since she'd read of the new design.

"Do you think they'll have any of Leonardo's paintings? I'd love to see his *Vitruvian Man*. It's based on the works of the architect Vitruvius. Who designed the art gallery?"

"Not Vitruvius, I can assure you. A man by the name of Walter Liberty Vernon. He also designed Maitland Technical College and our railway station, to name but a few of his achievements."

"I wonder if he took into account the measurements of man?" Why Michael rolled his eyes she had no idea.

"The cabs are over here." Michael stepped up alongside. "National Gallery if you please."

"How long will it take us to get there?" Jane asked as she settled into the cab. She was looking forward to pacing out the internal measurements of the building. According to the newspaper article there was an oval lobby. She'd never stood in anything but a rectangular room, but then, in all honesty, she hadn't stood in very many places at all.

"There you are—the National Art Gallery of New South Wales."

Jane's breath caught when she gazed up at the imposing Ionic columns. Truly a classic Greek temple, perfectly proportioned, silhouetted against the bright blue sky. The newspaper journalist hadn't lied when he'd called it a temple to art.

A temple that was totally overrun by people. "Don't get lost, Jane. Stay right by me," Michael said as they stepped from the cab and took the broad stone stairs as though walking into a church. The autumn light slanted across the sandstone, throwing a golden glow.

"Why is it so crowded?"

"It's the first viewing of the new exhibition for the best landscape painting of Australian scenery in watercolor or oils. Anyone associated with the Labor campaign received an invitation."

She might have guessed. Ever since Labor's victory in the 1910 state election Michael spent more and more time in Sydney. Both he and Elizabeth were great advocates for all things Australian, all people as well, no matter where they came from, and Michael had fought long and hard to see better working hours and conditions introduced, supporting the minimum wage and half-day trading on Saturdays.

Both he and Elizabeth went out of their way to help people less fortunate. It had taken Jane time to realize that it wasn't just an arithmetic test that had made Elizabeth pick her out of the orphanage; it was what Elizabeth did. Elizabeth and Michael were philanthropists.

A great crowd mingled under the skylights beyond the foyer. Everyone was dressed to the nines, the men in formal suits and the women in huge hats with enough feathers to render an emu naked.

"Have we really got to stand and wait to get into the exhibit?" asked Jane. "Couldn't I go and have a look around?"

"I think it would be a good idea if we did. Perhaps the queue will diminish. Come along."

That was one of the best things about Michael, he hated wasting time. Probably because he was always so frantically busy. In fact, Jane had been surprised when he'd suggested she come. When he was at home he spent most of his time at the auction house, not in his office but on the shop floor, talking to customers, or out the back chatting with John, the auction house manager, making sure everything ran smoothly. Despite his campaign to become a member of the legislative assembly at the next election, he still managed to find time to make sure everyone was happy.

Instead of turning to the right, Michael led the way to one of the smaller galleries off the main vestibule. Away from the crush of people, the light inside was particularly bright, reflecting from the glassed ceiling off the pale mint-green walls.

They stopped at the entrance and Michael read aloud from a plaque on the wall.

"'An exhibition of the first paintings purchased by Mr. Nicholas Chevalier and Colin McKay Smith in 1875.' Right, well, let's have a look. I was under the impression they purchased Australian paintings. The first, if my memory serves me correctly, was Conrad Martens, a watercolor of Apsley Falls."

Michael's cane tapped on the parquet floor as he began a slow tour around the perimeter. "Hmm. It would seem I was wrong. Why in heaven's name would they purchase paintings from England? I realize it was before Federation, but we're our own nation now. The Commonwealth of Australia."

Jane let Michael's political ranting wash over her as she made a quick circuit of the room. Seven paintings in all. All landscapes and nothing that looked remotely Australian, except perhaps the picture of a ship on a stormy gray sea. She stepped closer. *Sir Oswald Brierly, A fresh breeze off Revel, France 1875.* Not Australian. By the time they got out, Michael would be in full flight.

God help them!

She moved on to the next painting. A group of cattle grazing by a river. It could have been the Hunter River except for the fact that the light was softer, sort of older looking. *Henry Britten Williams, Cattle piece, a scene on the Wye, 1873.* What was the Wye? She needed an atlas. It frustrated her enormously when she didn't have all the facts at her fingertips.

The next painting was very much like the one of the cows by

the river, a country scene, the sort of picturesque village they put on Christmas cards except there was no snow and no robins in sight. She'd never understood why people sent greetings cards of England in the winter when in Australia the sun was blinding and the sky an incandescent blue.

She'd rather be taking a look around the building, maybe a little more of the city. There had to be more than these country scenes. The next one showed a thatched cottage with a girl leaning over the gate. Jane read the title: *Marigold Penter, Waiting at the village gate.*

Michael stepped up beside her. "No chance of mistaking that one for Australia." He let out a humph and turned to a page in the catalogue they'd been given at the entrance. "It's definitely England. It says the painter comes from the West Country. That she was one of the first female impressionists to be exhibited in Paris. Not my kind of thing. All this English rubbish." He wandered off, his cane *tip-tapping*.

"She is regarded as one of the most talented women in her field."

Jane spun around. A thin-faced man wearing a loose-fitting checked jacket, the sort that would send Elizabeth into the pits of despair, regarded her with a patronizing air.

"I beg your pardon?"

"Marigold Penter. My wife, the artist."

Her face flushed as she tried to remember if she'd said anything inappropriate or had simply thought it. She was probably the color of strawberry jam. Well and truly. What had Aunt Elizabeth said she must do when she put her foot in it? "I do beg your pardon." And change the subject. To what? "Have you had the opportunity to see the Australian landscape exhibition yet? Mr. . . ." She snatched another look at the card next to the painting. "Penter?"

"Langdon-Penter. No, I haven't. The crowds are a bit much." He sounded almost bored, his voice drawling. "The gallery purchased another of my wife's village series, and we have taken the opportunity to visit Australia."

Michael appeared beside her again. "Seen enough, Jane? I think it's time we went to look at the Australian paintings. This romantic English rubbish does nothing for me."

"This is Mr. Langdon-Penter." She glared at Michael. "His *wife* painted this picture."

The tips of Michael's ears turned an interesting shade of pink and he held out his hand. "Michael Quinn."

"Ah, Mr. Quinn! It is my pleasure." Langdon-Penter stepped in front of her with a self-confident smile and as good as elbowed her aside.

"I was just commenting on your wife's painting. Is it for sale?" Michael wasn't interested in buying the painting, not at all. Jane shot a look at him, caught his twinkling eyes.

"The gallery doesn't sell the works it acquires." Langdon-Penter drew back his shoulders. "They intend to show my wife's paintings alongside some of your Australian impressionists."

"Indeed. How very exciting." Jane flashed Michael a look of triumph. "Is your wife here?" She searched the crowd for someone who looked as though she might be an artist.

"No, she is not. I handle her business arrangements."

Michael threw Jane a warning look, knowing very well which way her mind had traveled. She'd spent enough time in Elizabeth's company to be well versed in her belief that women should manage their own affairs.

"Come along, Jane, let's go and see if we can see the Australian landscapes. Nice to meet you."

Michael bobbed his head and Jane slipped her hand through the crook of his elbow and off they went, leaving Mr. Langdon-Penter framing his next sentence.

The next two hours passed in a blur of pictures, strange smells, and too many people. Nothing that sparked Jane's interest. She got a mouthful from one of the suited gentlemen standing guard when she'd asked if they had any of Leonardo da Vinci's drawings. What she'd like was a nice long glass of Bessie's lemonade and maybe an egg-and-lettuce sandwich. Her stomach gave an assenting rumble.

When they finally stepped outside, Jane dragged in a rewarding lungful of the fresh air blowing in from the botanical gardens.

Michael drew to a halt. "What would you like to do now? A walk through the gardens? It's quite shaded, and there is a café in George Street where we can get a cup of tea, a late lunch, a strawberry ice perhaps. Elizabeth had a suggestion. She thought you might like to take a ride through the grounds of the university and see where you will sit the entrance exam, then we'll catch the Maitland train."

Before Jane could respond, Langdon-Penter appeared right in front of them, blocking the path. "What a coincidence. Maitland, you say? Small country town in the Hunter Valley, I believe."

Michael puffed out his chest as he always did when the subject of Maitland came up. "Hardly small. A population of over eight thousand. Maitland is a very progressive city, and we have an active Benevolent Society who are keen to sponsor exhibitions, particularly now we have such a wonderful display space in the new technical college."

Langdon-Penter held up his index finger with an air of self-importance. "I might be one step ahead of you. One of my wife's paintings will be on display at the technical college. A Major Witherspoon has arranged it."

Jane didn't miss the look on Michael's face. He and the major didn't agree on anything, most especially if it smacked of politics.

"A display of significant paintings purchased by the gallery. I'm sure you and your daughter would enjoy them."

"I shall mention the matter to my sister. She will be most interested. Does your wife sell to private collectors? I would enjoy viewing her other work."

Had Michael gone mad?

"Unfortunately we're leaving for Melbourne tomorrow. We have an appointment with the gallery there. Perhaps we could arrange a viewing on our return." Langdon-Penter rubbed his hands together, the skin on his palms making a rasping sound.

"Perhaps." Michael slipped Jane's arm through his and without another word started down the path.

"We are bringing the extended exhibition to Maitland after we finish in Melbourne," Langdon-Penter called.

Michael let out a long-suffering sigh and turned back. "Are you, by Jove! Good chap. Now, if you'll excuse me, Jane and I have business to attend to."

SIX

HILL END, 1863

Sitting in the back of a heavily laden bullock dray with no shade from the sun, wedged between a mound of flour sacks and more barrels than he dared contemplate, was not Michael's idea of heaven. The mere thought of all the ale made his stomach turn, made worse by the malty aroma that billowed around whenever the dray hit a bump in the road, which was often, real often.

Up on the box seat, three men fought for enough space to rest their bony bums, their voices getting louder and more raucous as they made short work of another flagon of rum. Ahead, a trail of wagons lined the track and behind an army of men on foot, some pushing wheelbarrows or hefting pickaxes and shovels and all manner of strange-looking devices. Mrs. Cameron was right. Hardly a woman or child in sight. A couple of impatient horsemen squeezed past, scattering the men on foot and blanketing everyone in a cloud of dust.

"We'll make it before nightfall if we're lucky." The teamster threw a half-hearted grin over his shoulder.

Michael hoped to God they would; all feeling in his arse had vanished days ago, and the hypnotic rhythm of the continual bumping and grinding had addled his brain and turned him into a rattling skeleton.

The farther they meandered westward, drifting through Sofala and Sallys Flat, the more eerie the landscape became, the hills all deforested, the gullies eroded. "What's all that?" He pointed to the pockmarked slopes.

"Mullock hills. That's what's left over after they've panned for the gold."

A scattering of bodies crouched in the gully, some up to their knees in water, their crude tents and shacks pitched close by. On the opposite side of the slope clusters of men toiled with picks and shovels.

The dray descended a steep slope and rounded a sharp bend. Michael's mouth gaped. Against a backdrop of mountains and gorges, the crush of people forced them to slow.

"Hill End up ahead."

Bathurst had been the only halfway decent town they'd passed, yet here in the middle of nowhere the streets thronged with people, no mistaking their many and varied origins. From the sounds of the voices there were more Irish than he'd seen since he'd left Liverpool, and where the Irish weren't, the Scots reigned, their lyrical tones ringing loud and clear.

A bunch of adventurous-looking young lads, shotguns slung over their shoulders, swaggered past, shouting a series of obscenities at a group of Chinamen, drawing attention to their round faces and strangely colored skin. Even their clothes marked them as different—conical-shaped hats and long shirts hanging over baggy trousers. Possibly not such a bad idea. Michael had itched his skin raw beneath his thick woolen trousers and shirt after sitting in the scorching sun for days.

The dray bumped along, past rows of tidy little houses, their gardens surrounded by picket fences crowded with flowers and fruit trees—a woman's touch without a doubt. All Mam's dreams might have come true in this place.

Across the street, outside the only two-story building he'd seen, a group of businessmen stood in their bowler hats and suits looking as though they ran the place.

And the noise. A continual pounding made his ears ring. "What's the awful noise?"

"The stamper battery. Only day you'll get any peace is Sunday." The teamster slowed the dray and the three men toppled out. "Come and sit up the front. Give you a sense of the town."

Michael climbed over the backboard and slid onto the box seat when the teamster pointed to a compact line of buildings clinging to the side of the ridge, running north to south, for about half a mile. "What's a stamper battery?" He had to shout to make his voice carry over the incessant thumping.

"A great big machine. They use it to crush the quartz."

"Is that where you find the gold?"

"Could be. If you strike it lucky. Reef gold, not alluvial. They've opened up a mine above the river, built a dam too. There's good money to be made. Said you wanted Diggers Rest?"

Michael nodded, his eyes bulging as he counted the number of pubs. Enough for every man Jack to take his fill. There was a telegraph office and a couple of large stores, rows of smaller shops, even a dispensary.

"Diggers Rest is up there. But there's better places than that."

"Nah. That's what I want, that's where me da is."

The teamster cocked a shaggy eyebrow and shrugged. "That case, I'll let you off here." The dray slowed and Michael hit the ground with a thud, his bag jarring his shoulder.

"Head down there a piece. It'll be on your left."

"Thanks, mate." Michael let the word *mate* roll off his tongue and lifted his hand in farewell. He liked the word and the look of this place, liked it a lot. The clerk's news about Mam and the brief note had put the fear of God into him, but now that he'd seen the town, especially those neat little cottages, his cloud of worry had lifted. There'd been a mistake. Had to be. How could a bloke from Sydney know what had happened to his mam nearly two hundred miles away? He could see her in one of those neat little cottages, cheeks plump and pink from the stove, all trace of the famine wiped away; she'd be right at home.

Diggers Rest was easy to find—a tumbledown weatherboard warehouse that looked as though the slightest puff of wind would send it toppling. Michael shouldered open the door and dropped his bag to the ground. The stench and the darkness hit him, and he stood for a moment inhaling the strange, smoky air.

"I'm looking for Michael Ó'Cuinn."

A wizened bloke standing at a long counter made of some sort of polished wood and stinking of sweat gave him a puzzled frown. Behind him, stacks of large bales and boxes were organized along the walls and small ceramic barrels lined the narrow shelves. "Quinn."

"Yeah. Quinn." What was it about these people? Couldn't pronounce a man's name? Perhaps that's why they called everyone mate.

"Who would you be?"

"Michael Ó'Cuinn."

The bloke gave a bark of laughter, though Michael couldn't see what was funny.

"Michael Quinn," he repeated, "he's me da."

"Is he now? He's upstairs." He flicked his head over his shoulder toward the even darker interior. "Wily old bugger."

A young boy, who didn't come much higher than Michael's elbow, emerged from the shadows, dropped a wooden frame full of beads onto the counter, and peered at him.

"Take him to Quinn, Jing."

"Upstairs?"

"Yeah! Up-bloody-stairs. It's his son."

The boy inclined his head to the back of the warehouse where a tiny lamp flickered and spluttered in the gloom. "Come, Mr. Quinn."

"Me name's Michael. Mr. Quinn's me da."

When they approached the dim doorway at the back of the warehouse, Jing knocked twice and waited until the door latch raised. He led the way up some gloomy steps to a small barred door without a handle. It'd need an ax to burst it open.

Jing put his mouth close to the door and uttered a string of low-toned words that sounded more like a song than anything else, and the door mysteriously swung open.

Michael turned back once they'd passed through, wishing he had time to study the ingenious system of cords and pulleys that controlled the door. More lamps spluttered and flickered in the gloom, and the air was heavy with a pungent floral odor. A grim-faced Chinaman sat in one corner brooding over a smoky little lamp, which he was feeding with fat from a tin. Arranged around the room a group of recumbent figures reclined, pipes at their mouths, inhaling the smoke.

"I'm looking for me da. Michael Quinn."

The old man waved his hand at the group.

"Me da . . ." His words petered out as one of the corpse-like figures rolled to a sitting position.

"Mr. Quinn." Jing crossed the floor to the platform and eased the old man upright.

It couldn't be Da. What had happened to the strapping man he remembered, the man who brandished a hurling stick like a weapon?

Not an ounce of flesh remained on his bones, his chest concave and his legs frailer than a splinter of wood, with vomit staining his threadbare shirt. "He's sick. Is it the consumption?"

Jing shook his head. "Ah-pen-yen."

"Ah-pen-yen?"

"Opium." The old man's hand rested on Jing's shoulder. "He is searching for lost heaven. To take away the pain."

Michael sank down on the bench, lips clamped against the roil of his stomach.

Tears welled in Da's eyes and he blindly reached for the clay pipe. "It's Michael, Da."

Blinking in the half-light, he rolled over and peered into his face. "Michael, me boy." The words wheezed past his cracked lips.

"Where's Mam?"

He sucked hard on the pipe and lay back, eyes closed, shutting him out.

"Da!" Michael reached for his shoulder, the withered skin dry and fevered beneath his touch.

"Come with me. I know." Jing reached out a hand, pulled him to his feet, and led him back down the narrow staircase.

Michael wasn't certain he wanted to hear the story from this diminutive boy with his smooth skin and narrow eyes, who looked a darn sight younger than he was, but there was little else he could do except follow.

When they reached the bottom of the rickety stairs, Jing led him to a corner of the store and sat him down on an upturned box. "Wait. I'll get tea."

He didn't want tea. He knew what he'd seen. Da wouldn't last long; the oily sweat smearing his emaciated body and the overpowering stench of vomit, mucus, and excrement told him more than enough.

Jing thrust a small cup into Michael's shaking hand. He inhaled the clear perfumed liquid and turned up his nose.

"Drink it."

Michael sipped the tea, winced as it burned down his throat. He wiped his mouth with the back of his hand and put down the cup. "What happened to me da?"

"He's no good." Jing tapped at his head. "Fell down and broke his head."

"He cracked his skull?" Didn't they have hospitals in this god-forsaken hole? "What did the doctor say?"

"He's finished."

"What happened to me mam? Where is she?"

"Very good lady. Come." Jing clattered down the dark corridor, through the doors and out into the sunshine, taking off at a fair gallop down the road.

"Wait a minute. Where are we going?" He wasn't leaving Da, nor was he leaving his belongings with these strange Chinamen.

"To see your mam. Good stone. Your da spent up big." He scooped out some shape with his hands.

Michael grabbed hold of Jing's arm. "Stop! Me mam, where is she?"

"Up the road a piece. Catholic burial ground."

The wind whistled out of his lungs, and he sank down in the gutter. Mam was dead and Da only a few steps behind. He squinted up at the boy. How would he know? He needed someone he could trust, someone who'd understand. "Where's the priest? Where's the church?"

Michael scrubbed Father MacCormick's large white handkerchief across his face, drew in several slow breaths, and tried to remember he was a man. Right now all he wanted was his mam's soothing smile and the gentle touch of her hand.

"There's nothing to be ashamed of, lad. It's come as a shock, I can rightly imagine."

"What about Da? Can't the doctors do anything? Should I take him back to Sydney? Get him away from the Chinamen and their filthy smoke."

"I doubt he'd make the trip. Be thankful you'll have the opportunity to say your goodbyes. Don't be quoting me, but the opium's the kindest way. Once your mam passed he turned to the bottle something fierce, stumbled and fell into one of the old diggings. Jing found him the next morning. There's naught they can do for him."

"Where's me mam buried?"

"Over yonder, and there's space alongside for your da; it's what he wants. Then you'll have to be deciding what to do with the business."

"The bullock dray?"

"Your da did well, Michael. Very well."

"He found gold?"

"In the early days, alluvial gold. He made a wise decision after that. His cartage business, more than one dray, and the Diggers Rest, they'll be coming to you."

Michael screwed the soggy handkerchief into a ball. "You're saying Da's a wealthy man. Did good for himself?" He couldn't imagine the crumpled bag of bones he'd seen making good of much. He'd rather remember him as he'd seen him last on Irish soil.

"Gold's all well and good, but the diggers need to eat, need the services your da provided."

Then what was he doing holed up in that awful attic sucking on an opium pipe?

"There's nothing you can do for him, Michael. He'll be called soon. He'll die a happy man. He and your mam talked about nothing but you and your sister. Is she with you?"

Michael's stomach turned upside down, threatened to spill the greasy lamb and damper he'd had that morning, only a few hours ago, when he'd imagined something far different. He sucked in a shallow breath. "Elizabeth's in Sydney. I left her there with a family we met on the ship. I didn't know what I'd find. The bloke in the immigration office made mention of Ma's passing."

"You're a sensible lad. Now, let's be going to see your da. He's better after a pipe or two, and you'll be coming back with me until we sort things out."

As much as he wished otherwise, even a fool could see Da wasn't long for this world, and Michael was more than thankful for the good father's support. Nothing was as he'd imagined. A fall down a mineshaft. What terrible luck. He'd dreamed they'd left all that behind in Ireland.

<hr />

Over the next few days, Michael worked like a man possessed. With Jing's help, he cleaned and scrubbed and moved Da downstairs into the room at the back of the warehouse. A local girl, Kitty, came to cook and clean, and Jing ensured that there was a supply of the little brown pellets, making Da's last days on God's earth as comfortable as they could be.

And when the time came, Father MacCormick laid him to rest alongside Mam in the little cemetery. Some things a man couldn't change, and so Michael turned his mind to his inheritance, because as surely as God was looking down on him, Da'd left him the means to make a decent life for himself and Elizabeth.

SEVEN

MAITLAND TOWN, 1913

"Jane, try not to bounce when you walk. It makes you seem overenthusiastic."

Jane slowed her pace. She didn't want to cause a ruckus; she wanted everything to go as smoothly as possible, especially since Elizabeth had suggested she accompany her to the technical college. Ever since she'd finished evening classes, her life revolved around accounts books and never-ending lists of figures. It wasn't that she didn't like the work, but it didn't stretch her mind the way it once had, and although she wouldn't dare admit it to Elizabeth, she was a tad bored. She needed a conundrum, something to solve, a puzzle . . . better still, a mystery. She'd cracked the last of Sir Arthur Conan Doyle's mysteries before Sherlock. Now, that would be the job! She'd definitely have the aptitude for that sort of challenge.

"Jane, you're still bouncing."

Yes, she was. She couldn't help it. The thought of the exhibition had her nerves vibrating. It wasn't so much the paintings from the art gallery—although they seemed to be the only thing anyone could talk about—it was the Tost and Rohu curiosities, taxidermied specimens, and fossilized remains. A prehistoric skull and jawbone reputed to belong to the fearsome prehistoric wombat, the diprotodon. She still hadn't found the time to visit the library at the School of Arts and check her facts, but if she remembered correctly, they'd been found over sixty years earlier and no one had paid very much attention until now.

Jane squinted up at the facade. Built of red brick with a steep slate roof, the building was hardly a temple to art, but it was impressive nonetheless. She'd read that a volcanic rock, trachyte, had been used for the steps, and every time she passed by she pictured them erupting, bubbling in a welter of steam and sulfurous gases. She took the three steps in a bound and stood waiting for Elizabeth, who insisted on adjusting her hat and pulling her gloves straight before she gave Jane a nod indicating that she should push open the door.

The high-ceilinged foyer illuminated by the stained glass skylight put her in mind of the hushed reverence of a church, which she promptly destroyed as her boots clattered on the parquetry floor.

Mrs. Witherspoon, guardian of the technical college, raised her head and came to her feet, fawning. "Miss Quinn, how wonderful to see you out and about and looking so bright and sunny."

Jane would hardly describe Elizabeth's steel-gray walking-out suit as sunny, but the boater with the mauve and green ribbon, a nod to Elizabeth's belief in women's rights, was a cheerful touch. Jane hefted her satchel onto the polished cedar bench top, which served as a desk, and removed the ledgers.

"I can't thank you enough for all your hard work." Mrs. Witherspoon's fingers compulsively smoothed the leather of the ledger as though she couldn't believe the miracle that had transformed the disorganized piles of papers and receipts she'd handed over into one neatly bound book entitled *Technical College Accounts*.

Jane had no idea why people found accounts so difficult. She still preferred numbers to words, though she no longer needed to rush for a dictionary every few minutes as she had when she was younger. Numbers had a practicality, a definitive no-nonsense, no-alternatives, no-misinterpretations black-and-white reality. She always found a certain security and comfort in the neatly lined-up columns and rows of the accounts ledgers.

"Jane is responsible for the work." Aunt Elizabeth's mouth curved in a semblance of a smile. "Jane, would you be so kind as to explain the nature of the ledger and how best Mrs. Witherspoon can continue?"

When Mrs. Witherspoon opened the book her face creased in a worried frown. She flipped through a few more of the pages. "Where does it tell me how much we owe and how much we have in reserve?"

"Jane, while you answer Mrs. Witherspoon's questions, I'm going to take a walk around the exhibition. I've heard nothing but good reports of the major's efforts to procure displays from Sydney. So good for the town."

Mrs. Witherspoon raised her head from the ledgers and simpered. "The news has traveled like a wildfire. There's never any need to advertise. Jane Tost and her daughter, Ada Rohu, are a force to be reckoned with. The ladies did exceptionally well for themselves. Their shop in Sydney went from strength to strength; they won numerous medals and awards for their meticulous taxidermy at international trade exhibitions. I do admire women in business, don't you?"

"Indeed I do." Elizabeth's face betrayed little but her desire to escape from Mrs. Witherspoon's incessant rambling.

"Mother and daughter, *Jane* Tost, what a coincidence . . ." Mrs. Witherspoon gave a girlish giggle as though she had singularly discovered something of great significance.

Raising her hand in a regal wave, Elizabeth sailed beneath the rose-adorned Tudor doors into the space now reserved for exhibitions.

"I'll leave you to discover the major's treasures," Mrs. Witherspoon called after her.

Jane swallowed her sigh. What she wouldn't give to be accompanying Elizabeth.

Mrs. Witherspoon brushed her hands together and turned back to the neat rows of figures in the ledger. "Such a clever girl. Have you finished your schooling?"

"Some time ago." Jane doubted anyone in the town would ever see her as anything but another of the poor little orphans Elizabeth Quinn had taken under her wing, despite the fact that Jane'd been almost running the auction house since Michael started his campaign for a seat at the next election.

"Now, see if you can explain these hieroglyphics to me. Major Witherspoon is convinced I am lacking." She tapped her finger against the side of her head and rolled her eyes.

Maybe Jane could agree with the major in some cases. "The column here is for outgoings and the next page is for incoming monies." Surely Mrs. Witherspoon could understand. "The items are in the left-hand column, then the allocations in the additional columns." She stifled a groan, hoping Mrs. Witherspoon would catch on. "Here's your income. It follows the same pattern." She turned another page. "Think of it like this—debits to the window, credits to the door."

If she didn't finish soon, Elizabeth would be over and done with the exhibits. She had to see the jawbone and skull. The mere thought that giant wombats had once roamed the country set her mind on fire. Imagine the size of their burrows!

". . . and the monies received in this column." Mrs. Witherspoon's forehead creased in a frown. "Is that right, Jane? Jane . . ."

"Correct, Mrs. Witherspoon. I think you've got it. Now, if you'll excuse me, I must go and find Miss Quinn. We are expected home for tea."

"Of course, of course. I might have to call on you again. I'm sure you won't mind."

Jane drew in a deep breath, almost choking on the dusty scent of attar of roses emitting from Mrs. Witherspoon's bulky person, and nodded. "Excuse me." She bolted though the open archway into the display room and came to a skidding halt.

There in the middle of the room, on a large table bathed in a dazzling stream of light from one of the floor-to-ceiling windows, was the skull and lower jaw of the gigantic marsupial—monstrously huge. It could have swallowed her whole in one terrifying gulp and made short work of every bone in her body with the two enormous tusk-like teeth.

She tiptoed closer, hand outstretched, her skin prickling with a mixture of awe and trepidation. Two curved incisors protruded from the lower jaw, thicker than her thumb and at least twelve inches long. She stretched out her arm, measuring the length of the skull—over a yard. How she wished they'd displayed the whole skeleton. She backed away, almost barreling into one of the glass-fronted cabinets crowding the dim perimeter.

She spun around. Each cabinet contained a different bird, set in its own environment, swooping from boughs or perched atop rocks. Between each display case hung an assortment of paintings and etchings, which, if the *Maitland Mercury* was to be believed, Major Witherspoon had procured single-handedly from the National Gallery for Maitland's benefit. No wonder Elizabeth hadn't reappeared. There was enough to keep a person occupied for weeks.

Jane ambled back to the diprotodon. The information on the card said that it was discovered eight feet below the surface on the Darling Downs, the giant teeth poking through a creek bed, and they estimated the specimen was over a hundred thousand years old. From the size of the skull it would have to be larger than a hippopotamus. Why had no one ever told her about this before?

The striking of the clock in the foyer brought her up with a shudder. Elizabeth—where was she? Jane made a circuit of the gloomy edge of the room and returned to the center. She glanced at the diprotodon's gnashing teeth, an odd, unsettling feeling prickling the back of her neck now that the beam of sunlight had faded and darkening shadows stretched out their fingers.

Elizabeth must have left while she was still talking to Mrs. Witherspoon. Jane made one more quick lap of the room and threaded her way toward the three massive Gothic arches near the back of the exhibition space, taking care not to nudge any of the cabinets. As she rounded the last set of display cabinets, her foot caught and she turned her ankle. Steadying herself, she bent down to fasten her laces.

In the corner of the room, in a damp-smelling space between two large cabinets, a figure huddled, knees drawn up to her chest, her hands cradling her bent head as though protecting it. A low noise like a moaning wind filled Jane's ears.

"G'woam. G'woam."

"Aunt Elizabeth." Jane edged closer, her voice barely more than a whisper, reached down, and gave Elizabeth's shoulder a gentle shake. Elizabeth flinched and tightened her grasp on her head and the hollow wail echoed. Sinking down, Jane put her arm around Elizabeth's shoulders. "What is it? Let me help you up."

Elizabeth didn't acknowledge her presence. Instead, her body rocked backward and forward, and the strange wailing sound intensified, filling Jane with a morbid sense of dread.

"Everything's all right. Come on. Stand up. Let's get you back home."

"G'woam. G'woam." Elizabeth's head sank deeper onto her chest, her arms shielding her head.

Jane's mind spiraled and she inhaled a steadying breath. It was Elizabeth. She knew it was—the neat, almost masculine gray suit told her so, as did the buttoned boots she always wore, but the voice . . . the voice wasn't Elizabeth's.

"G'woam. G'woam."

It sounded like a foreign language, one of the native tongues perhaps.

The awful wail intensified. Mrs. Witherspoon would come barging in any moment. She couldn't find Elizabeth like this.

Jane unpeeled Elizabeth's hand from her head, clasped her gloved fingers, and eased her back against the wall, then wiped the damp hair from her drained skin. The look of horror etched on Elizabeth's face terrified Jane more than the dreadful wailing. Beneath her glazed, staring eyes her skin sagged, and tracks scored the powder she so carefully applied to her face every morning.

What should she do? "Come on. I'll help you up, you've taken a turn."

At the sound of her voice, the tension left Elizabeth and she fell back against the wall. Jane eased her to her feet, slid her other arm around Elizabeth's shoulder, and led her through the strange cloying twilight out into the foyer.

She settled Elizabeth into the nearest chair, then walked to the desk where Mrs. Witherspoon stood poring over the ledgers. "Could I trouble you for a glass of water? Miss Quinn has taken a turn. The heat, I think. I'd like to call a hansom cab. It's too hot for her to walk home or take the tram."

"Goodness gracious." Mrs. Witherspoon rushed across the foyer and peered at Elizabeth. "What's happened?"

A flash of panic flickered across Elizabeth's face when Mrs. Witherspoon leaned over her. The dreadful woman simply made matters worse. Jane drew herself up to her full height. "Would you please fetch a glass of water and call a cab?"

There must have been something in her tone because the interfering busybody swiveled on her heels and as good as ran.

Jane crouched next to Elizabeth, lifting her hands and placing them in her lap. Despite the oppressive heat, Elizabeth's hands felt cold, yet there was a fine sheen of sweat on her upper lip.

"G'woam. G'woam." Elizabeth's hands gravitated toward her head again but Jane held them firm.

When Mrs. Witherspoon reappeared with a glass of water, Jane lifted it slowly to Elizabeth's lips. As she sipped, a slow tremble rippled across her shoulders.

Mrs. Witherspoon leaned forward, enveloping them in a cloud of her sickly sweet fragrance. "She's pale. Feverish possibly. Shall I call the doctor?" The intense scent of attar of roses must have acted like smelling salts because Elizabeth's eyes flashed open and within a moment cleared.

"Would you like another drink?" Jane held up the glass of water.

Elizabeth shook her head and stumbled to her feet. "I'd like to go home."

Jane held her fast. "Mrs. Witherspoon has called a cab. It will be here in a moment." She flashed a glance over her shoulder at Mrs. Witherspoon, who nodded her head and disappeared through the front doors into the street.

Elizabeth drew in a deep breath and smoothed down her skirt. "We'll walk. It's not even a mile." She stood up and strode to the door, head held high, as though nothing out of the ordinary had occurred.

Jane left the glass of water on the counter and rushed after her.

Mrs. Witherspoon must have been better at arranging transport than her accounts because a cab stood waiting.

"Can you follow us, in case we need you? Aileen House, Church Street."

The driver doffed his cap. "Right you are."

Elizabeth, showing no signs of her previous weakness, ignored the cab. "Come along, Jane. Hurry up. We've got no time to lose. I'm expecting the ladies from the Benevolent Society."

"I think perhaps you need to rest—"

"I'm perfectly fine. Stop fussing."

They trailed past the bookseller and stationers and Mr. Paskin's Musical Instrument Warehouse along High Street. Regardless of what Elizabeth said, her grasp on Jane's arm tightened with each step, and by the time they reached the bank she was placing each foot carefully, taking one step at a time.

Jane flagged down the cab. Elizabeth sank into the corner of the seat and stared straight ahead for the remainder of the journey.

With a sigh of relief, Jane pushed open the garden gate and led Elizabeth up the path, past the neatly tended standard roses to the front door. Before Jane could disentangle her hand, Lucy threw open the door. She took one look at Elizabeth and sprang into action. "Come inside, come and sit down. It's so hot out there."

"Aunt Elizabeth isn't feeling well. Could you please get her some water, and maybe some tea? I'll take her up to her room. She needs to rest."

Lucy rushed off without any of her usual complaints, and Jane helped Elizabeth up the stairs to her bedroom. She sat her down on the bed and removed her buttoned boots, puffed up the pillows, and helped her slide back against the headboard.

Elizabeth accepted Jane's ministrations, her eyes wide and staring in her pale face. Jane smoothed her hair back from her forehead, expecting to find her burning up, but her skin felt cool beneath her fingertips. If anything, she felt a little cold. Jane draped a cashmere shawl across her lap and perched on the edge of the bed. "Lucy will be up in a moment with some tea."

Elizabeth stared blindly at the window, her lips drawn in a tight line, then blinked rapidly as if trying to clear her thoughts.

"It's all right." Jane reached for the pale hand lying on the coverlet. "You'll feel better soon."

Elizabeth's lips trembled and a tear slid down her cheek.

Jane reached for the handkerchief on the bedside table and wiped it away. "You took a turn." She smoothed Elizabeth's forehead. "Sleep. It'll all be over when you wake." She straightened the pillow and tucked Elizabeth's cold hands under the shawl.

A gentle knock on the door heralded Lucy's arrival and Jane took the tray from her, ignoring her questioning gaze, and closed the bedroom door firmly.

Jane held the cup toward Elizabeth. "Be careful, it's hot."

Elizabeth shot her an embarrassed look. "I don't want anything."

Elizabeth pushed her hands flat against the mattress and eased her way down the bed, her eyelids drooping. Jane smoothed the cover on the bed and drew the curtains over the windows, picked up the cup of tea, and drank it herself.

Jane had never seen the normally competent woman anything other than perfectly groomed and composed. Lying there with her hair awry and the tear stains tracking her cheeks, she'd aged ten years. In all the time Jane had lived at Church Street, Elizabeth had never spent a day in bed. She was always up for breakfast with Michael, immaculately dressed, hair neatly styled, and when she retired at night, it was always at the same time, as though she had some internal clock and it would be a mortal sin to interrupt the preordained timetable of the day. She was as regimented and ordered as the numbers she bludgeoned into neat columns. Something had upset Elizabeth, but Jane had no idea what.

EIGHT

SYDNEY, 1866

Elizabeth rubbed the heel of her hand against the dirty pane of glass and pressed her nose against the window, watching and waiting. Four days of nonstop rain had turned Sydney's streets into a mass of smelly puddles and sticky manure.

It would have to be paid for later, these unexpected few days of reprieve from the washing. That was the way of it, now that Mrs. Cameron kept her home from school. There was never any time for reading, and she missed it something fierce. No books either, now that she couldn't borrow them from school. So she read the only one she had, over and over again, the one Michael had bought her for her eighth birthday. It was beginning to feel as though she'd waited as long as Sleeping Beauty for Michael's return.

In the beginning he'd come regular as clockwork every quarter, but now he had the extra dray he didn't always do the Sydney run. Said he was too busy rebuilding and he had to be in Hill End for his Saturday auction.

"What are you doing staring out of that window?" Mrs. Cameron's voice startled her and she whipped around. "There's work to be done. As soon as this rain stops we're going to be up to our armpits in washing."

Up to everyone else's armpits, more than like. Elizabeth wrinkled her nose, trying to rid herself of the permanent smell of sweat-soaked undergarments that permeated the downstairs room where Mrs. Cameron housed her ladies' laundry business.

She picked up the broom and half-heartedly ran it across the floor, swept the dirt out into the backyard, and closed the door before the floor got soaked. The next day there wouldn't be standing space. It'd be covered with piles and piles of bags full of sweaty, smelly unmentionables and voluminous petticoats, and by evening her skinned knuckles would be red raw from the lye soap after scrubbing away all manner of repulsive stains.

Mrs. Cameron swore by a lye and lard mixture blended with wood ash. But it turned Elizabeth's stomach, not that it was ever full enough to part with the meager meals they had these days.

The money Michael sent every quarter ought to feed the three of them a lot better, but Elizabeth knew where most of it went—straight into Mr. Cameron's pocket and down to the Fortune of War, where he spent all his time drinking since he'd lost his boat and his business.

"Have you finished down there yet?"

"Almost." She shot the last piece of dust under the cupboard and trudged upstairs.

"Come and take my shoes off. My feet are giving me hell's delight."

Sucking in a deep breath, Elizabeth knelt at Mrs. Cameron's feet and slid her felt slippers off.

"Me bunions are near killing me. I cannae get a decent pair of slippers for love nor money."

"You should ask Michael when he comes."

"Why would I do that?"

"Because he knows where to get everything. He told me last time that the auction house was selling all sorts of ladies' finery, now more people have moved their families to Hill End."

A curl of excitement wound through her. The next time Michael came she was certain he'd take her to Hill End. He kept putting it off, saying the cottage wasn't ready yet, and she couldn't sleep in the warehouse because it wasn't good enough, and there was no one to look after her while he was on the road. She'd just have to try and convince him she wouldn't be a burden.

"You can wipe that look off your face. God only knows when he'll turn up next. With all this rain the roads'll be clogged. He won't risk it just to see you, and besides, I need you here with me." That was true enough. Michael wouldn't risk the dray while the rivers were in flood, not because he didn't want to see her, but because the business depended on the drays. He'd explained that to her last time he'd visited.

When Michael did arrive, she was going to tell him the truth. Not stand there, mouth closed, accepting everything Mrs. Cameron said. When he heard she wasn't going to school anymore and had to spend her time up to her elbows in dirty washing, he'd whisk her away just like the handsome prince in her storybook. Away from the smelly laundry, away over the mountains where she'd be with Michael, where she belonged.

"There's broth on the stove. Go get yourself a bowl, then go down the road and get a couple of pounds of lard and some more lye. Once this rain stops we'll need more soap."

Elizabeth chased a piece of disintegrating potato around the bowl and contemplated the afternoon. If the rain stopped, the reek from the steaming streets would be foul. She upended the remains back into the pan and pulled her coat down from the peg behind the door, forcing her arms into the sleeves. It barely came down to her knees and wouldn't do up anymore. Proof, according to Mrs. Cameron, that she was getting more than enough to eat and should stop whining.

She made her way up along George Street, stopping now and again to peer into the windows. Last time Michael had been in town, he'd taken her to the Café Français on George Street, and she'd thought she'd flown to heaven. They'd sat at little metal tables, and when that first spoonful of strawberry ice had landed on her tongue she'd understood just how much more there was to life than smelly unmentionables and watery broth.

She swiped away the raindrop dangling from the end of her nose and ducked into the grocery store. "Two pounds of lard, please, and four ounces of lye. On Cameron's account."

The man behind the counter brought his nose level with hers. "Can't be doing that, love. Not until the outstanding's paid up."

"But Mrs. Cameron—"

"You heard me, no more credit. Tell Her Majesty to come down and talk to me if she don't like it."

Masking the grin on her face, Elizabeth dawdled a bit longer on the doorstep. *Her Majesty* wouldn't take no for an answer, but until she deigned to come down herself there'd be no lard and lye. That meant Elizabeth wouldn't be spending the next day elbow-deep in smelly unmentionables. Perhaps every cloud did truly have a silver lining.

When the shopkeeper's beady eyes began to make her skin prickle, she moved outside into the rain. Head down and collar up, she stepped onto the road and almost missed the huge bullock dray ambling down the road. Squealing, she darted back. It ground to a halt close to the corner of George Street.

"What the hell do you think you're doing? I could've squashed you flat." Michael's face glared down at her and her heart almost took flight.

"Michael!"

When he jumped down from the dray she threw herself at him and spread her arms wide as he swung her high in the air, round and round until the world turned upside down and her heart flew into her mouth.

By the time he put her down, the bullocks had trundled halfway around the corner and they had to run to catch up.

"I thought you'd never come," said Elizabeth. "It's been a thousand lonely days and I've missed you so."

"Nowhere near that. Don't exaggerate." Michael snatched her up and plonked her on the front seat of the dray, then swung up next to her. "You can't be lonely with all your friends at school. What are you doing out here in the pouring rain?"

"I had to buy lard, for the soap. We've run out and after the rain . . ." The words dried in her mouth as his eyes narrowed.

———— ≈ ————

"Answer me question. Why weren't you at school? If you've done a runner and ducked off . . ." Michael couldn't imagine why she'd skip school. She loved it. Two spots of color flushed her pale cheeks, accentuating her thin face.

"Elizabeth?"

Her lower lip trembled and she snatched at it with her teeth. "Oh, me little darlin', there's no need to cry. Let's get this dray down to the docks and I'll take you home."

He reached over and grasped her cold hand in his, turned it over. Angry, red swollen blisters peppered her skin. His words dried in his throat. By all that was holy, something wasn't right, and he'd be finding out what it was.

It took an age to get the bullock dray down to the yards. He threw a handful of coins at one of the urchins to keep an eye out and with Elizabeth's hand tucked firmly in his, marched her back down the street to the Camerons'.

Poor little mite didn't say a word, although he could feel her hand shaking. He brought his fist up to the door and hammered hard.

"I have to use the back door. We don't use the front anymore."

"What do you mean you don't use the front? I've never heard such nonsense." He hammered his fist against the peeling paint.

The door flew open. "Michael, come in, come in," said Mrs. Cameron. "Look at you, you poor thing. You look like a drowned rat. Come upstairs, we'll get the fire going and warm you up."

The woman was all of a fluster and she'd not taken a blind bit of notice of Elizabeth.

"Go and put the kettle on, child. Michael'll be wanting a cup of tea, or something stronger perhaps?"

She took his arm and brought him into the front room, which was as damp and miserable as the bottom of a mineshaft.

"I'll not be staying long. I've a mind to take Elizabeth and buy her some new clothes. That coat she's wearing won't hardly do up and half her arms are hanging out. Did you not get the last money I sent?" That had to be the answer. He'd left the last run to Mr. Li; maybe he hadn't delivered it. But that was a load of bollocks. He'd trust the Li brothers with his life, had trusted them with Da's.

"It's not as easy as it once was. We've had to cut back a bit, and then when Bill lost his lighter . . . Well, I've had to start a little business of my own to make ends meet."

"His boat?"

"Costs in Sydney are rising every day."

Ah! So that was the way of it. He turned to the door as Elizabeth brought in the tea. She'd pulled a graying smock over her dress and had a moth-eaten mob cap clamped over her curls. She looked like a kitchen drudge. "Dressing up for the occasion, are you, darlin'?"

Elizabeth flushed to the roots of her lank hair, making him realize how wan she looked. He hadn't noticed the dark circles under her eyes, and her hands were still shaking, those poor red hands. "Put the tray down and come over here, darlin'."

He sucked in a deep breath and pulled her to him, wrapping his arm around her waist. She snuggled into his chest like a bedraggled puppy.

"Think you better tell me what's going on, Mrs. Cameron. I don't like what I'm seeing."

"Going on? What are you suggesting?"

"House is as cold as charity. Elizabeth looks as though she hasn't seen a decent feed in weeks. Tells me she hasn't been to school." The anger rose in him. He leaned forward and looked the woman straight in the face. "That's not the arrangement. What about her hands?" He picked one up. It lay red and swollen in his palm.

"I told you. Been having trouble making ends meet. Elizabeth must do her share. She's one of the family."

All he wanted to do was scoop Elizabeth up, wrap her in his great-coat, and spirit her away, but how could he? Out on the dray he was doing the Bathurst run six days out of seven. There was no place for her to stay. The warehouse was only half repaired; his bedroll, when he'd time to use it, thrown down out the back wherever there was space. Eating out of Li's kitchen or whatever he could grab on the road.

He dropped his head into his hands. "Tell me what the problem is."

"I told you. Bill's lost his boat. Owed some money, had to sell it off. It'll pass, just a bad patch. I'm making ends meet, and Elizabeth's helping me. We've got a ladies' laundry business." Her cheeks flushed. "Not something I like to discuss with a man."

And then he understood Elizabeth's hands. "You're going to discuss it, and you're going to discuss it now. How much do you need?"

"Michael, Michael." Elizabeth tugged at his sleeve. "Can I come with you to Hill End, see Mam and Da?"

Oh, he was the worst kind of lily-livered fool! An irritated huff sprang from his mouth.

"I won't be no trouble."

"No, love. We'll sort this out. You need to go to school. We'll get you some new clothes tomorrow, and some warm boots and gloves." He had to get her out of the room, had to sort this out. She couldn't come to Hill End with him, not yet. He wasn't ready. He still needed time to find another full-time dray driver, buy the cottage on Tambaroora Road he'd got his eye on, make a home just like he promised. "Go and play with Lizzie now while I sort it all out with Mrs. Cameron. I'll be back tomorrow and I'll take you out."

"Off you go, Elizabeth. You heard what Michael said."

With a look that as good as ripped out his heart, Elizabeth pattered to the door and slipped like a wraith into the dark corridor.

Once the door was closed he stood up, back to the empty fireplace. "How much do you need? How much a month? I want her fed proper, clean clothes, no more laundry work, school every day." It was the least he could do to make sure Elizabeth was cared for until he'd found a cottage for them to live in and got the business under control.

NINE

E lizabeth pried her lids open and surveyed the room.
What was she doing in bed? She had no memory of taking a
nap. She never took a nap. Come to that, she had no memory of entering her bedroom. She threw back the covers . . . Nor of taking off her
skirt and blouse. Good heavens! She was dressed in only her chemise.

She pushed back against pillows, tugged the sheet higher, and ran
her tongue around her mouth. She might as well have swallowed a
mouthful of cotton wool.

Jane sat beside her, stubby fingers plucking at the bedspread and
her gaze fixed on some point beyond the window, more than likely
contemplating some obscure calculation. The girl had no imagination,
only a prodigious memory for anything to do with facts and figures.

It wasn't until Elizabeth cleared her throat that Jane gave up chasing rainbows and paid her some attention. "You're awake."

"I'm parched."

"You've been sleeping with your mouth open."

The girl had no sense of decorum. "May I have some tea?" The
tray sat in its usual place under the window, the ray of afternoon light
turning the porcelain cups translucent.

71

Jane wiped her hand across her face and struggled to her feet, looking too tired to ask any of her interminable questions. Elizabeth didn't mind them, but they were—had always been—incessant. The girl had such a thirst for knowledge and an insatiable interest in the most obscure facts.

Her curiosity didn't, however, extend to the niceties of pouring tea. Jane slopped the tea into the cup, her hand shaking. As the fragrant jasmine scent released, it brought back the memory of Elizabeth's first taste, the first time she'd drunk the brew, her face puckering at the strange flavor. She'd been so nervous, wringing her hands and hiding her shabby boots under her skirt, praying the fascinating boy with the pigtail wouldn't think her a fool.

Such a long time ago. She liked to think, even after all the time that had passed, they might one day meet again. A foolish thought. He'd be long gone, back to his family in China.

The steam billowed onto her fingers.

"It's hot. Don't spill it." Jane peered into her face as though examining a specimen under glass. "Are you better?"

Her well-meaning attempt to emulate the patronizing tone reserved for invalids fell short of the mark. Something must have happened to upset her if she was attempting to cultivate bedside manners.

Elizabeth brought the cup to her lips, sipped, and let out a long, satisfying sigh. How had she become a cantankerous middle-aged woman who took pleasure in drinking jasmine tea in bed in the afternoon?

"I'll get up in a moment. The Benevolent Society ladies will be here before long and I haven't completed the final entries in the ledger."

A most unusual flush blossomed on Jane's cheeks, making her appear as guilty as a chorister caught with his hand in the donation plate. "I sent them away."

"Whatever did you do that for? The afternoon's been planned for weeks. They needed to know the state of their accounts before the committee meeting."

"After your turn I thought it would be better." Jane resumed her bedspread picking, her bitten fingernails compulsively tracing the patterns in the satin. She must remind Bessie to find some bitter aloes. That would keep Jane's fingers out of her mouth.

The steam from the tea played against her nostrils as she sipped. Her *turn*. She wriggled her toes under the sheets, gave her shoulders a tentative shrug. Everything felt normal. "There's nothing the matter with me. What time is it?"

Jane glanced at the carriage clock on the mantle. "Six fifty-two."

So precise. What was wrong with an approximation? Beyond the window the light had faded to a pearly gray streaked with lilac while she'd slept the day away like an invalid.

"It's about time we had supper. I'll see you in the dining room."

"Lucy's bringing you something on a tray."

"Stop mollycoddling me. What's all this about?"

"You don't remember, do you?"

Far too astute. Always had been, despite her disheveled appearance and bitten fingernails. "Of course I do."

Did she? Elizabeth forced her mind to rerun the day. Breakfast. Kedgeree. She could hardly forget that. Her favorite. She'd spent some time reading the *Maitland Mercury*, completed the word puzzle, attended to some correspondence, and then delivered the ledgers to Mrs. Witherspoon.

"We walked to the technical college. You remember that, don't you?"

Of course, of course. "The woman had trouble understanding the ledgers. You explained."

"Yes. That's right!" The beginning of a smile tilted the corners of Jane's lips. "Then what happened?"

Matters became a little blurry. The more Elizabeth tried to force herself into the void, the faster her heart pounded and the angrier she became. Perspiration beaded her upper lip and the ghastly sense of vertigo threatened. Her heart tripped. "We walked home."

"What about the exhibition?"

With a will of their own, her hands came up and she ducked her head, the ringing in her ears growing steadily louder, making her teeth chatter.

Birds. Hundreds of them, wheeling and diving in a vast black cloud over her head, their dark-feathered wings closer and closer, beating against her cheeks, an overwhelming darkness, thick, inky black.

"Aunt Elizabeth?" Jane placed the teacup on the bedside table and dabbed at the spilt tea with a towel.

"I remember the birds." She forced her hands down into her lap. The nauseating stench of excrement, the terrifying swooping wings. Avian eyes, dark and shiny, watching and waiting. A torrent of confusion flickered behind her eyelids like a Magic Lantern show, invading her senses and creating a tide of confusion.

"Ah!" A wealth of knowledge seemed contained in Jane's single syllable. "I deduced it might have been the birds. I did wonder about the diprotodon but rejected that conclusion."

Elizabeth slammed the door on her bewildering emotions. Such weakness was not to be tolerated. "It's a foolish phobia." The illogical and totally irrational fear she had—ornithophobia Michael called it, though it wasn't a word she'd ever found in any dictionary or medical treatise. Not that the word mattered. It was a horror she'd never managed to overcome.

The large glass cases crowding the musty space had made the

air close around her. She remembered grasping the tight collar of her blouse and the perspiration trickling into her eyes, making them sting. "I shouldn't have gone into the exhibition hall. I thought perhaps since they were specimens, dead, inside display cases, I could manage." Now everything made sense. The birds had caused her dilemma.

"What happened after that?"

This cross-examination was beyond tedious. As tedious as her crippling fear. Which was nothing she wished to put on display. "We walked home. I should like to get up now. Please leave."

"Aunt Elizabeth." Jane moved closer and Elizabeth reared back against the pillows. For a moment, she feared Jane might touch her. The last thing she wanted was for the girl to feel her damp, goose-flecked skin. "It would be far better if we talked about this. We must try and ascertain the cause. Mr. Freud is greatly in favor of dialogue—"

"Modernistic claptrap. Leave now."

"I was only trying to help." Jane rammed her hands into the pockets of her skirt. "Shall I contact Michael?"

It would be comforting to know he was in the house, not swanning around playing politics, but the last thing she would do was admit her weakness. "You most certainly will not. He has matters to attend to in Sydney."

The door clattered closed and only her well-honed sense of control prevented her from hurling her treasured teacup against the wall.

TEN

"H urry up, child." Mrs. Cameron's voice drifted down the stairs to the laundry.

Elizabeth heaved a sigh, pegged the last of the washing onto the line, and threw the basket into the corner. As much as she loved being back at school, it meant she spent almost all the rest of her time down in the dungeons, dangling over the row of steaming coppers.

"We have a visitor."

A visitor! Michael! It could only be Michael. She unwrapped her pinafore, threw it on the floor, and galloped up the stairs.

And there he was. Just as he'd promised in his last letter.

His big, strong arms lifted her off the ground, and he spun her around and around until Elizabeth thought her head would burst.

"Stop! Stop!"

The world slowed and she rested against his arms, staring up into his face. So many lonely days since she'd waved goodbye. She planted a great big kiss on his cheek and slid to the ground.

"Let me look at you, me darlin'."

How she wished she wasn't wearing her old dress. She didn't want to have to explain to Michael that she simply wouldn't stop growing and none of her clothes lasted more than six months. She pushed her hands into the pocket of her pinafore.

"Oh, you're a sight for sore eyes, and haven't you grown?"

"I am fifty-four inches tall. At least I was last week when Mrs. Browne measured us all." Elizabeth straightened her shoulders and tried to stand still. "That's four feet and six inches. I am tall for an eleven-year-old, though I'm a little more—three months and twenty-three days more. It's a leap year."

"By the sound of it you've been studying your lessons."

"Oh yes, I have. Mrs. Browne says I am the best arithmetic girl she's ever had. I'm special because girls' brains don't develop like boys so they find calculations difficult."

"This Mrs. Browne told you this nonsense, did she?"

"It's not nonsense, it's scientific fact."

"You can explain this scientific fact while we are on our picnic."

"Picnic? What picnic?"

"A picnic with a prince."

"A prince, a real live prince?" Or had he brought her another book of fairy stories?

"None other, all the way from England. Prince Alfred."

"You'll not be taking her to Clontarf. There'll be hundreds there." Mrs. Cameron, the killjoy, glared at them both. Of course she'd try and stop Michael. Elizabeth slipped her hand into Michael's big paw and gazed up at him, trying to make her eyes plead.

"She'll be fine with me, and I've got a basket downstairs with lemonade and strawberries and—"

"You spoil that child."

"How can he? He hasn't seen me for one thousand lonely days."

"For goodness' sake, Elizabeth, how you exaggerate. You sound like one of the princesses in your story books." Mrs. Cameron rolled her eyes.

"If you're going to call me a princess I must dress as one. I can't meet a prince in rags." She tried for a curtsy, which brought a huge bellow of laughter from Michael. "What do I call him? Prince Alfred? Your Royal Highness? Is he a royal highness?"

Mrs. Cameron let out a loud huff and folded her arms across her fat bosom. "He's Queen Victoria's son, and you won't get within spitting distance of him. I can promise you that. And you'll need tickets. Heard tell they cost a pound each."

Michael patted his top pocket. "Ten shillings for ladies."

He had the tickets, got it all planned. Oh, how she'd missed Michael. A girl couldn't want for a better brother.

"Waste of money, if you ask me."

With Mrs. Killjoy Cameron's words ringing in her ears, Elizabeth raced upstairs. It was perfect. The sun shone down from a crystal-clear sky and she was going on a picnic to meet a prince! She hadn't a moment to waste.

She stripped off her patched pinafore and struggled into her Sunday best. If she closed her eyes tightly she could pretend it was white and she had a crown of flowers for her hair. But as Mrs. Cameron kept telling her, poor Irish couldn't pick and choose; they had to make do.

The beastly buttons were impossible so she squashed her straw hat onto her head and traipsed downstairs. She was going to have to ask someone to do her up.

She edged around the door where Michael was deep in conversation with Mrs. Cameron, the two of them standing like ruffled roosters, hands on hips and faces red. It was always that way. Either something she'd done or something about money.

Elizabeth slipped out the back into the scullery. "Molly, can you help me?"

"What would you like me to do for you, my pet?" Molly threw the next load of clothes into the copper.

"Can you button me up, please? I'm going to meet a prince and I need to wear my Sunday best."

"You and your stories. Turn around."

She couldn't be bothered to explain, as long as the buttons were done up. Besides, Michael might invite Molly; worse still, he might invite Mrs. Cameron. She wanted him all to herself. "Hurry up."

"I'm trying. I'm trying." Molly's damp fingers fumbled on the long row of buttons. "You need to put your hat straight too. Here, turn around." She fussed and tutted until Elizabeth wanted to scream. "You tell that brother of yours it's time you had a new dress. This one's way too small. Turn around again and put your shoulders back."

Elizabeth stood straight and arched her back until Molly finished fastening the buttons. "You're done." She gave her a quick pat on the back. "Off you go and enjoy your prince. Say hello from me to that lovely brother of yours."

Not bothering to reply, Elizabeth shot down the hallway and barreled into the front room. "I'm ready."

Michael turned, his face red and angry, and snatched up the basket. "We'll be going. I'll have her back before dark. Come along, Elizabeth."

She slipped her hand into his and had to almost run to keep up with his big, long strides. "How are we going to get there? Where're we going? I've forgotten the name of the place."

"Clontarf. It's on the other side of the harbor. We'll go down to the Quay and get a ferry."

"A ferry! I've never ridden on a ferry. Will the prince come too?"

"He's got his own ship, the *Galatea*. It brought him all the way from England. It's moored down here; we'll see if we can see it. They've got a special steamer for him to use today. Over there."

He pointed at the smartest ferry Elizabeth had ever seen, bedecked with hundreds of tiny fluttering flags. "You've got to hold tight to my hand. I don't want to lose you." Michael's angry look had faded and he'd stopped galloping, which was a good thing because her legs could hardly keep up.

In the all the lonely days, he'd changed. Grown taller and broader and looked more important. How she wished she could go with him to Hill End instead of staying in Sydney. Every time she asked, he'd say *next time . . . maybe soon . . . one day . . .*

It wasn't all bad with the Camerons, but as she'd got older she had more and more jobs to do and school every day until lunchtime. Without a doubt, today would be the best day of her life.

The trip across the harbor was as magical as she'd imagined. Their ferry was jam-packed full of people, but Michael found a spot for them out of the wind. Before long they rounded the bay, and there before them was a long, sheltered stretch of golden sand. Trust Michael to know the best of places. The skin on her face felt stretched from all the sunshine and smiles. It was so good to have her brother back.

Giant tents ringed the beach and a band, playing breathtaking music, had set up under a clump of trees. So many people. There were thousands. Elizabeth tried to count but got lost sometime after the first hundred because they kept milling about. "How many people do you think are here?"

"They said they'd sold fifteen hundred tickets. We'll sit ourselves under these trees, and when the prince comes out of the tent we'll get a good look at him."

"What's he doing in the tent?" She wanted to see him now. Maybe she'd practice her curtsy a little. She bent slowly, crossing her left leg behind her right and keeping her back straight, like she'd seen Molly do with her tongue rammed into her cheek, when Mrs. Cameron's back was turned. She toppled over.

"Up you get." Michael set her on her feet. "He's in the tent having lunch with the other dignitaries."

"Can we go in there?" She dusted off her skirt.

"Sit yourself down, darlin', and have some lemonade. There's sandwiches too."

"No, no look. They're coming out."

Like a massive animal, the crowd surged forward. Elizabeth's heart was beating so hard she thought she might fall over. "I think he's coming to say hello to me. I can't see."

Michael swept her up and held her high, and she got her first good glimpse over the heads of the pulsing crowd. Her prince, walking toward her. He'd seen her, she was sure of it, even though he was busy chatting to a woman wearing the biggest hat imaginable.

So handsome! Elizabeth waved her hand. He turned and sauntered across the green toward the clump of trees where the band had set up. He had a piece of paper in his hand, which he held out to one of the men.

"What's he doing?"

Michael shrugged his shoulders.

The woman jammed in next to them muttered, "It's a check, a donation for the Sailor's Home, to mark his appreciation."

Oh! Elizabeth didn't care about that. She wanted to go and meet him. She'd curtsy, and maybe he'd smile at her and ask her name, offer his arm and walk her across to the band. Maybe he'd dance with her!

By the time the prince and his entourage had finished a whole lot more talking and speeches, she was ready to jump out of her skin; she had to get closer. He was so handsome with his golden hair, uniform frock coat, and dazzling white trousers.

Suddenly someone cried out.

A man sprang forward, lifted his hand, and pointed straight at the prince's back.

A gun!

A sharp crack echoed and Elizabeth slammed her hands over her ears as her feet went from under her. Was she dead?

Michael reached down, swept her into his arms, and forced his way through the crowd. "Come away, my darlin'. You don't want to be looking."

Alive and safe in Michael's arms, she peered over his shoulder.

Another shot resounded, and another, and her prince collapsed onto his hands and knees.

"No. Let me go. They shot my prince. Is he dead?" She wriggled and squirmed, but Michael held her tight.

The crowd parted and a group of men carrying the limp body of her prince struggled up to the tent.

"No, not dead," a voice called.

"There you go, my darlin'. He's not dead." Michael lowered her to the ground and his rough fingers wiped away her tears.

"They've got the dastardly ruffian," another voice reported. The crowd yelled its approval and surged forward, almost flattening Elizabeth. "Lynch him! Hang him! String him up!"

In front of her, a man stood, his arms pinioned behind him, his head hanging low. The crowd roared and pushed closer, ripping at his clothes, spitting on him.

A loud scream cut the air.

Michael scooped her up again and she buried her head in his shoulder as he barged through the crowd. By the time she dared look, they'd reached the wharf.

"I've got to put you down for a minute."

The moment her feet hit the ground, Michael bent double, his breath coming in great heaving gasps.

"Stand right by me." He coughed and spluttered. "Don't move."

"Did they shoot you too?"

He sank down onto his knees and pulled her close. "No, me darlin', I'm not hurt, only winded. They're bringing him aboard now."

They manhandled the prisoner down onto the wharf. His white waistcoat hung in tatters, and a bloody trail marked the gangplank as they dragged him aboard and threw him in a bedraggled heap.

How had everything changed so quickly? One minute everyone was so happy and now the sounds of crying and wailing, shouting and screaming reverberated all around, as if the crowd wanted to rip the man apart.

Sometime later, the crowd waiting around the tent parted and a hush fell. A mournful cry trickled out of Elizabeth's mouth as a group of sailors bearing a litter carrying her prince edged their way onto the deck of his waiting steamer.

The sound of pounding blood in her ears receded and she slumped down onto the grass. Michael pulled her into his arms. "We'll stay here and wait while everyone sorts themselves out, then we'll find our ride home."

———————————≈———————————

What a disaster. The day he'd planned so carefully from the moment he'd read about the prince's visit had ended in a debacle. Not that he'd got much time for the British monarchy. They'd too many questions to answer about Ireland. He'd done it for Elizabeth, done it because he knew she'd like the idea of seeing a real prince, what with that imagination of hers. Now here she was, as tired and disheveled as the flags on the prince's steamer.

Michael had worried the diggings were no place for a young girl, but clearly Sydney was as bad. Worse perhaps. At least in Hill End people had their mind set on gold, not murder.

And now it was getting dark and they'd been waiting in the queue for the ferry for hours. He shuffled forward; maybe they'd make this one, maybe not. Elizabeth's head had fallen to his shoulder and she was fast asleep. She didn't weigh much more than a small bag of chaff.

"Last one. Come on, mate. We'll squeeze you in. Let you get the little girl home. She looks tuckered out."

The gangplank wobbled as Michael walked aboard, and for a moment he imagined the black oily water closing over their heads, just like the stowaway who'd fallen overboard in Liverpool. "There you go." A hand under his elbow pulled him aboard.

"Go up in the wheelhouse. Room for you to sit the girl down."

"Thanks." He pushed through the door into the warm space. He wasn't the only one who'd been lucky. There were a couple of constables in there too. They shoved along and made room for Elizabeth, and Michael propped his shoulder against the cabin wall while the ropes were loosened and the ferry nudged away from the shore, out into the harbor.

"Saw it all, did you?" one of the constables asked.

He nodded. "Right near the front." He pointed to Elizabeth curled up on the seat. "She wanted to see a real live prince. Any idea what prompted the man to shoot him?"

"Thought you'd have a fair idea. Being Irish."

No self-respecting Irishman would give a toss what happened to a prince of England, but he hadn't expected anything to happen in Australia. "Beg your pardon?"

"Who are you trying to fool? O'Farrell, that's the bloke's name. Told everyone he'd done it for the Fenians, for Irish independence."

He shrugged. "Never been much for politics." Da had, back in Ireland. Michael had been too young to pay much attention, more worried about where the next meal would come from.

"Yeah, well, you better keep your head down because this'll go a lot further. What's your name?"

"Michael, Michael Ó'Cuinn."

"A good Irish name. Where are you from?"

"Hill End."

"I'd be going back there quick smart if I were you. They're looking for O'Farrell's accomplices and there's talk of a reward, a big reward."

Michael stared out at the oily water bubbling out from beneath the ferry. Talk about give a bloke a bad name.

The moment the ferry hit the wharf he lifted Elizabeth into his arms and went out onto the deck. He wanted to be first down the gang-plank and get her back to the Camerons' safe and sound. It took longer than he expected to make his way along George Street. At every pub bodies spewed onto the road, and there was only one thing on people's lips. Bad news travelled faster than the Devil.

When he reached the Camerons', Elizabeth was still fast asleep. He knocked on the door and tried the knob. Locked tight. He stepped back and the window upstairs opened.

Bill Cameron's head appeared. "Surprised to see you here."

"I've brought Elizabeth home."

"No, you haven't. Bugger off! We ain't harboring crazy Fenians."

"But—"

"Shove off, Mick." The window slammed shut.

Michael raised his fist to hammer on the door, then let it fall. Elizabeth lifted her head and smiled sleepily at him. "Are we home?"

"Not yet, me darlin', not yet." To hell with the Camerons. He'd sort them out tomorrow. He'd got a room booked at the Clarendon. He'd bed Elizabeth down there. Chances were, everything would have blown over by the morning.

———— ≈ ————

"Where am I? Michael, Michael, wake up!" Elizabeth sat in the middle of the bed, panicked eyes staring at him.

He shot to his feet, every muscle tense.

For a moment his befuddled brain refused to function. He rubbed his hand over his face and examined the chair where he must have spent the night. Elizabeth's hat lay on the floor on top of his coat and her boots were tossed by the bed. She was a mess—dress all screwed up and her hair hanging down her back like a banshee.

Beyond the window, the sky was a pearly gray. "Snuggle back down for a minute or two. It's early yet."

The crash on the door sent his heart into his mouth. "Ó'Cuinn. Michael Ó'Cuinn. Open up."

He tucked the blanket around Elizabeth's shoulders and went to unlock the door. Before he'd even reached for the handle it flew open, catching the toecap of his boots, flattening him against the wall.

"Michael Ó'Cuinn, you're under arrest for Fenian conspiracy."

"What?" He shrugged them off, held his hands high.

Elizabeth's wide, frightened eyes stared at him over the blanket. "What are you talking about?"

"You were at Clontarf, in the company of O'Farrell."

"Aye. I was at Clontarf. I saw what happened."

It was too much for Elizabeth. She threw back the blanket, her face bone-white. "Is my prince dead?"

Michael shrugged and stared at the belligerent constable.

"You'll be coming down to the station."

"I'll come, but I have to take me sister home first." The heftier of the two men spun him around, pushed his face against the wall, and yanked his arm up his back. No! Elizabeth didn't need to see this. He had to get her somewhere safe. No matter what Bill Cameron had said the night before, Mrs. Cameron would take her in; she'd said she loved her like a daughter. He wasn't sure he believed her anymore, but anything was better than this.

"You're not going anywhere. Where's the girl got to go?"

"Up the road a piece, to Cameron Victuallers."

"Right you are. It's on the way."

The pressure on his arm slackened. "Get your boots on, Elizabeth."

She slid off the bed, slipped her feet into her boots, left the laces dangling. He couldn't do much about it with his arm rammed up his back. They trundled him down the stairs like a sack of potatoes and out into the street.

It took only moments to reach the Camerons'. "Let me take her in. Sort things out."

"Not a chance, lad. I'm not having you run off." The bloke rapped on the door and Mrs. Cameron's head appeared at the window, as though she'd been waiting. "He wants you to take the girl in. All right with you?"

Mrs. Cameron slammed the window shut.

"Stay here, Elizabeth. Mrs. Cameron'll be down in a moment."

"No." She hung onto his free hand. "I'm staying with you."

"No, darlin', you can't, not now. I'll be back to see you. Just sort these fools out." His arm wrenched in the socket. The door opened a crack and Mrs. Cameron's hand shot out, grabbed Elizabeth, and pulled her inside.

"Michael, I want . . ." The slam of the door muffled the rest of Elizabeth's words and the constables propelled him down the road. Why on earth had they picked on him? There had to be thousands of Irish in Sydney.

Turned out, most of them were at the police station. It was crowded as all get out. They threw him into a packed cell, reeking of excrement and unwashed bodies, with a bunch of other blokes, every one of them Irish.

"What the hell's going on?" Michael slumped against the only vacant space on the wall, standing room only.

"Some bugger's got a fly up his arse." A big redheaded bloke spat neatly into one of the few empty spots on the floor. "Reckon this assassination is some Fenian plot to overthrow the queen."

"Ain't the assassination attempt that's got everyone riled up. It's the reward."

"Reward?"

"Thousand pounds for information leading to conviction of any of O'Farrell's accomplices. Whole world's ratting on an Irishman."

"That's a load of rubbish. O'Farrell didn't have any accomplices. I was there."

An uncanny silence settled on the cell. "You were there, man?"

"Aye. I was."

"I'd say the rest of us'd be in the clear."

A laconic voice called, "You'd be telling us what you did."

For Christ's sake, even his compatriots thought he was guilty.

He let out a long, slow puff of air and recounted the story.

ELEVEN

MAITLAND TOWN, 1913

Despite Elizabeth's turn, she was back in the garden well before breakfast the next morning, dead-heading the roses, apparently none the worse for the events of the previous day.

"What time did Mr. Quinn say his train would be arriving?" Bessie dropped Jane's two eggs into the boiling water and added a splash of vinegar.

"He said he'd get the nine thirty."

"Which will get him back here when? Not everyone carries the train timetable in their head, you know."

"Twelve fifty-two."

"Lunchtime. Right." Bessie nodded. "What about the doctor?"

Jane hadn't thought to call Dr. Lethbridge while she sat with Elizabeth as she slept. When she'd finally decided to ignore Elizabeth's wishes and telegraph Michael in Sydney, he'd told her to ask Lethbridge to call at two o'clock.

"I wish I'd thought to call him yesterday."

"Can't be calling the doctor every five minutes. Here, take this to the dining room and I'll ring the bell. Make sure you put it on the warmer. Miss Quinn likes her breakfast kedgeree hot."

Jane took the evil-looking mess of fish, rice, and hard-boiled eggs and made her way down the hallway. She'd hoped she'd manage to snaffle a piece of bread and jam in the kitchen and cite some excuse about having to be at the auction house. She simply didn't want to face Elizabeth. The look on her face the night before had said it all.

"Good morning, Jane." Elizabeth swept into the dining room, placed her basket of roses on the window seat, and took her usual place at the head of the table. "What's for breakfast? I'm exceptionally hungry."

"Kedgeree. Or toast if you'd prefer something lighter."

"Kedgeree would be lovely, thank you."

Jane filled the plate and set it in front of Elizabeth, who gave a terse nod and toyed with her fork while Jane helped herself to some toast and her hard-boiled eggs, neither of which were particularly symmetrical. Not a good omen for the remainder of the day.

After Elizabeth's uncharacteristic behavior the previous evening, Jane wasn't sure how she should behave. She sliced the top off the first egg with more force than she intended and scooped the dribbling egg yolk from the side of the cup with her finger.

"Manners, Jane." Elizabeth rapped her fingernail on the table to emphasize her point.

Very encouraging. She reached for the napkin and wiped her fingers.

"Did you establish a new time for the meeting with the ladies of the Benevolent Society? I completed the accounts last night. It's going to take more than a soupçon of diplomacy to convince them they have insufficient funds to stage the annual moonlight concert."

"Something else to do this morning."

"Speak up, Jane."

"I said I would confirm this morning." She would have to re-schedule the meeting because of Dr. Lethbridge's visit.

"Very good. Make it next week, and while you're out perhaps you'd be so kind as to call into the technical college and collect my hat. I must have dropped it."

Jane bit down on her toast and contained the curl of excitement. The perfect excuse to have another look at the diprotodon, and she'd call into the School of Arts and see if she could find any additional information in the library.

"I'll leave you to finish your breakfast. I intend to complete my tour of the garden while I consider the Benevolent Society's position. They simply can't afford to fund that concert."

Jane swallowed the remains of her tea with a frown. The last time she'd seen the accounts they had been in the black. She loaded up the tray to take out to Lucy, and she'd see if Bessie needed anything from High Street; a bit of shopping would give her the perfect excuse to stay out a little longer. If she wanted to visit the library it was the only solution.

In no time Jane was wheeling her bicycle out through the garden gate and into the street. Besides, she liked the cooling breeze and, pro-viding she pinned her hat tightly down, she could cover the distance in half the time.

Taking care to avoid an overpacked dray and a rattling tram, Jane skirted a group of gossiping women and turned right into High Street, chanting in time to her pedaling, "Pears soap, a loaf of bread, half a pound of tea. A ham hock and VoVos, just for you and me!"

Some days she'd prefer to spend her time in the kitchen rather than cooped up with Elizabeth and the accounts. She understood the importance of a good business grounding and she had only gratitude for the way Elizabeth had helped her, but she'd never imagined herself poring over dusty old ledgers day after day.

She coasted to a halt outside the telegraph office and ducked into the general store next door.

The bell had barely tinkled before Mrs. Dodd pounced on her. "How's Miss Quinn today?"

"She's perfectly fine, thank you, Mrs. Dodd. It was the heat." Not the truth, because despite the brave front at breakfast, something was not right. Shadows under Elizabeth's eyes, and her hands had shaken as she lifted her teacup. It seemed so odd for someone who was so controlled to have a fear of anything, never mind birds. "I need half a pound of tea, a ham hock, and a packet of Iced VoVos."

Mrs. Dodd bustled around making a stack on the counter. "Much cooler today, thank heavens. Is that all, dear?"

There was something else. Jane ran through the rhyme she'd concocted. "A bar of Pears soap for Miss Quinn." She handed over the money and tucked the packages under her arm.

"A thank-you wouldn't come amiss."

"What was that?"

"A thank-you."

For goodness' sake, she had no time to waste. "Thank you."

With the items clutched tightly, she eased her way through the door and placed them into the basket on the front of the bicycle, then scooted off the footpath and onto the road. Next stop, the technical college.

The moment Jane entered the foyer, Mrs. Witherspoon raised her head from the ledger and scowled at her. "I'm still having difficulty with some of these figures."

"I've come to collect Miss Quinn's hat. She left it here yesterday."

"How is she feeling this morning?"

"Better."

Mrs. Witherspoon made no effort to hand over Elizabeth's hat;

she remained behind the desk peering down at the ledgers, tapping a pencil against her teeth.

"Did you find Miss Quinn's hat? A straw boater with mauve and green ribbons?"

"Hat? No. No, I didn't. She didn't have one on when you left. I remember thinking how thick her hair was." A faint flush rose to Mrs. Witherspoon's cheeks. "I'm sorry. It was such a shock to see her, well, to see her so disheveled. She always appears to be in command of the situation."

"I'll go and have a look in the exhibition hall. Maybe the cleaner found it."

"Cleaner? No, she comes in on Wednesdays."

Jane bolted through the Tudor doors, trying to control the *tap-tapping* of her boots on the floor. *"Never run when you can walk. Never walk when you can ride."* She had the not walking when she could ride bit under control, now the bicycle was well oiled and the tires pumped, but the first part of Elizabeth's instructions was still a daily trial. She couldn't wait to see the diprotodon again. Her hand span measured six inches. If she made an estimation and checked at the library, it would give her some indication of the truth of the matter. A calculation around the length of the femur, fibula, and tibia in the leg, along with the humerus, radius, and ulna, could allow an estimation of size based on the bones of the hand or foot. Could she create formulae to confirm the size of the diprotodon?

She danced into the exhibition hall and turned to the left, then ground to a halt. A large wedge-tailed eagle with outspread wings scrutinized her with an intimidating squint. She bent closer and read the card pinned to the front of the display case: *Shot at Lochinvar by Mr. T. Kelly, while in the act of making away with a lamb.* Her stomach churned. Maybe Elizabeth's fears weren't so far-fetched.

TEA COOPER

The adjacent case contained two magpies so lifelike she couldn't help but push her ear against the glass to see if she could hear them caroling. The silence was overwhelming. Not a laugh from the kookaburras in the next display case either, though their eyes gleamed with anticipation as they peered, frozen in time, at a small lizard set on a rock. There was no doubt about it, Tost and Rohu deserved every one of the international awards they'd won.

In between the cabinets, a series of paintings hung on the walls in ornate gold frames. The first, *Madonna and Child* painted in heavy oils, was nowhere near as exciting as the prehistoric skull. On the other side of the room were more paintings, mostly oils; an etching; a beautiful cathedral labeled *Antwerp*; and a mountain stream. *Nelson New Zealand*, the plaque on the wall told her. Jane meandered toward the middle of the room and drew up short. She had to find Elizabeth's hat, then she could concentrate on the diprotodon. Her heart stuttered as she passed under the imposing Gothic arch into the shadowy and musty space, then a flash of color on the floor caught her attention. She bent down and there was Elizabeth's hat, half hidden under one of the last cabinets close to the corner. Once she'd extricated it, she straightened up and came face-to-face with another painting, different in style to the heavy oils and etchings.

She peered more closely. A weathered church tucked into the fold of the hill surrounded by ancient headstones, tilted like old men's teeth, every patch of lichen highlighted. Several sarcophagi, chipped and worn, and to one side a large circular burial vault.

Jane moved a little closer. All the other pictures had cards next to them describing the painting, but not this one. There was something about it that appeared familiar. She glanced over her shoulder. Mrs. Witherspoon was nowhere to be seen, so she hoisted the picture from the hook, turned it around, propped it against the wall, and crouched down. A small piece of paper glued to the back rewarded her ingenuity.

MARIGOLD PENTER, THE VILLAGE CHURCH, 1889, OIL ON CANVAS

And then she remembered. The wife of the self-confident man who'd annoyed Michael at the gallery in Sydney. It must be one of the pictures he'd been talking about.

She studied the vibrant colors and wide brush strokes, the way the light glanced off the church windows, and the long shadows thrown by the circular vault, then she spotted the girl, almost hidden beneath the wide branches of a tree.

She could hardly tell the color of the clothes the girl was wearing, all a pale gray-blue, almost as though she were fading away. It looked as though Lucy had spilt bleaching powder all over her. "Quite strange."

She bent down to replace the painting.

"Let me help." A young man with sparkling eyes and a slightly sunburned face regarded her with a lopsided grin.

He rehung the painting, tipped his head to one side, and straightened one corner. "My mother painted this picture."

"Oh! I met your father, at the art gallery in Sydney before Christmas." He looked nothing like the man, with his big broad shoulders and smiling face. "He said your mother might have an exhibition in Maitland."

A slight flush tinted his cheeks. "Ah, yes, he mentioned meeting you and your father, Mr. Quinn."

"Michael is not my father. I'm an orphan, at least I was until Aunt Elizabeth and Uncle Michael rescued me."

"Oh. I'm so sorry."

"Nothing to be sorry about. I count myself lucky. My name's Jane, Jane Piper."

"Timothy Penter." He held out his hand. After a moment's hesitation, she grasped it.

"I'm here to evaluate the space for the full exhibition, part of Mother's tour."

"Her tour?" For heaven's sake, she sounded like a parrot.

"Several galleries are interested in my mother's paintings, so we have taken the opportunity to visit Australia." He had a slight burr to his voice, a little more wholesome than his father's, very different from Michael's Irish accent.

"Are you from London?"

"West Country."

She must have frowned because he added, "England."

"Oh! I see. Do you like Australia?"

"Haven't seen much except from the train window. Sydney, Melbourne, and now Maitland. Mother and Father are still in Melbourne. Father sent me here to look things over."

"Doesn't your mother decide where she shows her paintings?"

Perhaps that wasn't the right thing to say, because his eyebrows disappeared into the shock of hair falling across his forehead.

He stuck his hands into the pockets of his rumpled jacket and leaned against the wall. "If Mother had her way she'd spend her time in Paris. Father makes her business arrangements. This trip was his idea."

Ambling across the room, he paused in front of one of the other paintings. "These are not Mother's style at all. Traditional oil paintings, painted in a studio. Mother favors painting *en plein air*, as do the other impressionists. They aim to portray an overall visual effect rather than the minute details. Step back a little and you'll better appreciate the picture."

Jane did as he suggested, although the shadowy light made it difficult. She'd never given any thought to whether artists painted in a studio or out in the open air. "When will your mother's exhibition open?"

"After the Melbourne exhibition, the paintings will be shipped here. That's my job. Father has an acquaintance he's trying to track down. I don't think he fully appreciated the size of the country."

"This exhibition is due to run for another three weeks." Jane pointed to the sign on the door.

"I have to confirm the arrangements with Major Witherspoon. Have you any idea where I might find him?"

"He spends a lot of time in Sydney. He's a politician." Although completely on the other side of the fence from Michael. "I'm sure Mrs. Witherspoon can help you. She's outside in the foyer. Are you going back to Sydney today?"

"Train leaves in a couple of hours."

"Come and have a look at the diprotodon. It's fascinating. I'm about to go to the library and see if I can find any further information. Perhaps you'd like—"

"Jane!" Mrs. Witherspoon's flustered voice echoed through the cavernous space. "Have you finished in there?"

"It sounds like she's worried."

"Mrs. Witherspoon is a bit of a nervous Nellie. My aunt had a turn when we visited the exhibition. She's probably worried I've had an accident or that I'm up to no good." Whatever had possessed her to say that? "Coming, Mrs. Witherspoon."

Throwing Timothy an apologetic smile, Jane hurried out into the foyer.

"Ah! There you are. You're to go straight home. Mr. Quinn wishes to speak to you."

What a shame. She'd hoped she might chat a little more with

Timothy Penter. Now she'd finished evening classes she rarely had the chance to talk to anyone her own age.

"Nice to meet you." Timothy raised his hand in a salute as she scuttled outside, Elizabeth's boater bouncing against the side of her leg, reminding her of her priorities.

TWELVE

Sydney & Hill End, 1868

It took several days and numerous hours answering question after question before Michael finally established his innocence. In fact, he wasn't sure he had. O'Farrell's notebook was found full to the brim of Fenian nonsense, but Michael's name didn't figure, so they let him go.

The government passed the Treason Felony Act, making it an offense to refuse to drink to the Queen's health, but went no further. The poor bloke, O'Farrell, came up before the court and was convicted, even though his defense maintained he was mad as a hatter, and sentenced to hang. Michael had no intention of staying around to witness that.

The moment they released him he shot up the road to Cameron's warehouse. Elizabeth would be upset and he'd have to break his promise, but he had to get out of Sydney and back to Hill End as fast as he could. There were papers stuck all over the town—every door and every shop window—proclaiming the Irish menace and the evils of Catholicism. The whole situation made his flesh creep.

"Michael!"

He slithered to a halt, spread his arms wide as Elizabeth flew down the street.

"I thought you'd never come, I've been waiting and waiting."

He lowered her to the ground and took a good look at her. She had her Sunday frock on again but she looked nothing like she had the last time. Her hair was a mess of knots and tangles, her face as filthy as a guttersnipe. "What are you doin' out here, darlin'?"

"Waiting for you. I knew you'd come."

At least she had faith. There'd been times in the last few days when he thought he'd never see the sky again.

"Why are you out here on the street?"

"Mr. Cameron doesn't want papist spawn."

"Elizabeth Ó'Cuinn! I'll wash yer mouth out. What are you doing out here?"

"I told you. Mr. Cameron didn't want me in the house. He said I had to wait for you out here."

How would Cameron have known he'd get released and when? "What have you been doing for food and a bed? I've been locked up for days." What was wrong with Mrs. Cameron? No one would treat a daughter that way. Unbelievable. This O'Farrell had caused more trouble than his foolish assassination attempt was worth.

"Sleeping in the shed out the back. Molly snuck me some food on her way home every day." Elizabeth put her hand in his and stared at him for the longest moment, fixing him with a penetrating stare from her huge blue eyes. "You won't leave me again, will you?"

"Aye. I'll not be doing that."

She squeezed his hand. "Are we going home?"

"That we are, me darlin'." His fingers tightened in return, sealing the deal.

"To see me mam and da."

No, no, no. He'd forgotten. Time to face up to the truth.

"I'm glad I'm going home with you. The Camerons don't want

me anymore." Her brilliant blue eyes filled with tears. "Everything changed when Mr. Cameron lost his boat."

Had he opened his eyes to the truth about the money-grubbing couple, he'd never have left her there for as long as he had. Something he'd regret for the rest of his days.

———❧———

Several days later Elizabeth sat next to Michael on the bullock dray, all clean and scrubbed, wearing the new coat he'd bought her in Bathurst, striped stockings, and good thick boots. Her hair blew in the wind, and in one hand she clasped the tattered remains of Lizzie the doll. He'd done little for her in the last six years; he'd trusted the Camerons. He wouldn't be making that mistake again. Elizabeth was his responsibility, and by all that was holy he'd make sure she never came to harm.

"I'll make it right. I promise. I'll make it right. But first I have to tell you something."

"It's about Mam and Da, isn't it?"

The child was wise beyond her years. "How do you know?"

"They're dead. If Mam and Da were alive they would want to see me and would've come and gotten me long ago."

The silence hung between them, and for the first time he was thankful Mam and Da were gone.

"It's strange. I know I'm meant to be sad, but I don't remember them. Not at all." Her face screwed into a ferocious frown as if she could will her memory to function. "I've got you, though."

He was all she had. "You were a wee young thing when they left. Why, you barely came to me knee."

"I remember my birthday on the ship. We had such fun. I remember when we got to Sydney." Her face paled. "Why did you leave me behind, Michael?"

"I thought I was doing what was best. A girl needs a woman's touch, and I thought Mrs. Cameron would look after you better than I could. I didn't know what I'd find in Hill End, nor if I could provide for you."

"What happened to Mam and Da?"

"The consumption got Mam, and Da had a fall, cracked his skull." That was more than enough. He'd take her and show her their resting place, introduce her to Father MacCormick, enroll her in the school, make sure she attended church every Sunday. The cottage was as good as ready. They'd be a family, the family he'd promised he'd provide. "We'll not be thinking on it anymore. I've got plans for you."

"So have I. I'll get a job. I can read and write and my arithmetic's good. I'm a good worker, but not in a laundry. I can't do that again. I'd like to work in a real shop."

"You'll do nothing of the kind. My plan is school for you, until you learn all there is to learn, and then you'll come and work in the business. You won't set foot on the streets without me, understand?"

"You expect me to stay locked up? I might as well have stopped with the Camerons."

Michael drew in a belabored breath. No, he couldn't lock her up, but he couldn't leave her to wander Hill End on her own. "You'll go to school in the mornings, like everyone else. In the afternoons, you stay at home."

"By myself?"

"No, with Kitty. She does a bit of cleaning and washing and cooking for me." She'd pick Elizabeth up from school, bring her home, give her some lunch, and they could do the things women did.

"Then you'll come home when you have finished work. Just like a real family." Elizabeth clapped her hands together and threw him a smile wide enough to make his heart sing. "Are we going home now?"

"To the warehouse first. I've got to make sure they managed."

"Can't they do without you?"

"We'll find out. I've got to go and have a natter with Li Jing, then we'll call in and see Father MacCormick about school."

"Who's Li Jing?"

"Me right-hand man."

She frowned, looked down at his hands on the reins. "What's wrong with your hands?"

"Nothing. It's his mind I need, just like a rabbit trap." He brought his hands together in a sharp clap and, as he'd expected, Elizabeth jumped, eyes wide with surprise.

"Don't do that!"

"Come on, darlin', grab your scarf. The wind's sharp enough to slice a four be two." He pulled the dray to a halt and jumped down.

The Diggers Rest no longer resembled the broken-down building he'd inherited. He'd put in the hard yards, repaired the building, bought goods from those strapped for cash and building materials and tools in Bathurst and auctioned them off. He'd left the upstairs room, where he'd found Da on that first day, well alone, and let the Chinamen pay him rent.

He hadn't tried to compete with the existing businesses; instead, he'd turned the back of the old warehouse into a cheap boarding house for the constant stream of hopefuls who turned up in the town.

Now he had three drivers working for him and held an auction every Saturday. He'd never once been tempted to search for gold. Jing's folks had it right. He'd taken a page from their book early on. Father

MacCormick was of like mind. Better business providing for the diggers, just as Da must have decided. They couldn't work without tools, food in their bellies, clothes on their back, and a roof over their heads. That's what the auction house provided, and their business provided for him, and would take care of Elizabeth too.

And every day he gave thanks to Da because now he had a fine business and owned the whole lot outright. Never mind the cottage he'd picked up for next to nothing.

"Look at that!" Elizabeth shrieked above the thundering of the stampers.

"Look at what, me darlin'?" He reached up and swung her down to the ground.

"The man over there. Is that a camera? Shall we have our picture taken? There's a man in Sydney who makes daguerreotypes. Have you ever seen one?" She clasped her hands close to her chest. "So clever. A little piece of glass with the person trapped inside forever."

"That's a bit fanciful even for a girl like you with all your fairy stories."

"Wouldn't it be lovely to have a keepsake of someone you'd loved and lost?"

"Better not to have lost them in the first place. Come with me now. There's plenty of time for that later."

"I'm never losing you." She slipped her arm through his and gave a little skip. He'd have to learn to shorten his stride if he was going to have Elizabeth walking on his arm. By all that was holy, it was good to have her here with him.

Elizabeth's eyes were wide with curiosity when they arrived outside the Diggers Rest. She didn't turn her nose up at the overcrowded warehouse as he'd expected. But she'd never done what he'd expected, had she?

———— ≈ ————

The smoky, perfumed air made Elizabeth's nose prickle. Then she heard the noise—not the stampers now that they'd moved inside, but a strange clacking sound. She squinted down the length of the warehouse and spotted a long, high bench running along one wall where a boy sat flipping beads from side to side across a frame that looked like a child's toy. Beads threaded on a series of rods that he moved so fast they blurred before her eyes.

Michael stretched out his arm and clasped the boy's shoulder. "Elizabeth, this is Li Jing."

The boy shot off the stool and greeted her with a bow, keeping his eyes down. He wasn't as tall as her, and the wrists poking from his black sleeves seemed as frail as a chicken's leg. "Miss Elizabeth, welcome. Mr. Michael told me all about you." His lean face broke into a smile, then he spun around and pulled a stool from under the bench.

She slapped her hand over her mouth, trapping the gasp. His black hair, drawn back from his wide forehead, was fastened in a braid that snaked almost to his waist.

"Jing does the accounts for me," said Michael, "and keeps an eye on the place when I'm out and about."

Jing clanked the beads one final time, made a few jottings on the paper in front of him, then gave the frame a quick flick, sending all the beads down to the base, away from the center bar.

The sound sent a shaft of curiosity spiraling into Elizabeth's stomach, dissolving her nervousness.

She stepped closer. "What is it?"

"That's Jing's toy. Says it makes his calculations faster. I reckon he likes the noise." Michael crossed his arms and rested his hip against the desk, his lips twitching.

Jing didn't move a muscle, didn't react to Michael's teasing; instead, he pushed the frame toward her. "Suanpan, Miss Elizabeth."

"What do you use it for?" She stretched onto tiptoe to better see the shiny black beads on the polished rods.

"You tell me three numbers, the biggest you can think of. Maybe as much gold as they'll pull out today."

"The very biggest?"

He nodded and grinned at her. "And the very hardest."

That was a little difficult. Not many numbers were hard, as long as she wrote them neatly and kept them in line. "Two hundred and ninety-nine thousand, three hundred and fifty-six."

Jing's fingers flew across the beads, rearranging them. "And?"

"Nine thousand, six hundred and seven."

More clanking. He looked up and gave her a shy smile.

"Two hundred and seventy-seven thousand, three hundred and twenty."

Before she had time to blink, Jing sat back and folded his arms, the beads all rearranged on the frame. "You tell me the answer." He waved his hand at the beads. "We move the beads up or down toward the beam. These rearranged ones are counted. These are not."

"I have to write it down." Elizabeth ran her finger across the beads.

"Don't move them. What do you think?"

She gestured to the highest row of beads. "Is this the thousands?" A strange intensity lit his eyes, as though she had in some way surprised him. "Clever girl. Five hundred and eighty-six thousand." He gestured to the other beads. "Two hundred and eighty-three." He flicked the frame again and the beads slid to the bottom.

She snapped her mouth shut, her mind reeling. "Can you show me how to use it?"

"Not now, me darlin'. We've got to go and see Father MacCormick about school." Michael grabbed at her hand. "Say goodbye to Jing."

Elizabeth reluctantly lifted her hand in farewell and allowed Michael to tug her toward the door.

"Jing, see that our bags are delivered to the cottage and the dray unloaded. We'll take a walk down to the church, find the good father, then I'll be taking Elizabeth home."

Once they stepped out onto the street the noise of the stampers made any further conversation impossible, but Elizabeth was more than happy to take in the sights.

Men with picks and shovels slung over their shoulders laughed and shouted as they walked down the streets, their eyes bright, and all around her an air of excitement drifted on the breeze. A young boy rode past on a bicycle and shouted a greeting, which Michael returned with a lift of his hat. Elizabeth had imagined Hill End would be small and quiet compared to Sydney; instead, the place thrummed with activity and everyone seemed to know Michael.

"Here we are." He held open the gate and inclined his head to the path running up to the front door of a cottage. She skipped ahead and waited.

The door swung open.

"Ah! And you'll be Elizabeth, I'm guessing." A razor-thin man with wispy white hair and wire-framed spectacles bent down and peered into her face.

"Yes. Elizabeth Ó'Cuinn." She drew herself up to her full height.

"Michael, me boy, how are you?" They clasped hands and shook as though their life depended on it. "You'll have news of the ruckus in Sydney then?"

Michael gave a bit of a shake of his head. She guessed he wasn't going to talk about the Fenian rubbish in front of her. He'd refused on the trip down despite her incessant questions, said it wasn't anything for her to worry about. Mr. Cameron's ranting had given her most of the answers so she'd let the matter rest.

"Come inside then, come inside. I've got some ginger beer for the young lady."

"We'll not be staying long. I want to make sure Elizabeth can come to school tomorrow."

"So she's here to stay, at long last?"

"Aye. Sydney's no place for a young girl."

"School won't be a problem. I'll speak to Mr. Whittaker in the morning. What'll you be doing in the afternoons? Classes finish at noon."

Elizabeth took the glass of ginger beer Father MacCormick offered. She might as well be a lost dog in need of housing the way Michael and Father MacCormick kept going on about where she'd be and what she'd be doing with her time.

"I'm going to ask Kitty to come every day, pick up Elizabeth, take her home for lunch, and stay until I return. Joe Lawson's doing the Sydney runs for me so I'll not be going far."

Father MacCormick clapped Michael on the shoulder. "Good man, we don't want her coming to any harm. If you have any difficulty she can always spend the afternoon with me."

"I'll be fine by myself at home."

"You won't need to be by yourself. It'll be me or Kitty." Michael threw her a wink and her heart gave a skip. Putting the glass down, she slipped her hand into his.

"We'll be getting along now. I'll be walking her to school myself in the morning."

"Right you are." Father MacCormick pressed a bunch of flowers into her hands. "These are for your mam and your da." He tipped his head toward the churchyard next door. "I'll be seeing you tomorrow, young lady."

———— ≋ ————

Father MacCormick's bunch of flowers scuppered Michael's plans to avoid the cemetery, coward that he was.

Elizabeth skipped ahead, her thick hair bouncing against the back of her coat, her striped stockings flashing in the frail winter sun. Showing her Mam's and Da's graves was never going to be easy, and he dreaded the questions she might ask, but it was better to get it done.

"This way, darlin'." He led the way through the headstones to the small plot encircled by a low fence, one of the first things he'd done after Da's funeral; the least he could do when he found out what Da'd left for him.

"'Here lies Aileen Ó'Cuinn, the light of my life and the love of my heart.'" Elizabeth read the words, her voice catching at the end. "He must have loved Mam very much. Did they love me?"

His throat dried as he framed his answer. "How could anyone not love you, me little darlin'?"

"'Michael Ó'Cuinn, a giant of a man and a father to cherish.' Was he truly a giant? Taller than you?" She turned her wide blue eyes up to him and something tugged at his heartstrings.

"Aye, that he was, but not by much. He was a giant in his heart more than anything."

She bent down and placed the flowers in the middle of the headstone and ran her finger along the last inscription. *Never to be parted.* She gave a little sniff and tucked her hand into his. "I hope we're never parted, Michael. I should wilt just like unloved flowers if I ever lost you."

"It's not going to happen. That's my promise."

"Shall we go home now?"

"Aye, that we will. Kitty will have something for us and we'll settle you in."

Leastways, the cottage was warm and cozy and Elizabeth would come to no harm.

THIRTEEN

MAITLAND TOWN, 1913

M ichael, there was no need to call Dr. Lethbridge, nor was there any need to come rushing back from Sydney. I thought you had meetings."

"You're much more important, Elizabeth. Come and sit down and tell me what happened." He raised his teacup and arranged his encouraging smile.

The last thing Elizabeth wanted to do was to revisit the whole debacle, not once but twice, because she had no doubt Dr. Lethbridge would ask the same questions.

"There's nothing to tell. I'm sure it was the heat, the darkness, the unfortunate smell. The stuffed birds are so lifelike I thought I felt their wings graze my cheeks. I don't wish to discuss it. The heat made me tired. I was perfectly fine after a rest."

"I can't remember you ever being tired. You can talk it over with Lethbridge. In the meantime, I don't want you exerting yourself. He'll be here before too long. Where's Jane?"

"She went into town to retrieve my hat. I left it at the technical college."

"Is there anything I can get you?"

"No." Attempting to assure him that she was fine, she pulled her feet under the chair and sat tall, her hands grasped tight in her lap to still their shaking. "Satisfied?"

"Marginally. I'll be back when Lethbridge arrives."

"No, you will not. I have no intention of having you present while I speak to the doctor."

"Oh, what am I to do with you? Very well. However, I shall ask him for a full report."

She wandered over to the window where, beyond the glass, a tiny blue wren performed a series of antics in the bird bath. It didn't bring on a paroxysm of terror, so why had the birds at the technical college sent her into such a panic? She had the strangest sensation she was missing something that was just beyond her reach. This fear of birds, this ornithophobia, she didn't understand it. "Michael, have I always been afraid of birds?"

"For as long as I've known you."

"What a strange thing to say. You've known me forever. Did something happen to me as a child, before we came to Australia?"

He cleared his throat. "Because someone is afraid of something— spiders, heights, birds—doesn't mean they had a nasty experience earlier in their life."

"I felt as though the birds would smother me, as though they were choking me, and the dusty smell was dreadful. It snatched at the back of my throat and made my eyes water."

Michael listened, his arms folded across his chest, with the same studious consideration he always showed. "Maybe you are remembering something I know nothing about. I haven't always been by your side."

"I can't remember a time when you haven't, except for all the lonely days you left me with the Camerons in Sydney."

"Not that old argument again. I thought it was for the best, and as it turned out, circumstances had changed." He patted her hand and smiled down at her. "Get some rest, and let's see what Lethbridge has to say. I'll go and find Jane."

Which, of course, was Michael's way of saying he intended to cross-examine her. There wasn't much to add, unfortunately.

Garden birds didn't send her into a panic, neither did the ducks on the river, nor an occasional chicken pecking its way through the vegetable garden. Not that she'd like to pick them up the way Jane did. There was a nasty pigeon tree in the middle of the street in Hill End; she'd always taken the back way home to avoid it. It didn't send her into a blind panic. It was the flocking she feared. Never before had she reacted so violently, as though she didn't know herself. And the smell! She could still taste the dreadful stench of bird excrement in the back of her throat. Where had it come from? The birds were dead. Taxidermied. Stuffed.

There was such a disconnect in her thoughts, yet she couldn't pinpoint the reason. The weather was warm yet she kept trembling, and she could hear her own breath and feel her pulse pumping beneath her skin. All the everyday sounds hummed around her: the clatter of china from the kitchen as Lucy washed up the lunch dishes, the clang of the tram bell as it meandered down the road, and the sound of laughter drifting across the road from the group of chattering schoolgirls.

"I expected to find you upstairs." Lethbridge's deep voice broke her reverie. He scrutinized her with an inquisitive gaze.

Elizabeth surreptitiously swiped her hand across her mouth. "I am well."

"Let me be the judge of that. Relax and tell me what happened."

She simply couldn't bear the thought of revisiting the whole circus.

"There's nothing to tell. I think perhaps I fainted. I was well enough to walk home. Jane will testify to that." Where *was* the girl? "I woke this morning feeling perfectly fine."

Lethbridge opened his bag and pulled out the ghastly stethoscope contraption he used on Michael.

"There's nothing the matter with my heart, I can assure you."

"Would you like Jane in the room while I examine you?"

"No, I would not."

"Very well." He placed the contraption on her back and her chest, asked her to breath in and out, grunted a fair bit and removed the pieces from his ears. Then he took her wrist, feeling for a pulse.

After a few minutes, he stood up. "I have to agree with you; I can find nothing wrong. Have you had any headaches, disturbed vision, or other peculiar sensations?" he asked, tapping into her thoughts with uncanny accuracy.

"No." She had no intention of mentioning the periodic racing of her pulse, the moments of vertigo, nor the strange smell she couldn't shake.

"There is only one other conclusion I can draw. It's a little delicate."

"Spit it out. I'm not some pampered ninny who can't be told the truth."

"Women of your age . . ." He cleared his throat, turned to the window, and fixed his concentration on some point beyond the garden.

"Women of my age?" she prompted.

"The change of life. Symptoms such as overheating, difficulty sleeping, disturbed memory . . . This can lead to nervous exhaustion and hysteria." He continued to stare out of the window. "Have you been suffering any of these maladies?"

"For goodness' sake. Hysteria? Next you'll be demanding I prove my sanity and threatening me with the attic."

"Nothing of the kind. However, I would like to suggest plenty of rest and a substantial diet—dairy products and red meat."

"Don't let Bessie hear you say that. She prides herself on the meals she provides and I am more than happy to substantiate my approval."

"Have you had any difficulty sleeping?"

"No, none at all," Elizabeth replied, thankful he was still facing the window and couldn't see her heated cheeks. She'd barely slept the night before, too concerned the despicable hallucinations would return. Spent most of the night staring out into the darkness until the sky lightened.

"I'll leave you a sleeping draught and call in again in a few days. If your symptoms worsen I expect to be notified immediately. Now I shall go and put Michael's mind at rest."

"While you're here, be kind enough to remind him to carry his pills. I noticed he left them at home while he was in Sydney."

"Touché." Dr. Lethbridge quirked a smile. "Stay seated. I can find my way to Michael's study."

———≈———

"Is there nothing we can do to prevent a recurrence?" Michael asked Lethbridge.

"There is simply no way of telling. If it continues we can look at some further treatment."

"What kind of treatment?"

"There is a place on the river, beyond Morpeth; their rest cures are held in high regard."

"You mean the asylum? I can assure you I will not be committing Elizabeth to an asylum, not based on one episode of understandable cause." They were well-respected, wealthy members of the community. People like Elizabeth didn't end up in an asylum.

"Understandable cause?"

"She did tell you about her fear of birds?"

"No, she didn't mention it."

"My word. She can be closer than a clam when the mood takes her."

"Are you certain you don't have any idea what this fear stems from?"

"None at all." And that was the truth. "There was one occasion, years ago, when we were in Hill End. There was a hollow tree at the intersection of the main street. People would leave notes pinned to it, and there were several nesting boxes for the carrier pigeons. At dusk when the birds returned they'd swoop. We happened to be passing at the time. She turned tail and bolted home. After that she avoided the place. I didn't pay much attention. Impressionable young girl, full of fantasies."

"How old was she?"

"Around eleven, maybe twelve. A year or so after she arrived at Hill End. It's only recently we've kept chickens. Elizabeth was never keen. Lucy and Jane deal with them."

"In my professional opinion it is simply the stage of her life she has reached. Women of a certain age frequently have a trying time. I've told her I'll call in again later in the week. Now it's your turn."

The man was a nuisance, and Michael would put money on the fact Elizabeth was behind it. Lethbridge waved his stethoscope around like some sort of an Indian cobra. "Come along. *Angina pectoris* is not to be taken lightly."

"I have the medication with me at all times." He patted his top pocket and hoped he wouldn't be asked to show proof. The last time he'd seen the little brown bottle of pills they were on the dresser in his bedroom.

"Carry them. Do you understand me?"

"Yes, *Dr.* Lethbridge."

Lethbridge pulled a ferocious frown. "Neither of you are getting any younger, and I intend to ensure Maitland has the benefit of your combined skills and expertise for many years to come. I have no idea what the town would do without you, or what I would do, for that matter."

"Can I offer you a drink?" Michael reached for the bottle of whiskey at his elbow, then thought better of it. "Tea, perhaps?"

"Thank you, no. A bit of restraint with the hard stuff wouldn't go amiss. Concentrate on some gentle exercise, an evenly paced walk every day," he added. "I'll see myself out."

Once Lethbridge departed Michael dropped his head into his hands. He had no idea what had caused Elizabeth's turn, and try as she might to pretend there was nothing wrong, he could sense her confusion. This fear of birds had never caused such a reaction before. He'd played it down in front of Lethbridge, but it hadn't occurred to him to warn her about Tost and Rohu's exhibition—he'd even recommended it. Shame Witherspoon hadn't stuck to paintings.

Which reminded him. He walked to the door. "Jane!" Lucy came scuttling along the corridor.

"Where's Jane?"

"She got back a minute or two ago."

"Tell her to come to my study."

With Jane's ability to reduce a problem to the bare essentials and apply basic logic, she must have a rational answer. Perhaps Elizabeth's turn was nothing more than a momentary lapse. She seemed her usual self now, and Jane hadn't thought it necessary to call Lethbridge the night before.

Asylum. Heaven forbid.

Five minutes later Jane's head appeared around the door.

"Ah, come and sit down," said Michael. "Can you shed any light on yesterday's events?"

Jane scrunched up her face and shrugged. "I don't think so. I was talking to Mrs. Witherspoon about the accounts. When we'd finished I went to find Aunt Elizabeth. She was sitting in the corner on the floor with her head in her hands. She was extremely upset."

"Was it the birds?"

"I can't think what else it could be. She seemed to recover quickly and insisted on walking home, though I asked the hansom cab to follow us and she finally agreed to a ride."

Michael grunted what she hoped was his approval.

"She slept for the rest of the afternoon. I shouldn't have worried you. I'm sorry."

"It was entirely the correct thing to do. I'll call into the technical college and have a look at this exhibition myself. I have a meeting this evening; I'd like you to stay at home with Elizabeth."

———≫———

Michael picked up his hat and his cane from the hat stand and pulled the front door closed behind him. An evenly paced walk, Lethbridge advised. It would take about half an hour to walk to the technical college via the telegraph office. He'd have a word with Mrs. Witherspoon and take a good look at this exhibition before he talked to Elizabeth again. The sooner the birds were gone, the better.

Walking was all very well, but by the time he arrived at the telegraph office he'd raised his hat so many times his arm was in danger of dropping off and his heart was pumping faster than he'd like. Curses! He'd forgotten to pocket the pills before he left.

"Good afternoon, Mr. Quinn. How is Miss Quinn today?"

"Much better, thank you, Mrs. Shipton." It would seem all the townsfolk had heard about Elizabeth's turn at the technical college. Bunch of time-wasting gossipmongers. "I've come to see if there's anything for me."

The woman behind the counter turned to the neat rows of wooden cubbyholes behind the desk and pulled out an envelope.

"Your private correspondence was delivered to the house this morning. This arrived only a few moments ago. Joe would have delivered it later this afternoon."

Michael took the small brown envelope from her outstretched hand. "I've been expecting this," he mumbled, slipping it into his breast pocket.

"From Liverpool, England. Nothing wrong, I hope." Mrs. Shipton peered at him over the rims of her spectacles.

Why she asked, he had no idea. At this precise moment, she knew more about the contents of the envelope than he did. She read every telegram received and frequently broadcast the information before Joe had the opportunity to deliver it. "No, nothing at all."

"Well, I don't know." She gave an irritated huff and turned her back, giving him the perfect opportunity to escape.

Next stop, the technical college, and then he'd be free to see what his inquiries had produced.

"Good afternoon, Mrs. Witherspoon."

"Mr. Quinn, how delightful. How is Miss Quinn today?"

Michael bit back a sigh. "Better, thank you. I would like to have a word. Dr. Lethbridge is investigating Miss Quinn's episode, and I wondered if you could shine any light on the matter."

"Me?" The woman patted her hair and straightened her spine. She eased around the desk, enveloping him in a cloud of something horribly floral, dead roses perhaps.

"Did you notice anything unusual about Miss Quinn's demeanor?"

"No, nothing at all . . . until Jane brought her out of the exhibition."

"Perhaps you could show me around."

"It would be my pleasure," she simpered. "Tost and Rohu are a force to be reckoned with." She came to a halt in the doorway and flung out her hand. "The exhibition is due entirely to Major Witherspoon's tireless efforts on behalf of Maitland Town, as I'm sure you'll appreciate."

A lot of stuff and nonsense. Due entirely to the major's efforts to win support for the Commonwealth Liberal party in the area. Michael closed his lips firmly. He was not here to debate the merits of Maitland politics.

"The exhibition will run for another three weeks." A bell tinkled in the distance and Mrs. Witherspoon emitted a tiresome sigh. "You'll have to excuse me. Have a look around and I'll be right back."

"Can you tell me exactly where Miss Quinn was standing when she suffered her turn."

"No, I can't. I wasn't here. Jane and I were going over the accounts. I did, however, call a hansom cab." She lifted her nose. "Miss Quinn refused to get in it."

The bell tinkled again in the distance.

"Excuse me, I won't be a moment." She disappeared through the arch, taking her cloud of dusty roses with her.

The exhibition wasn't large, but the contents were extraordinary. In the center of the room the diprotodon skull took pride of place, and behind it was a massive eagle, which could well have been the cause of Elizabeth's distress. There were snake skins, one at least fourteen feet in length, furs, various other taxidermied birds, and a series of carved emu eggs.

Elizabeth was happy to eat eggs, but the chickens had to be kept cooped up. She'd threatened to sack Lucy when they'd wandered into her rose garden, and she'd insisted Jane remove the bird table she'd put up hoping to encourage the king parrots.

Then there was the pigeon tree in Hill End. Ridiculous. He was clutching at straws. He had to have a serious talk with Elizabeth. Perhaps if she faced her demons she'd be happier.

It was most peculiar. All the birds were displayed behind glass, yet Elizabeth had insisted she'd felt their wings graze her cheeks in the darkness. It made no sense.

Shafts of sunlight illuminated the exhibits in the front section of the room. Michael sniffed and detected no strange smell, other than the remnants of Mrs. Witherspoon's rose-scented person.

After making one more circuit, he walked out to the desk where Mrs. Witherspoon was in close discussion with a group of women. Their conversation stopped short as Michael approached. He nodded, replaced his hat, and left. The last thing he wanted to do was get caught up in another round of commiserations and inquiries. It was all most peculiar—and here in Maitland, the one place where he thought Elizabeth would be safe.

FOURTEEN

HILL END, 1870

M ichael couldn't believe the ease with which Elizabeth slipped
into his life, into the life of Hill End. Every morning he'd walk
her to school and every afternoon he'd return to a cottage filled with
laughter, warm food, and the happiness Mam had promised so long
ago when she and Da first heard about the assisted immigration
scheme. He couldn't fault them for leaving, for trying to make a better
life for them all. They'd made the right choice; they just hadn't lived
to see their plan come to fruition.

"I'm home."

The door banged, echoed in the silence. Michael sucked in a breath,
his nostrils twitching.

Burning!

He raced out the back to the kitchen and pulled the pot from the
stove. Charred remains greeted him. "Kitty!"

Back inside the house, the cold wrapped around him, the fire in
the grate nothing but a few dying embers. "Elizabeth! Kitty!"

He thundered up the stairs, throwing open the door to Elizabeth's
room, to his own.

Nothing. No one.

With his heart thundering he slammed the door and shot out into the street.

A couple of boys playing with hoops, a baby crying in its mother's arms while she chatted unconcerned over the fence.

"Mrs. Dalley, Mrs. Green." He slowed to a halt. "Have you seen Elizabeth?"

They shook their heads.

"What about Kitty? Did anyone see Elizabeth this afternoon?"

"Davy!" One of the boys with a hoop lifted his head. "Seen Elizabeth? Was she at school?"

Of course she was. He'd dropped her off himself, just like always.

"Yeah." The boy turned back to his hoop, sent it bowling across the street, narrowly missing Ah Chu, vegetable baskets dangling from his timber shoulder yoke.

"Have you seen Elizabeth?" Michael called to Ah Chu.

"She came, got some vegetables. Down at the garden."

"When? What time?" He dashed across the road, fists clenched, resisting the temptation to shake some information, any information, out of the man.

"After school finished."

"With Kitty?"

"No, she's home. Her man's sick. Broke his leg in a rock fall."

Michael let out a groan and took off up the street. Why hadn't Kitty told him? Where would Elizabeth go? If she was down at the gardens on the creek, anything could have happened. What if she'd taken a shortcut through the old diggings, honeycombed with disused shafts, sinkings, and mounds of upturned dirt. Da's face, his indented skull, flashed in his mind and he took off up the road.

"Jing! Jing!"

"Mr. Michael." Jing appeared at the front of the warehouse.

"I can't find Elizabeth. Lock up. Come with me." He bent double, hauling the cold air into his lungs.

"All locked up. Time to close."

Michael shot a look at the darkening sky. Soon it'd be impossible to see anything, never mind a young girl wandering alone in a town full of drunken miners and ne'er-do-wells. "Ah Chu saw her down at the gardens at lunchtime."

"With Kitty?"

"Nope. Joe's sick. She didn't fetch Elizabeth." Left his darlin' alone. Mary and Joseph, anything could have happened.

"I'll go down there." Jing indicated the sprawling shanties of the old town. "You go to the church."

The church, yes. Father MacCormick, he'd help. Without responding, Michael took off.

The sun had long gone, but not the incessant thumping of the stampers; they rang out, keeping time with the pounding of his feet. He screamed to a halt outside the church, his breath clouding the cold night air. No lamplight shone in the father's house; the churchyard was covered in darkness.

Slumped against the sagging fence, Michael scanned the churchyard. "Elizabeth!" His voice hardly broke above the thundering stampers. He snatched more air into his lungs. "Elizabeth!"

A flash of white.

He vaulted the fence. Stopped dead.

"Here." A frail voice wafted in the darkness, then another glimmer of white. He spotted her slumped against the wall of the church, a crumpled mess, and bolted across the graveyard. "What the hell are you doing here?" He started to pull her to her feet.

"Michael, stop it! Stop it! My foot . . . I can't . . ."

He scooped her into his arms, heart hammering, fury swelling in his gut. "Who did this? I'll beat the living daylights out of him."

"Michael, put me down." She struggled free, slid down, groaning when her foot touched the ground.

Something akin to a sob spluttered from his mouth, fury turned to fear.

She swiped at his face. "Don't cry."

He knuckled the tears from his eyes. Grimaced.

"I stumbled over Mam and Da's gravestone. I squashed the flowers Ah Chu gave me. I called and called. Father MacCormick didn't hear me."

The air fell out of his mouth, a massive sigh of relief.

"My ankle hurts." She stood like a broken bird, balanced on one leg, the palm of her hand against the church wall, supporting her weight.

"We'll get you home." He scooped her up, tucked her close to his heaving chest.

"My apron." His balance shifted as she bent down. "I waved it, like a distress signal. Did you see me?"

"Aye, my darlin', I saw it."

"I dropped the vegetables. I need them for your supper."

"I don't need anything excepting you safe and sound. Let's go." He snatched up her apron, left the vegetables, and strode off into the darkness.

Michael's heart thumped against Elizabeth's cheek as he cradled her so close it almost hurt. Almost. Not as much as the throbbing in her ankle. He didn't say a word as he thundered back up the street. She'd known he'd come, not that he'd take so long.

It wasn't until he lowered her into the chair by the long-dead fire and unlaced her boot that his face softened. "Made a nasty mess of that." He eased off her boot and stocking, revealing a throbbing purple mess around her ankle. "You sit tight. I'll stoke this fire and bind that up."

"I cooked supper." Her voice quavered and tears gushed down her cheeks. "I'm sorry, Michael." A huge sob wracked her body. "Don't be cross. Kitty couldn't come. She sent a message. Mr. Whittaker wanted me to stay with him but I told him I had to get supper ready for you."

"Oh, me little darlin'. Don't you worry. Sit tight."

He pulled off his coat and placed it around her shoulders. The smell of him—woodsmoke, soap, and a little bit of something from the warehouse—wrapped around her, keeping her safe.

———≈———

Elizabeth woke to the warmth of a blazing fire, tucked under her quilt with her bound foot throbbing.

"I've brought you some supper." Michael put the tray down on the floor and slipped his hands under her arms, easing her into a sitting position. "There's a boiled egg and a cup of tea and some bread and jam. That'll see you right."

"I made lamb hot-pot. We forgot the vegetables."

"Long gone, me darlin'. Can't leave it cook forever. Eat up." He cracked the top of the egg and handed her the spoon.

"I can do it. I'm not a little child."

"No, you're not, but we can't be having you wandering alone.

Seems Kitty's going to be busy for a while, so you're going to have to forget school and come to the auction house until that ankle's better."

Elizabeth started to complain about missing school but thought better of it and stuffed her mouth full of egg. There was nothing she'd like better than spending time at the auction house!

"At least that way if I'm busy, Jing can keep an eye on you. Once your ankle's healed and Kitty's sorted, you'll go back to school."

"What about my lessons?"

"There'll still be lessons. Jing can go and pick them up every day until you're better."

———※———

Elizabeth loved being at the auction house. She had her lessons done in a flash, didn't have to wait for all the dawdlers and the plodders, and for the rest of the morning Jing taught her the workings of his suanpan.

Every day he'd wait patiently until she finished her schoolwork, then he'd produce the ledgers and together they'd work their way through all Michael's outgoings and tally all his incoming receipts.

It was close to the end of the month, and a pile of pieces of paper Elizabeth had found in Michael's coat pockets covered the bench. She smoothed and sorted the receipts into date order and entered the figures in the ledger.

At the very moment she reached for the suanpan to calculate the total, a gust of cool air blew through the open doors and the papers took flight. She flattened them under her palms.

Jing grinned at her. "Quick hands. Quick mind."

"Not quick enough. I haven't totaled them."

"But I have." He drummed his long fingers against a scrappy piece of paper.

"How did you do that so quickly?"

He threw her an infuriatingly mysterious look. "I'll show you. Later, later. We've got people."

"Top of the morning to you."

Elizabeth hadn't noticed before, but Michael's voice had changed. It was deeper and more important. He stuck out his hand and a weathered, stringy man with a drooping moustache clasped it.

"Michael Quinn?"

"How can I help you?"

The man looked over his shoulder and beckoned; a small woman with a baby clasped to her chest and a toddler hanging off her leg stumbled in. "It's me wife and bairns. They'd be needing a place. Folks say you can help."

"That I can. Come on in."

Michael shepherded them through to the back of the warehouse. "You'll be wanting a cup of tea and maybe something to eat. Sit yourself down."

He pulled the huge metal teapot from the fireplace at the back of the warehouse, poured three cups of tea, and set a plate of biscuits in the middle of the table.

"Leave them be, Tommy. We ain't got money for it." The woman slapped at the boy's hand.

"Help yourself, lad. There's nothing worse than a grumbling tummy."

The biscuits disappeared in a second and Elizabeth's gut roiled in sympathy, bringing with it a flash of memory, the touch on her tongue of barley sugar, flickering candles, and Michael, a much younger Michael, his arm cradling her against him, keeping her warm.

"We've got a room for you. It's not big, but it'll do the four of you." He flashed a look at the hangdog man leaning against the doorjamb.

"Won't be needing it for long, just long enough to sell what we've got. Then we're outta here. It's no place for the likes of us. Need money, big money behind you to get anything but scratchings these days, and them Chinamen take all those." He sent a squinty-eyed look in Jing's direction.

Michael ignored his comments. "You'll be wanting a ride. You won't be walking back over the mountains with the little 'uns."

Elizabeth doubted the woman would even have the energy to make it out of town. Sweat beaded her pale brow, and with the wind whistling through the open door, it couldn't be the heat causing her discomfort. As if noticing Elizabeth's scrutiny, she wiped her face on her apron, smudging dirt across her hollow cheeks.

"I'll give you a decent price for your goods and chattels," Michael said, "and throw in a bed for the night and as much stew as you can handle. There's a dray heading for Bathurst tomorrow. We could organize a ride."

"I ain't riding with no Celestials." The man rammed his hands in his pockets and glared at Jing.

His wife turned her pleading eyes on her husband.

"Your choice, that's me offer." Michael folded his arms across his chest and raised one eyebrow. Elizabeth knew the look, even though she hadn't seen it for a long time. "Take it or leave it."

Before the man had turned to go, the woman pulled herself to her feet and stood behind her son, the baby clasped tight in her arms. "We'll take your offer, Mr. Quinn, and we'll be thanking you, if'n it's a good offer for the goods. There's spades and shovels and bedding, pots and pans. A good size tent, canvas."

"Sit yourself down and have a cup of tea. Me and your man'll go outside and organize things. Me sister will look after you."

And so Elizabeth learned another side of Michael's business. Not only buying and selling and transporting goods, Father MacCormick said Michael made a good auctioneer because he had the gift of the gab. It wasn't so much that—he knew what people needed, what they wanted, and he looked after them, the same way he cared for her.

FIFTEEN

MAITLAND TOWN, 1913

The house was in darkness by the time Michael slipped his key into the door. He took off his coat and hat and hung them on the hall stand, stuffed his gloves into the pocket, and threw his scarf onto the table. As much as he enjoyed the local Labor party meetings, he was feeling his age, even though Jane now worked full time at the auction house and had relieved him of many of his responsibilities. His occasional visits were mainly for show to appease those who still insisted a woman's place was in the home.

He switched on the lamp on his desk, reveling in the soft glow from the green shade, and poured himself a glass of whiskey before settling in the chair.

Elizabeth had turned fifty-five the year before; she was ten years younger than him, and despite her perpetual insistence to the contrary, the feeling he'd failed her preyed heavily on his mind. Everyone believed he was responsible for their financial security, but in fact it had been Elizabeth who'd managed, during the depression of the 1890s, to cement their future by investing in seemingly risky ventures that in the long term had thrived. She'd gambled with the skill of a veteran bookie—not on the horses, nothing as flighty as that, but on land, bricks and mortar, and floundering businesses, arranging mortgages and rescuing cash-strapped farmers. They'd come out of it head and shoulders above everyone else.

He'd always imagined she'd marry one day. She'd had her fair share of suitors, but whenever Michael had raised the question she'd maintained family came first, and since he was the only family she had, the matter didn't merit discussion.

And that was the crux of the problem. It was time he told her the truth. And he had no idea how to do that.

It would be selfish and cruel to take away everything she knew, everything she'd worked for. She'd expect answers where there were none. If the knowledge were broadcasted she'd be subject to the most appalling gossip and innuendo. They'd have to move on. Start again. But he couldn't. They couldn't. It was too late in life. He had to find some answers.

He pulled the small brown envelope from his pocket, hoping against hope it contained the information he needed. Closing his eyes, he rocked back in the chair, remembering the sensation of her tiny, trusting hand slipping into his and her pleading eyes.

When Elizabeth had asked him if she'd always been afraid of birds, his stomach had turned and he'd almost admitted the truth. Instead, he'd stood there, incapable of responding because he simply didn't know.

He'd waited far too long.

Perhaps the answer lay in the small envelope.

He set the whiskey glass down on the desk and withdrew the telegram. The thin piece of paper rustled as he unfolded it.

REGRET TO INFORM UNABLE TO ASSIST.
100 YEAR CLOSURE PERIOD FOR RECORDS
IDENTIFYING INMATES. WORKHOUSE
ADMINISTRATOR. BROWNLOW HILL, LIVERPOOL.

One hundred years. Michael clenched the telegram into a tight ball and let his mind drift back to that evening fifty years ago, when he'd strolled down the road, his heart full of promise and the future stretching like the road to heaven before him . . .

A fine mist rolled in across the Mersey, dampening the dim twilight. The bloke in the immigration office said the sun always shone in Australia. Michael couldn't believe that. Not every day, not all the time, otherwise what would they do for water? A little bit of sunshine, once in a while, could go a whole lot toward making a man happy.

Just a few more days and he'd have the paperwork in his hands. He'd earned the money faster than he'd thought possible. Two pound for himself and one for Lizzie. He'd taken any and every job on offer and worked so hard he never had the energy to find somewhere to lay his head. In doing that he'd neglected Lizzie. He'd not kept his promise to see her once a week; it had been three weeks since the last time, way overdue.

Fingers crossed Miss Finbright would be on duty. She'd make sure Lizzie was waiting for him. She wasn't like the other dragons who guarded the workhouse. She knew what it was like, having grown up there herself. She knew how much his visits meant to Lizzie.

He climbed over the metal railings and slinked through the shadows behind the chapel to the side wall of the girls' dormitory. The clock on the tower chimed six and the door opened a crack.

"You there, Michael?"

"Aye, that I am." He stepped into the light of her lantern.

"Lizzie has a new friend. Mind if she tags along?"

"'Course not." He tucked his hand into his pocket and counted the number of barley sugars he had. More than enough for Lizzie to share.

"I'll bring them down. It's a bit chilly. Take them to the chapel; you'll be sheltered from the worst of it. Won't be long."

She pulled the door to, leaving him scuffing up and down, stamping his feet. Lizzie would forget the cold when he told her he'd got a sailing date. She couldn't remember Mam and Da, but he'd kept them alive by talking about the past. A little girl needed family. A boy, too, even if everyone thought him a man.

"Here we are." Miss Finbright held the lantern high, illuminating the two pale faces in the bright glow. "I'll leave the lantern with you and be back on the dot of seven. Make sure you listen for the clock tower."

"Right you are, miss." He flicked her a wink, made her cheeks flush, then pulled Lizzie into his arms, hugging her tight. "How are you, me little darlin'?"

"Cold." She burrowed into his chest. "Have you got something for me?"

"That I have. Some of those sweeties you like, and . . . just you wait and see. Who's this, then?"

The little slip of nothing hung her head, and Lizzie shrugged. "Miss Finbright calls her Girlie, but she doesn't like it."

He slid Lizzie down to the ground and crouched in front of the pathetic little piece of misery. An aroma stung his nostrils; she could do with a bath, never mind a decent feed. "What's your name, darlin'?"

Her nose wrinkled a little and she licked her blue lips.

"She won't tell. She won't tell Miss Finbright, won't talk to no one."

Poor little mite. From the look of it, someone had put the fear of God into her. Probably got a beating for refusing to talk. "Righto then, let's get out of this mizzle."

Cold, thin fingers wrapped around his hand, and a swish of good feeling warmed his blood as he led them down the path.

The heavy door groaned when he shouldered it open and the three of them slipped inside the chapel.

"Come and sit down over here and let's see what I've got in me pockets." He tucked his heavy coat over the back of the pew and made a bit of a nest for the two girls, then emptied his pockets. "I've got some news for you, Miss Lizzie."

One of the men down at the docks had given him a couple of oranges. He'd never seen anything like them before. He'd eaten one but saved the other for Lizzie. If he'd known there'd be two of them he'd have saved the second.

Before he could begin to take the peel off, Lizzie grabbed the fruit and sank her teeth into the skin.

"Urgh! It's horrid." A sweet smell filled the cozy space.

"Give it here. You don't eat the skin. Watch this." He slid his finger into the hole her teeth had made and peeled back the thick skin, then broke it into segments, just like the bloke on the dock had showed him.

"There." He held out one segment. Lizzie shook her head. "It's nice, real sweet. I promise."

Before she had a chance to change her mind it disappeared, and there was Girlie chewing away with a look of pure pleasure on her peaked face.

"Your friend likes it. Come on, Lizzie, you try it." He held up another segment. "You're going to have to get to like them. They grow in Australia and are real good for you."

She tentatively took the piece and held it up to her nose.

"I've got news, good news."

"Are we going soon?"

"Sooner than soon, just five more days."

Lizzie held up her thumb and then her fingers, one at a time. "Five like me. That's a long time." She nestled against him. "You said soon."

"Not five years, me darlin', five days. You go to sleep tonight, then the next night, the next night and the next and then next." He held up each of his fingers and watched Lizzie's brow crease as she tried to make sense of it all.

Not so her friend. With wide eyes she watched each of his fingers, nodding her head, bright as a button. He slipped his hand into his pocket and brought out two barley sugars.

Lizzie fell on them, her interest in their long-promised sailing date pushed aside. He could understand that. It had been nearly two years since the day Mam and Da had left, and promises grew thin.

Girlie sat with her head cocked to one side, tracking his every move, her serious gaze never wavering. He tried waggling his eyebrows, offering her a smile, then finally put his hand in his pocket and drew out two more sweeties. Unlike Lizzie, she didn't pounce on them; she just sat there.

Palm out, he offered them. Eventually she took one and slid it into the pocket of her smock. "Aren't you going to eat it?" Michael asked.

She shook her head and moved a little closer to him, her blue-tinged lips trembling. He pulled his coat from the back of the pew and wrapped it around her shoulders.

"Will Mam and Da be in Australia waiting for us?" Lizzie's puffed cheeks stuffed full of barley sugar moved as she spoke.

"You know they will. They promised."

"Sometimes people break their promises."

Poor Lizzie, she had so many disappointments in her short life. She couldn't remember Mam or Da, only Aunty Nuala, and she'd been taken. A string of pledges that came to naught.

"I'll never break my promise to you."

"You might."

"No, I won't. I promise you we will go to Australia in five days, and Mam and Da will be standing on the dock waiting for us."

Lizzie nodded her head, tugging her lip with her teeth.

A whiplash of wind tore around the back of his head and the lantern flickered. Miss Finbright stood in the doorway plucking at her apron. "I'm sorry, Michael. It's time for the girls to come inside. Matron's doing her rounds early. Don't want any trouble."

He swung Lizzie to the ground, then slipped his hands around Girlie and lifted her down. She clung like a limpet.

"You too. Time for bed."

She buried her head in his shoulder.

"I think you've made a conquest. I don't suppose she told you her name?" Miss Finbright took the fragile bag of bones from his arms.

"Not a word."

"I'm not sure she's all there." She tapped the side of her head. "Sometimes the shock of being left is more than they can stand. She's old enough to speak. Must be nearing five." She reached out and lifted the girl's hand over her head and tugged her fingers down toward her ear. The little mite let out a wail.

"You're hurting her."

"No, I'm not. It's the only way to tell in cases like this. Lizzie, can you touch your ear?"

Lizzie lifted her hand over the top of her head, her fingers grazing her ear.

"See. We know Lizzie's turned five and there's no mistaking it. Length of the arm in relation to the size of the head. That and their teeth."

Michael groaned. She might have been talking of a horse.

"Come on, Lizzie. Let's go." She held out her hand and Lizzie happily took hold of it and threw him a wave. Girlie just stood there gazing up at him.

"Off you go. I'll see you next time." The words were out of his mouth before he'd thought too much about it. Next time he and Lizzie'd be heading down to the docks.

Michael tossed the telegram aside. So much for memories. He'd been over it a thousand times, seeking a minute scrap he may have missed over the years. Time to attack the problem head-on. Procrastination was not a virtue, no matter how one camouflaged it.

There was only one person who could help and she might well be dead.

He picked up the Waterman fountain pen Elizabeth had given him for Christmas, sent all the way from New York, and pulled a piece of paper from the drawer of his desk. His hand hovered over the page as he admired the embossed address at the top of the paper and the sophisticated styling—more of Elizabeth's handiwork. She had become so much a part of his existence he couldn't bear to imagine life without her.

With a sigh, he unscrewed the cap.

Dear Miss Finbright,

Please do not think me forward in writing, but I would like

to lay at your feet a conundrum that has plagued me for many years.

Michael twisted the pen in his fingers. He was evading the issue. If he sent a letter framed thus it would prolong the entire matter.

A blot of ink fell from his nib and spread before it soaked into the cartridge paper, a replica of the stain on his heart.

I hope you will not consider this letter a liberty, particularly as it is many years since we last met, and I doubt you will remember me.

He'd been a scrap of a lad. He'd thought he was a man at fifteen, but his decisions had been those of a child. What if the woman was dead? He had no idea how old she might be.

More procrastination. He couldn't be having it. He must put the guilt behind him. He could change nothing.

And this is where I must humbly request your tolerance and assistance.

He still couldn't face what he had done, nor could he control the shaking of his hand. If only he could talk to her face-to-face.

I am planning a trip to England . . .

Was he? Why, yes, of course he was. It would be the perfect way to introduce Elizabeth to the truth. A trip to Liverpool. London, even. He rocked back in the chair and thought a little longer.

Then it came to him. Bath. They would take a trip to Bath.

Elizabeth was forever speaking of the place. Over the years she had developed a passion for the novels of Jane Austen and spoke constantly of the city. They could travel to London as well, attend the opera, visit the British Museum, stay at the Ritz; it had only recently been refurbished in keeping with the Ritz in Paris. Yes! Paris. They would travel there too. It would do them both good. A change of scene. Jane was more than capable of running the business, and the auctioneering skills of the manager, John, far surpassed his own these days. Ever since he'd contracted the ridiculous ailment the previous winter he'd felt under the weather, lacking energy and suffering pains.

. . . and would very much like the opportunity to meet with you. I have often wondered about the little girl Lizzie befriended.

Yours most sincerely,

Michael Ó'Cuinn

Michael poured himself another generous slug of whiskey. He would send the letter care of the workhouse and ask them to forward it, then he'd make inquiries about travel and book tickets. When that was done, he would tell Elizabeth of his plans.

———≈———

Jane wheeled her bicycle around the back of the auction house and propped it against the shed. The cancelation of the meeting with the Benevolent Society was the only good thing to have come out of Elizabeth's turn. Jane hadn't argued when Elizabeth mentioned the society's lack of funds for their moonlight concert, but she knew that wasn't correct. Elizabeth never made mistakes but she was certain there was a discrepancy in the accounts.

She let herself in through the back door of the auction house and skipped upstairs to the room she'd taken over as her office some months earlier.

In the early days, when Elizabeth and Michael first arrived in Maitland, they'd lived above the auction house. The homely simplicity of these rooms pleased Jane. Plain painted walls and scrubbed wooden furniture. The kitchen table had become her desk; it gave her space to order her thoughts, spread herself out, unlike the little desk in her bedroom. She needed space to think.

Ever since Michael had become involved in the Labor party, he'd spent more and more time in Sydney or in his study at home, and rarely used his former bedroom in the building overlooking the street. Elizabeth's old bedroom they used as a storeroom, and, much like its one-time occupant, it remained ordered and perfectly neat, the boxes of records and accounts stacked against the back wall.

Jane liked the privacy and the peace upstairs. Settling into the wooden chair, she opened the drawer in the middle of the table and took out Elizabeth's abacus.

Learning to use the abacus was one of the first things Elizabeth had insisted upon when Jane moved into the house on Church Street. During the Christmas holidays, with the weather unbearably hot, the back veranda provided the coolest place in the house, and one day Jane had been sitting there, pondering the percentage chance of her being accepted by the toffee-nosed girls at St. Joseph's when school reconvened. Elizabeth, in that way she had, must have noticed her misery and decided to divert her thoughts because she'd drawn up a chair and produced this frame supporting a series of beads. She sat with it on her lap, her hands smoothing the worn timber, and explained how it worked.

At first Jane had taken it as an insult, thought perhaps Elizabeth didn't share Michael's belief in her mathematical ability—the only characteristic she'd been remotely proud of. It had taken only a moment for the simplicity of the abacus to thrill her, and as the summer progressed she'd come to understand its capabilities. Since then she'd used it almost daily. Elizabeth had never actually given it to her, but she seemed happy enough to leave it with her.

Jane retrieved the manila folder containing the bank statements for the Benevolent Society and untied the pale blue ribbon: blue indicated the completed work; green marked unfinished business. She opened the folder and ran her finger down the entries. She couldn't make any alterations without Elizabeth's signature, but she could check the original statements. The sooner she put her mind to rest, the sooner she could fit in her trip to the library to research the diprotodon.

Her fingers flew with satisfying ease, the *clink-clank* of the beads bumping against each other soothing her disquiet. In a matter of moments she'd located the problem. Somehow Elizabeth had transposed a set of figures. Seven hundred and ten pounds had become one hundred and seventy pounds. Carefully she re-totaled the column in the ledger, neatly inscribing her initials against the corrections. No wonder Elizabeth thought they had insufficient funds. What an embarrassment!

Once everything was rectified, Jane slammed the ledger shut and tucked it under her arm. Sadly, she'd have to mention it to Elizabeth and have her initial the corrections before she went to the library. Elizabeth was a stickler for accountability.

With a glance up at the clock, Jane closed the door behind her and clattered down the stairs. Monday was her day to check the tills and issue receipts for the cash. While she was here it would be best to get it out of the way.

An hour later Jane pushed open the kitchen door and bumped into Bessie.

"Mind your feet. I've washed the floor."

She tiptoed across the linoleum. Such a waste of time washing the floor every day with the number of people who came in and out.

"Where's the bread?"

Jane ground to a halt. Blast! she'd forgotten all about it. "I'll go back and get it later. I've got to go and see Aunt Elizabeth."

"I suppose I'll have to send Lucy." Bessie let out a huff of annoyance.

"This is more important. I'm sorry."

At this time of day Elizabeth would be at her desk in the sitting room, overlooking the garden. Jane pushed open the door.

"There's a problem with the accounts for the Benevolent Society. I need your signature on the corrections I've made."

She marched across the carpet and came to a halt in the middle of the empty room.

How strange.

Leaving the ledger on the desk, she ran up the stairs and knocked on Elizabeth's bedroom door. Receiving no response, she peered inside. Where was she? Surely she hadn't had another turn? Jane stepped out onto the veranda and glanced down into the garden, breathing a sigh of relief when she spotted Elizabeth sitting on the bench seat under the apple tree staring at nothing, at least nothing Jane could see. Most peculiar. She wasn't even reading.

Two minutes later, with the ledger tucked under her arm, Jane approached Elizabeth. "How are you feeling?"

"For goodness' sake. Is there nothing anyone can say without requiring a minute description of my demeanor?" She untwisted a piece of red thread from her finger and gathered it into the palm of her hand. "What have you got there?"

"The Benevolent Society ledger. I found a mistake."

"Balderdash."

"I reworked the statements and found an error."

"Give it to me." Elizabeth pulled the ledger from her hand and settled it on her lap, flicking through the pages. "And sit down." She ran her finger down the columns and stopped short at Jane's initials. "Why did you make these changes?"

"The numbers were transposed. That's why you thought they hadn't sufficient funds to stage their moonlight concert."

"Numbers don't lie."

Unless they were incorrectly entered. And Elizabeth had entered the numbers. "It's an easy mistake."

"I don't make mistakes."

"Are the payments up-to-date? Because if they are, it's not going to cover July. If you moved the excess from June and take the earnings from May it all should balance nicely."

"Where are the statements?"

"I've checked the statements and made the corrections. I need you to sign off on them."

The ledger and all the papers fell to the ground as Elizabeth jumped to her feet. "Do not contradict me, young lady." With her face the color of Bessie's famed plum jam, Elizabeth marched back into the house, the screen door banging behind her. Jane sat for a moment, clasping her shaking hands. Elizabeth never, ever lost her temper.

SIXTEEN

HILL END, 1871

Time passed in a flurry of people, some arriving, some leaving, some striking it rich and others losing their all. Elizabeth hardly spent any time in the little weatherboard house with the neat white fence and the shingle roof. Once her ankle healed and she returned to school, Jing met her at the gate and, after a lunch of clear soup and tasty little dumplings, they'd get to work on the auction house accounts, keeping track of Michael's expenses—making sure he left something for them to live on and didn't give everything away. Jing would work on the ledgers for some of the other businesses in town. No matter how often she tried to tempt him away from the desk, he remained disciplined as he patiently completed long columns of figures.

Every Saturday afternoon they'd raise the flag outside the auction house, and on the dot of two o'clock, Jing would ring the bell and the warehouse would fill. Plenty of the new arrivals had money and happily spent it on secondhand tools and materials, and every week the rent on the rooms above the warehouse came in.

Elizabeth promised Michael right at the outset she wouldn't venture up the stairs, and she kept her word until one day her curiosity drew her to the door with no handle. She didn't get far; Jing appeared by her side, stealthy as the resident cat, and led her away from the origins of the strangely exotic smell that permeated the entire building.

Elizabeth pulled the suanpan toward her now and ran her fingers over the smoothly rounded beads. The simplicity of it still thrilled her. She could add and reckon faster than most, but with the aid of the beads it took only a fraction of the time. It was so simple, painfully logical. Beautiful, in fact.

It hadn't taken her long to master Jing's beads. Every day he made her practice. He'd throw random numbers and questions at her, and shriek with pleasure when she came up with the answer. Questions like how many minutes were between the twenty-first of February and the eleventh of November?

And when she'd ask if it was a leap year or not, he'd look askance. Of course it made a difference. Why would anyone think differently?

But one afternoon everything changed. When Elizabeth sat down, Jing produced a list of questions and challenged her.

"We race." He pushed a smoothed paper bag and the stub of a pencil across to her. "On your marks, are you ready? Let's go."

She'd flown through the equations without any trouble and sat back in the chair before she'd looked up at him. When she did, he was sitting, arms crossed, a neat list of numbers, no workings, and the answers neatly inscribed on his paper bag. He'd even written them twice, once in Chinese and once in Arabic numerals.

His smug smile said it all.

No one ever beat Elizabeth at school. She pushed back the chair, wishing she could storm out. No. It would be bad manners. Although she might be good with numbers, her manners left a lot to be desired, or so Michael liked to remind her. He believed Jing's manners were exceptional. "You work much faster than I do. Do you think I'll get smarter as I get older?"

"You're smart now. Mr. Whittaker says there's no more school for you," said Jing.

"What do you mean no more school? I like school."

"He says you've finished, nothing he can teach you. You can learn more here with me."

"So you'd be my teacher?" As much as Elizabeth enjoyed Jing's company, she also liked the routine of school, even if she did spend most of the day helping the younger children. The auction business had grown so much in the last few years. She hardly saw anything of Michael. Even though he no longer did the run to Sydney, he was forever in Bathurst, and Kitty had to come and stay on the evenings he was away. If Elizabeth could do more in the auction house, then he might have more time to spend at home, more time with her.

"Do you want soup?" Without waiting for a response Jing ladled some soup into two small bowls and slid one across the work bench to her. He pointed with his spoon. "Eat."

Small pieces of chicken drifted between white cabbage and carrots. The steam and the sweet spice of ginger and sesame filled the air between them, making Elizabeth's mouth water. Sometimes Jing brought dumplings—lovely dewy dough filled with spicy red pork, or little tiny parcels wrapped in the finest skin. They were her favorite; they usually ate those earlier in the day with a cup of jasmine tea. The first time Jing had offered her a cup she'd spat it straight back out. It was nothing like the tea Michael liked to drink, but over time she'd come to relish the delicate perfumed flavor.

"What do you think Michael will say?" she asked, sipping the broth—everything she knew it would be, fragrant and delicious.

Jing made a sucking noise and lifted his head from the bowl. "Mr. Michael told me to see Mr. Whittaker. Tell him he agrees you won't be coming back to school, you'll be working with me."

A swirl of anger displaced the warmth of the soup in her belly. Why hadn't Michael spoken to her? "He didn't ask me."

"Mr. Michael, he's the boss." Jing's chopsticks clattered against the bowl, neatly capturing a floating piece of chicken.

Nevertheless, Michael might at least have mentioned it. He could hardly claim she was a child now, especially if he thought she should leave school. "When will Michael be back from Bathurst?"

"Not until tomorrow afternoon. Kitty will stay with you tonight."

There it was again—this constant need for someone to watch over her, all arranged without her knowledge.

Elizabeth picked up her bowl and drank the last bit of broth. "Thank you, that was delicious."

She slipped off the stool and wandered to the door. Bright shafts of sunlight slatted down across the new timber floor and the sound of raucous jeering drifted down the dusty street.

A boot came flying through the door and landed at her feet with a thud. She bent and picked it up in time to see a young boy skidding up the road, waving his hands and screaming at the two much larger laughing boys who were taunting him.

"I've got it here." Elizabeth held the worn boot up by its laces and waved it in the air.

The boy's head dropped and he shuffled to a halt, standing like a forlorn rag in the middle of the road.

"Come on, quickly. There's a dray behind you."

Without bothering to look he limped across to the warehouse, one foot bare.

She tipped his chin, saw the tears trickling down his face. "What's your name?"

He sniffed. "Song."

There were few Chinese children in Hill End. Mostly men came

THE GIRL IN THE PAINTING

in search of gold, leaving their families behind. They were a familiar sight, working together on alluvial diggings, creating water races, panning to extract the ore; diligent, hardworking, and tireless, willing to work the tailings left by other miners. They kept to themselves and lived in the Chinese camp, a crowded mass of tents below Red Hill.

It was only then Elizabeth noticed the trickle of blood seeping onto the floor. "Come with me, Song." She took his filthy hand in hers and led him into the shop. Poor little mite.

"Good afternoon to you." Jing settled the beads on his suanpan and studied the little boy, then swept him up and plonked him onto one of the stools. "Have you been a bad boy?"

Song shook his head and another tear welled.

"He's cut his foot. I'll go and get something to clean it up."

Leaving him with Jing, she ran through the warehouse into the kitchen that had replaced the blackened old fireplace and camp oven of earlier days. She filled up an enamel bowl with some warm water from the kettle and tipped in a generous slug of iodine, collected some clean rags, then, as an afterthought, lifted the lid on the stack of bamboo baskets and pocketed a couple of Jing's pork buns.

By the time she returned, Song had a lopsided smile as he slid the beads on the suanpan while Jing spoke to him in a low voice. Elizabeth couldn't distinguish the words but they sounded soothing.

"Here we are." She handed Song a pork bun, then dunked the rag into the warm water and sat down next to him. "Put your foot here on my lap."

She might as well have asked him to run the next auction. His mouth dropped open and he almost lost the chewed remains of his pork bun.

"Come on. I can't fix this if you won't let me see it."

Jing threw her a questioning look, and when she shrugged her shoulders, he lifted Song's foot and placed it gently in her lap. The poor little boy's muscles tensed and he almost fell backward off the stool. Layers of dirt covered the sole of his foot, as though he'd never worn boots. Elizabeth wiped the rag across his skin in search of the wound. The blood welled and led her to a nasty slice between his toes. He flinched as she dabbed it with the cloth. "Be brave. I've got to clean it. Why didn't you keep your boots on?"

Song sniffed and looked away.

"He only wears his boots at school. He takes them off for the walk home," Jing answered for him.

"That's ridiculous!"

"Makes them last longer."

"Where's the other boot?"

"The boys took it."

"For goodness' sake. Why?" She turned to Song but he didn't answer. Instead, he sat, head hanging, his cheek pouched with the remains of the pork bun.

"It's not good enough. I'm going to do something about it, see if we can find his other boot. I'll ask at the school." She patted Song's leg. "Who took your boot?"

He mumbled something to Jing and slid down from the stool.

"What did he say?"

Jing's lips quirked. "That it was a waste of time worrying, and besides, he hates his boots. They're too small and hurt his toes."

"Then we'll get him another pair." Michael wouldn't mind, probably wouldn't even notice; a pair of boots wouldn't make a dent in this month's earnings if the incoming totals were anything to go by.

Jing let out a long-suffering sigh. "It won't make any difference. He'll get a belting when he gets home and that'll be the end of it."

"But it wasn't his fault. He didn't do anything wrong." She handed the single boot back to Song, slipped her hand into her pocket, and brought out the other pork bun. He clamped it in his hand and balanced on one leg, the white bandage blazing against his dirty foot.

Elizabeth reached for her hat. She'd go down to the school and have words with Miss Drake. It was all very well allowing the Chinese to attend the National School, but not if they were bullied.

"I'm not going to let it rest. If Song were Cornish or Irish or German—any other race—Miss Drake would have the matter sorted in moments and the bullies punished."

"Law no good for Chinamen."

Elizabeth hated it when Jing aped the sing-song pidgin the Europeans used when they spoke of the Chinese, but she couldn't argue with his attitude. Only the week before, two Chinese men had been jailed for an attack on the constable outside the church. No one gave them a chance to explain themselves. Michael reckoned it served them right, but Michael was blind about anything to do with Father MacCormick. "I'm not going to let it rest," she repeated.

"Where are you going?"

"To the school, to see Miss Drake, I told you."

"Don't. You'll make it worse. Tomorrow Song will be in more trouble."

"Mr. Whittaker wouldn't let it happen at the Catholic school."

The quiver of a smile flickering on his face unsettled her. "You can't change anything."

"What's so amusing?" It was almost as though he was challenging her. Testing her. "The least I can do is see him home safely."

"I will take him."

"No, I am coming too."

"Mr. Michael won't like it."

"Then we will go together."

———— ≈ ————

The road wound past the pigeon tree Elizabeth usually avoided. For some reason the birds in their nesting boxes made her flesh crawl and she hated the smell of their droppings. Today she didn't care. With Jing leading the way and Song dangling from his hand she felt quite safe. She'd never strayed beyond the cottage before. They'd driven the road when they'd arrived, but ever since she'd hurt her ankle Michael had set her boundaries: home, school, the auction house, and the local shops. Truth be told, she was pleased to have an excuse to explore, and if she was in Jing's company Michael could hardly complain.

As they walked away from the new town the noise of the stampers diminished. Jing slowed and waved his hand in a wide arc. "My home is over there."

In all the time Elizabeth had spent with Jing, it had never crossed her mind to ask where he lived. With his father and his uncle, she knew, but not where. "Why don't you live in town?"

"When they doubled the license fees for the Chinese they also said our camps had to be away from the new town."

How ridiculous!

Rough timber fences surrounded many of the dwellings, and once they left the road, Song took off, his sore foot forgotten, and disappeared into a maze of narrow laneways.

Ahead of them, perched on the only piece of high ground, stood a slab and mud building, much larger than any of the canvas tents and shanties. Flags flew from the roof and large, bright red pieces of paper hung on either side of the ornate timber doors, fluttering in the breeze.

"What's that?"

"Joss house, the temple."

"What are all the flags for?"

"Greetings, good wishes, and notices about news and meetings."

Small pieces of red paper littered the ground in front of the doors. Elizabeth bent down and picked one up.

"Firecrackers from the celebration last month. Come." Jing pushed open the door and led her inside.

The familiar smell from the warehouse coiled around her, mixed with the reek of Chinese tobacco and something else sweet and cloying. "What's that smell?"

Jing gestured to the windows where a row of slowly burning sticks, a little like miniature bulrushes, sent a coil of heavily scented smoke into the air. "Incense."

Not much different from the incense Father MacCormick liked to throw around every Sunday. In fact, the restful peace was no different from his church, yet in the shadows at the back a group of men sat clustered around a table, clouds of gray smoke from their pipes suspended above them. Heads down, they argued ferociously over some sort of game involving piles of small white tiles that clattered and clanked as the men slid them across the tabletop with mesmerizing speed.

"What are they doing?" Elizabeth kept her voice low.

"Gambling. Mahjong."

"In the church?" She smothered a laugh. She couldn't imagine Father MacCormick approving one of the miners' poker nights.

One of the men looked up and said something to Jing. He replied, then led her out of earshot to show her a row of porcelain figures lined up on a table in front of a scroll covered in perfectly formed black lines and slashes.

"I don't think I should be here."

"The joss house is for everyone. To protect us, help us. We pray for fortune, health, and safety for ourselves and our family at home and burn joss money for our ancestors."

"They burn money?" Michael wouldn't approve of that.

"Joss money. Bamboo paper with a small gold square." He sketched the shape with his fingers. "We send the money to our relatives to make sure their stay in the afterlife is comfortable."

The faces of the porcelain gods stared at her and her skin prickled. Was sending money any different from leaving flowers on Mam's and Da's graves every week? Perhaps more useful. "How often do you do this?"

"Birthdays, special holidays, funerals." He waited a little longer, then took her arm. "Come. It's time I took you home. It will be dark soon."

The heat had gone from the sun as they stepped outside the joss house, the air full of the smoke from cooking fires and the smell of spices. Perhaps Jing's father and uncle were sitting somewhere, waiting for him to come home. Why had she never wondered about his life outside the warehouse? He was always there before her in the morning and stayed to lock up when Michael or Kitty took her home.

"Where's your house?" Elizabeth asked.

He sketched a vague line in the air. "A little farther down the lane toward the creek."

"Will you show me?"

A frown flashed across his face. "No. Not tonight. It's late." His look stopped her arguing.

"My father and my uncle would not be happy." He held out his hand. "Kitty will be wondering where you are. We must hurry."

She studied his long fingers, then threw caution aside and placed her hand in his. His clasp tightened, and their fingers interlaced. He picked up the pace and headed back onto the Hill End road.

Elizabeth gave a skip and tightened her grasp. It seemed the most natural thing in the world to be walking along hand in hand with Jing.

They found Kitty hanging over the gate, scanning the road with a scowl to match the clouds gathering behind the hills. "Where do you think you've been?" she bellowed with her hands slammed on her ample hips and her voice overpowering the thump of the stampers.

Elizabeth groped for some excuse. If she told Kitty she'd been to Chinatown she'd never hear the end of it.

"I've been at the warehouse."

"All locked up and the pair of you—"

"Mrs. Kitty, I beg your pardon." Jing jumped to her rescue. "We had some deliveries to make and I thought it better to take Miss Elizabeth with me than leave her alone at the warehouse. I know how valuable your time is and did not wish to impose."

Kitty eyed Jing through narrowed eyes, then let out a loud huff. "Well, hurry along now." She pulled the gate open and grasped Elizabeth's hand, hauling her into the garden.

"Goodbye, Jing. See you tomorrow," Elizabeth called over her shoulder as he disappeared into the twilight without another word.

Kitty slammed the front door and turned on her. "Are you out of your mind? Gallivanting around the streets with a Celestial?"

Elizabeth snatched her hand free. "I wasn't gallivanting around the streets. If you really want to know, we were helping someone." A flicker of annoyance grew in Elizabeth's chest. What right had Kitty to complain about Jing? He'd done nothing wrong. It was her idea to go with him to take Song home and besides, she'd had the most interesting afternoon.

SEVENTEEN

MAITLAND TOWN, 1913

Jane hopped up onto the footpath, narrowly avoiding the wheels of the buggy as the burly auction house manager screeched to a halt. "Come with me."

"What is it, John?"

He bent the switch double. "Mrs. Witherspoon's mad as a cut snake."

"Mrs. Witherspoon?" The woman was such a nuisance. Gathering her skirts, Jane climbed up into the buggy. "What's going on?"

"There's some bloke with a wagon full of paintings. Claims he's been told he could store them at the technical college, and she's as good as blockaded the door."

The buggy swerved as it rounded the corner, scattering a group of women waiting at the tram stop.

"I don't see what it has to do with us."

"She reckons it's all Mr. Michael's fault, that he *disrupted* Major Witherspoon's arrangements."

"Oh, for goodness' sake."

"You can't turn up and expect to hang your paintings whenever you feel like it." Mrs. Witherspoon's strident tones echoed down the street, and before John drew to a halt, Jane leaped down from the buggy.

"You agreed the exhibition could take place in three weeks, and that you would store the paintings until then."

It was the voice Jane recognized first, the lovely burr. Timothy Penter. The artist's son.

"Major Witherspoon has arranged for the current exhibition to run for a longer period. We have had such a response, people coming from as far as Newcastle and Singleton. We simply don't have room to store your paintings."

"But you didn't see fit to inform me."

"Well, no. I . . ." Mrs. Witherspoon flushed. "Major Witherspoon referred the matter to Mr. Quinn."

"I can't leave all these paintings sitting here. It's going to rain." As Timothy spoke, great drops as big as pennies plopped onto the footpath.

"Timothy. Timothy Penter. How lovely to see you." Jane produced her best imitation of Elizabeth's soothing tones. Her ploy worked because Mrs. Witherspoon closed her mouth with a snap. "I don't expect you remember me. We met a month or so ago."

She gestured to the technical college, then held out her hand.

Timothy's face flushed a bright red, the tips of his ears almost glowing.

"Miss Piper. Of course I remember." He grasped her hand in both of his.

A large crack of thunder rolled down High Street and the rain began to fall in earnest. Timothy let out a groan and attempted to pull some sacks across the pile of paintings in the back of the wagon.

"You can't leave them in the rain. Bring them to the auction house, we've plenty of room there. Mrs. Witherspoon, you go inside. I'd hate you to get wet. We can sort this out later."

Already the stuffy woman's hair was trailing down over her face and a large drip hung from the end of her sharp nose. Jane managed what she hoped was a winning smile. It had little effect as she was elbowed aside and Mrs. Witherspoon barged through the doors and disappeared. It would be interesting to see how long it would take the news of this to spread. Another bout of gossip might get Elizabeth out of the limelight.

The rain fell in sheets as Jane ran back to the buggy. "As quick as you can, John. We don't want the paintings to get wet."

Several minutes later they drew up outside the auction house. Jane jumped down and reached for the first painting from Timothy.

"Can you manage? It's heavy."

She took the weight, fingers clasped tight around the protective calico covering, and made for the door.

"Where do you want them?" John asked, three paintings clasped in his brawny arms.

"I've got no idea." Where on earth could she put them? People were crammed into the auction rooms seeking shelter from the rain. "Let's just get them inside first. Then we'll take them upstairs."

"Right you are."

John propped the paintings against the wall and shot back outside. Jane traipsed after him.

Poor Timothy smiled wryly, his hair plastered to his head. "You go inside. I can manage."

"Nonsense. Pass me the next one."

He jumped down from the back of the wagon and pulled another painting down. As she took it, his face was so close she could see the laughter in his eyes. "You're enjoying this."

"It's not every day I get this close to the girl of my dreams."

Jane as good as reefed the painting from his arms and shot through the door, her face burning. The girl of his dreams! For goodness' sake, what was the matter with him?

Pulling her soaking hair back from her face, she bolted back to the door in time to hold it open for both John and Timothy.

"That's it. We've got them all." John eased four huge paintings down.

"Thanks very much." Timothy stacked them against the wall. "Father will kill me if anything happens to them. I need to get the covers off in case the damp affects the paint." He untied the largest of the calico bags.

Jane eyed the crowd watching with interest. "It would be better if we could take them upstairs." Not only would there be no room for any of the customers to get through the door, they'd all get an early preview. "You don't want everyone seeing them before the exhibition."

"Good point." John heaved several paintings into his arms and took off up the stairs.

"Sorry about all of this," said Timothy. "The weather looked fine, only a little overcast when I hired the wagon at the station."

"Are your parents with you?" Jane asked.

"They're taking a bit of a tour. I brought the paintings here from Melbourne."

"Let's get the rest of these upstairs and they can dry out."

They ferried the remaining paintings up the stairs and stripped them from the calico bags. All the while a strange ambience whirled, making her chest tighten and her breath come in short, sharp gasps. Timothy reached for one of the calico bags and wiped his dripping hair. Raindrops clung to the hair on his forearms where he'd rolled up the sleeves of his shirt.

"Let me get you a towel." She coughed to clear the wobble in her voice. "Sit down." She gestured to the chair as she skirted the table. "I'm sorry about the mess. I'm looking for a way to simplify our accounting system." She shot the beads across the abacus and they clattered into neat rows.

"What's that?"

"An abacus. A Chinese device. It makes accounting much faster. Now, tell me what the problem is. How long will you be in Maitland?"

"I don't know. Mrs. Witherspoon is most insistent we can't go ahead. They have extended the previous exhibition. I'm not sure quite what to do, or what it has to do with Mr. Quinn."

Probably nothing at all. Mrs. Witherspoon was likely using Michael as a scapegoat.

"Mother was planning to stay in Maitland for a while and do some painting. We'll have to cancel and I'll return to Sydney. But I have no way of contacting them and nowhere to store the paintings. We intended to rent some rooms, somewhere to stay. That's my job. Find accommodation. Organize the exhibition." He pushed a shock of damp hair back from his forehead and slumped in the chair.

"You must stay with us." Oh, perhaps not. It depended on Elizabeth. She might not want a group of strangers in the house right now. Although it might bring back a bit of interest in her life. Give her something to think about instead of taking all those draughts Dr. Lethbridge kept recommending. One to make her sleep, another to wake her up. It couldn't be good for her. "I'll have to speak to my aunt. She's been a bit poorly."

"We couldn't impose."

"Let me know if you have any difficulties." Jane jumped up. "Wait! I have the perfect solution! We'll hold the exhibition here."

"Here?"

"Downstairs in the auction hall. It would be perfect. Your mother could use one of the rooms up here as a studio." She cast a look around; it would need a little bit of a clean-up. "There's a room through there

THE GIRL IN THE PAINTING

with a large window overlooking the street, which would make the perfect studio. People would line up to see her exhibition and the artist in residence." Words bubbled out of her mouth, the entire idea filled her with such enthusiasm. "I'm sorry, I'm jumping to conclusions. It might not be what you want."

"It sounds marvelous." Timothy pushed himself to his feet. "Maybe you could speak with Mr. Quinn and I could call tomorrow."

"I shall look forward to it. Don't forget to let me know if you have difficulty finding rooms. Aileen House, Church Street is where we live."

"Thank you." He threw her the most rewarding smile, deep dimples marking his cheeks.

His gratitude, charming as it was, embarrassed her; she hadn't expected him to be so enthusiastic. "It's all settled. I look forward to seeing you tomorrow." She tried to sound businesslike but couldn't control the smile on her face or the lift in her voice.

By the time Jane cycled off down the road, the rain had stopped and there was no sign of Timothy. It did nothing to diminish the bubble of excitement growing inside her.

As Jane expected, Michael was in his study when she got home.

She knocked on the door and walked straight in.

"Jane, you're home early." He pushed a large manila folder into the drawer and stood up.

"I know, and I'm sorry to disturb you, but I have some exciting news."

"Do you? Better pull up a chair and tell me all about it." He nudged the folder to the back of the drawer and closed it.

"Timothy Penter turned up today."

"Timothy Penter?"

"Do you remember Mr. Langdon-Penter, the man we met at the

National Gallery in Sydney? Timothy is his son, and Timothy's mother, Marigold Penter, painted one of the paintings we saw, and there's another on display at the technical college. Major Witherspoon canceled because he'd extended the Tost and Rohu exhibition. Apparently he'd spoken to you about it."

"Not that I remember."

"I expect Mrs. Witherspoon got everything muddled. It doesn't matter. I have a solution, and I'd like to talk to you about it."

———— ≈ ————

Michael's hand drifted to the drawer. "Now might not be the best time. I've a few things on my mind." For a moment he had an overwhelming urge to confess his secret to Jane. With the clarity of youth and her overblown sense of logic she'd surely get to the bottom of it.

"Timothy brought all the paintings, from Melbourne."

"I'm sure something can be arranged . . ." His mind was filled with the prospect of the trip to England; Melbourne and paintings were the last thing he wanted to talk about. "We'll discuss it in the morning."

"It's too late. Mrs. Witherspoon told him to take the paintings away, and it was pouring with rain so I let him leave them upstairs at the auction house. I've had this truly wonderful idea."

She pulled the chair closer to his desk, her eyes sparkling with enthusiasm, something Michael sorely lacked. "Mr. and Mrs. Penter are on the way here from Melbourne. Timothy has no way of contacting them, and they are expecting to arrive for the exhibition and spend some time in the area. Mrs. Penter wants to paint Maitland. We can't let them down. It would reflect very badly on the town. I think we should host the exhibition."

There had to be somewhere else. The church hall? No, it was undergoing repairs.

"We could hold it in the auction house and offer Mrs. Penter studio space. Apart from anything else, people would flock to see her latest work, if only for a chance to see the upstairs of the building." She sat back, her arms folded.

"Upstairs, you say. There'd be some cleaning up to do." Long overdue, too, and perhaps if he went through his old office he might find the papers he was missing.

"John, Timothy, and I could get it done in no time. Mrs. Penter does most of her painting outside, but she could use Elizabeth's old bedroom as a place to keep her paints and canvases. It has a lovely big window that lets in lots of light, and we could use your old office for the auction house business. It would be perfect, an excellent drawcard. We haven't done anything different for a while."

She had him there. Business had become a little stagnant. He stood up. "Thank you, Miss Piper, for your excellent advice. You have a project on your hands. Now, when are the Penters arriving?"

"We've got about three weeks to organize everything. Timothy's looking for rooms. He planned to set up the exhibition while he waited for his parents to arrive."

"We should offer them accommodation here. We have plenty of guest rooms."

A faint pink tinge highlighted her face. "I've already said that, if he can't find anywhere suitable."

"Elizabeth would benefit from some company." It might pull her out of her strange mood, give her something new to think about while he organized their trip. "Do you feel she's recovering?"

Jane sat for a moment chewing her lip, which was unusual—not so much the lip-chewing but the lack of response.

She screwed up her face, then sighed. "I don't want to . . ."

"If there's something wrong with Elizabeth, I need to know."

"It's not so much that anything is wrong physically, but she's different."

"Different?"

"I found a mistake in the Benevolent Society ledgers."

"We all make mistakes."

"Aunt Elizabeth doesn't. She was most upset when I pointed it out."

"I see. Anything else?"

"She seems distracted. She sits in the garden for ages staring into space, twisting a piece of thread around and around her little finger, and to be honest, she's been very short-tempered."

"She's always impatient. You know that as well as I do."

"No, not impatient. Her temper suddenly snaps and she loses control."

None of that reassured Michael. He doubted Lethbridge would see it as a good sign either. This exhibition might well be the very thing to perk Elizabeth up. Perhaps he'd commission a painting of her rose garden. She'd love that.

"Very well. See what the boy comes up with, and get to work tomorrow bright and early cleaning everything out."

Elizabeth wouldn't be the only one to benefit from a new venture. Michael felt inspired too.

EIGHTEEN

HILL END, 1872

E lizabeth rested her shoulder against the doorjamb, raising her hand and waving at the shouted greetings of the children as they paraded down the road. So much had changed in the last few years. Some were saying Hill End was now the largest inland town. It certainly seemed like it. They'd finished the new school and built a new Catholic church, many of the roads had gutters and footpaths, and there were more pubs in town than a drunkard could count.

The town was booming. Mines dotted the barren stretch above the river: noisy and smoky, they flourished as never before, and finally the accusations against the Chinese miners—that they were diverting water, over-mining, and taking opportunities intended solely for the Europeans—had waned.

Several men had left the Chinese camp and moved into Hill End, and Jing's uncle had opened a shop next door to the Diggers Rest. It did a brisk trade, mostly due to his reputation for honesty. Elizabeth and many of the women were more than happy to shop there. The week before, he'd presented her and all his other customers with a blue earthenware jar nestled in a delicate wicker lattice. When she'd taken it home and opened it, she'd found the most delicious preserved ginger inside, the flesh plump and soft, the sticky syrup pure heaven.

Michael's drays carted their imported goods from Sydney, same as he did for the other business owners, and he spent half his time at least in Bathurst. The focus of Elizabeth's life had shifted; she didn't miss him as she once had. The sun no longer rose and set with his every whim.

"They've opened another pub; that makes twenty-seven, and there are over two hundred registered mining companies now. I don't know how we'll fit anyone else in." She flipped the newspaper aside.

"A long way from the place I first came to." Jing picked up the teapot and poured the fragrant liquid into the two cups, then handed one to her. They'd finished the weekly accounts early and were sitting outside on the new veranda enjoying the spring sunshine. She stared down into the tea and plucked the single straggler floating on the top.

Elizabeth brought it to her mouth and bit down on the stalk. "Do you remember my mam and da?"

He turned his head and stared into her eyes. "I remember your da most. He was a good man. Helped my uncle when we came."

Jing didn't often talk about the past so she nudged him on. "You can't have been very old."

"Old enough to come with the men."

"And leave your family behind."

He brought his head up with a snap. "We look after our families."

"Oh yes, I know. I didn't mean to suggest that you didn't."

It was common knowledge the Chinese sent gold home to support their families and their villages. Rumor had it that they packed the bones of their dead relatives with gold before sending them back to China for burial. Something Elizabeth didn't like the idea of at all.

"I keep records for all the families of the gold they send home," said Jing. "Quinn Accounts does very good work."

"There's no stopping Michael. It's just as well the Sydney bankers moved in, otherwise we'd be running Quinn's Bank." Savoring the refreshing jasmine tea, she took another sip and almost choked when a roar of excitement billowed up the street from the direction of the mines.

Jing jumped to his feet and stood shading his eyes, staring down the road. "What is that?" He held out his hands and drew her to her feet.

The roar built in the air, carried down the street, overpowering the constant noise of the stamper batteries, or had they stopped? "What's going on?"

A band of men with their picks slung over their shoulders swarmed down the street, shouting and carrying on as though the world had ended.

Jing grabbed her hand and tugged. "Come on. Let's go and see."

The men approached, a raucous army, their hoarse voices filling the street, and behind them a dray pulled by four bullocks.

Jing dragged her aside and her mouth dropped open. Mr. Holtermann stood on the back of the dray, waving like Prince Alfred, one arm draped around the biggest lump of quartz, gold streaks sparkling in the sunlight, almost as tall as the big man himself and nearly as wide. "Where did they find it?"

"Hawkins Hill. Star of Hope Mine. Last night, they said. Blimey. What I wouldn't give . . ." One of the miners standing on the footpath took off his hat and wiped a dirty hand across his brow. "Reckon that'd be worth over twelve thousand quid. It'd have to weigh six hundred pounds at least."

"Not bad for a barber!" Jing's warm breath grazed her ear.

"A barber?" she whispered back.

"That's what they say, until he teamed up with Beyer and they sank the mine."

"I don't think there's much call for barbers in Hill End." She gazed at the crowd of men, all with beards almost reaching their chests, then turned back to Jing, the blackbird sheen of his hair and the honey tones of his skin accentuated in the bright sunlight. He smiled down at her, and her stomach gave the strangest twist.

"Look over there." Jing pointed down the street.

"It's Mr. Merlin with his camera. Let's go and have our picture taken."

"I think he's too busy with Mr. Holtermann and his nugget."

"No, come on. I've wanted to have my picture taken ever since I first came here."

"Shouldn't we wait for Mr. Michael?"

"No. It's perfect. I can surprise him."

After much pushing and shoving they finally arrived outside Mr. Merlin's photographic shop. Elizabeth gazed up at the sign spanning the shopfront and pushed open the door before Jing could say a word.

A boy, not much older than she was, stepped out from behind a curtain. "What can I do for you?"

"We'd like a *carte de visite*."

"A calling card? Merlin ain't here right now."

Jing tugged at her arm but she ignored him. "You're Alfie Blyth, aren't you? We went to school together."

"Who are you? Didn't used to talk to girls."

"I'm Elizabeth Quinn. My brother owns the auction house."

Something in his demeanor changed and he straightened his shoulders. "And?"

"We'd like to have some *cartes de visite* made to advertise the business, like the ones the tobacconist in Clarke Street has. First we'd like a sample, something I can show my brother."

"Elizabeth, we'll come back another day." Jing turned for the door.

"Well, maybe I could do something for you. Why don't you step through here?"

With a triumphant grin, Elizabeth towed Jing after Alfie through a curtain to the back of the shop.

A chair stood in the middle of the room with a potted plant next to it. "You sit down here, Miss Quinn."

She settled herself on the chair while Alfie stuck his head under a black cloth and looked at her through the camera. "Are you ready?"

"No, wait. Jing, come and stand next to me."

"Mr. Michael won't . . ."

"What rubbish. Come and stand here."

"Haven't got all day if you only want a sample." Alfie peered out from under the black cloth.

"Quick, Jing."

He stepped up behind her and she looked up at him. "Hold it right there. Don't move until I tell you."

Her lips twitched as she took in the startled expression on Jing's face, then she caught his eye. He relaxed and smiled down at her.

"There we are. All done." Alfie pulled a plate from the side of the camera. "I'll bring this around when it's ready and Mr. Quinn can decide if he wants more."

Jing couldn't get out of the shop fast enough. Elizabeth followed more slowly, stopping to study the pictures on the wall. It was a very good idea. Just what Michael needed, a way of promoting the business. He could leave cards in Sydney and Bathurst, hand them out to people who passed through the town. She'd make sure he came down to get his picture taken as soon as he returned.

By the time she was back in the street, Jing had vanished. People still crowded the roads, the news of Holtermann's nugget on everyone's lips. Elizabeth returned to the auction house and found Jing with his head buried in a pile of papers. He didn't acknowledge her arrival.

"Why are you cross with me?"

"That wasn't a good thing to do."

"Whyever not?"

"That boy, Alfie, he is not supposed to take the pictures."

"How do you know? He's Mr. Merlin's assistant." And more than likely he thought he'd done a good thing for the business. After all, Quinn Family Auctioneers and Accountants had a great reputation. It wasn't as though he wouldn't get paid.

———— ≈ ————

Michael tightened the lanyard and grinned up at the flag snapping smartly in the breeze. Two o'clock every Saturday afternoon, before the miners had the chance to celebrate the end of the working week. The old timers reckoned you could set your clock by the auction house's flag. Michael hadn't missed raising it since he'd brought Elizabeth home. He tucked in his shirt and rammed his broad-brimmed hat down on his head, ready for business.

Jing hauled out the tea chest, set up the table and his abacus, then helped Elizabeth out, settling her in a chair with as much care as if she were an aged aunt. She beamed up at him, eyes sparkling. Michael had never let her stay for the auction before, didn't want her mixing with the rough crowd that gathered every Saturday, but Jing would see to her, he'd no doubt about that. Since she'd left school they'd become the best of mates and saved him a heap of worry, let him continue what he did best. He'd trust Jing with his life.

He clambered onto the tea chest, Jing rang the bell, and off Michael went into his patter, raising the crowd to fever pitch, selling everything from tents to tin pots, shovels to shirts, and today even a house, if it could be called that. The shanty wasn't much, but it provided shelter, and the building materials alone would fetch a tidy sum.

Rubbing his hands together, Michael rocked back on his heels. The biggest clearance rate they'd ever had, and unless he was very much mistaken, the cash box would be overflowing. "How did we do?"

"Lots of buyers. Everyone thinks they're going to find more like Mr. Holtermann. The mines are taking on more workers, and people are flooding into town." Jing patted the cash box. "I'll take it down to the bank when I close up. Don't want to leave it in the warehouse."

"Good lad. I've got to go and have a word with someone down in Germantown. Tell Elizabeth I'll be home in time for tea."

———— ≈ ————

"You go home, unless you want these." Jing brought out a stack of bamboo boxes and placed them on the desktop.

Elizabeth opened the lid and inhaled the delicious scent, knowing each little parcel would be filled with finely chopped vegetables. Jing waved a pair of chopsticks in front of her face and grinned at her.

So tempting, but Michael would be waiting. Kitty hadn't been to their house once in the last week. Her husband's leg was causing him grief again so her sister, Susie, came in the morning and tidied up and prepared something for their evening meal.

"I need to go. Thank you for the offer. I'll see myself home."

"Bright and early tomorrow. We have accounts." Jing patted the pile of papers pushed onto the metal spike.

They didn't only take care of Michael's business; some of the others in town and the manager from Star of Hope mine had asked them to look after their books. Since Holtermann's find, everyone in Sydney wanted to buy shares in the mines and that meant a set of figures for every business. Something most of the managers couldn't fathom.

However, if they'd been told a girl and a Chinaman were behind Quinn's Accounts, and not Michael, they would have run in the other direction. They didn't, though, because anything with the name Quinn attached to it was good as gold. Quinn Family Auctioneers and Accountants. Michael insisted in keeping the "family" bit in there; after all, if it hadn't been for Da, he wouldn't have had the start.

"Bright and early." Elizabeth reached for her notebook and the *carte de visite* slipped onto the table.

Jing grabbed it before she had a chance to stop him. She wasn't sure why she hadn't shown it to him when Alfie delivered it. There was something about the look on her face and the way he was staring down at her. It didn't look very businesslike at all.

"What did Michael say?"

"I haven't shown it to him yet." She reached to take it from him, but he wouldn't let it go. She turned her head to glare at him and stopped.

After a long moment he held it out. "You keep it." He brushed a strand of hair from her face, his fingers light as a feather against her cheek, and smiled in a way that suggested it should be their secret. Before he could do or say anything more, she pushed the card into her notebook and made for the door, her cheeks glowing with unexpected warmth.

The avenue of trees cast a pleasant shade on the dusty road. Elizabeth clung to the edge to avoid the never-ending parade of drays, people, and horses, and as always skirted the pigeon tree.

Halfway down the road, she crossed behind a sprung carriage and opened the small latched gate in the picket fence. The little garden never failed to bring a smile to her face. She carefully saved all of Mam's flower seeds that she'd grown in containers behind the warehouse and replanted them every October once the frosts had passed. They flourished in the shade beneath the apple and pear trees.

An open door greeted her, along with the mouth-watering smell of chicken pie. Ah Chu had delivered some delicious carrots, parsnips, and cabbage that morning. Hopefully Susie had remembered to put them into the pie.

"Michael! I'm home."

He sat in his usual place at the small table in the back room, a sheaf of newspapers spread out in front of him.

"What are you reading?" He rarely had time for the newspapers, but his attention seemed riveted on the advertisements. She peered over his shoulder. "That's not the local paper."

"Nope. *Maitland Mercury*."

"Maitland. Where's that?"

He rocked back on the chair, smiling. "You might have a great head for figures, but your geography's less than useless."

"No chicken pie for you if you're going to be rude."

He let out a bark of laughter and jumped to his feet. "I've been thinking."

"Hmm." The chicken pie had a lovely golden crust, and she set it down carefully in the center of the table. "Can you put knives and forks out?"

Michael pulled open the drawer in the table, all the while peering down at the paper. "Time we expanded."

"Again? I'm not sure now is the right time. Prices are high. Ever since they found the reef gold, people have been pouring into town. A room at the hotel costs almost as much as one in Sydney. Did you know there are over eight thousand people in the area now?"

"I wasn't thinking about Hill End. Something farther afield."

"Bathurst!" She'd only ever been there once, on the way from Sydney after poor Prince Alfred had been shot. She still remembered that day, the sun on the water, her handsome prince. She'd read in the paper that he'd married the Grand Duchess Maria from Russia. So much for childish dreams. He'd set his sights a bit higher than a girl from the gold fields. "Bathurst would be a perfect place to set up a business. Everyone travels through the town on their way to the Turon."

"No. I think we might be seeing the end to the boom before long. The Sydney business community hasn't got money to spare for gold-mining ventures. If anything's going to happen, it's got to come from London, and I can't see that."

"You want to go back to England and raise capital?"

"No. I've been down in Germantown. One of the blokes, his wife, Eliza, comes from a town called Maitland. She reckons it's the perfect place. Access to Sydney by land and sea, through the port of Newcastle and the Hunter River. They say there's even a train from Newcastle to Maitland." His eyes glowed with promise. "Says it's second only to Sydney. Big enough for an auctioneering business, small enough to make a mark."

"You want to leave Hill End?" Elizabeth's breath caught. She didn't want to leave. She loved the town, the life. She belonged, knew who she was. And there was Jing. The first person she'd met when they arrived in Hill End, her closest friend. He'd taught her everything she knew. "Where's this place? Have you got a map?"

"It's in the Hunter Valley, north of Sydney. We'll go and have a look. Take the train. Have a bit of a holiday. How would you like that?"

Her heart raced and her skin tightened. "I don't like trains."

"What do you mean you don't like trains? You've never traveled on one. They're the way of the future. Just like my plans. Maitland's a fine town by all accounts."

Elizabeth rubbed at her goose-flecked skin and swallowed the bitter taste in her mouth. She didn't want to leave Hill End. She turned on her heel and left Michael to the chicken pie.

———≈———

"Where are you?" Jing waved his fingers in front of her face, bringing her out of her dismal reverie.

Elizabeth stuck the pencil behind her ear and rested her chin on her hands. She couldn't concentrate on the rows of figures, couldn't even add two and two, never mind total expenses for the goods coming up for auction or work out the reserves. Jing had taken the suanpan from her; he knew her too well, knew her mind had wandered.

"Why so sad?"

"I'm not sad . . ." At least she didn't think she was. It was all Michael's fault. All this talk of leaving Hill End. Six months after Holtermann's find and none of the mines had hit a decent seam. There was an air of despondency about the town. Talk of greener pastures, new fields, Victoria. Even farther away than this hunters' valley Michael kept talking about.

She sucked in a breath. "Michael wants to leave Hill End." Her voice belonged to someone else. She opened her mouth to explain, but her breath caught, cutting off the remainder of her words. When Jing's arm wrapped around her shoulder, the tears began, great, wet tears trickling down her cheeks, rendering her incapable of thought. He pulled her against him and smoothed her hair from her face, saying nothing. Sighing, she rested against his chest.

How long he held her, she had no idea. Slowly the breath returned to her body and her world came back into focus. She turned to the workbench and picked up the suanpan, running her fingers over the smooth, worn beads, finding reassurance in the familiarity of the movement.

Against her back, Jing's heart thudded, no longer in time with the stampers but faster than before. Heat radiated from him. "Where does Michael want to go?"

"Some place called hunters' valley, two hundred miles away." Hundreds of miles from where she wanted to be.

He reached around her and pushed away the suanpan. "We must all go home one day."

"You? You'd go back to China?"

"My family is there."

"Your father and your uncle are here."

"Not my sisters, or my grandmother, my aunts. We will never belong here. It is lonely to be without a family."

"Some Chinese have been here for many years, brought their families." Her voice hitched again. Only the week before, one poor man had killed himself, so lonely and sad he couldn't stand it a moment longer. He wouldn't be going home.

"We will all go home," said Jing.

"Not those who're buried here."

"They will go home too. The agent will take their bones back to lie with their ancestors."

"But there's hundreds buried in Moonlight Gully." The Chinese burial ground lay alongside the river on a pretty bend where the willows hung.

"Eighty-two, not hundreds. Only those who could wait no longer and those who had an accident. We all go home, take our gold, find a wife . . ." He turned and stared at her, the corners of his mouth turned down, his eyes soft and sad.

"You could stay here." Her heart gave a start, blood pumping wildly as the plan slipped to the forefront of her mind. "You could come with us to this hunters' place. Help Michael and me set up a new business. Would you?"

"Maybe one day."

"What do you mean, one day?"

He pulled a piece of red thread from his pocket. "I will tell you a story, a Chinese story. The Chinese gods know who will meet and who will help each other, so they take a thread, like this one, and tie it around the little finger." He twisted the thread around her finger and held the other end between his index finger and thumb and pulled it taut. "No matter how long, no matter where in the world this thread stretches, maybe it tangles, but never, never breaks." His breath fanned her cheek. "I will always find you."

Her hands rose of their own volition and rested on his broad chest. Through his soft shirt, the steady rhythm of his heart reverberated against her palms. A smothered groan rumbled in his chest and his warm breath tickled her neck.

She turned her head and he brushed back the hair from her face. His fingers wandered light as a feather over her cheek and along her lips. Only the emotion in his eyes gave any indication that her proximity affected him. Sighing in pleasure she rested against his chest, frightened that words would break the idyllic moment.

She inhaled the familiar scent of jasmine tea and soap, and something else, something familiar yet at the same time unknown, exciting. The air shifted, and with a mind of its own her body leaned closer.

Michael pushed open the door and stood for a moment, waiting for his eyes to adjust to the light. He'd had another chat with Eliza Cox, the wife of one of the miner's he'd help set up. She'd grown up in the Hunter Valley, and her family still lived there, but she'd followed Hans, the German she'd fallen in love with the moment she set eyes on him, to Maitland. Maitland was the biggest town in the area, bigger even than the port of Newcastle. The old public house would be perfect for his plans.

The bottom floor would make a fine auction house, and the upstairs had two bedrooms and one other huge room that would make an excellent living space and still have room for a small office area. It was time to move on. They'd put in the work and set down roots in Maitland, and he'd make the life for Elizabeth that she deserved.

"Elizabeth, Jing! Everything ready for the auction tomorrow?" Michael's mouth dried and he rocketed across the room. "What the . . . Get your hands off her."

Elizabeth shot around to the other side of the desk, cheeks flaming.

"What on earth is going on? Come here." He grabbed Elizabeth's arm and pulled her close. "Get out of here, Jing, and don't come back."

Jing picked up his beads and vanished through the back door. The one person he believed he could trust to care for Elizabeth. How wrong could a man be?

"Jing, I . . ." Elizabeth struggled frantically against Michael, landing a hefty kick on his shin.

"You'll do nothing but stay put, right where you are. Did he hurt you, touch you?"

"Of course not! I'm all right." She gave a little shake and unfolded her arms.

She could pretend all she liked, but Michael could tell from the pitch of her voice, higher and frailer than usual, that she was upset. And there was no mistaking the look in Jing's eyes, the look in every man's eyes when they saw Elizabeth. She'd grown into a beauty, but Jing . . . his best mate, the bloke he'd trust with his life. "What was he thinking?"

Her face puckered in a frown. "I told him you wanted to leave. About this hunters' valley. I don't want to go. I don't want to leave Jing. Please let him come with us?" Her voice wavered and she brushed at her eyes.

She wanted Jing to come along? Michael's blood chilled. It couldn't happen. He'd seen what happened to women who chose an Oriental—abused by others, forced to live as outcasts. That would not be Elizabeth's fate. Not now. Not ever.

An unfettered fury billowed in his chest at Jing's duplicity. "No more of your nonsense. We'll be moving to Maitland as soon as I can sell the business." And with that his mind was made up.

She let out a monstrous wail and dropped to her knees, sobbing fit to bust.

"Oh, me little darlin', it's not so bad. We'll make a good life there. I'll build you a house, a beautiful house. You'll have fine clothes and live as you were meant to. As Mam and Da intended. We'll start again, a real auction house. None of this secondhand, hand-me-down rubbish. We'll live upstairs first, and when we make our fortune I'll build you the house of your dreams! Now, what do you think about that, me little darlin'?"

"Can Jing come?"

No, he most certainly couldn't. He exhaled slowly, composing himself. "They're different, darlin', not like us. They look different, work different, think different."

"Not Jing."

Yes, Jing. The scheming little mongrel. He'd trusted him. Trusted him with his money, his secrets, and Elizabeth.

Michael swallowed the red rage, clamped his teeth. "As soon as I've tied everything up, sold the warehouse, we're leaving. They'll want Jing here. Do the books, like he's always done. We'll go to Sydney and take the train. It'll be like the old days. Remember? Just you and me."

"I love him."

The sweat dried on his skin, leaving him cold. Whatever was she thinking?

"No, you don't. You've got to understand he's not for you. He's from another race, another culture, another country." Michael ticked each item off on his shaking fingers. "And another religion! By all that's holy, understand he's different."

"Jing's worked for you for years, ever since you first came here. His family looked after Da. You're as biased as Bill Cameron, labeling people. You're nothing but a bloody Fenian upstart!"

The insult sent Michael rocketing to his feet. He was no Fenian. He'd never had time for all that nonsense. He treated all men the same. But this was about Elizabeth. This was different.

"Jing's a Celestial, and he'll always be a Celestial. I'll not have you labeled a Chinaman's whore."

"You can't make me leave."

"I can, and I will. I am your brother. You are my responsibility."

"Not if I marry."

"Until you marry. And that ain't going to be any time soon."

NINETEEN

MAITLAND TOWN, 1913

The morning after discussing the exhibition plans with Michael, Jane left home and arrived at the auction house before anyone else woke; she had to be back at Church Street in time for the meeting of the Benevolent Society. She let herself in through the back door, ran up the stairs, and surveyed the chaos. Canvases took up every spare inch of the room, the calico bags that had protected them hung over the backs of the chairs, and an unusual smell had infiltrated the room, something metallic, chemical.

Shrugging out of her jacket, she contemplated the surroundings, trying to imagine the paintings hanging downstairs with neat labels as they had done at the technical college.

Jane was standing looking out of the window when footsteps sounded on the stairs and Timothy stuck his head around the door. "Am I too early?"

The sight of him brought a smile to her face. "No, not at all. I was hoping to clear this up a little. I've spoken to Mr. Quinn and he's more than happy for the exhibition to take place here. Have you found somewhere to stay?"

"Yes. Two rooms at the Wheatsheaf. Small, but adequate."

"I'm sure your mother would love this room. The light is wonderful."

The early-morning light spilled from the window across the floor, bathing the room in a gentle glow.

"She would." His face broke into a cheerful grin. "My work is almost done."

His eyes were soft and crinkly at the corners, as though he'd spent time squinting against the sun, or perhaps an easel. "Do you paint?"

"Me? No." He gave a dry laugh. "I'm the gallery slave, and sometime framer."

She struggled not to lose herself in the gray depths of his eyes. "What about your father?"

"I doubt Father knows one end of a paintbrush from the other."

Jane gestured to one of the two chairs at the table and sat down. Timothy folded his long limbs under the table and leaned forward. "I've been thinking about you."

Her face flamed. "Have you?"

"What happened to your parents? You said the Quinns rescued you."

She exhaled, a strange sense of disappointment swirling. "No idea. I was dumped, like an old suitcase, on the doorstep of the orphanage in the dead of night. I always hoped Florence Nightingale was my mother and would come and rescue me." She tried for a laugh, but only managed a pathetic groan.

"I'm so sorry."

She couldn't pine for something she'd never known, yet sometimes it would've been nice to know who she was. "The Quinns took me in when I was nine years old. They're like family to me."

Why, for heaven's sake, was she telling him all this? She never discussed her feelings. She stuck to numbers and organization—much, much safer.

"Enough of that." She pulled the diary toward her and dragged her hair back. "Have you any idea when your parents will arrive?"

"I expect them late next week."

Jane ran her finger down the list of auctions. "We have a few more auctions planned. General goods, foodstuffs, and haberdashery and fabrics. There's a lull at the beginning of next month. How long do you think the exhibition should run?"

"Normally two weeks or so. It depends on interest and whether Father has arranged anything I'm unaware of."

"Well, I'll block out two weeks. How does that sound?"

"Perfect." His wide, friendly smile made her feel as though she'd solved every one of his problems. "You must let Mother tell you about her paintings. I'm sure she'd offer lessons as a thank-you."

Jane let out a loud, open-mouthed laugh. "Painting is not my thing."

"What is your *thing*?"

"Calculations, mathematics, and most especially da Vinci and Fibonacci."

"'Without mathematics there is no art.'"

The words rendered her speechless. Jane was more used to reactions like Bessie's, and she'd never managed to interest Michael in Fibonacci. As for Elizabeth, well, it was hard to tell; her polite face was the most Jane had ever received. "Yes! Luca Pacioli said that. He was a contemporary of da Vinci."

"You'll enjoy talking to Mother."

"I'm sure I will. So many of da Vinci's paintings are based on the Golden Mean. The *Mona Lisa* is a perfect example. Where did you learn about Fibonacci?"

"Mother. She studied art in Paris and likes to apply the principles in her landscapes. She maintains it is more pleasing to the eye. Even though it may look an apparently natural arrangement, there is much more to her compositions than you would imagine."

Jane clasped her hands together, rested her chin on her knuckles, and let out a long slow sigh. "You have no idea how much I am going to enjoy talking to you."

"Thank you, ladies. I shall ask Jane to explain in more detail and let you know."

Elizabeth closed the front door on the ladies of the Benevolent Society with as much restraint as she could muster and stormed down the corridor.

"Lucy!" Where was the nuisance, and more to the point, where was Jane? She knew perfectly well the meeting was at ten this morning. "Lucy!"

"Yes, miss."

"Your cap is askew."

"Beg pardon, miss."

"I'm looking for Jane. Do you have any idea where she is?"

"At the auction rooms. She left real early this morning, before breakfast. Something to do with some paintings."

"She was meant to be here. Go and find her."

"Yes, miss." Lucy opened the front door.

"Don't use the front door."

"Yes, miss."

What was the matter with everyone? Michael's strange behavior, locking himself in his study insisting he had work to do; Lethbridge's ongoing rubbish about women of a certain age, a perfectly sleepless night, and now this. She lifted her fingers to her throbbing temple and closed her eyes against the blinding waves of dizziness.

"Why don't you go and have a lie down, miss. I'll bring you a nice cup of tea."

Her head swirled. She could do with some peace and quiet. "Maybe you're right."

Elizabeth climbed the stairs to her room and sat down in the chair overlooking the garden. She reached for Jing's red thread.

A flight of parrots wheeled and squawked in the trees, their jeweled colors lighting up the dark line of trees marking the slow, winding curve of the river. She pressed her palm flat against the glass. Not a quiver or a tremble, not a trace of fear. Why had she reacted so violently to the exhibition? Gritting her teeth, she played it back. She remembered walking into the exhibition hall. The large eagle with the wide wingspan hadn't caused any adverse reaction, nor had the kookaburras with the lizard on the rock. Nothing there. She remembered passing under the Gothic arches to look at the paintings. One of Antwerp, a cathedral somewhere, and . . .

The smell, the dreadful smell. She slammed her hand over her mouth against the rising surge of bile and staggered across the room, collapsing facedown on the bed. "G'woam! G'woam!"

Hands reached for her shoulders, shook her.

"Miss Elizabeth! Miss Elizabeth! Oh, heavens above. Here, let me help."

"Take your hands off me, Lucy. I am perfectly fine." Her tone sent the girl scuttling from the room.

It took a good half an hour for her breathing to settle and her heart to achieve some sort of normal rhythm. All the while her mood alternated between dread and despair; if she didn't get to the bottom of this she would be headed up the river, straight into the waiting arms of Lethbridge and his cohorts at the asylum.

She had to act. She had to find some way to control these sudden moments and the overpowering sense of helplessness they engendered.

TWENTY

HILL END, 1873

Elizabeth didn't want to deal with Michael's anger. She wanted to sort out the tangle of emotions wrapping tendrils around her heart. The way she'd felt when Jing held her close, his warmth, the sparkle in his eye, the dimple in his cheek when he smiled. The palms of her hands still tingled from the warmth of his skin. She smoothed them together, trying to recreate the sensation of his beating heart. If Michael hadn't interrupted them he might have kissed her. She ran her tongue over her lips, imagining the touch of his mouth on her skin.

"Elizabeth?"

"Hmm?" She wriggled, the cotton of her blouse rough against her skin. Skin that prickled and shimmered with an unnatural sensitivity.

"Elizabeth!" The front door banged. "Elizabeth! Where are you?" Michael's boots thumped down the hallway and the door flew open, bringing the scent of the night, the smell of damp and wood-smoke.

She plastered what she hoped was an attentive look on her face.

"I want to talk to you. About Jing."

She stood bolt upright, backed against the kitchen table, color flooding her face anew. "What about him?"

"What's going on?"

187

"Nothing's *going on*." Nothing except the delicious feelings Jing's closeness brought. "We work together, spend time together. He's my friend." Her only friend. "I was upset and he was comforting me."

She had to make Michael change his mind. She was certain if he made Jing an offer of work, he would come with them. She knew he would. Hadn't he told her they'd always be tied? She ran the piece of red thread through her fingers and flopped down on the kitchen chair.

Michael reached her in two long strides and stood staring down at her. "Oh, me little darlin', don't be lying to me." He ran his rough hand down her damp cheek. "I'll have his guts for garters. Leading you on like that."

"He didn't lead me on."

"It's a load of nonsense, Elizabeth. How many times must I tell you? You can't. You just can't love him. It'll give people the wrong idea. Young girl like you needs to take care."

"I'm not a girl. I'm nearly sixteen. A woman."

Her pig-headed brother didn't even deign to answer, simply tipped the corner of his lips in the infuriating way he had and lowered himself into the chair, his long legs stretched out in front of him and what looked suspiciously like a satisfied smirk on his face.

"Plenty of women get married at sixteen."

"You'll not be getting married."

"You can't stop me if I—"

"When you've calmed down, how about you listen to what I'm saying?"

She flopped back down on the chair. "I'm listening."

"I've solved the problem, and if you'd bear with me for five minutes and stop all the shenanigans, I'll explain."

She let out a long huff of air. "Stop smiling." How could he smile? She'd never been so miserable in her life. She glared at him.

"Very well." He pulled a long face and frowned. Within a moment he gave a big, deep rumbling laugh. "Would you be ready now?"

"Yes. Yes, I am."

"I've sold up."

"Everything? Now?" This insane idea of his about going to . . . She couldn't even remember the name of the place.

"Aye, everything."

"Why on earth would you do that? Hill End is still booming. Holtermann's find will lead to others. It's the most ridiculous decision you've ever made. Property prices are the highest they've ever been." She flew out of the chair and pulled the ledgers from the pile on the table. She fanned the pages. "We've got plenty of money in the bank. We don't owe anyone anything. We own this house and the Diggers Rest; the top floor is earning a good rent, and it's slap bang in the middle of the best street. You own three drays and employ five people. You've invested all your time and effort in the auction house." She threw up her hands in despair. "And you've sold!" He was insane.

"For someone who's supposed to have a handle on the business, you've missed the point, me little darlin'."

"Don't call me that. I hate it." It made her feel like a lap dog, some sort of treasured pet without a mind of her own. "How have I missed the point? You told me your aim was to make something of our inheritance, not give it away. Why sell now when property prices are still rising . . ."

"Think for a minute, me little . . ." He bit his lip. Good. Maybe he'd take notice of what she'd said. "Prices are going to fall. They haven't had a decent strike since Holtermann's. He's resigned, left town. Sydney bankers are pulling out."

He didn't know what he was talking about. Michael freely admitted she had a much better head for business than he did. His skill was with people, not numbers. That's why he made such a marvelous auctioneer. Father MacCormick said he could sell fool's gold to the assayer.

"We're selling at the top of the market. I sold the Diggers Rest to Li & Co. They've been after it ever since they bought the shop next door, want to expand, and I've sold the cottage to one of Holtermann's mates, fellow by the name of Bayer, who seems to think the walls are plastered in gold."

"You'll get more if you wait. Another find or two and prices will jump again."

"That's as may be, but I've had enough. It's time to leave."

She threw her arms around his neck. "Then Jing can come too." If he was happy to sell to the Li family, he couldn't have anything against Jing.

"No."

She reared back as though scalded, heat flooding her face.

He brought his fist to his mouth and made some sort of trumpeting fanfare noise. "I've made an offer on a place called the Potters Inn in Maitland."

She moistened her lips as the implication of Michael's words sank in. "A pub. For goodness' sake, you spend your time complaining about every single one of the twenty-seven pubs in Hill End." The words spluttered from her mouth.

"Ah, but this one's different. It's going to be our auction house. Right in the middle of town, it is. On High Street."

The man was truly mad. Elizabeth snapped her gaping mouth closed and glared at him. "You don't know what you're talking about." She pushed the chair out of her way.

Spinning on her heel, she slammed out of the house into the cool of the garden, every nerve ending aflame.

———❦———

When Elizabeth woke the following morning, an unnatural silence hung over the house. Michael often left early, but usually Susie would be slamming around, getting the chores done as quickly as possible. Elizabeth rolled over and peered out of the crack between the curtains. Surely she hadn't slept that late. She'd lain awake half the night trying to come up with a solution. But if Michael had already sold, there was no point in trying to change his mind. It was too late.

She had to see Jing. Just because Michael was leaving Hill End didn't mean she had to. She didn't need Michael to earn a living. She and Jing could continue the accounts business, and then when they'd made enough money, they could marry, have children, live in the cottage.

The thought made her heart sing. She threw on her dress, pulled a brush through her hair, and slipped on her shoes. Slamming the door behind her, she took off down the road to the warehouse.

When she arrived she found a rusty old chain and padlock through the door handles. It was never locked, not at this time in the morning—the sun was well up. She cast a look at Li & Co next door. They were open for business. A crowd of women stood at the counter, and Jing's uncle was doing a roaring trade as usual. Michael must be out and about, maybe gone to Bathurst. Elizabeth couldn't remember what he'd said. It was mid-week, so he wouldn't have to be in town for the auction. But where was Jing? Why hadn't he opened up?

She slipped around the back to the kitchen and let herself in. There was no fire in the stove, no steaming kettle. The bamboo tray sat on the table where it always did; the tin of jasmine tea, the little teapot and cups, but nothing more. No stack of bamboo steamers full of pork dumplings, no metal container with her favorite chicken and vegetable soup. Despite the warmth of the morning, a chill prickled her skin.

She pulled the stool over to the row of shelves and climbed up, bringing down the empty blue-and-white ginger pot Mr. Li had given her. It rattled when she shook it, and with a smile she lifted the lid and took out the key.

Elizabeth returned to the front doors, slipped the key in the padlock, and loosened the chain. The door swung open and she stepped inside.

The darkness struck her. She'd never arrived at the warehouse first, never unlocked the building, never locked up. Jing always did that. Throwing a quick glance over her shoulder, she walked down the carefully swept floor to the work bench, her heart thundering in her chest.

The stacks of ledgers had all vanished; the piles of paperwork gone, tidied away. The only thing that remained on the workbench was Jing's suanpan. She lifted it, inhaling the scent of sandalwood.

As she placed it back on the table a piece of paper caught her eye. She picked it up and unfolded it.

Inside was a line of perfect Chinese calligraphy, more like pictures than words. Elizabeth twisted it one way and the other. Jing had taught her to write numbers in Chinese script but nothing more, and none of these marks looked like the numbers she knew.

Where was he? An unpleasant twist in her stomach sent her scurrying next door to Li & Co, the piece of paper clutched in one hand and the suanpan in the other. She pushed open the door and skirted the crowd. There had to be at least a dozen women before her and only Jing's uncle serving behind the counter.

She eased through the door to the back room. The air was blue with tobacco smoke and incense, and at the table sat Mr. Li, pipe in hand. Elizabeth cleared her throat, but he made no move. She took a step toward the table. "Mr. Li, excuse me."

Very slowly he lifted his head. He offered no greeting, none of his usual cheerful smiles. "What do you want?"

She stopped still, her hands clasped in front of her, throat dry from the smoke. "I'm looking for Jing."

"Not here." He sucked on his pipe and turned his head to the back door.

"Do you know where I can find him?" She dared another couple of steps toward the table and came up short when he spun around.

"Bathurst."

Bathurst? Jing never went to Bathurst, never left Hill End—not once in all the years she'd known him. "Do you know when he'll be back?"

Mr. Li shrugged his shoulders.

It was only then she remembered the note in her hand. She held it out. "Can you tell me what this says, please. I think Jing left it for me."

His eyes narrowed and he opened his palm, not moving from his position at the table.

Sucking in a breath, she took another two steps toward him. Her heart was thundering like a drum. The darkness, the swirling smoke, the heavy cloud of perfumed incense made her feel distinctly queasy and more than a little scared. She placed the paper in his hand and waited, her fingers curled around the beads of the suanpan as though they could offer some protection.

"It says suanpan yours." He wadded up the piece of paper and tossed it down on the ground.

With a cry Elizabeth bent and picked it up, stuffed it into the pocket of her skirt.

"Go!" He pointed a long finger at the door. "Go!"

Not waiting to be told a third time, Elizabeth fled through the crowd and outside into the soothing sunshine. Once her breathing settled, she went back to the warehouse and checked to make sure she hadn't missed anything. Then she went out the back to the kitchen and collected the teapot, the two cups, the tin of jasmine tea, and the blue-and-white ginger pot. She packed them into one of the woven bamboo boxes that held the kitchen supplies, attached the heavy chain to the door, locked up, and made her way home.

The banging and crashing coming from the front room told her Michael had arrived home, so she hurried upstairs and buried the bamboo box beneath her petticoats, where she was certain he wouldn't find it, then ran downstairs.

She barged into the room and slammed her hands onto her hips. "What have you done?"

Michael pulled himself to his feet and looked sideways at her. "Done? I'm packing up. The Li brothers have signed the deeds; the warehouse is theirs. We've got two days to be out of the cottage before Bayer's brother takes over."

"That's not what I'm talking about, as you very well know." All her pent-up emotion and anger bubbled to the surface, and she took two steps toward him and slammed the flat of her hand against his chest. "I hate you!"

His large hand wrapped around her wrist and forced her hand down to her side. "Come and sit down."

"Jing's gone. Gone to Bathurst. You sent him away."

"I did no such thing."

"I spoke to Mr. Li. He told me."

"I'll put money on the fact he didn't tell you I'd sent Jing away, because I didn't."

She rocked back on her heels. "Well, who did?"

"Come and sit down and we'll sort this out."

"I don't want to sit down, and stop talking to me as though I am a half-witted nincompoop."

"Oh, that's the last thing I think you are, me little—"

"Don't call me that!" She spat the words at him, spun on her heel, and turned her back to him. "I'm not your darling."

Outside the window the poppies nodded their stupid heads against the blue cornflowers, the same blue as her ginger pot. She clamped her lips tight. She would not cry. Crying was for girls, and she was no longer a girl. She was a woman. A woman with a heart in grave danger of breaking.

"Why has Jing gone?" Her voice hitched on a painful note and she bit down on her lip, relishing the coppery taste of her blood.

Michael let out a long-suffering sigh and the chair groaned in sympathy as he lowered himself. "The Li brothers decided it was for the best."

"Why? Why would they do that?"

"Elizabeth, me—It's for the best. He's gone. Not coming back. By the time we reach Sydney he'll be on the high seas, heading home."

Unable to control her scream of despair, Elizabeth flew up the stairs and burrowed under her eiderdown.

TWENTY-ONE

MAITLAND TOWN, 1913

Jane rammed a piece of bacon between two crusts and rushed for the back door.

Bessie blocked her path. "Where are you going in such a hurry?"

"To the auction rooms."

"Without breakfast?"

She waved the doorstep sandwich. "I'll have a cup of tea when I'm there."

"Who is going to keep Miss Elizabeth company? Mr. Quinn's in Sydney again."

"She doesn't want company. She's still in bed; I checked on my way downstairs. Her door is closed."

Elizabeth spent more and more time in her room, and when she wasn't, she sat outside on the veranda staring into space.

"I think Dr. Lethbridge is coming again today," said Jane. "It might be a good idea to mention what's going on."

"Not my place."

"Bessie, please." She turned on her most angelic smile, the one that always earned her an extra slice of cake. "I've got so much to do. The

196

last of the auctions is today and we have to set up for Mrs. Penter's exhibition."

Any excuse to leave the house. Since Elizabeth's turn, her episodes of vagueness and apparent detachment had multiplied from an hour here or there to days when she didn't leave the security of her room. It made Jane uncomfortable. Timothy and the distraction of the impending exhibition were a godsend.

"Oh! *We* do, do *we*?"

"Of course, Mr. Penter will be helping. It's his mother's exhibition, and he knows how she likes her work presented."

"You watch yourself, young lady. There's enough gossip going on about this family without you adding more."

"Gossip? What gossip?"

"Never you mind. Off you go, and I'll pass the message on to Dr.Lethbridge. You can explain your absence to Mr. Quinn when he gets home."

Jane slithered out of the door and pulled it closed behind her. She hadn't seen hide nor hair of Michael for days. When he was home he was locked in his study, and the rest of the time he was in Sydney doing whatever it was he did. She'd run the last two auctions almost single-handedly because John was busy with deliveries; standing up in front of the crowd with a gavel in her hand was not anything she planned to do again in a hurry.

A crowd greeted her at the auction house. Not the usual drop-ins checking the upcoming sale goods, but people huddled in groups chatting, or so it seemed.

It wasn't until she reached the bottom of the stairs that the buzz of conversation halted and all faces turned toward her. The silence was positively strange, like the time years earlier when she'd walked into the dining room in her nightgown when Michael and Elizabeth had guests for dinner. Jane glanced down at her shirt and blouse and straightened her tie. Nothing seemed amiss.

John must have sensed her confusion because he left his position at the front of the room and came over to her. "Morning, Miss Jane. We didn't know if you were coming."

The bell over the door tinkled as a group of women left. No bags in their hands, no carefully wrapped packages. Most peculiar.

"I'm here for the auction."

"Is Miss Quinn feeling better today?" His voice rose to a boom and the faces turned again.

For goodness' sake, did everyone in the town need an update on Elizabeth's health? "What's going on, John?" Jane hissed the words, hoping they wouldn't carry.

"Nothing for you to worry about, Miss Jane. A few people inquiring after Miss Quinn. They haven't seen her out and about, so they're a bit worried."

More like Mrs. Witherspoon and her cronies spreading gossip. "She's perfectly well. I'm here for the last auction and then I'll begin setting up the exhibition. Mr. Penter will be along soon . . ." She let her words drift away. Something about the inquisitive looks on people's faces told her she'd said something wrong. "We may as well start since there's such a crowd, John. Are you ready?"

Her words seemed to flick some sort of switch and the rumble of conversation picked up again. A few more people crowded in the door, and it was as though the atmosphere had magically been wiped clean.

"Gotta go and get the ledgers and the cash bags," said John. "I'll come with you."

Perhaps if she could get him alone for a minute he might tell her truthfully what was going on.

He stepped into his little cubbyhole of an office and swung open the safe to remove the cash bags. Michael had always insisted John deposit the money in the bank every afternoon, said if it was known around town, no one would bother breaking into the premises. He'd been right. They'd never had a break-in, although it might have more to do with John's six-foot frame and wide shoulders. In a previous life he'd been a coalminer. Elizabeth had offered him a job when he and his wife moved into town so their children could attend school. He had worked his way up to manager of the auction house, but he still had a room out the back. He made a formidable night watchman, even though his stature contrasted sharply with his passive nature.

Jane closed the door behind her and rested her shoulders against the frosted glass panel. "John, tell me the truth. What was everyone talking about?"

"Miss Quinn's turn. Told you."

"There's more to it than that, isn't there?" she persisted. "What specifically about Miss Quinn's turn?"

John huffed and puffed for a moment, then threw himself down in the swivel chair. "I'm not one to go with gossip . . ."

"But . . . ?"

"Miss Quinn's turn reminded people of the past. Of when the pair of them first came to town."

"What's so unusual about that?" It was years earlier. Forty years, and goodness only knows how many months and days.

"Bit strange, brother and sister living together for so long and neither of them"—he cleared his throat—"getting married like."

"Getting married? Why would anyone care about that?"

"Not something I like to discuss with a young lass." John's skin took on a sort of purple tinge, as though he'd caught his breath and couldn't sort it out.

"I think you better tell me." She wasn't going to have gossip spread around about Elizabeth, especially not because she'd got overheated and had a bit of a turn. Although the whole episode, and her behavior since, had been most peculiar.

"Might be better if you talked to Mrs. Cohen."

Jane had no intention of talking to the dispatch clerk. She couldn't stand the simpering ninny who spent her entire time pandering to Michael's every whim.

"I'm talking to you, John. Come on. Otherwise I won't pass on any more tips for the races."

Her words hit him right where it mattered—his hand reached for his breast pocket. He always brought the form guide for her to have a look at before race day. It was all easy, logical. The winner could be picked if she took a moment or two to study it. He'd offered numerous times to place a bet for her, but she'd never bothered; knowing she was correct was enough.

"This is going to have to be between you and me," said John. "I don't want no one knowing about this conversation."

"Come on, you know I can keep a secret." She raised one eyebrow and smiled into his eyes. It was one of Elizabeth's traits. Asking a question without doing so.

It worked.

"Thing is, some people say there's more to Mr. Quinn than meets the eye. Irish, they always have the gift of the gab. That's what made him a good auctioneer. Can make you believe you can do or be anything you want to be."

True enough. He'd done that for her the very first day she'd met him.

"Thing is, there's lots of people saying that's what he did. Turned up here with a fistful of money, bought the old inn for a song, turned it into one of the most profitable businesses in the area. Built a fine house for Miss Quinn, but like I said, neither of them married. Kept themselves to themselves, they have."

"How can you say that?" Most of the people employed in the auction house had a background like hers and John's, from the orphanage or down on their luck. Then there was Michael's work for the Labor party—it benefited hundreds of people.

"Haven't you ever wondered, miss?"

"Wondered what, John?"

"Why Mr. Quinn would take you into his home?"

"Because I topped the arithmetic exam, everyone knows that. They sent me to school and evening classes so I could work for them, take over from Miss Quinn."

"Why would they want to do that?"

"Because I'm good with numbers and because . . ." Jane plonked down into the chair in the corner, her heart beating twenty to the dozen. "What are you saying?"

John cleared his throat. "Have you never questioned where you came from? Who your mother was? Your father?"

Of course she had. At the orphanage it was a constant topic of conversation, not only for her but for everyone. Where they came from and why they were unwanted. Somewhere she had a mother and a father, and if they didn't want her, so be it. She'd thought about it when she was young, but if no one had come forward by now it was unlikely it would ever happen.

John moved to her side and rested his large hand on her shoulder. "Better it comes from me than one of those old crows out there." He straightened up, dragged in a breath. "Some say Mr. Quinn's your father." His words came out in a rush.

It took her a moment for them to sink in. "My father?" And then a memory of Timothy's father at the gallery in Sydney popped into her mind. What had he said? . . . *You and your daughter.* Michael hadn't corrected him.

"If that was the case, why wouldn't he have told me?" She couldn't control the tremble in her voice.

"Maybe he's intending to and hasn't got around to it. The answer to his telegram only arrived a while ago."

"What telegram?"

"The one from England."

This was ridiculous. She stood up and smoothed down her skirt, much more in control of the situation now she'd considered the probability. "What has my parentage got to do with Miss Quinn taking a turn?" The whole town had gone crazy. Nothing better to do than invent ludicrous rubbish.

"I'm sorry, Miss Jane. I didn't mean to cause no offense."

"It's not your fault, John, and thank you for telling me. I'm not going to take any notice. Mr. Penter will be here soon and we have an auction to run."

She pinned her hat back in place, effectively ending the conversation, and walked onto the auction floor with sufficient aplomb that would make Elizabeth proud.

Jane kept her head down and recorded every one of the prices with meticulous care while John ran through the lots. In little more than an hour the sale was over and the money collected, keeping her far too busy to say more than a brief "good morning" to any of the townsfolk or dwell on John's strange words. Once the crowds cleared she packed up the ledger, took the stairs two at a time before anyone could interrupt, and pushed open the door to Michael's office, John's words echoing in her ears.

The familiar smell wafted—tobacco and the musky sweet aroma of malt whiskey. She stepped inside and closed the door.

Unlike his study at home, Michael's desk was perfectly clean. She dropped down into the chair and ran her hands along the worn timber armrests, swiveling from side to side.

Could Michael be her father? The thought had her rattled. If he was, who was her mother? Not Elizabeth. Apart from the fact she was Michael's sister, she and Jane had nothing in common either. Elizabeth was tall, statuesque, and always impeccably turned out. Jane was short, mousy, and plain, just like her name.

The drawer on the right-hand side of Michael's desk squeaked as Jane opened it. A mass of broken pen nibs and blunt pencils rattled and rolled. She shut it with a disparaging sigh, not knowing what she was searching for. The drawer below revealed nothing of any significance. Turning to the left-hand side she repeated the process. A pile of unused paper and a couple of new notepads.

Resting her elbows on the desk, she dropped her head into her hands. Michael had spent a couple of hours in here the week before, clattering and banging away. What could he have been doing? She had to be missing something. But what? Had this telegram John spoke about anything to do with it? She pushed back the chair and paced around the room, coming to a halt in front of the fireplace. Above it hung a painting of the *Cutty Sark* under full sail. She ran her finger over the timber frame, tipped it from the wall.

Michael was so predictable.

Stretching up onto her toes, she lifted it off the wall and placed it carefully on the floor. Recessed into the wall was a small safe. She turned the lock and heard the tumbler mechanism click, then tried to pull it open. It held fast.

Jane's heartbeat quickened; she had no idea what she expected to find in the safe. They say everybody has a secret. Was she Michael's?

She paced the length of the room. For all Michael's ability with people, he was a simple man. The combination couldn't be difficult to fathom. But what would he have used? His date of birth? Too simple even for Michael. More likely Elizabeth's birth date.

"Eleven, eighteen, eighteen . . ." Jane paused, then gave the tumbler the final turn to fify-seven. With a satisfying *clunk* the door swung open.

Standing on tiptoe she peered inside, ran her hand around the base, certain it would be where Michael would keep anything private. Her hand came to rest on a roll of papers. She pulled them out, untied the string, and unrolled the papers.

Tens, if not hundreds, of IOUs—every one of them for debts never called in. So typical of Michael and Elizabeth's generosity and compassion. And nothing there to indicate Jane was anything more than another of their charity cases.

She gave a disgruntled huff and flopped down in the chair. What had she expected to find? Some letters telling Michael he'd fathered a child in England and she'd been left at an orphanage, her mother incapable or unwilling to care for her? How foolish! Next she'd be looking for some reference to Florence Nightingale.

"Miss Piper, are you there?"

Timothy! She'd forgotten he was coming after the auction. She leapt to her feet, pushed back her hair, and straightened her skirt. "I won't be but a moment."

She pushed the bundle of papers back into the safe, swung the door closed, gave the tumbler a twist, and lifted the *Cutty Sark* above the mantel.

"Can I help? That looks heavy."

"No, no, I've done it." She stood for a moment with her back to him, willing the flush to fade from her cheeks, then turned. Whatever had possessed her? What if Michael or Elizabeth had come in instead of Timothy?

"Why don't you come and sit down for a minute. You look exhausted."

He held the door to Michael's office wide as she stumbled out, a horrid mixture of shock and confusion swirling in her stomach. What had she expected to find? Blast Mrs. Witherspoon and her gossiping jackdaws. She slammed the palms of her hands down on the table.

"I do hope this exhibition isn't creating too much work for you," said Timothy. "You must tell me what needs to be done, not take on everything yourself."

"It's not that. It's . . ." Oh, for heaven's sake. She dropped into a chair, her head in her hands. Crying, like a baby. She never cried. Not when she'd been sent back to the orphanage and the people had adopted Emmaline instead, not when Michael and Elizabeth had taken her in, not when she'd got beaten over the knuckles for answering back in Religious Instruction, not even when Sister Mary Ann had accidently slammed her fingers in the dormitory door.

Agonizing sobs wracked her body, making her shoulders quake. "I'm sorry. I'm so sorry." Timothy put his arm around her, tentative at first, and as she leaned into him, he drew her closer.

"What can I do?" He pressed a large white handkerchief into her hand.

Jane dragged in a deep breath, opened her mouth to speak, but nothing came out, nothing except a mournful howl.

"Sometimes it's better to cry. Let it all out." He pulled her closer against his chest, patting her back. No one had ever done that before, held her that way. She let her head drop to his shoulder, inhaled the warmth and comfort of him until gradually her breathing returned to normal.

"Let me make a cup of tea. Tea fixes everything."

She grimaced, scrubbed at her face with his handkerchief, dragging in the sweet smell of sunshine and soap. "Yes, please."

The familiar sound of the burner and the clatter of the teacups soothed Jane.

Timothy placed two cups and the teapot on the table. "Is there any milk or sugar?"

She drew in a disgusting sniff. "I'm sorry. There's sugar on the shelf up there but no milk. I don't take sugar."

"On this occasion I think some sugar would be a good idea. Now, tell me. I'm a good listener."

What could she say to him? *It's possible the man I thought was my benefactor is in fact my father, and he's never cared enough to claim me.* She didn't even know if it was the truth. Gossips, the whole lot of them.

"I feel such a fool." Another infuriating sob lodged halfway up her throat. "I never cry."

"Drink your tea, it'll help. It always does." He pushed the cup toward her and she inhaled the sweet steam, taking a careful sip, then another, feeling the sugar seep into her system.

She had to talk to someone and it couldn't be Elizabeth, nor Bessie or Lucy. Better perhaps this man, who knew nothing of her life. She dragged in a deep breath. "I've let the local gossip get to me."

He sat down, rested his elbows on the table and his chin on his hands, and said nothing, just stared into her eyes, encouraging her to continue.

"I told you I grew up in an orphanage." He nodded. "It's never bothered me. I've been so lucky living with Michael and Elizabeth, the Quinns. They've given me everything I could ever hope for, but today, today . . ." Another sob threatened. "Someone told me Michael might be my father. I went into his office, that's what I was doing when you arrived, foraging through his papers, breaking his trust, breaking into his safe . . ."

"And?"

"And . . . well, nothing! I don't even know what I was expecting to find. I need to know. Know if it's true, and find out what a telegram from England has to do with me."

"Is there any reason why you shouldn't ask him?"

Jane put down the teacup with more force than she intended. Such a simple solution . . . unless it was more than gossip. What if Michael didn't want to claim her? What if there was something lacking in her, which was why he hadn't told her? Some way she'd disappointed him. She couldn't bear it.

"At least you'd know."

"What if he isn't my father?"

"Then nothing has changed. You said you're happy with your life. Why let a bunch of puggle-headed fools make you miserable?"

"Puggle-headed?"

"Aye. Foolish, stupid, drunken."

"I don't think Mrs. Witherspoon and Mrs. Shipton are drinkers."

"Wouldn't put it past the Witherspoon woman."

"You can't say that!" A picture of the two women rolling down High Street flashed before Jane's eyes and she burst out laughing.

"There. That's better, isn't it?"

A long sigh wound its way through her body and she relaxed back into the chair. "Thank you, Timothy. Thank you. I've no idea what came over me."

"You were all at sixes and sevens, nothing to be ashamed of. Now, what are you going to do?"

"I'm going to go home, see if Michael's back from Sydney, and talk to him."

"I'll come back tomorrow. Mother and Father won't be arriving for another week so we have plenty of time to prepare for the exhibition." With that he threw her a smile and disappeared downstairs.

Beyond the window, the light had almost faded. Once downstairs, she called a quick farewell over her shoulder to John and jumped onto her bicycle. With her satchel thumping against her back she pedaled like crazy, nerves doing a wild dance in her stomach. She must have covered the distance back to the house at about ten miles an hour. She cycled right through the back gate and up to the laundry and threw her bicycle against the wall.

"Where do you think you've been?" Bessie grumbled as she came through the back door.

"I'm sorry I'm late. There was . . . there was a problem after the auction." Almost the truth.

"Mr. Quinn's home and they've eaten early. You better go and make your apologies."

Jane left her satchel hanging on the back of the scullery door, then scuttled into the sitting room, her mind full of questions she didn't dare raise in front of Elizabeth.

TWENTY-TWO

MORPETH, 1873

E lizabeth brushed Michael's arm away when he attempted to escort her down the gangplank as though she were a frail miss, incapable of putting one foot in front of the other. A stiff breeze whipped across the river and she clamped her new straw hat firmly down on her head, determined not to lose it. Michael had bought it for her in Sydney, and although she had no intention of telling him, she liked it. In fact, she'd enjoyed every moment of the trip from Hill End.

When they'd arrived in Sydney they'd spent a day looking around, and Michael had bought them both a mountain of new clothes from a very smart shop. Then they'd boarded a very neat little ship, sporting not only sails but a steam-driven paddle. As usual, Michael had been ahead of himself—the rail link between Sydney and Newcastle was still a far-off dream, due to the small matter of a missing bridge across the Hawkesbury River and a large unfinished section of rail line. Not that Elizabeth minded. For some reason the thought of traveling in a roaring, pumping, and smoking iron monstrosity made her bones quake. Instead, she'd spent the night in a very comfortable sleeping berth in a cabin with three other women, and when she woke in the morning they'd already arrived in Newcastle. They'd eaten an early breakfast out on the deck—fresh bread and the sweetest fish she'd ever tasted—overlooking numerous small islands, before gliding up the river.

The land, thickly wooded down to the water's edge, abounded in all sorts of birds: pelicans with their big baggy beaks, plovers, curlews, cormorants, and more kinds of ducks than she'd ever imagined. Why would anyone want to travel in a dirty, noisy, smelly train?

"I can manage quite well, thank you," said Elizabeth. "I'm not an invalid."

"I'm not suggesting you are, me little—" The word dried on Michael's lips as she glowered at him.

Just as well, because if she'd told him once she'd told him a million times—she wasn't his "little darlin'." She was a grown woman.

"This is the beginning of our new life, and you'll be needing to behave like a lady."

She couldn't help but bristle at his tone. She needed to *behave* like a lady, not a foolish girl who'd fallen in love with a man Michael decreed totally inappropriate.

He waved his hand at the two men lugging their trunks up from the wharf and took her arm. "Well, here we are! Are you excited?"

She offered him a half-hearted smile and gave his arm a squeeze. She was excited, and to pretend otherwise would be ridiculously churlish. It was thrilling to be embarking on a new adventure, even though her heart lay shattered somewhere beneath her new blue coat. No matter what Jing said about fate and red threads, she'd given up hope of them ever meeting again.

It wasn't only Michael who disapproved of her friendship with Jing. Mr. Li thought her as much of an infidel as people believed the Celestials to be. Celestials—*phat!* They were people. What did it matter which god they prayed to, the shape of their eyes, or the color of their hair?

The Li family were as biased as anyone else. One day, she promised, one day . . .

She skipped a few paces to keep up with Michael's long strides. She'd find Jing. All she had to do was believe and the red thread would bring them back together. In the meantime, she would make the best of it.

"Tell me about the Potters Inn. You said I had to wait until we arrived, but now we're here, you've got no excuse."

Michael drew to a halt next to a smart sulky and tipped his hat to the stable hand, who scrambled down and dropped the step for Elizabeth.

"It's less than a half hour ride into town. We follow the creek, then turn onto High Street and cross the bridge apparently." He flicked the whip across the horses' rumps and they took off at a brisk trot. With his wide grin and his dark eyes flashing, he looked like the brother she remembered from her childhood. "The Potters Inn operated as a hotel from 1820 until a few years ago, then the license was canceled and the owner decided to sell the building." The words tumbled out, his Irish lilt increasing with his excitement. "We'll be small, expand slowly. I've got my eye on the two buildings next door as well."

"Can we afford it?" Surely the expenses would be enormous, and Elizabeth knew exactly how the balance sheets looked.

"We'll not be having a problem. I've a couple of deals under way. One I shall be showing you in a moment or two, and I've heard about a business that has to close their doors. I'm going to buy their stock to get us started. Mostly haberdashery and notions. That's where you come in."

"Me? I don't know anything about haberdashery and notions." Shovels and pick handles, tents and canvas, but notions! She'd never had the time or the interest in buttons and bows.

"That's as may be. You know all about looking after the accounts and bookkeeping. We'll employ someone to help, although I'll be doing the auctions myself. According to Eliza Cox there's nothing of the kind in Maitland. One place where everything anyone could want can be found. Sydney and Newcastle are within easy reach when we're ready to restock."

It all sounded dreadfully . . . well, dreadfully Michael. Wishful thinking. Although he was right about the accounts—thanks to Jing, she could do that.

She smoothed her hand over the bag on her lap and tried not to think too hard about that last awful day. She knew Jing hadn't left of his own accord and that he hadn't wanted to leave her. No matter what Michael believed, she'd never forget him. Jing hadn't only been her teacher, he'd become her closest friend.

Michael reckoned she was too young to have feelings for a man. She wasn't. She wouldn't give up; she'd keep pestering. He couldn't do without Jing, and she couldn't imagine life without him.

The sulky made short work of the well-graded road, and before long the pelicans and gum trees inhabiting the swamp lands adjacent to the creek gave way to buildings, far more substantial than anything in Hill End.

"That's the jail over there." Michael flourished the switch and the poor horse picked up the pace, leaving Elizabeth with little time to ponder the massive sandstone walls and the vertically barred windows. "Not so pretty from the inside either, I'll be bound, but nothing you'll need to be worrying your pretty head about. There's only been three breakouts since it opened, nigh on thirty years ago, and all the escapees found themselves back behind bars before they had time to enjoy their bid for freedom."

With every roll of the wheels, Elizabeth's imagination soared.

She'd rather believed Michael had painted some halcyon picture of this famed Maitland Town, but now she could understand his enthusiasm. Sydney might be the biggest town in New South Wales, but her memories of Sydney bore no resemblance to the neatly laid-out streets and substantial two- and three-story buildings and businesses lining High Street. Drapers, clothiers, banks, ironmongers, and booksellers, never mind the inns and churches—more denominations than she'd dreamed existed—and even a cathedral. A Catholic cathedral. No wonder Michael was smitten.

The sulky slowed to a halt outside a two-story white stone building with windows above a veranda that kept the sun from the downstairs. Even though the paintwork was peeling a little, the windows were boarded, and a large chain and padlock secured the double front doors, Elizabeth could see its potential.

Michael jumped to his feet, arms spread wide like a showman. "There you are. Accommodation upstairs. Good-size rooms and a kitchen downstairs, at the back. Once we've settled in and made a bit, I'll build you the beautiful house I promised. I have a mind to live on Church Street. Eliza Cox said it was where all the people of means reside. It's down here." He flicked the switch across the horse's back and the sulky drifted along the road, past more shops and offices, and into a street lined with the most impressive houses and flourishing gardens.

They drew to a halt outside two imposing houses. Michael tilted back his hat and stared up. "These belong to Owen and Beckett, business partners in the general store."

How could anyone earn enough out of a general store to be able to build something like this? The thought made her hair stand on end and her skin prickle. The two houses, mirror images of each other, appeared fit for royalty.

"Heard tell there's wallpaper in the dining room and a harmonium, grand marble fireplaces, and cedar furniture all polished up shiny as a mirror."

Those would be the stories he'd heard from Eliza Cox, without a doubt. Who polished all the furniture?

"Even the butler's got his own special pantry."

Intricate cast iron, as fine as the prettiest lace, adorned the upper verandas with double doors and fine timber shutters, all fenced by neatly trimmed bushes with bright shiny leaves. Nothing like the timber palings and dusty gardens of Hill End.

"See that vacant block of land?" Michael gestured beyond the two houses to an empty paddock.

A good acre and a half, unless she was mistaken, and in the distance a line of trees where she imagined the river ran.

"That'll be ours. Surprise! I'm going to buy it! That's where we'll live, and the house we'll build will be bigger and better than any Maitland Town has ever seen."

Michael's ideas were far grander than anything she'd dreamed. Her heart leaped, then stilled. The only fault in his entire plan was the fact it didn't include Jing.

And there it was. Elizabeth would have to be happy. This was better than anything Hill End could offer, and no Jing. Michael's blood still boiled at the thought of what might have happened. He'd seen the men's leering faces and heard the women's malicious chatter when she'd walked down the street.

Not good enough for Elizabeth, not good enough at all.

Life would be different now, though. He had work to do to make their name in this new place. He had plans, big plans, and money behind him, thanks to Da and a bit of hard work.

From the look on Elizabeth's face he'd made the right decision. On their way through the town her head turned this way and that, taking in every new sight. He pointed out the music shop, the Mechanics Institute, and the offices of the *Maitland Mercury*, the very newspaper he'd read in Hill End when his plan had first taken shape. Then the School of Arts with its sign proclaiming, "Evening Classes." There'd be more Elizabeth could do to round off her education. She'd had the brains handed out to her, fair and square.

"Did you hear me, Michael?"

He slowed the sulky. "What's that, me little darlin'?"

"If we're starting afresh, you have to stop calling me that. It makes me feel as though I'm still in pinafores."

"I can be doing that for you. Now, what was it you were saying?"

"Back there, at the School of Arts, the sign said they had book-keeping classes. I could go."

"Aye, that you could, if you think you'd like to. Or maybe learn how to play the piano, or take some painting lessons, something be-fitting a fine lady."

"I'm not sure I want to be a fine lady. Look at the two women walking down the street there. Their hats are as big as houses and . . . look. Look at their behinds!" She clapped her hand over her mouth but failed to quell her shriek of laughter.

It was so good to hear her laugh again. "Bustles, those are. The latest fashion."

She frowned at him. "No wonder ladies faint so often. Those nipped-in waists and big behinds probably damage their internal organs."

He'd gone to a lot of trouble to find out about ladies' fashions. He wasn't going to have Elizabeth looking anything but her best, even if it did mean a little bit of light-headedness. Michael Quinn and his sister were going to make their mark.

His fingers itched to get his hands on the keys and begin. The agent in Sydney had told him they could collect them from the shop two doors down. A surge of eagerness swept through him and he climbed down from the carriage and held out his arms to Elizabeth.

"Michael, stop! I'm not a child anymore. You can't be seen swinging me around and around like a whirligig."

"Oh, I'll be doing whatever I like. 'Tis an exciting day." The mere sight of the building had his blood pumping, except for the name. Potters Inn—it would have to go. The only pots he intended to see would be the ones passing under his hammer.

She was right. No more whirligigs. Elizabeth was growing to womanhood. New town, new place. She'd already turned sixteen, and they needed to establish themselves. The pair of them were on their way up.

Here was his chance to do right by her. Make up for his rash decision, his lie. Aye, that's what it was. A lie. One he'd regret until the good Lord called him home. When they were settled, when he'd built her the house, given her everything she deserved, he'd sit her down and explain why he'd acted like Christ Almighty and taken her life into his hands.

TWENTY-THREE

MAITLAND TOWN, 1913

Elizabeth was nowhere to be seen, and only a sliver of light shone under the door of Michael's study. Without giving herself time to second-guess her reasoning, Jane knocked.

"Come in." Sitting in front of the fire, a glass of whiskey at hand, Michael looked up, stubbed out his cigar, and stood. "Jane, thank goodness you're home. We were beginning to worry."

"I'm sorry. Can I talk to you?"

"Of course you can. More plans for the auction house?"

"No, nothing like that. This is a bit more personal, and I'm sorry if I'm going to sound impolite, but I need to ask you something before I lose the courage."

"Goodness me. That sounds dire. Come and sit down."

"I'll stand." She drew in a deep breath. "Michael, are you my father?" There, she'd done it. Timothy was right, it hadn't been too difficult.

Michael's face turned puce and he closed his eyes.

"Are you all right?" Where were his heart pills? She'd never seen him have an attack. Elizabeth had warned her if he did, she was to find his pills in his top pocket and make sure she tucked one under his tongue. She darted forward and slipped her hand into his inside pocket, right over his heart.

His eyes flashed open and he wrapped his fingers around her wrist. "I'm not having an attack, Jane."

As though scalded, she wrenched her hand free and stepped away. "I'm so sorry, so very sorry."

Why was he sorry? Sorry he hadn't told her? Sorry he hadn't had an attack? She sank down onto the rug in front of the fire.

He lifted her chin, stared deep into her eyes. "No, Jane. No, I am not your father. Believe me, if I were, I would be a proud man. Nothing would make me happier."

"Oh!" The air left her body in a sudden whoosh. She wasn't Michael's daughter. The knowledge hit low in her gut like a punch. So much for the townsfolk. She should have known. Since when did gossips deal in truth?

"If you were my flesh and blood I would never, not in a heartbeat, leave you to grow up in an orphanage."

She wasn't sure how she should feel. Was she disappointed? There wasn't anyone she could think of she'd like better than Michael to be her father. She'd fallen into the same old trap as all the girls at the orphanage did. Grasped at dandelions.

"Jane, look at me."

She lifted her head, dashed away the tears collecting in the corner of her eyes.

"What made you ask the question? It's not like you to jump to conclusions."

"I'm a fool."

"No, you are not. That is the last word I would use to describe you."

Easier to tell the whole truth. "When I arrived at the auction house today everyone was staring at me." How foolish she sounded. "I asked John what was going on. He said since Elizabeth's turn, and the telegram from England, people were saying there was something odd about you and Elizabeth, that you had something to hide. They thought it might be me."

———— ≈ ————

Jane sat like a fallen sparrow on the rug, picking at the fringe, her face bone-white. Poor little mite. "I'm so pleased you came to me and asked," Michael said. "Honesty is one of your most admirable characteristics." Not a quality he could attribute to himself.

"I didn't come straight to you." She sat up tall, threw back her shoulders. "I went into your office and looked through your desk. I opened the safe."

"Did you indeed, and how did you manage that?"

"It wasn't difficult to guess the combination." Her lips puckered and the color came back to her cheeks. "Elizabeth's birthday."

The date Elizabeth believed was her birthday, the date he'd given her, all those years ago.

"What did you find?" A handful of old IOUs. Nothing more, unless he was mistaken. He'd moved all the old paperwork—their immigration papers and Mam's and Da's early letters—to the house when he'd cleared out his office.

"I'm sorry, Michael. It was underhanded. I've never done anything like that before. I promise you."

"I believe you, Jane." Although in many ways he wished she had found something. He'd like to share his burden with her, ask her advice and see how she might apply her logic to the conundrum. "Now we've sorted that out, tell me how you think Elizabeth is."

Jane picked up the poker, prodded the fire, and for once had the look of someone choosing her words. "She's not getting any better."

"Something more than the scare at the technical college?"

"Much more. She's lost, well, she's lost her bounce, which is a silly thing to say, because she's always telling me I shouldn't bounce. She has no enthusiasm, no interest. It's as though she's somewhere else. I keep finding her sitting staring out of the window, as though she's thousands of miles away."

Perhaps she was. "Jane, what's the earliest memory you have?"

"The earliest?"

"Yes, the first thing you can remember."

"Being in the orphanage. In the dormitory, all of us in cots, rows and rows of them. The way the single ray of light played and threw shadows. They changed as the day passed."

"That's a strange thing for a little girl to remember."

"The bars made patterns on the walls. I remember threading my sheet through the bars to change the pattern . . ." She let out a huge splutter of laughter.

It was such a relief to see her back to her usual self. What a dreadful thing for the poor child to suffer, to imagine he was her father and hadn't wanted her. The thought brought him up short. How could he tell Elizabeth if he had no answers? Thank God he'd plucked up the courage to write a proper letter to Gertrude Finbright. How he hoped the workhouse would forward his letter and she might have an answer for Elizabeth.

"You should have seen Sister Mary Ann's face! I am so glad you rescued me," Jane said. "What's your first memory?"

"Mine? Of me mam, sobbing her heart out. Me uncle Seamus. He'd been taken, accused of all sorts of rubbish by the bloody English. Mam had found out Da was caught up in it too. That's what made their minds up to come to Australia, as if the famine weren't enough. They left us with my aunty, and the plan was for us to join them once they'd established themselves. But my aunty died of the consumption, and so Lizzie was settled in the workhouse 'til I could earn enough to pay out the tickets. Took a lot longer than any of us expected."

"Lizzie? I've never heard you call Aunt Elizabeth Lizzie. That's what she calls her old doll."

How had that slipped out? "Enough of all this nonsense. You must be hungry, missing supper like that. Go and find Bessie and see what she has for you."

He stoked the fire, reached for the whiskey bottle, and topped up his glass. The flames twisted and flickered and took him back . . .

———≋———

An ominous red glow tinted the sky.

Without a second thought he'd taken off, his boots clattering against the cobblestones, his breath billowing in front of him in misty clouds. The flames had to be coming from the workhouse. There were no other buildings along that stretch.

He skidded to a halt and clambered over the fence, feet slipping against the coated iron. Hit the ground with an awful thump, snatched a breath, full of burning timber and something sweet and musky, putrid and leathery, something he'd not think on.

Skirting the exercise yard, the boys' dormitory, and the building where they housed the old men, he pushed through the crowd. Giant flames swept up into the night sky, sending sparks like fireworks high into the air.

"Out of the way." He elbowed through the crowd until he was almost at the front. Jesus, Mary, and Joseph. What the hell . . .

A crowd of quaking bodies huddled together as one of the wardens called out a list of names.

"Ellen Brown, Alice Baker, Susan Alcock . . ." Each name was greeted by a frail echo. "Lizzie Ó'Cuinn."

Silence, then a low murmur. "Lizzie."

The air whooshed out of his lungs. She was safe.

"Here. Make use of yourself. We're going in." The line of men passing buckets pushed him forward.

The warden grabbed him by the shoulders. "Michael, me boy. What're you doing here?"

"Looking for Lizzie."

"She answered her name. Give us a hand." A bucket was thrust into his grip and a hefty shove sent him toward the line.

God only knew how much time passed in a flurry of buckets, water, and heat, until finally the chapel and the girls' dormitory gave an almighty groan and the rafters collapsed inward in a mass of sparks and dust, leaving only the silhouette of the ravaged chapel spire.

Bent double, Michael hacked the smoke-ridden air from his lungs and peeled off his sodden jacket. When he straightened up, he caught sight of the group of girls huddled under the tree. He had to find Lizzie. Take her away. She wasn't staying here. Not now, not when they'd be boarding the ship first thing in the morning. He didn't care what anyone said, he'd be taking her. Right this minute. He'd packed her new clothes into a bag, all as the clerk at the immigration office had told him.

He ducked around a cluster of women in all manner of nightclothes and made his way to the group of girls—a couple of older ones, ten, maybe twelve years old, arms wrapped around the younger children, hugging them tight, and in the middle of them all was Miss Finbright.

His eyes scanned the group. "Anyone seen Lizzie? Lizzie Ó'Cuinn?"

Faces pinched and pale turned to him.

"Lizzie Ó'Cuinn. Anyone seen her?"

A pair of eyes big and round as saucers stared at him. He bent down. "D'you see Lizzie?"

Her little friend sniffed, wiped a great blob of snot down her nightdress. His heart plummeted right down to his soaking boots. He ploughed through the mass of people, forced his way to the front, and stopped short. A row of bodies laid out in the dirt. Two of them adults from their length, others smaller.

"Lizzie, Lizzie Ó'Cuinn." He grabbed the jacket of some officious-looking man ticking names off on a long list. "I'm looking for Lizzie Ó'Cuinn."

"Name's ticked off. She answered the roll call. Must be over there somewhere with the other girls."

He had to find her. A wave of remorse shot through him. He'd promised Mam he'd care for her. Fine job he'd done of that. He should have kept her with him, not left her at the workhouse.

The hollow skeleton of the girls' dormitory towered against the lightening sky. He searched and searched, asked everyone he saw, and still he couldn't find Lizzie.

"Michael, what are you doing here? I thought you'd gone." Miss Finbright stood before him, a doused lamp in her hand, her face streaked with soot and a mass of hair hanging down her back.

"I can't find Lizzie."

"She's here somewhere. Her name is marked off. They've taken the girls into the women's dormitories. You go and get some rest, come back in the morning. I'll find her."

He had to take her word for it. What else could he do? Lizzie had answered her name; she'd be inside. "Thank you, Miss Finbright."

"Gertrude. Call me Gertrude."

"Gertrude." He grasped her hand in both of his. "I won't forget everything you've done for us."

"You're a fine man, Michael Ó'Cuinn."

Hardly a man, more an overgrown boy, but her words made him stand taller.

"You'll make someone a fine husband."

"And you'll make a wonderful mother."

Why in God's name had he said that? It must have been the right thing because her face lit like a beacon against the stark skeletal remains of the chapel.

"Come back tomorrow. Everything will be all right. I promise you."

TWENTY-FOUR

MAITLAND TOWN, 1913

At the end of four days, Jane's hands were raw and every muscle in her body ached. They'd swept and cleaned and polished, and the auction room glittered, the windows putting Michael's cut-glass decanters to shame.

John and Mrs. Cohen had helped transform the auction rooms into a reputable gallery. Mrs. Witherspoon could take it and stick it in her unmentionables.

Elizabeth still said she was fine, but her words and her demeanor said the opposite. However, she was determined to see the exhibition, and Michael thought it might be good to get her out of the house, stop her incessant introspection and strange moods.

The Penters still hadn't arrived from Melbourne, though Timothy assured Jane they'd be there by the end of the week. The preview would be a trial run. A chance to show Michael what she'd accomplished, and give Bessie, Lucy, and the auction house staff an opportunity to view the paintings because they'd be up to their eyebrows on opening day.

Timothy arrived late—not an endearing habit. Eight minutes and twenty-two seconds after the time they'd agreed upon. Jane was all aflutter.

"It looks marvelous." He made a quick tour of the room, unnecessarily straightened a couple of the pictures, then stood back and surveyed the room. "I've arranged for a photographer on opening night. Mother will like a record when we return to England."

Return? The thought hadn't crossed her mind. She fancied the idea the Penters might find Maitland so appealing they'd stay.

"When will that be?" She shook away the plaintive note in her voice, plastered a smile on her face.

"No idea. It depends on Father. I told you, he calls the shots."

She wasn't going to involve herself in any discussion. Already she had the feeling she and Timothy's father wouldn't see eye to eye—it went back to that very first meeting at the gallery in Sydney—though she couldn't say exactly why.

"Michael and Elizabeth and the staff are coming in about an hour for a preview. A sort of dress rehearsal."

"To make sure the subject matter of the paintings is appropriate." Timothy threw her an outrageous wink.

"Of course they are! I just thought it would be a nice thing to do for the staff. They're going to be busy on opening day with refreshments and ticket sales, and Michael and Elizabeth want to have a preview as well." Surely she didn't have to explain.

"I'm teasing you, Jane."

Codding, as Michael would say. She never understood it. Better to move on.

"The light is best in the afternoon. As good, if not better, than the technical college." And no Mrs. Witherspoon sticking in her out-of-joint nose.

He took two steps closer, grasped both of her hands, and looked straight into her eyes. "I want to thank you for all you've done."

Her lips dried, along with her ability to speak. The past days working with Timothy had been full of laughter, and she'd enjoyed every moment of their time together. "I hope we haven't forgotten anything."

"Does it matter? As you said, it's a dress rehearsal. Besides, it might be a little late. Here they come."

Michael's cane tapped on the floor as he and Elizabeth walked in, arm in arm, looking very much the guests of honor. They stopped in the middle of the room and Michael gazed around, then nodded his head. "A remarkable job, young lady. Congratulations."

"Uncle Michael, Aunt Elizabeth, I'd like to introduce Timothy Penter. His mother is the artist, Marigold Penter."

A smile lifted the corner of Elizabeth's lips. "It's a pleasure to meet you, Timothy, and I look forward to meeting your father and mother. I believe they'll be with us in a few days."

"Yes, I'm expecting them very soon." He handed Michael and Elizabeth a copy of the catalogues they'd had printed and gestured to the first of the paintings.

"You go with them. Everyone else is arriving." Resisting her need to let out a great whoop of excitement, Jane pulled the doors wide and a raucous babble of voices filled the room. "Catalogues for everyone." She handed them out, taking no notice of the snooty look on Lucy's face, and tried very hard not to comment on John who, dressed in a suit and tie, escorted his wife across the room as though he were the sole guardian of the Crown Jewels.

Michael made a slow tour around the perimeter. "I have to admit I prefer the work of our Australian painters, particularly the Heidelberg School. Streeton's landscapes and Roberts's wonderful *Shearing of the Rams*. Much more my cup of tea."

Ignoring Michael's patriotic rambling Jane made a quick circuit of the room, checking for problems. Give it another five minutes and Michael would be in full flight.

God help them!

It was only when Jane stepped up to straighten one of the paintings that a strange humming noise registered.

Elizabeth stood, her gaze riveted on one of the pictures. Jane moved to her side. "What did you say?"

The humming stopped and Elizabeth lifted her head with a sigh. "Such a lovely scene. Look at the cottage with its thatched roof, and the beautiful garden with the apple tree. It makes me want to step inside and sit under the tree."

She'd never heard Elizabeth say anything so, well, so fanciful. She was all practicality and common sense. Jane was the one who was often accused of being preoccupied, though not with paintings.

Elizabeth moved on to the next and stood staring, her arms clutched tight around her waist. Jane slipped into the space beside her and followed, a little tired of the bucolic scenes. More thatched cottages tucked into the fold of the hill and village scenes.

If asked, Elizabeth couldn't have described the color of the clothes worn by the girl sitting under the tree. Perhaps a gray blue, almost as though she might fade into the distance. Up in the window of the cottage, another face pressed against the glass, chin in hands, staring down. "The girl has such a look of longing on her face. I want to reach out my hand to her. I feel such a sense of peace when I look at this picture. It's gentle. A calming scene. As though no harm could come to anyone. Yet there's a sense of wistfulness about it. Does this place exist? Do we know where they were painted?"

"Timothy says they live in the West Country, in England, although his mother has spent a lot of time in Paris."

Trust Jane to know, such a voracious appetite for information. The pictures were almost too idyllic to be true. Mullioned windows, picturesque dormers, and thatched roofs, neatly designated fields edged with stone walls and flowering hedgerows. None of the dusty, barren paddocks of Australia stretching further than her imagination. "I'd like to know exactly where."

Bessie stepped up alongside Elizabeth. "They remind me of the stories me gran used to tell about home. Said it was like a fairy tale. Everything so pretty. Little stone cottages and trees, so many flowering trees. Apple orchards they were."

"Apple orchards, you say?" Elizabeth studied the painting.

"Miles and miles of them, and the bees buzzing so loud they hurt your eardrums, that's what she said."

"Where was she from, your grandmother?"

"Down southwest of London somewhere. They sailed from Plymouth. Convict, she was, accused of stealing a handkerchief. She did no such thing." Bessie shook her head. "Still had to serve her sentence. Seven years for picking up a handkerchief, if you please. Just fourteen she was."

"Look at the girl at the window—she has such a sad face."

"Looks angry to me, maybe even jealous. As though she'd like to be out there under the tree."

"I wish I knew why." Elizabeth's skin tingled and her breathing slowed.

"Look over there on the hill. There's gypsy caravans, and look at that, them two walking down the path. It's like a tunnel the way the leaves on the trees meet. Nice life for children."

The urge to cry came over Elizabeth, tears welled and left a big ache, blurred by something she didn't understand. She moved on to the next painting.

A church, a crooked fence, long-forgotten gravestones, and in the foreground a circular building, the light glancing off the slate roof. The picture wavered and shimmered like the horizon on a scorching summer's day.

A violent explosion of sound sent her heart leaping against her ribcage. Birds, hundreds of them. Wheeling and diving in a vast black cloud, their feathered wings beating against her cheeks, the darkness, overwhelming darkness, black as night. She stumbled back against the wall, gulping in deep, unsteady breaths of dusty air, her face damp with perspiration, her head swelling with the constant pounding in her ears.

She drew herself upright. The pounding louder, more rhythmic. The colors in the painting blurred, blended in swirling distortion.

The linoleum spiraled up to meet her.

———≈———

"G'woam. G'woam."

"Aunt Elizabeth."

"Give her some air."

"She needs smelling salts."

An eternity before the room flickered into focus and reality trickled back. Jane's face hovered, her fingers grazing Elizabeth's forehead as if checking for a fever.

Elizabeth's mind snapped into the moment. Next she'd be in a darkened room having cold compresses, cups of tea, and nasty little glasses of laudanum forced on her.

"I'm perfectly fine. Help me up." All the fuss and carry-on would drive a saint to purgatory.

"Was there something about the paintings that upset you?"

Michael crouched by her side, his body warmth and strong arm comforting her as always. She let out a long, slow breath.

"Everything's going to be all right. We'll make sense of it all," he said.

"I feel as though it's the picture of my dreams. The scudding clouds, the woodlands, and the hedgerows are so familiar." Elizabeth swallowed her strange, strangled cry.

"That is the painting from the technical college," Jane said.

Was it? She didn't remember seeing any of these paintings at the college, only the birds in their glass-fronted cabinets swooping. She wrapped her arms tightly around her body to still her sudden tremor, clamped her lips to prevent the wail building in her throat escaping.

She was slipping, everything dark, as though her balance had somehow deserted her.

"Come and sit down." Michael led her to the chair in the corner of the room and she sank down, couldn't prevent her hands coming up to protect her head.

The focus of the room wavered again, drowned by the noise, the beating of wings filling her head.

"What is it?" Michael's voice hitched, a tinge of panic in the raised inflection. "Look at me. Are you having trouble breathing?"

Every one of her muscles strained, her stomach churned, and the raw, aching gasps wracked her body.

Her thoughts blurred, twisted, and tumbled together. She wanted Jing, someone to hold her, assure her she wasn't alone. Where was Jing? She blinked away the yearning.

Her instinct told her to forget the paintings, never look on them again, to get rid of the memories they evoked. The same way she'd tried when Michael made her leave Jing. It was the only way to cope. Not let the past crowd out the future.

She brought her hand to her mouth, burying her knuckles between her lips, trapping the strange cry while tears poured silently down her cheeks.

Michael wrapped his arm tighter and drew her closer until the terrible tension in her body lessened, her breathing settled, and the distant murmur of their voices began to make sense.

"What's she saying?"

"I've no idea."

"It was the same thing she said at the technical college."

"John, call a cab. I'm taking Elizabeth home. Jane, you close up."

TWENTY-FIVE

"I'm sorry to drag you out on a Sunday afternoon. I'm at a total loss." Michael raked back his hair.

"Please don't concern yourself. Explain to me again what happened." Lethbridge paced across the room, then came to a halt in front of his desk.

"Nothing different. I hoped time would help Elizabeth recover, but she seems to be getting worse. She's made mistakes in the ledgers, railed at Jane when she pointed them out. Now this. A repeat of her initial turn at the technical college. And she keeps repeating this strange cry—'G'woam! G'woam!'"

"As before, I can find nothing physically wrong with her. She's complaining of a slight headache, that's all. I've given her a sleeping draught. We are going to have to come to a decision—she cannot spend the rest of her life in a laudanum-induced haze."

"This idea of a rest cure is not an option. I am not having Elizabeth locked away in some establishment for the mentally unsound."

"You're overreacting. A month, maybe two, in a different environment might be exactly what she needs. Carefully administered drugs will allow her mind to settle. It's a private establishment on the banks of the Hunter River. A delightful house built in the 1840s. It caters to women who . . ." Lethbridge cleared his throat. "Nostalgia can, in itself, become a death sentence." He laced his fingers into his waistcoat pockets and rocked on his heels. "I have no doubt it's the change." He muttered the words through tight lips, his cheeks burning with embarrassment.

The change. What change? Elizabeth hadn't mentioned any change.

"It can be simply arranged. We need two doctors, myself of course, and one other to agree with the diagnosis and sign a certificate."

"A certificate for what?"

"Cases of melancholia at this stage in a woman's life are not unusual. Particular emphasis is placed on the natural environment aiding the recovery. Nostalgia is not a diagnosis to be ignored. Untreated it can lead to the victim wasting away and losing their ability to adjust and cope with daily life, falling into a deep depression, becoming consumed by sadness, apathy."

Whatever was he talking about? It came to Michael in a flash. Lethbridge thought Elizabeth had lost her marbles. "No. The answer's no." Elizabeth was no more senile or demented than he. "If you can't come up with any alternative, I shall take her to Sydney for a second opinion. Better still, London. I have a mind to travel to England."

"You are in no condition to consider that option." Lethbridge let out a disgruntled sigh. "If you won't entertain the rest home for Elizabeth, we must go over the events, yet again, and see if we have missed something."

Michael would have to come clean, but how to approach it? His heart gave an unwelcome stutter. "There is something that perhaps might shed light on the matter."

"Something you haven't told me?" Lethbridge dropped into the chair opposite and studied him, then pointed a long finger.

What was he? A recalcitrant child? "Is it possible an event in the past could trigger these attacks?"

"It's possible. It depends on the magnitude of the event and the outcome." The man was far too knowing. His eyes narrowed, pinning Michael to his seat. "How long have we known each other?"

And what had that to do with anything? A man was entitled to his privacy. A woman too.

Lethbridge didn't wait for his answer. "My first memory is the time Elizabeth forced you to see my father. A small accident with a ladder and a broken clavicle, unless I'm mistaken. Slates on the roof. Almost forty years ago."

Was it so long ago? Why on earth had he procrastinated until it had reached this point? "You're not mistaken."

"And we have been friends ever since."

"We have."

"In that case I think you should, for friendship and for Elizabeth's sake, tell me what the hell is going on." Lethbridge's voice reached a crescendo.

Michael pushed out of the chair; he needed a drink, a large drink. He waved the decanter in Lethbridge's direction and much to his surprise, didn't receive a lecture on consumption, but instead a nod. He splashed the amber liquid into two tumblers and handed one over.

"To friendship." He clinked Lethbridge's glass and took a long, slow pull at the whiskey, embracing its welcome warmth, and before he could change his mind said, "Elizabeth is not my sister."

Lethbridge gave a splutter, knocked back the rest of his drink, and mopped his mouth with his handkerchief. "Then who the hell is she?"

"That is the conundrum. I don't know."

"You don't know?" Lethbridge waved his glass in the air and Michael refilled it, and his own. "Start at the beginning, man, and take it slowly. It's going to take a while to sink in."

"You've heard the story of the past. I've no need to go over that again. Arriving in Australia, Hill End, and here, Maitland."

Lethbridge nodded, his eyes firmly fixed on his face as though trying to read him. From the look of his tortured frown he might have been speaking Gaelic.

"Me sister Lizzie, God rest her soul, died in a fire at Brownlow Hill, Liverpool, in 1862, the day before I set sail for Australia."

"Liverpool, the telegram Mrs. Shipton's been yammering about. The one the entire town is debating."

"Aye, that's the one. The chapel and the girls' dormitory went up in flames. Lizzie got caught inside with twenty-one others. She burned to death." The horror of it still made Michael's gorge rise. Only the whiskey held the agony back.

"Who the hell is Elizabeth?" Lethbridge repeated.

He shrugged his shoulders. "A little girl Lizzie took a shine to. They shared a bed."

"But what's her name? Where did she come from? They must have records."

"That's what I don't know, and the reason I sent a telegram to the workhouse. I hoped they could tell me, but there's a hundred-year moratorium on the release of their records. I've written to someone who might have some information. As yet I've had no response. I have to find out who she is and how she ended up in the workhouse."

"More to the point, how did she end up on a ship with you?"

"Aye, well, that'd be the bit I'm not so proud of. I was standing in line, consumed by grief and misery, waiting to get my papers checked. I gave them to the clerk, and next I knew the little mite was holding on to my hand. The bloke asked if she was my sister, and well, she looked at me like I was her savior, and so I said yes. How was anyone to know? And Lizzie wasn't going to be coming aboard. She never made it out of the dormitory." He choked back another mouthful of whiskey. By all that was holy he was a fool.

"Has she no memory of boarding ship?"

Michael shrugged his shoulders.

"You've kept it a secret from her for all these years? Surely it must have plagued you."

"Aye, it did, does, but so does the thought of losing her. Right from the very beginning all I wanted was to see her safe. It was bad enough losing Lizzie. I couldn't hand her over to the authorities, poor little mite. She had no one. I didn't even think about what I'd say to Mam and Da—the longer I left it, the harder it became." A massive sob wracked his body, the memories he'd held back for so long squeezing the core of his being.

"Take a moment, no need to rush."

Michael shook his head. Now he'd started he had to finish. He'd held it back for too long. He recounted the early years, told Lethbridge about the note waiting for him at the immigration office, how he'd left Elizabeth with the Camerons while he went in search of Mam and Da, and how he'd eventually taken her to Hill End. "I wanted her with me."

Lethbridge's eyes narrowed. "You're not going to tell me something that might be better for the confessional, because—"

"No. I've nothing to be ashamed of. Nothing the good father needs to hear. We've lived as brother and sister, nothing more."

Though he'd nearly lost her to the Chinaman. He'd behaved as though he were God and bundled her out of Hill End. It was simple jealousy, not the loathing for Orientals he'd allowed Elizabeth to believe. He couldn't bear the thought of giving her up.

"Other than the fact you kidnapped her and gave her a new identity."

"I don't look at it like that. She didn't have any family. Been dumped at the workhouse. I saved her from that dreadful place."

"Old habits . . . Sounds a bit like young Jane." Lethbridge grunted. "What name did the workhouse give Elizabeth?"

"They called her Girlie, though she wouldn't answer to it. It wasn't until we crossed the equator that she spoke more than the odd word. I gave her the doll Mam had made for Lizzie. I always thought one day she'd remember, but she hasn't. It's only recently, since the trip to the Tost and Rohu exhibition at the technical college, that matters have gone awry."

"How old was she?"

"I don't know that either. Miss Finbright, she's the one I'm trying to contact, said she wasn't yet five."

"How did she know?"

Michael reached up with his hand over his head and touched the top of his ear. "She said it wasn't until a child turned five they could touch their ear. That happened the day we crossed the equator. I told her that was her birthday, four days after Lizzie's."

Lethbridge groaned and staggered to his feet. "Didn't your embarkation papers show Lizzie's date of birth?"

"She was listed as a female child, me sister, between the age of four and seven years. The papers didn't show anyone's exact date of birth."

"Have you got any more of that whiskey?"

"I need to tell her."

"Indeed you do." Lethbridge scratched at his chin, chewed his lip, screwed his face into a frown. "Do you believe these events, these turns Elizabeth is experiencing, are sparked by some past memory?"

"I don't know, but something is going on." Michael paused. Speaking to Lethbridge had lifted the weight he'd carried for so long. "She's not her usual self. Something must have prompted it."

"Memory is a strange thing. There's not a lot any of us remember from our early childhood, and anyone who tells you differently is relying on what they've learned since, from their family or these days from photographs, not true memories. Sometimes something happens that triggers the past, but it's like a dream, faded and blurred."

"More like a nightmare in Elizabeth's case."

"True enough, given her reaction. You think it was the birds that triggered the first episode, or the paintings? Did you note anything particular about the paintings?"

"English pastoral scenes. Not my sort of thing."

"Think about how you're going to tell Elizabeth."

"I don't know how to tell her. It might make her worse."

"It may."

"She's not going to the asylum."

"Full circle." Lethbridge gulped a mouthful of whiskey. "Tell me more about these paintings."

"Nothing to tell. The exhibition was meant to be held at the technical college. Major Witherspoon extended the Tost and Rohu exhibition and failed to mention it to Timothy, so Jane offered the auction house."

"Who is Timothy?"

"The artist Marigold Penter's son. They live in England, the West Country. Her paintings are all of her local village and surroundings."

"Give me a day or two. I want to see if there's anything written up. Freud is making a mark in this area. New findings. The mind's a tricky thing. He might throw some light on the best way to reveal the truth to her."

"You'll keep it to yourself?"

"I would hope you know the answer to that." Lethbridge tossed back the remainder of his drink. "I'll see myself out."

Michael topped up his whiskey glass and sipped it slowly, savoring the flavor. How had it come to this? All he'd ever intended, from the first moment he'd set eyes on the poor little mite, was to keep her safe.

TWENTY-SIX

O h! She was sick of lying in a darkened room, tired of feeling so thoroughly exhausted, tired of the monstrous lethargy the laudanum provoked, as though she lay trapped in amber. If she could manage a decent night's sleep, matters might improve.

The moment Elizabeth closed her eyes the smell returned—birds and a bygone time forcing her to fight through the clouds of memory. She stood barefoot and shivering in the darkness. Birds flapping their wings overhead, the sound amplified, the air stinking of mildew, excrement, and fear.

Trying not to focus on the pain in her head, the rolling of her stomach, and the dryness of her throat, she rode the moment. So dark she couldn't see her own feet. Arms clamped by a pair of huge sweaty paws. Thrown through a narrow doorway into a nasty black hole. She was floating, maybe flying, tired, too tired to open her eyes. The rough stone wall hurt her head.

A door slammed.

She lurched back into the present.

Was it too much to ask for some peace and quiet? "Come."

Michael stood before her, his face creased in concern. "How're you feeling?"

"Not too bad. I'll be up soon."

"Bit late for that. Why don't I tell Lucy to bring you a tray?"

"I'm so tired of this. I feel as though I'm suffocated by a thick haze. Everything is out of reach, intangible."

Michael moved the chair closer to the bed and sat down. Most unusual. She couldn't remember him ever entering her bedroom, never mind sitting down, making himself at home. Although she couldn't ever remember being confined to her bed. The odd head cold, an off day, but nothing that required invalid status.

"I need to speak with you." His grave voice pushed aside her own concerns.

"Are you unwell?" Not the pair of them, surely. "Have you been taking your pills?"

"It's not me. I have something to tell you, something I should have told you years ago." He sat there wringing his hands, gazing down at his interlaced fingers.

For some strange reason his demeanor sent a flash of energy through her. What had he done? Gambled away their assets? Not a chance. Not without her knowing. She had everything tied up tighter than a Victorian corset. Maybe he'd found some worthy cause, got carried away, and donated every penny. She wouldn't put it past him. Heaven forbid. Or was it something to do with Jing? They never spoke of him.

She twisted the frayed red thread around her fingers under the counterpane. "Spit it out. It can't be that bad."

He cleared his throat, pulled at his cravat.

"Michael, for goodness' sake."

"How much do you remember of the past?"

The past? "Which particular part of the past?"

Her eyes flicked to the little blue-and-white china pot sitting on her bedside table. Surely he wouldn't mention Jing. As far as Michael was concerned, that was long gone, albeit the only time they'd had any sort of altercation. That and the time he'd made a ridiculously enormous donation to the Labor party—to appease his conscience, she'd always insisted, because they'd done so well for themselves. What a strange thing to ask. "My earliest memory?"

He shook his head, took a deep breath. "I haven't told you the truth."

About what? "Michael, you're frightening me."

A faint humming sound assaulted her ears, followed by a tinge of dizziness. She closed her eyes, clenched her teeth. Her world shifted, then stilled.

She snapped open her eyes. "Well?"

He sucked in a deep breath, exhaled, stretching the buttons on his waistcoat. "You are not Elizabeth Quinn. You are not my sister. Not Elizabeth Ó'Cuinn."

The atmosphere in the room swelled, taking every breath of air. "Of course I am," she gasped. "What makes you say that?"

"Elizabeth Ó'Cuinn died on September seventh, 1862."

"That's the day before we left England."

His head shot up. "You remember that?"

"I remember what you've told me. When we arrived in Sydney you left me with the Camerons and forced me to suffer thousands of lonely days." Her overly dramatic words brought a touch of a smile to his face. "You took me to see the prince and got arrested for sedition. I remember that as clearly as yesterday." She'd always prided herself on her memory. How could she not be Elizabeth Quinn? "You've made a mistake."

"No," he said softly, "it's not a mistake."

"Then who am I?" She could feel her very core unraveling, as though someone had grabbed the end of a thread and pulled, whipping her soul away.

"That I don't know. I'm sorry."

Sorry! Was that all he could say? A flash of fury ignited. "You're apologizing? You tell me I'm not the person I believe myself to be, and you are apologizing? Not the person I was yesterday, not the person I've been for the last fifty-odd years."

She shook her head, batted away a lock of hair falling over her eyes, and stared past him, through the window to the garden beyond, the roses, the life they'd built together as brother and sister, and all that time she'd been living a lie. Did he have any idea how foolish he made her feel? How hurt?

"How can I trust you? I don't know if I ever will again."

He reached for her hand and she turned from him, blocked him out as she'd never done before, not even when he'd taken her from Jing. He didn't move, just sat there waiting.

"Why did you lie? More to the point, why would a fifteen-year-old boy steal a child? Something must have happened, something I can't remember."

That provoked a slight smile, more a grimace. "I didn't steal you. There was a fire at the workhouse where you lived. Lizzie, my sister, perished. The next day the boat sailed. I had no alternative but to leave."

Lizzie? Lizzie her doll, sitting up there on the shelf where she'd sat for a lifetime of lies, gathering dust.

"Lizzie or Elizabeth?" The man was making no sense. "How did I get to be with you? A four-year-old doesn't make the decision to sail off into the wide blue yonder with a stranger. Didn't the workhouse want me?" Her voice hitched again.

"You were always headstrong."

"That's no answer and you know it, Michael Ó'Cuinn."

"I was standing in the line, on the gangplank waiting to board, my mind elsewhere and my heart broken. I handed over my papers and looked down you were next to me, grasping my hand. The bloke asked if you were my sister and I said yes."

"That was it?" It sounded foolish. "Why didn't you tell the authorities?"

"I couldn't bear the thought of returning you to that place. It was a nightmare. Cold, miserable, lonely. Reeking of death and destruction. It was too late for Lizzie, but not for you. Just when I was starting to think better of it, they found a bunch of stowaways, belted the living daylights out of them, threw one of them overboard, dragged the others off the ship in chains. I couldn't let them do that to you." He dropped his head into his hands.

She smoothed her hand over his hair and he lifted his head. "Thank you, Michael. Thank you for saving me and for looking after me." But he shouldn't have kept the truth from her. "Why didn't you tell me?"

She felt drained, empty. Why couldn't she remember? "I don't remember the workhouse, or Lizzie, or the fire, only being onboard the ship and arriving in Sydney. I'm sure I do. Or is it because you've told me? Tell me, tell me again right from the start."

He massaged his chest, right above his heart, with the heel of his hand, as though it pained him to tell her. "I told you. I was handing over the immigration papers and there you were by my side. They asked if you were my sister, and I said yes."

"It can't be that simple. How did I get there? Did you know me?" The whole idea was preposterous. Far-fetched.

"I'd met you. You and Lizzie had struck up a friendship at the workhouse."

"You must know my name, my own name."

"I don't. They called you Girlie at the workhouse, although you wouldn't answer to it. You didn't speak, except to say Lizzie's name."

He tipped his head to the doll sitting on the shelf above her dressing table, as faded and worn as she felt. "Not until we crossed the equator."

"On my birthday. My fifth birthday. Or does that belong to someone else too?"

"I gave it to you. It was the day you touched your ear."

"The day I touched my ear?" Was there nothing that belonged to her? Not her name, not her birth date, not the man she believed to be her brother.

"I'd been told when a child could reach over their head and touch their ear they were likely five years old."

"Poppycock. Something must have made me leave the workhouse and follow you."

"Do you remember the fire?"

The mere word made her inhale and she fancied she could smell smoke, and something sweet and fleshy, like Bessie's Sunday roast.

"Why didn't I die with your sister?"

He dropped his head into his hands. "I have no idea."

"You must know." How could he sit there and tell her all of this without having any answers?

"We thought Lizzie was safe. When they called out all the children's names, she answered. I helped put the fire out, but then I couldn't find her afterward. They sent me away. Told me to come back in the morning. They'd taken the girls in with the women. They said she was safe, she'd answered her name . . ."

Michael's voice faded and dulled, drowned out by the roar of flames dancing against the ink black sky, and the smell, that awful smell.

"Lizzie Ó'Cuinn. 'Lizzie!'"

Her heart stopped pumping as the moment rushed back. She'd answered, called Lizzie's name.

TWENTY-SEVEN

"Jane, come into my study." Michael grabbed at the doorframe, ignoring the sudden wave of dizziness. Seeing the pain he'd caused Elizabeth, his inability to supply her with any answers, drove him to distraction, and whiskey—more whiskey than he'd drunk in a long time.

"I'll be along in a moment." Her feet thundered on the stairs and a door slammed.

How he envied her boundless energy and fine mind. He'd tell her to cherish it, make the most of it. He hadn't appreciated his own youth, and now he felt like Methuselah. Old age had crept up, stealthily, while he wasn't looking.

Jane ground to a halt in the doorway. "Yes?"

"Come in and sit down. I have to talk to you."

Her face steadied and a small frown puckered between her eyes. "Is it Aunt Elizabeth?"

"Yes and no. It's not what you think. She's still not herself, however Lethbridge is investigating alternative treatments. I need your help." He pulled out the sheath of papers stacked in the manila folder and deposited them on the desk with a determined thump. "Have you spoken to Elizabeth lately?"

"Not since yesterday morning. I've been down at the auction house. Helping Timothy." A flush rose to her cheeks.

So that was how the land lay. Nothing like young love to bring the bloom to a girl's cheeks. "I had to give Elizabeth some unfortunate news." Wasn't that the biggest understatement of his life. Jane plopped down into the chair and pulled her feet up under her skirt. Not only a bright mind, but the flexibility of youth. It strengthened his resolve.

"I've been doing some research and I need your help."

Her head came up and she pinned him with a stare. He'd caught her attention, as he intended. "Yes?"

"I did something many years ago of which I'm not proud."

He'd never thought of himself as someone who had trouble with the truth, trouble spitting it out. He'd always taken responsibility for his actions, and now he was floundering around. Spit it out, man, spit it out.

"I'm trying to find out who Elizabeth is."

"Everyone knows Miss Elizabeth Quinn."

She'd said that once before, on the first day they'd met at the orphanage, when he'd sat stunned by her sharp inquiring mind and her similarity to Elizabeth. Was he doing the right thing? It wasn't as though he was going against Elizabeth's wishes. Jane was the closest thing they had to a daughter. He needed to be truthful with her. She should know he wasn't the man she thought him to be.

"Elizabeth Ó'Cuinn was my sister. She died in September 1862, in a fire in a workhouse in Liverpool, England."

Parched, he licked his lips and reached for the glass of whiskey, took a long slug while he studied the series of emotions playing across Jane's face.

"Then who is . . . ?" The name stuck on her lips and she gestured behind her, up the stairs to where Elizabeth lay in her bed, chasing memories she couldn't catch because he'd played God.

"I don't know."

"Does she?"

"No."

"She believes she is Elizabeth Quinn?"

"Not anymore. I told her last night."

"She's lived all her life thinking she was someone she's not? You must know who she is. How did you meet her? Where did she come from?"

For the third time he had to recount his foolish, misguided actions. He repeated the story as succinctly as he could. Jane sat, eyes trained on his face, not speaking, although he could almost hear her mind absorbing every word, lining up each fact in a neat column. When he'd finished he pushed a manila folder toward her.

She uncoiled herself from the chair and spread the contents out onto the floor, read through the immigration papers, pushed them aside, picked up the telegram, smoothed the creases, then tossed it aside, ran her finger down the list of notes, and looked up.

"Have you had a response from this Gertrude Finbright?" She waved the draft copy of his letter in the air.

"Not yet. I don't know if she's alive or dead. I thought maybe a trip to England might trigger some memory for Elizabeth, a meeting with Miss Finbright even. I hold out little hope she will have any additional information. I clearly remember the first time I saw Elizabeth. They'd called her Girlie. She wouldn't speak, wouldn't answer to that name, wouldn't tell them her own. I don't think anyone knew where she had come from."

"Lack of speech is a fairly normal reaction to a stressful event in a child that young. Dr. Freud says early infant trauma can scar a person for life. Have you got a pencil?" Jane got up from the floor and came to stand by his desk. "And a piece of paper. Let's write down everything we do know."

She cleared a space on his desk and pulled up a chair. "You don't know her exact date of birth, but we can presume toward the end of 1857."

"She must have been born in Liverpool, otherwise she wouldn't have been in the workhouse."

"No, you can't presume that. Close by, perhaps, but not necessarily Liverpool. There's nothing to back that up. You came from Ireland and ended up in Liverpool." Jane chewed the end of the pencil. "You said she didn't speak until you arrived in Sydney."

"Until we crossed the equator on the eighteenth of November."

"Her birthday. There's no specific date on these papers. Just says 'female child, four to seven years.' How did you know?"

"I didn't. I made it up. No one queried it. Why would they?"

"Did she call herself Elizabeth?"

"By then she answered to the name."

"Didn't she know that Elizabeth had died?"

"She called my sister Lizzie. We all did."

"The immigration papers say Elizabeth."

"Lizzie's baptismal name. Da was outraged, naming his daughter after a Queen of England, but Mam insisted, said if it was a new life, we needed to shake off the shackles of Ireland. It was the last thing we did together as a family before Mam and Da left. He made such a show of it all—first her baptism, then a gathering. He called it a going-away gathering and promised another when our turn came and we arrived in Australia."

"So you called her Elizabeth and she accepted that?"

His mind creaked and groaned as he thought back to the day so long ago when they'd boarded ship. "I told her we were going home."

While Jane shredded the end of her pencil, Michael poured himself another glass of whiskey. Like an old friend, it helped dull the ache in his heart. Now more than ever he regretted his foolishness; not in bringing Elizabeth to Australia—never that, they'd made a good life together—but for lying to her all this time.

"Did she have an Irish accent?"

Jane's question brought him upright. "When she first spoke? No, now that you mention it, she didn't. Softly spoken, a lilt in her voice, but no, not Irish."

"You still sound Irish. Elizabeth doesn't. She sounds, well, nothing specific, a mixture of this and that, I've always thought. Cultured. Did Lizzie have an Irish accent?"

"That she did."

"G'woam."

"I beg your pardon?"

"G'woam. What does that mean? Elizabeth cried out 'G'woam, G'woam' when she saw the birds at the technical college and at the preview."

"I've not a clue what it might mean."

Jane wrote the word on the paper, drew a large circle around it. "We'll have to find out. Is there anything else you can think of?"

"Other than the birds? No. She's never liked birds, didn't like the pigeon tree at Hill End."

"Didn't like the Tost and Rohu exhibits." Jane's eyes narrowed and she continued the infuriating tap on her teeth with the pencil. "Didn't like the preview of the paintings."

"Marigold Penter doesn't paint birds. I fail to see the link."

Michael couldn't keep up anymore; his head was hammering fit to bust. He was so tired, and his heart was galloping faster than the favorite at Randwick. He rubbed at his chest, felt in his pocket for the bottle of pills, and opened it under the desk. He slipped one under his tongue, letting it dissolve, then washed the taste away with the remains of his whiskey. No point in alarming Jane; the pain would pass, it always did.

"I've got to go down to the auction house," she said. "See if Timothy has everything he needs. I might talk to him. Maybe he'll have some ideas why his mother's paintings might have produced a reaction in Elizabeth."

"I'd rather you didn't."

"Whyever not?"

"Because I've spoken to you in confidence. It's not something that should be bandied around. Elizabeth would be devastated. In fact, I think you better let her tell you herself."

"Why don't you tell her you've told me?"

Perhaps he ought to. "Please, Jane. Help me find out who she is. She has to know."

———— ≋ ————

When Jane arrived back at the auction house, Timothy was nowhere to be seen. It left her feeling annoyed; she'd hoped he'd be waiting for her.

She lit the downstairs lamps and sat on the chair in the middle of the room. Despite the fact she'd helped hang the paintings, she still hadn't taken a good look at them, nor did she understand what it was that had upset Elizabeth.

It was obvious they were all by the same artist; not that she knew much about art, she'd been too tied up in more interesting subjects, unladylike subjects by some standards. Bookkeeping, the study of the planets, Darwin's and Freud's theories, Fibonacci and da Vinci. No one had taken much notice of the girl who sat at the back of the room behind all the men, providing she remained inconspicuous.

The paintings all showed simple outdoor scenes. No fine detail, just touches of bright color giving a fleeting impression, a glimpse of everyday village life portrayed with great intimacy. As though she were peeping into someone's innermost thoughts. Bright and vibrant and, as Timothy had told her the first time they'd met, they were better viewed from a distance.

Taking one step at a time, Jane moved along the line of pictures. A similar sky, stone walls, the same thatched cottages and winding paths. In one painting, a young man and a child walking hand in hand through a tunnel of overlapping leaves; in another, a series of covered wagons, fine dabs of red paint giving them an almost festive air, and the church, with the village in the background.

There had to be something else. She threw herself down on the seat and stared at the paintings. There had to be a pattern. Something that linked them, something that had upset Elizabeth. Then she noticed the one common factor. Somewhere in every picture was the wistful young girl in the pale dress.

She glanced at the clock. It didn't look as though Timothy was going to keep his promise. It was time she went home. Maybe Elizabeth was feeling better and they could discuss the pictures.

Twilight bathed the town. A fine mist rose from the river, bringing a chill to the air as she cruised along Church Street on her bicycle. She was late, but maybe if she was lucky, Bessie would have saved supper for her; otherwise, she'd have to make do with bread and cheese.

She tucked her bicycle inside the fence, taking great care not to disturb Elizabeth's roses, and reached for the door handle. Locked! Bloody Lucy, making sure everyone knew she was late. Jane lifted her hand to thump on the door and her fist fell away.

An ominous black satin wreath hung in the center of the door. It was a trifle faded, as though it had been there a long time, yet she'd never seen it—not on the day Michael had first invited her to tea, not in all the years she'd lived with the Quinns.

A flight of bats swirled out of the fruit trees next door as she slipped around the side of the house to the kitchen. Curtains were pulled across all the windows at the back and upstairs, and the kitchen door was firmly locked. It was never closed. Bessie went off at half cock if it wasn't kept open, still reckoned an inside kitchen was an abomination.

The bats skimmed over the house, making her muscles tense, so she slammed the palm of her hand against the door. It opened a crack. Lucy's hand shot out and pulled her into the dim interior, and her stomach turned to lead.

To steady herself, she rested against the wall. Bessie sat at the table, her head in her hands, making some sort of retching sound. Then she saw Lucy's face. "What's going on? Why are you crying?"

"It's the master, Mr. Quinn." Lucy wiped her index finger under her nose, then down her dirty pinafore.

The bats, still roosting in the back of her mind, took flight. "What about him?"

Bessie lifted her head, her face the color of uncooked pastry and her hands shaking. "Dead." She buried her face again and her sobs rose to a crescendo.

"Dead? Where is he?" She pushed past the table and headed for the door. What a load of nonsense. She'd only been talking to him a few hours earlier.

"In his study." Lucy tugged at her arm. "You can't go in."

"Of course he's not dead; he just needs his pills. Have you called Dr. Lethbridge?"

"He's with Miss Quinn now."

"Why is he with Aunt Elizabeth? Why isn't he with Michael?"

"Because he's dead!" Bessie hissed the words. "Haven't you got an ounce of compassion in you? Stop asking questions. It's all you ever do."

"He's fine. I was with him earlier—" She bit off the words. If no one was going to take care of Michael, she'd have to. A little pill from the small brown bottle in his top right-hand pocket, under his tongue, chased down with a nip of whiskey, would see him right.

A strange buzzing filled her ears. She shook her head and shot through the door into the morbid dusk blanketing the house.

Creeping along the hall, hand on the chair rail, she barreled straight into Dr. Lethbridge.

"Ah, Jane. Elizabeth is going to need some help. I've given her something to make her sleep; however, it will be a while before it takes effect."

Elizabeth! Why was it all about Elizabeth? What about Michael? She'd never liked Lethbridge, especially after her bout of chicken pox when he'd made her bathe in potassium permanganate. It had turned her skin a strange brown color and made all the blisters itch and pop. She scratched at the small hole in her forehead where the first blister had erupted. She hadn't been able to resist picking off the scab.

"Michael needs his pills." She tilted her head toward the study door, firmly closed as always, but a waft of tobacco and whiskey seeped out.

She raised her hand to the doorknob.

"No!" Lethbridge's fingers tightened around her hand. A sinking feeling sent her stomach plummeting.

"Go and sit with Elizabeth. She needs you. The undertakers, Mr. Fry and his brother, will be here soon, and when they've finished you can see Michael."

"I want to talk . . ." To her horror her voice cracked and her eyes overflowed, tears streaming down her face.

"He's gone, my dear. There's nothing you can do. His heart."

"What about his pills?" There couldn't be anything wrong with Michael's heart, except perhaps it was too big, full of a compassion she didn't always understand. "He wasn't sick." She couldn't remember Michael ever taking to his bed, not even when he was laid low by the chills and fevers the previous winter.

"He wasn't a man to complain, but he was suffering from chest pains, indicative of congestive heart failure. I had prescribed amyl nitrate, which he reported reduced the severity. He was not a young man."

"He was not an old man."

"I'm so sorry. He was a good man, one of the best." Lethbridge gave her shoulder a squeeze. "Go to Elizabeth, she needs you."

She counted every one of the stairs and the fifteen paces along the landing to Elizabeth's bedroom. Her knock wasn't answered so she opened the door and eased inside.

As in every other room in the house, the curtains were pulled, but a sliver of moonlight breached the darkness, showing a mound in Elizabeth's bed. What was she supposed to do? Jane knew her failings—she never said the right thing at the right time. She was the last person Elizabeth would want. Settling for the safety of silence, she dragged the chair closer to the bed.

Now what? Comfort. Soothing pats. That's what Timothy had done for her.

She reached out her hand and tentatively touched Elizabeth's shoulder. Once, twice. The mound under the blankets didn't move. Was that a good sign, or bad? For want of anything else, she continued the pats a little longer.

Elizabeth made some sort of a noise, halfway between a hiccup and a sob, and her head appeared above the eiderdown, her face devoid of color. Nothing like the real Elizabeth, whose upswept chignon never had a hair out of place. Her brilliant eyes were opaque with grief. Her pupils dulled to a sort of storm cloud color, the whites lost in a puddle of reddened tears.

"No one to hold my hand now." Her gaze remained fixed on the window as she spoke, but the fragility in her voice touched Jane, and when Elizabeth lifted her hand from beneath the sheets she reached out and took hold of it.

Elizabeth's fingers tightened around hers, squeezed hard. "Dr. Lethbridge said you'd fall asleep soon."

Elizabeth let out another heaving sigh and her eyelids fluttered. Jane sat as the moon rose above the treetops, the bones in her hand grating against each other, until Elizabeth's grip loosened and her mouth became slack.

For a moment, Jane feared it was all too much for Elizabeth and she, too, might die, but the odds on that seemed more outlandish than John's race-day favorites. Finding some sort of consolation in the familiarity of the form guide, she reran the odds in her head while Elizabeth's hand rested in her own and her regular breaths continued. It wasn't until the door creaked open a fraction and Lucy's tear-streaked face appeared that she extricated her hand and tiptoed away from the bed.

"Bessie said you're to come down and have a cup of tea. There's work to be done before morning and she needs everyone's help. The doc said Miss Quinn'd sleep 'til morning."

———— ≈ ————

It wasn't until the following morning when Jane entered the dining room that reality finally hit. Instead of a neatly laid table and breakfast on the sideboard, Michael's body lay in an open casket on the table and the cloying scent of lilies filled the room.

She bolted, slamming the door behind her, and skittered out to the kitchen. There was some bread and jam on the table next to a cold teapot. Where was everyone? She lifted the curtain and peered out into the yard where Lucy stood over the boiling hot copper—one of Macbeth's witches, stirring a horrible dark brew.

"There you are." Bessie appeared, arms full of shiny black material. "I've got a job for you."

"What's Lucy doing?"

"Tsk, tsk. For someone so smart you can be mightily stupid sometimes. Dyeing. Here. Take this." She pushed the material into Jane's arms. "I want you to thread a new wreath for the front door. Had to borrow that one from the good father."

"Can't we get one from the auction house, or ask the undertakers?" She hadn't the vaguest idea how to thread a wreath.

"Would have thought you knew they didn't sell things like that at the auction house. You spend enough time down there."

The comment didn't merit an answer. Her mind whirled faster than Lucy's evil brew. She'd never had anything to do with death, never thought much about it. She wanted to ask Dr. Lethbridge about this amyl nitrate—perhaps it had caused Michael's death. He hadn't seemed the remotest bit sick—preoccupied by the conundrum of Elizabeth's identity but not sick.

"You get on with that wreath. None of us can set foot outside until we've got something respectable to wear."

She hated black, and she was sure Elizabeth did too. But she was nowhere to be seen; her door had been firmly closed when Jane had tiptoed past.

"I'll be back in a moment." She scooted down the hallway and eased into Michael's study. The familiar aroma brought tears to her eyes. Papers covered every surface, books stacked in piles on the floor, rolls of maps . . . a treasure trove. She stayed for a while absorbing the essence of the man, of the room, so different from the ruthless organization of Elizabeth's desk. So much about him she'd never appreciated.

She snatched back a sob and picked up the manila folder containing the papers Michael had shown her, *in confidence.* The phrase settled in her mind. Better these weren't left lying around for everyone to see. She'd keep them safe until Elizabeth saw fit to tell her secret. It was the least she could do for Michael. He'd done so much for her. If only she hadn't taken off to find Timothy, who hadn't even bothered to appear, Michael might still be alive.

Closing the door behind her, she scooted up the two flights of stairs to her attic bedroom and pushed the folder under her mattress.

On the way down she stopped outside Elizabeth's bedroom, hovered for a moment, spotted the breakfast tray sitting untouched outside the door. She picked it up and took it back to the kitchen, where Bessie shook her head and exchanged the tray for a pile of slippery black satin.

———≈———

For two days silence enveloped the house, thick enough to slice. No one spoke. Numerous cups of tea were handed out but nothing much to eat. Not a breath of fresh air. Nothing but the all-enveloping cloud of misery. It couldn't go on forever, wouldn't, because when Bessie finally permitted speech, she informed them the funeral was scheduled for two days hence and would be a huge affair. The auction house would remain closed—even for receiving goods, which Jane wasn't too sure Michael would be pleased about. Two of the bigwigs from the Labor party were coming by train from Sydney, never mind the constant stream of people who had been in and out of the house for the prayer vigil. Father Cochran had as good as moved in, and still Elizabeth hadn't made an appearance.

It wasn't until the morning of the funeral that Elizabeth finally came downstairs. Jane walked past the dining room and instead of Michael's casket, found Elizabeth sitting at the head of the table, swathed in black, with a piece of toast in front of her and a cup of her favorite perfumed tea.

She had no idea what to do or say, so she buttoned her lip, helped herself to the most symmetrical eggs she could find, and remembered to use her napkin. Elizabeth didn't speak. Not by so much as a twitch did she acknowledge Jane's presence.

———≈———

As the funeral procession wound its way along High Street toward the cathedral, Jane kept her eyes firmly latched onto Elizabeth's straight back. Nobody walked beside her, and when Bessie encouraged Jane to go and take her arm, Elizabeth's withering look as good as singed her. After all, she wasn't family. She might live in the Quinns' house, but she wasn't *family*. Neither she nor Elizabeth had a family, no matter what the rest of Maitland Town believed.

Crowds packed the sides of the road. She caught sight of so many faces she knew, their names too; the names she wrote on their pay slips every week. She always divided the little brown envelopes into two piles: those who, like her, had come through the orphanage, and those Michael and Elizabeth had employed from the myriad people who descended on Maitland once they'd realized their plans of finding fortune on the goldfields were nothing but an unrewarding dream.

The sun beat down on her head, unseasonably hot for May, and behind the monstrous black veil Bessie had insisted she wear, sweat trickled down the sides of her face and pooled at her collar. If they'd turned right instead of left outside the house, they'd be at the cathedral by now, but for some reason that escaped her it was necessary to parade through the town. Two miles and one hundred and seventy-six yards. At normal walking pace it would take forty-two minutes; at the rate they were traveling much, much longer than two thousand, five hundred and twenty seconds of sweat-soaked agony. Michael wouldn't have wanted that.

"So everyone can pay their respects," Bessie had assured her when she'd questioned the sanity of the idea. It showed how well Bessie knew Michael. She let out a puff and the veil billowed like an enraged thundercloud.

The cathedral was packed to the gunnels, and Father Cochran droned on and on . . .

"Arriving in Maitland with his sister, Elizabeth, Michael set about building a reputable business, an aim he achieved with a great deal of success and always to the benefit of others, becoming one of the founders of the Maitland Mutual Building Society and a member of the board of directors. He was one of the largest landowners in the district, and has for many years been prominently identified with all movements having for their object the welfare and progress of Maitland, particularly in the areas of flood mitigation, the railway and tramway extension, and the great campaign for federation. He will be sadly missed . . ."

Jane fought the overwhelming desire to leap out of her seat and speak up. Nothing Father Cochran had said was incorrect, but he'd somehow neatly forgotten to mention Elizabeth's contribution to Michael's success. Jane had no idea he was one of the largest landowners in the district. She'd simply taken everything for granted. She squirmed, wishing she'd taken the time to ask more questions. He and Elizabeth were a closed book as far as their earlier life was concerned. If Father Cochran was to be believed, Michael's soul would be winging its way to heaven on gilded wings.

———— ≈ ————

The cortege slowed as they entered Campbell Hill Cemetery, and everyone jostled for a position around the gaping great hole in the ground. Father Cochran intoned some Latin and threw around his incense burner, making Jane's eyes water and her throat scratchy. The next thing she knew, they'd lowered the coffin into the ground and she was flinching as everyone threw a handful of dirt on top of poor Michael.

She didn't hold with all this religious nonsense about life after death. Once you were dead, you were dead. They half admitted it with their ashes-to-ashes business, so she couldn't see why they'd rattle on about rebirth and sitting on the right hand of the Lord.

"Come on, Jane, it's time we left. We're needed back at the house for the wake. There's plenty to do." Bessie handed her a large white handkerchief. "Dry your eyes now."

Jane mopped away the moisture that covered her cheeks.

"John's brought the auction house van to give us a lift back to the house so we get there first, and Miss Quinn's going in the big car with those political men."

Once they reached the house they piled out of the van and Bessie marched right up to the front door, slipped the key into the lock, and walked in. "You and Lucy go around the back."

Lucy stuck her nose in the air. "Well, pardon me, Miss Hoity-

Toity thinks she'll be putting on airs and graces now Mr. Quinn's gone."

Jane didn't want to think about Lucy's comment. It had only occurred to her when they were standing around the grave that there might be changes. Maybe Elizabeth wouldn't want her now. She tossed her veil over her head and let the sun shine down on her face. Why would that happen? It wouldn't. Once she'd finished her bookkeeping course, the auction house had been her responsibility. Elizabeth stuck to her charity work these days, and besides, she'd made a promise to Michael to find out Elizabeth's origins. It was a promise she intended to keep.

"Come on. Get a move on." Lucy flattened her against the door and stomped into the kitchen.

Jane didn't want to follow her inside the dark house with its overpowering smell of lilies and naphthalene. She'd prefer to stay outside. She sank down onto the step and rested her hands on the sandstone worn into a smooth parabola from the countless feet scurrying in and out of the kitchen. Perhaps if she reckoned the depth and the wear rate of the sandstone she could fathom how many people had walked up the steps since the house was built. Pleased to have something other than death and misery crowding her mind, she closed her eyes and tilted her face to the sun.

"'Scuse me, miss."

She snapped her eyes open.

A young boy stood shuffling from leg to leg, waving a small folded piece of paper under her nose. "This the Quinns' place? I knocked on the front door. No one answered."

"That's because the house is in mourning."

"I got to leave this. For Miss Quinn." He shoved a small, thin package into her hands and took off.

Jane turned it over, examining the carefully tied string making four neat rectangles against the buff-colored paper. She ran her finger around the edge. An envelope of sorts, no glue holding it in place, no name except for a string of neatly inscribed characters that for some reason made her think of Elizabeth's abacus. She lifted the paper to her nose and inhaled the lovely fragrance, tugged at the string. Nestled inside lay a small piece of paper with a golden metallic rectangle in the center. She ran her hand over the smooth, shiny surface, then carefully replaced it inside the envelope.

"Come on. Inside. We've got work to do." Bessie glared at her through a crack in the door.

Jumping to her feet she tucked the package into her pocket. "I need to see Aunt Elizabeth."

"She's not back from the cemetery yet. And I need some help with these sandwiches."

TWENTY-EIGHT

They were all there, the townsfolk, the gossips, and the not-so-gossips, drinking tea and eating the mountains of cakes and sandwiches as though it were the highlight of their week—year even.

Jane could still feel Michael's presence, the smell of his whiskey and his sandalwood soap cutting through the sugary treats, stale sweat, and naphthalene.

"Miss Quinn."

Jane started at the drawling masculine voice—not Michael, not Lethbridge. She looked over her shoulder and into the eyes of a vaguely familiar, gaunt-faced man, nursing one of Michael's Waterford crystal tumblers full of whiskey.

"My condolences. Your father was a fine man." No, not that again. Not today.

Timothy quirked some sort of a grin at her from across the room; she wasn't sure if it was good or bad.

"Who are you?"

"We met at the gallery in Sydney. Langdon-Penter. Timothy's father."

It seemed so long ago, a day she would cherish now that Michael was gone even if the pompous man in front of her had infuriated him. "Mr. Quinn was not my father. I am an orphan, at least I was until he rescued me. My name's Jane. Jane Piper."

What might have been a frown wrinkled his forehead "Your adopted father perhaps would be a better way of putting it."

She studied his face, looked for something of Timothy; certainly not the steely eyes, she thought, as the soft gray of Timothy's gaze fixed on her across the room. "Mr. Quinn was my benefactor."

"Another of his good works." Langdon-Penter took a swig of whiskey and held it in his mouth.

"I don't see myself in that light."

"The man was well known for his altruism. The Labor party, the fight for working hours, the Benevolent Society, the orphanage. So many boards, so much time spent on the betterment of others. Especially during the depression, one of the largest landowners in the area. Not bad for a poor immigrant Irish boy."

He might have been repeating Father Cochran's eulogy, although she hadn't seen him—or Timothy—at the church. Oh, how she wished Michael was standing here beside her. "Were you at the funeral?"

"My wife and I arrived in Maitland early this morning." He took another mouthful and looked around the room. "They'll be reading the will later. You'll be a wealthy woman before long."

The odious man! Why would he say that? "I don't expect to inherit anything of Mr. Quinn's estate. It will pass to his sister." Who wasn't his sister at all, and at that moment was standing across the room looking more than a little forlorn. "Please excuse me, Miss Quinn needs me."

Placing her teacup on the table, she turned her back on him. How could someone as personable as Timothy have such an obnoxious father?

"Aunt Elizabeth." She laid her hand on the frail black-clad sleeve, felt a tremor. "Would you like me to take you upstairs? This must be more than you can stand." It was more than Jane could. She'd never

THE GIRL IN THE PAINTING

attend another funeral unless it was her own; wouldn't have much say in that.

"I think I would, Jane. I think I would. First I must make my apologies."

"There's no need to do that. I'm sure everyone will understand, and if they don't, I'll come back and explain."

"Very well. Thank you. I am tired."

"Did Dr. Lethbridge leave you some more of the sleeping draught?"

"I don't like it. It makes me feel . . ." Her voice cracked and she cleared her throat.

Poor Elizabeth, first finding out she wasn't who she thought she was, and then Michael dying before they could learn any more information. Jane would solve the mystery. She must. If she could reduce the facts to a simple equation, she knew she'd find the solution. "Yes?"

"Disorientated. Odd. And the dreams, I have strange dreams."

"Let me help you upstairs."

Jane opened the door to Elizabeth's darkened bedroom, the curtains still drawn as befitting a house in mourning, and led her to the bed. "Can I get you anything?"

"No, I'd like to rest." Elizabeth eased herself onto the top of the bedcovers. She reached out to the bedside table and picked up the blue-and-white jar. She pulled it close to her chest, lifted the lid, and withdrew a twisted piece of red thread. Once she'd wrapped it around her little finger, she replaced the lid and traced the collection of black symbols on the front of the jar.

Jane's hand shot to her pocket. The envelope was still there, the writing similar. She pulled it out. "Someone delivered this after we got back from the cemetery. I wasn't sure who it was for."

Elizabeth extended a shaking hand.

"Is it for you?"

A faraway smile lifted the corners of Elizabeth's pale lips. "I believe it might be." She pulled off the string and removed the sliver of paper.

"What is it?"

"A tribute from one man to another, a sign of acknowledgment." She rested back on the pillows, closed her eyes, a smile on her lips and the red thread wound tight around her little finger.

Biting back the surge of curiosity, Jane hovered by the bedside. After a few moments Elizabeth opened her eyes. "There's a box of matches in the dressing table drawer. Would you bring them to me, please?"

What in heaven's name . . .

By the time she'd retrieved the matches, Elizabeth had the blue jar open on her lap and was folding the golden square of paper and its backing neatly into a little package. She dropped it into the jar and held out her hand for the matches. She struck one and dropped it into the jar. The paper caught, and the scent of burning tinged with incense and sweet ginger filled the room.

"What are you doing?" She'd burn the house down. If the jar tipped and set the bedcover alight they'd be toast, although the tears streaming down Elizabeth's cheeks might go some way to extinguishing the flames.

"I'm sending it to Michael. It's a gift for the afterlife. Joss money."

What hocus pocus! Hell and damnation. She'd have to call Lethbridge. Where was he when needed? Downstairs helping himself to Michael's whiskey with Mr. Langdon-Penter?

She took two steps to the door and stopped. She couldn't call Lethbridge. If he saw Elizabeth like this she'd be up the river and off to the asylum before dawn.

"Go downstairs and make my apologies. See if you can get everyone to leave."

Elizabeth's steady voice broke into Jane's thoughts and she whipped around. No sign of tears, the blue-and-white jar with its lid firmly in place sitting on the bedside table, and only the scent of ginger and incense to prove she hadn't dreamed Elizabeth's strange behavior.

———≈———

Elizabeth lay back on the pillows, inhaling the scent of the past. Her hands cradling the tattered *carte de visite* she kept in her bedside drawer, Jing gazing down at her with such a look of love in his eyes. She had no need to look at the picture, every moment of their time together remained as clear as crystal.

How did he know of Michael's passing? Where was he? So many times she'd wanted to try to contact him, beg his family to allow her to write to him. He wouldn't have wanted her to do that. Michael had told her Jing had promised to sever all communication, but with Michael's passing, did that promise hold?

She still had the note Jing had left with his suanpan. Before they'd set out for Maitland she'd taken it to Ah Chu and asked him to translate it. She found out Mr. Li had lied by omission. The note hadn't only said the suanpan was hers. It had said that his heart was hers and he was leaving the suanpan because it was something she could keep forever.

Jing could help her make sense of the swirling confusion in her mind. Maybe he knew something of her past. Something Michael hadn't told her, something she couldn't remember.

The knock on her door made her jump. If it was Jane back again, or worse, that dreadful girl Lucy with her starched apron and knowing smile, she'd scream. "What is it?"

Lethbridge's face appeared around the door. "I thought I'd check on you before I left. Make sure you had everything you needed."

Everything except the one thing no one seemed able to provide. "I have, thank you." She slipped the *carte de visite* into the drawer and gestured to the bottle of laudanum.

"It will help you sleep."

Exactly what she didn't want to do. She wanted to make sense of the swirling confusion in her mind. She'd never felt so adrift, not since that dreadfully embarrassing episode at the technical college, and then at least she'd still had Michael. What she wouldn't give to step back in time.

Surely Lethbridge's diagnosis wasn't correct. *Women of a certain age.* What a load of poppycock. She'd overheard his suggestions for a rest cure. Rest cure! Rubbish. He was talking about the asylum. She knew all about it. A dreadful place. It was somehow slightly ironic that she should have begun her days in a workhouse, an institution, and now she might end them in another. Well, there was no Michael to save her. She was going to have to take matters into her own hands.

Lethbridge hovered over her like a persistent fly, offering a glass of his mind-numbing panacea. She turned her head away. "I don't want it. I want to talk."

He had the good sense to put the glass down and draw up a chair. "Of course."

"I don't believe I am losing my mind."

"I have never suggested that you were. Michael's passing is enough to upset anyone, and the stress of your turns . . ." He cleared his throat.

Her *dilemma*. She much preferred that word. After all, it was a dilemma—an embarrassing or perplexing situation. "What do you know about memory? Jane mentioned a Mr. Freud . . ."

"It's a difficult field. Many people doubt the validity of the new research."

"But childhood memory. How far back do people remember?"

"Most childhood memories recede, however something unpleasant can manifest as a phobia. Your fear of birds is a case in point."

"Surely if something traumatic had happened I would remember it." Michael had talked about the fire at the workhouse, and though she didn't recall it, she had no overwhelming fear of fire. The local bushfires outside Maitland had hardly been pleasant and the town had filled with smoke, but they hadn't sent her into this mind-numbing paralysis like the detestable birds.

"Repression is a protective mechanism," said Lethbridge. "The unpleasant memories are pushed out of your consciousness until a later event—the trip to the Tost and Rohu exhibition, in your case—elicits a response."

"That doesn't account for my reaction at Mrs. Penter's preview. There were no birds in her paintings." For a fleeting moment the beating cloud of swooping birds dipped and shifted in her mind. Perhaps it was time for another dose of laudanum.

"My feeling is that something happened to you in the first three, maybe four years of your life . . ."

He paused as if waiting for her to admit some guilty secret. She didn't want to be someone other than Elizabeth Quinn. She liked being Elizabeth Quinn, and now she was no one. She didn't even know her birth name, for goodness' sake. If she wanted his help she was going to have to tell him everything, as much as she didn't want to. It seemed so wrong to slander Michael, now that he was no longer able to explain himself. This aversion to birds had to have been caused by some event she couldn't recollect.

"Freud's observations indicate that not only do we not remember anything from birth to three years, we also have a spotty recollection of anything occurring from three to seven years of age. There are various theories as to why this occurs: some believe that language development is important, that the ability to speak helps us cement memories."

"Lethbridge, may I tell you something in the strictest confidence?"

"Of course, doctor-patient privilege is no different from that of the confessional. I would have hoped you knew that."

"This is difficult because not only does it affect me, but also Michael, his memory."

She expected her words to cause some sort of a reaction, some spark of interest. Instead, the man sat there, arms folded, waiting.

"I am not who I seem."

Still he didn't react. For heaven's sake, was she signing her own admission certificate? She clamped her lips tight and turned to the window.

The touch of his fingers on the back of her hand made her jump. "Elizabeth, Michael told me."

The air whooshed out of her lungs in an embarrassing display of relief. "So you won't think that these turns are an indication of my doolally status?"

"No, Elizabeth, no, I don't. Mind you, I have never thought that you were *doolally*, simply overwrought and suffering as many women of your age do. Nostalgia is a real complaint."

"Since Michael told me, I am firmly convinced that my . . ." she paused, "*dilemma* is related to something in my past, something that occurred before I met Michael, before I can remember."

He gave her hand another pat. "In that case, I think we should make a date to revisit these occurrences, speak in depth about them, but not, however, until you have had the opportunity to mourn Michael. No matter whether he was your biological brother or not, he was your closest family. You need time to grieve and allow yourself to recover."

"I have to admit that my fear is selfish; I am worried about my reputation. The entire town knows me as Elizabeth Quinn, Michael's sister. The thought of the ensuing gossip when they realize I have been living with a man who wasn't my brother, wasn't in any way related to me, terrifies me. Everyone will think the worst. And what of Jane? Her reputation will be ruined. She'll have no hope of marriage, having lived under our roof."

She ran her hand over the counterpane. She hated to be cowardly, but the thought of the rumors, the sly behind-hand remarks, made her sick at heart. She contemplated her drumming fingers and stifled a moan.

"There is no need for anyone to know anything you don't wish to tell them. I can assure you, they won't be hearing it from me." He handed her the small glass. "Drink this. It will help you sleep, and when you feel more yourself we will discuss it further. In the meantime, I shall continue to peruse Mr. Freud's writings."

He rubbed his hands together as though he relished the opportunity. Perhaps she should have taken notice of Jane when she mentioned this Mr. Freud. Perhaps it wasn't the modernistic claptrap she had first thought.

She brought the glass to her lips and swallowed. The drug offered its release almost before Lethbridge had closed the door.

TWENTY-NINE

Jane had only intended to spend a few minutes sitting quietly outside on her favorite cane chair before she went and put an end to the interminable round of tea and sandwiches and whiskey. Where had Langdon-Penter gotten the whiskey? How dare he help himself? He must have been into Michael's study.

"I wanted to offer my condolences."

She looked up into Timothy's eyes, full of sympathy and caring, unlike his odious father, and offered a wan smile. "Thank you."

"Mr. Quinn was a fine man. I'm so very sorry."

Yes, he was a fine man, but how would Timothy know that? Or his father, for that matter? Perhaps he was being polite, offering platitudes. At least he wasn't asking about inheritances.

"Had your father met Michael before the exhibition?"

He scratched his head. "I don't know."

"Has your father ever been to Australia before?"

This was most peculiar. Jane had the distinct impression Timothy wasn't telling her the truth. She remembered Michael introducing himself after his dreadful faux pas about the painting, and it had seemed as though Langdon-Penter had known who Michael was.

"No, this is our first visit, Father's first visit."

"I didn't realize Michael was so well known. He made a name with his work for the Labor party and workers' rights, but I didn't know his reputation extended beyond Australia."

Timothy shrugged his shoulders. "Does it matter? It all turned out for the best. The exhibition at the auction house has come up well. Mother is thrilled." He gazed at her with his strange eyes, like his father's but muted, a softer gray that darkened with concern. "I'm sorry, I'm being thoughtless. With Mr. Quinn's passing we will postpone the exhibition, a gesture of respect."

She hadn't given it a moment's thought. Was that what one did? Would the auction house stay closed? What would happen to everyone who worked there? There were no auctions scheduled for the next couple of weeks because of the exhibition, but John would expect to be paid, as would Mrs. Cohen, and there would be goods coming in and the deliverymen would need to be paid.

"No. We'll stay open." Michael wouldn't want the people who worked for him to be short; whole families depended on their income. "We'll make a few adjustments in memory of Michael." Take his portrait from the dining room and set it down at the auction house, maybe drape some of Bessie's black material around the frame.

"Are you sure it wouldn't be an imposition?"

"The invitations to the opening have gone out, advertisements to Newcastle and Singleton and in the *Maitland Mercury*. The weekend will be your busiest time. No, we will stay open and the exhibition will go ahead."

There. She'd made her first independent decision. Elizabeth was in no frame of mind to do it. Besides, Jane wanted the opportunity to ask Mr. Langdon-Penter some more questions. Something didn't sit right.

The following morning Jane left well before breakfast. The scent of Michael's whiskey still hung in the air, and the heavy melancholy permeating the house was more than she could bear. There was little point in waiting for Bessie to make breakfast. They'd been up until all hours cleaning after everyone left, and even then, Jane hadn't been able to sleep. Her notebook was minus most of its pages and the floor of her room covered in tattered pieces of paper.

She didn't understand Michael's sudden revelation about Elizabeth's background. Why now? But it was too late for him to answer any questions. She was going to have to solve the puzzle. It would be her tribute to Michael. A way of thanking him for all he had done for her. She would sort out this mess.

Except that she couldn't. She had all these facts scattered through her mind and nothing added up. Elizabeth's strange behavior over the scrap of gold paper had frightened her. Who set light to a condolence letter? Well, it was hardly a condolence letter, simply a piece of paper covered with Chinese symbols. Chinese writing. Chinese gold. And what had a display of taxidermied birds and Mrs. Penter's paintings have in common? Nothing, except Elizabeth's reaction and that strange wail. *G'woam. G'woam.*

She wheeled her bicycle around to the back of the auction house and propped it against the wall. The door was unlocked. She'd like to meet Mrs. Penter; she hadn't seen her at the wake with Mr. Penter and Timothy.

Standing in the middle of the room, she turned slowly. The exhibition looked magnificent. There was nothing the Penters could complain about, and the opening would give Mrs. Witherspoon and her band of gossipmongers something different to occupy their empty heads.

It wasn't until she'd completed two full turns of the room that Jane spotted a tall, spare woman in a plain navy dress in the corner of the room adjusting one of the paintings. There was something familiar in her bearing.

When she turned, Jane realized her mistake. She'd never seen her before.

The woman smiled and held out her hand. "Marigold Penter."

She was nothing like Jane had imagined. She would stand head and shoulders above her husband and she had an almost regal bearing.

Jane took her hand. "I'm sorry I haven't had time to introduce myself. I'm Jane Piper."

"Not at all. I understand. It's such a difficult time. We lost my mother not long ago. I feel responsible for adding to Miss Quinn's pain. I do hope she is . . ." Her words petered out.

"Timothy tells me you're happy for my exhibition to open. It's kind of you, but if you and Miss Quinn feel it would be disrespectful, I understand."

"No. The exhibition must go ahead." Hopefully she spoke for Elizabeth too.

"Is that your decision to make?"

A streak of anger flashed through her and she drew herself up to her full height. "Indeed it is. I have been running the auction house since Mr. Quinn began campaigning for the Labor party. The decision rests with me."

Not the truth—she'd always asked Michael's opinion in the past, but he wasn't here now, and Elizabeth wasn't in a fit state to consider the matter.

Mrs. Penter's face broke into a conciliatory smile. "I beg your pardon. I constantly complain about my husband interfering in my business affairs and here I am doing the same. Thank you."

Jane shrugged her words aside. "Mrs. Penter, could I ask you a few questions about your paintings?"

"Please, call me Marigold, and yes, of course. I'd be delighted."

Jane made a quick circuit of the room and came to rest in front of the picture of the church. "This is the painting that was displayed at the technical college."

"Yes, Timothy thought it would be better here with my other work. It's called *The Village Church*. The National Gallery has made an offer."

"Can you tell me about it?"

"As the title says, it's the view of the village church from the hillside. St. Mary the Virgin. The church dates back to the thirteenth century, but it was rebuilt in the sixteenth."

"I noticed there's always a girl somewhere in each of your paintings, sometimes hardly visible, indistinct, yet always there."

"The paintings do tell a story. My story."

Marigold's gentle tone made Jane feel as though she were about to be led down a secret pathway.

"So the girl is you?"

She gave no response, simply moved to the next picture—a figure sitting in the window staring out at a tree covered in blossom.

"She looks so very, very lonely."

"She was never alone, although she felt lonely."

Marigold's words intrigued her. She wanted to learn more. She could almost hear Elizabeth tutting in her ear, telling her not to ask questions, not to be so invasive. To hell with it, her curiosity was aroused. "It took me a while to find the other girl in this one. She's here behind the tree, as though she's hiding."

"Very perceptive." Marigold's lips formed a tight line as though Jane had hit a nerve.

"Why is she hiding?"

Marigold sat down on the bench with a sigh. "She's watching from afar."

Sweat prickled the nape of her neck. "It looks too idyllic for anything sinister to happen."

"One never knows. I wanted to portray a sense of curiosity coupled with the fear of the unknown."

When Jane turned from the painting, Marigold's eyes had filled with tears. She'd done it. Asked too many questions. "I'm sorry. I didn't mean to upset you."

Marigold dashed a tear away and smiled. "Excuse me. I painted this picture after my mother died." She pointed to another picture that Jane hadn't paid much attention to before. An older woman sitting in a chair under the same apple tree, in her lap a piece of embroidery, but where was the girl, the girl who was always in the painting?

Jane moved closer. "I can't see the girl in this one."

"You're observant, my dear. Most people take each picture as they find it. They don't see the pattern in them. There is no girl in this painting. She's gone."

"And the old woman accepts that she's gone."

"Gave up hope." Marigold shot to her feet. "Please excuse me." Without another word she left, head down, almost running.

Jane let out a sigh. She desperately wanted to ask more questions, but she could hardly chase Marigold down the street.

Once she'd made a final round of the exhibition, checking each painting for the girl, making notes on a scrap of paper she'd found in John's office, she ran upstairs and put on the kettle. She needed to think, needed a bigger piece of paper. Something nagged at the back of her mind, something she couldn't place.

Thank goodness for the new kettle. It heated the water so much faster. As she sipped the black tea, her tummy let out a huge rumble. Breakfast. Of course, she'd forgotten she'd had no breakfast. She burrowed into the cupboard under the sink and came out with a half-eaten packet of soggy VoVos. She dunked one into the tea, watched the little bits of coconut twist and swirl, and pulled out her pencil and a clean sheet of paper.

What was it? The elusive thought she couldn't trap?

"I saw you cycling down the road. I thought you'd g'woam."

Everything stilled and the hairs on her arms raised as Jane lifted her head. Timothy stood silhouetted in the doorstep. "What did you say?"

"I said I saw you cycling down the road and I thought you'd g'woam."

"Say it more slowly."

He ambled through the door, half a frown marring his forehead and a bit of a grin tipping the corner of his mouth. "G'woam . . ."

His accent broadened a rolling sound that usually made her feel warm and comfortable. Now she was icy cold.

All the hairs on her arms leapt to attention. *"G'woam?"*

"Go . . . home." He enunciated every sound, his accent more like his father's than ever before.

"That's not what you said. You said 'g'woam.'"

He shrugged. "It's hard to hear the accent you grew up with."

She snatched a breath, eased the words between her lips. "Where was that?"

He swept his hand behind him, indicating the exhibition downstairs. "The West Country. A little village nestling below Ham Hill, deep in the Somerset countryside where it's been for the last . . . God only knows how many centuries. Since the beginning of time. Norton-sub-Hamdon. Five miles shy of Yeovil, a million miles from civilization."

That was it. The word was English, spoken with a Somerset accent.

Jane scooped up the pieces of paper, then shot down the stairs and belted along the road on her bicycle, her legs pumping the pedals so hard her thighs burned. She needed a map, a detailed map of England. She'd left poor Timothy standing in the middle of the room with no explanation. She couldn't tell him without revealing Elizabeth's *dilemma*, and she'd promised Michael she wouldn't talk about it. Besides, she needed some time to process the information. She skidded to a halt outside the School of Arts, threw her bicycle down on the footpath, and ran up the steps.

"Slow down, miss." Mrs. Peabody slammed her pudgy finger against her mouth and hissed. "I've got the fossil books you requested here. No need to go and disturb everyone."

"I need to look something up."

Walking as fast as she could, she slipped around the corner into the reference section. She found section 910—Geography and Travel. Thank the Lord for Melvil Dewey. Numbers always held the answer.

She ran her fingers along the spines of the books until she reached 912: *Graphic representations of earth, atlases.* She let out a small whoop, pulled down the *Times Atlas*, and sank onto the floor. She flicked through the pages until she came to *England, towns, railways, and settlements.* Perfect, except she'd need a magnifying glass, more light. She heaved the book up onto the table and angled the page to catch the light. Where was Somerset? The West Country?

Somerset! The word jumped out at her. Bath, Bridgewater. That sounded like the dreadful novels Elizabeth liked to read. Oh! And Michael's planned trip. How could she have forgotten that? He'd intended to take Elizabeth to England.

"Got it!"

Loud rumblings and Mrs. Busybody's sibilant hiss greeted her shriek.

"Yeovil," she whispered. *"Five miles shy of Yeovil,"* Timothy had said. She ran her finger down the marked road and there it was. Norton-sub-Hamdon!

She rocked back in the chair.

"Stop swinging, you'll break the chair legs."

Jane lurched upright. "I'd like to borrow this."

"Under no circumstances." Mrs. Peabody glared over the top of her rounded spectacles. "Reference books are not available for loan, and if you continue to disrupt other readers I shall be forced to ask you to leave."

Jane ran her index finger over the map. Liverpool wasn't hard to find, tucked about halfway up, above Wales, and Ireland across the water.

"I hope your hands aren't grubby." Interfering woman, peering over her shoulder. "What's so interesting about the southwest of England, may I ask?"

"Nothing, nothing at all."

Jane clamped her lips tightly together and ran her finger up the left-hand side of England. Gloucester, Monmouth, Hereford, Shropshire—the names sounded like an English history lesson; she'd loathed history almost as much as geography.

If Mrs. Busybody got wind of what she was doing it would be around town faster than a dust storm, and twice as dirty.

"Curiosity, Mrs. Peabody, nothing more. The scale of maps, very important. Numbers don't lie."

"You and your numbers." Mrs. Busybody's surfeit of chins wobbled as she let out a disgruntled huff and wandered away.

The ripping sound as Jane pulled a page from her notebook had Mrs. Busybody throwing more filthy looks in her direction, so she made a great show of waving it in the air and replacing it in her pocket. She drew a rough map on a clean page and wrote down the distances and the towns along the way.

"We're closing for lunch now."

Where had Mrs. Busybody come from, sneaking up behind her like that?

She slammed the atlas shut and rammed the piece of paper into her pocket, then lifted the atlas and dumped it into Mrs. Busybody's hands. "Thank you so much."

With her nose in the air and mimicking Elizabeth's gliding walk, Jane swept from the library, not a bounce in sight.

———≈———

Elizabeth patted the last strand of hair into place and stepped back to check her appearance in the mirror. Black did nothing for her complexion, made her look sallow. There was little she could do about it. No matter what she thought, it was important to keep up appearances, and she had no intention of being cooped up like some ailing grandmother, trapped in the past by a melancholy so strong she could barely lift her head from the pillow. Poppycock!

At long last she'd managed a decent night's sleep, possibly thanks to another of the draughts Lethbridge continued to recommend. Her mind was clear. No more of this doolally nonsense; it was time to try and make some sense of her jumbled thoughts. In a perfect world she'd sit down and talk things over with Michael; however, that wasn't an option, and, unless she had misunderstood him, he had nothing further to offer on the subject. She was going to have to call upon Jane.

But first there were other matters to deal with. Messrs. Brown and Brown had said they would be there for the reading of Michael's will and Jane would need to be present.

The house was ridiculously quiet and dark, and Elizabeth knew she'd have to put up with it for a little longer for the sake of propriety. The question was, where should the reading take place? The dining room was the obvious spot, sufficiently formal, not too intimate, and besides, she couldn't face Michael's study yet.

A knock on the front door brought Lucy. Elizabeth glanced at the grandfather clock in the hallway, the hands still marking the time of Michael's death. The Messrs. Brown would be on time, no need to check. They were sticklers for punctuality.

"Lucy, slow down. That'll be Messrs. Brown. Please show them into the dining room and then go and find Jane and ask her to join us."

She sat down at the head of the table, folded her hands in front of her, and took several steadying breaths as the two like-as-peas black-clad men trooped into the dining room and took the chairs she indicated.

"Lucy, see to Jane, please, and ask Bessie to come in as well."

"Yes, miss."

In deference to the occasion, Lucy managed to close the door quietly.

"Our condolences, Miss Quinn." One of them, she wasn't sure whether it was the father or son, nodded his balding head. "We won't take much of your time. Mr. Quinn's will is in order."

And there shouldn't be any surprises, except perhaps for Jane, because she and Michael had updated both of their wills not three months earlier.

"There you are, Jane." Elizabeth indicated the chair next to her. "Come and sit down."

Jane's eyes widened. Her cheeks were flushed as though she'd been outside in the sun and her hair was mussed.

"I'm sorry I'm late. I got tied up at the auction house."

"Shall we proceed, gentlemen?"

As Elizabeth anticipated, the entire process was over and done within a matter of minutes. Bessie broke down when she discovered

THE GIRL IN THE PAINTING

that her years of steak and kidney pies had earned her a tidy one hundred pounds. Then Jane, poor Jane. It was the first time Elizabeth had ever seen her speechless. So she should be. Michael had been more than generous, given her a substantial salary increase and full control of the auction house. No more than she deserved; after all, she'd been doing the job for some time now. Once she turned twenty-one she'd also have a neat little nest egg that would see her through university and beyond.

"Aunt Elizabeth, I want to thank you . . ."

"Don't thank me, it's all Michael's doing, and nothing more than you deserve." She dusted her hands together, more for her own benefit than anything else.

While the Messrs. Brown droned on, she'd come to a decision. If Michael trusted Jane with his auction house, then perhaps she should follow his implicit advice. There was no doubt of the girl's capabilities, and she had such a clear and precise mind.

Once the Messrs. Brown left, she called Jane aside. "I wonder if you could spare me a few moments."

A flash of something that may have been impatience flittered across Jane's face. "Of course."

"Dr. Lethbridge suggested, as did you, that Mr. Freud's work might have some bearing on my dilemma." She cleared her throat. She refused to use the word *turn*; it made her sound like some eighteenth-century namby-pamby who was constantly reaching for the smelling salts. "There is another piece of information I would like to share with you."

Jane leaned forward, her face animated.

"I believe my peculiar behavior may have something to do with repressed memories triggered by the visit to the Tost and Rohu display at the technical college."

"I agree." Jane rummaged in the pockets of her skirt, crackling paper and sending pencil shavings to the floor. "I've made a few notes."

"Don't interrupt. I haven't finished. Before Michael died, he gave me some information that has changed my outlook and my priorities."

"I have made several deductions that I believe may be helpful."

What was the girl prattling on about? A rash of goose bumps flecked her arms as reality dawned. "You know?"

Jane slammed her hand over her mouth. "I'm so sorry. Michael asked me to wait until you told me yourself, but I think I may have some relevant information."

Michael had no right . . . First Lethbridge, and now Jane. Had he broadcast the situation to all of Maitland?

"Who else knows?" she hissed. Bessie? Lucy? Mrs. Witherspoon? The people at the auction house?

"To the best of my knowledge, no one else. Michael asked me for my help. I have a file and some paperwork, and I have uncovered a few facts that I think may be pertinent."

Jane emptied the contents of her pockets all over the table and sorted through various scraps.

The focus of Elizabeth's eyes wavered as the table disappeared beneath the disgusting jumble. "I've never felt so confused before. So untethered, as though I've been cast loose in a swirling mist."

"Stay here a moment. I have to go upstairs and get something else." Without waiting for her assent, Jane flew from the room, her boots pounding on every single one of the treads all the way to the attic.

Elizabeth's heart screamed, almost as though someone had ripped it out, creating a wound she'd never known she carried. Abandoned. With Michael's death that wound had become a gaping great hole. She stifled a cry, shattering the brick wall she'd unwittingly built to protect herself.

It wasn't until Jane plonked a manila folder down on the dining room table and turned the cover that she managed to compose herself.

"Right, here they are." Jane opened the folder and spread out a series of papers.

"These are Michael's." Elizabeth would recognize his spidery scrawl from a hundred paces. "You have no right to take them from his study."

The girl at least had the grace to flush.

"I know, but he showed them to me. I had to get them safe."

What was she talking about? "Keep them safe?"

"I didn't want anyone else to see them."

"Bessie and Lucy wouldn't dare to disturb anything in Michael's study."

"I know. I don't know why I did it. Just a feeling."

Good heavens. Since when had Jane paid any attention to feelings?

"There's something about Langdon-Penter."

Penter? Wasn't Penter the name of the artist? Ah! The son. "I thought you liked the young man."

Jane's face rivaled a beetroot. "That's Timothy. I'm talking about his father."

"Why would this Langdon-Penter fellow be interested in anything in Michael's study?"

"I don't know. We met him at the National Gallery. He seemed to know Michael, but Michael didn't recognize him. Then he helped himself to Michael's whiskey at the wake. I'm certain he had been in Michael's study. Everyone else had tea."

"That's outrageous!" Suddenly Elizabeth was on her feet pacing the room, her sluggish blood coursing once more through her veins. "These English! They all think they have some God-given right to make themselves at home. We should have second thoughts about this exhibition." She swiveled around and caught an impish grin on Jane's face. "What's so funny?"

"It's good to see you back, Aunt Elizabeth."

She couldn't control the undignified humph that slipped between her lips so she folded her arms and sat tall. Jane was right. She did feel motivated, more herself than she'd been since . . . not since Michael's death, since before that ridiculous event at the technical college.

"Tell me about these papers." At long last something was happening. Thank God for Jane.

Jane picked up the first. "These are the immigration papers from when you and Michael left Liverpool."

There it was in black and white—Michael Ó'Cuinn and his sister, Elizabeth. Elizabeth existed, except she wasn't Elizabeth. It was a most peculiar feeling. It showed the destination as Sydney, and the names of Mam and Da, except they weren't, were they? Not her mam and da. Her whole life built on a lie.

She pushed them aside and took the next sheet of paper Jane produced, covered in scrawl, with crossings out and dobs of ink and the general thinking-on-his-feet sort of attempt to compose a letter that Michael always went through.

"What is it?"

"The draft of a letter Michael wrote to a woman called Gertrude Finbright." Jane tipped her head to one side and raised an eyebrow in question.

"Who is she?" A shaft of jealousy licked through her. Ridiculous. If Michael had a lady friend, who was she to complain?

"She worked at Brownlow Hill, the workhouse in Liverpool. He contacted her after he received this telegram from the authorities. They refused to release any information about inmates, so he wrote to her, asking if she knew how you came to be in the workhouse."

The dreadful buzzing noise came back, and she was walking that path, her feet skimming and twisting as someone bundled her along. A boy, not a man, reeking of the farmyard. She shook the image away. She'd confront it later after Jane had her say.

"What else?"

"Not much. Michael made some tentative plans to take you to England to further his inquiries, visit the area, and take you to Bath."

"I have always wanted to go there."

Jane Austen, her guilty pleasure. How she loved those books. Michael was the only person who'd known about her chosen reading material; every time he returned from Sydney he'd have another novel tucked in his pocket. The rest of the town presumed she spent her life buried in accounts ledgers and Michael's political treatises. It seemed there was a lot the good folk of Maitland didn't know about her. A lot she didn't know about herself.

Concentrate, she must concentrate. "You said you had some thoughts."

"I'm not sure how much you remember of either the exhibition at the technical college or the preview. I feel there is a link."

"Surely you're mistaken. There weren't any birds at the preview, only paintings."

"Correct. However, there was one of Marigold's paintings at the technical college, and it was also on display at the preview."

"And? Come along, Jane, stop toying with me."

"I was hoping you might remember seeing it."

Try as she might, Elizabeth couldn't place one specific picture. There had been so many different paintings at the preview, and then, well, truth be told, things got a little confused—her *dilemma* again. "Tell me."

"The painting of the village church."

Something hovered in the back of Elizabeth's mind, something she couldn't place, and her heart picked up a pace or two. She clasped her hands tight, hoping Jane wouldn't notice her sudden shaking. Darkness, overwhelming, inky black. Birds wheeling and diving in a vast cloud, their feathered wings beating against her cheeks. Her hands started to come up, to protect her head.

"Do you remember?"

Jane's words snapped Elizabeth back to the present. "I fail to see how this moves us forward. The whole world knows I have an irrational fear of birds. How is a church relevant?" She shook the vision away and willed her hands to still. "I've had enough. Ask Lucy to bring me some tea upstairs."

"There is one more thing, Aunt Elizabeth."

She stalled, hand on the doorknob, her temper spiking. "What is it?"

"G'woam."

Her lips echoed the word, against the thrumming of her heartbeat. "What about it?"

"You were crying the word. I didn't know what it meant."

Neither did she. "Do you know now?"

"It's the way people from the West Country, in England, pronounce *go home*. I think perhaps you came from there originally. Michael said you didn't have an Irish accent."

"That seems a stretch."

Jane shook her head. "I intend to find out. It's what Michael asked me to do. From what I can piece together, Michael's sister, Lizzie . . ."

"*Lizzie Ó'Cuinn!*"

Towering flames lit the night sky and a smell, such a strange smell, meaty and sweet. Bile rose in her throat. She gagged.

"*Lizzie.*" She'd answered so Lizzie wouldn't get a hiding.

"That's how he referred to her in the letter to Gertrude Finbright. He also asked if she has any memory of the little girl Lizzie befriended."

The hairs at the base of Elizabeth's skull rose, and a sensation akin to pins and needles stretched her skin. She couldn't think about that for the moment. Later, in the quiet of her bedroom. Perhaps it was one of Dr. Freud's repressed memories.

"How is that going to help?" She felt even more alone now. Not Ireland, not Liverpool. Every connection she'd had with Michael whisked away.

Jane shrugged her shoulders, and if Michael had known any more he'd taken it to his grave. Her head felt as though it were stuffed with old newspaper.

"Isn't there anything you remember? Your earliest memory?"

Apart from a towering inferno, answering to someone else's name, and wheeling birds? "I remember arriving in Sydney on the ship, the sky was as blue as a sapphire. I remember the Camerons."

"The Camerons?" Jane jotted down the name.

"Cameron Victuallers. I lived with them until Michael took me to Hill End. It was the best day of my life when they kicked me out."

There was nothing the matter with her memory. That part of the past was crystal clear, including some things she'd like to forget, like whiskery Bill Cameron and his vile words about the Irish.

"Why would they do that?"

"Prejudice. Everyone was up in arms about O'Farrell, an Irish Catholic who tried to shoot Prince Alfred. Anyone with the slightest tinge of green was labeled a Fenian."

"Do you remember anything before Sydney?"

Nothing she was ready to admit until she understood what these strange delusions signified. "Nothing." The pounding in her head increased.

"What has happened to these Camerons?"

"Jane, Jane. Stop! I can't put up with this anymore. All these un-answered questions are crowding my mind. I need to lie down. I'll let you know when I want to discuss this further."

She had to calm down. Her blood was galloping around her system like the Sydney milk train and her hands wouldn't stop shaking. Perhaps a dose of Lethbridge's laudanum might help.

THIRTY

Elizabeth didn't reappear for the rest of the day. Jane hid in her room out of Bessie's and Lucy's reach, poring over Michael's notes and gaining no insight into anything of any consequence. The only remaining hope was receiving a letter from Gertrude Finbright, and she knew that a response in less than eight weeks was nigh impossible, presuming the woman was still alive and Michael's letter had reached her.

The town hall clock struck five as Jane reached the auction house. She wanted to see Timothy; she owed him an apology for the way she'd rushed out on him. Perhaps they could sit and talk, maybe take a walk along the river. She'd like to find out a little more about Somerset. Timothy would have some local knowledge and, short of a trip to England, as Michael had planned, secondhand information was the next best thing.

Blazing light greeted her as she walked through the back door. John sat tucked in his cubbyhole, his feet propped on the desk and the form guide spread on his lap.

"I thought you would have gone by now."

"They're still in there, arguing about this, that, and the other. Offered my help, but it seems there's more to it than that. That fellow's a pain, pushing his weight around, laying down the law."

"Timothy seems easygoing to me." A silly giggle escaped her lips and her cheeks heated.

John threw her a quizzical look. "Nah. Not the lad, his father. Anyone would think he was God's gift to the world the way he carries on."

"I expect it's all a teacup storm. I'll see what I can do."

"Wouldn't waste your time, if I were you. Family argy-bargy. Sounds like they might be a bit strapped for cash. What do you think about Piastre in the two o'clock tomorrow?"

"I haven't had a moment to look." Jane held out her hand for the racing form. Why would the Penters be short of money? Timothy made it sound as though they were wealthy. He talked of the family estate and his mother's time in Paris, and the trip to Australia for three of them must have cost a pretty penny.

A blood-curdling yell echoed, followed by a string of curses that would make a dray driver blush, and did make John blush.

Jane took off down the corridor, John hot on her heels, and skidded to a halt in the doorway to the auction room.

Langdon-Penter stood, aggression oozing from every pore, confronting poor Marigold.

"I'm not giving up. My future depends on this. What about the promise you made to Maggie?"

"I don't want you to give up, you know that. But at least let the exhibition go ahead. Apart from anything else it might help cover the cost of the trip." Marigold pushed her pale hair back, her eyes blazing like chips of lapis lazuli.

"Those paintings aren't worth the canvas they're painted on." He swiped his hand in a wide arc, narrowly missing Marigold's head.

With an ear-splitting crash, one of the larger paintings fell to the floor.

Marigold moaned, sank down, back to the wall, knees pulled to her chest, her hands covering her head and her shoulders heaving. Timothy's leap to protect her seemed well-rehearsed, because Langdon-Penter ripped his attention from his wife to his son. "If you . . . you lily-livered little snot had done what you were meant to do, we wouldn't be stuck in the middle of this godforsaken country town trying to get answers from a dead man." A dead man? Was he talking about Michael? Answers to what?

"Mr. and Mrs. . . ." Jane took two steps, but John's heavy hand restrained her. "Let me go." She shook him away. "Someone's got to break this up. Marigold shouldn't have to—"

"Stay," he hissed and dragged her back behind the door. "Right dodgepot, if ever I saw one. Wait a bit."

The picture of Langdon-Penter's bony fingers cradling Michael's favorite Waterford crystal tumbler flashed before Jane's eyes. The man had made her flesh creep from the first moment she'd come across him at the National Gallery. There was something about his self-assurance, his know-it-all manner and drawling accent that made her skin crawl.

"Ó'Cuinn must have known something."

"Father, we're beaten. Admit it."

"You're the one likely to be beaten. Your fault. No one else's." Langdon-Penter slammed his fist against the wall, sending several other paintings rattling and missing Timothy's head by about half an inch.

Marigold hauled herself to her feet. "Stop! The man is dead. We can't do anything more."

Langdon-Penter stood, not a muscle moving except for his piercing eyes. "We'll see about that." His gaze switched between Timothy and Marigold, then he closed his eyes, his shoulders relaxed, and a look of satisfaction settled on his face.

"Timothy, help me pick up the painting." Marigold's voice held a note of resigned sufferance, as though the scenario was all too familiar. "It will need repair."

As he hauled his mother to her feet, Timothy straightened and his eyes narrowed. A flush of heat stole across Jane's face. They'd spotted her standing in the doorway.

Caught surely as a crayfish in a trap, eavesdropping. There was only one thing to do. Drawing on every lesson Elizabeth had ever taught her, Jane stepped into the room. "Can I be of any assistance?"

"This is family business. Stay out of it." Timothy's father took three steps toward her.

She stood her ground. "What's going on?"

The odor of deceit hung in the air. Jane hadn't liked the way Timothy had answered her question about whether his father knew Michael. It hadn't rung true. It was so disappointing. She thought she'd made a new friend, thoroughly enjoyed his company. From what she'd just heard she'd been taken for a fool.

"Miss Jane, might be better if you head off home. I'll sort this out."

She brushed John's arm away. Nothing this side of Hades would make her walk away now. There was something afoot, something she didn't understand. Loose ends dangled like frayed threads and every step led to the paintings on the wall, and from those paintings to Elizabeth and Michael.

She straightened up. "Is there something I can help you with? Questions you need answered?"

Langdon-Penter waved her away, his gaze flickering. "No problem. No problem at all."

Jane didn't believe him for a moment.

When Jane arrived home she went straight to Elizabeth's room and tapped on the door.

"Come."

She stepped into the room. Elizabeth sat in the chair by the window, the blue jar on the windowsill in front of her, running the red thread through her fingers.

"How are you feeling?" Jane asked.

"Much improved. I haven't had any more of that rubbish Lethbridge keeps trying to pour down my throat. I've been thinking about your Mr. Freud."

This was better, so very much better. She didn't want to upset Elizabeth again, couldn't fathom how to approach the subject of the argument at the auction house.

"If the visit to the Tost and Rohu exhibition triggered my . . ." Elizabeth's lip curled a little as though loath to admit to her fragility, ". . . *dilemma*. What traumatic event does it stem from? It has to be something that happened to me before I came to Australia, before I was Elizabeth."

"That's what we have to find out. I'm hopeful a reply will come from Gertrude Finbright soon. I don't want to upset you, but can I ask another couple of questions?"

Elizabeth inclined her head.

"Did Michael know Langdon-Penter?"

Elizabeth frowned and gazed out of the window. "He never mentioned him to me. I thought you organized the exhibition for his wife. Why do you ask?"

"Something he said." Jane cleared her throat. "I overheard a conversation. Not really a conversation, more of an argument. It sounded very much as though he'd come to Australia specifically to find Michael. He said his future depended on it."

"I doubt Michael would be very difficult to find. His name's been splashed all over the national papers ever since he agreed to stand as a member of the Legislative Assembly, and there was a glowing obituary in the *Sydney Morning Herald*, and the *Age* as well." Which might account for Langdon-Penter turning up at the National Gallery and then at Michael's wake. "He seemed very annoyed not to have had the opportunity to speak to Michael again. In fact, he was furious."

A flash of pain crossed Elizabeth's face, making Jane regret sharing her thoughts. "Can I get you anything? More tea? Would you like your supper brought up here?"

"No. I'll come down; however, I don't want this discussed within earshot of Bessie or Lucy, understand? I won't have Michael's memory tarnished."

The following day, in a sudden flurry of industriousness, Elizabeth decided the Benevolent Society books should be audited so Jane hadn't had the opportunity to return to the auction house. She tried numerous excuses; none convinced Elizabeth.

Time for one last try. "I have to go down to the auction house. The wages need to be done."

Elizabeth lifted her head from the ledger. "You did the wages two days ago. However, I'm sure that young man would appreciate some company."

The corner of her lip twitched, making the color rise to Jane's cheeks. Timothy Penter might not appreciate her company after she'd witnessed his father's appalling behavior. But she was going to force it on him and get to the bottom of the story.

Without giving Elizabeth a chance to make any further comments, she left and headed down to the auction house. She found Timothy wandering up and down High Street, hands pushed deep into his pockets and his head down.

Resisting the temptation to thump her hands on her hips and demand answers, Jane drew in a steadying breath. "Can we talk?"

He grunted something that might have been an acknowledgment, so she led the way around the back of the auction house and upstairs.

"It's about yesterday, the argument with your father. There's something I don't understand . . ."

A grim smile ghosted across his face. "I haven't been entirely honest with you."

And if that wasn't the biggest understatement, she didn't know what was. She swallowed the string of questions hovering on her tongue. Perhaps she should let him go ahead.

"Father had business with Ó'Cuinn."

"Quinn. Michael Quinn."

"Yes, he called himself Quinn, but he was Michael Ó'Cuinn once. Father knew him from England."

"Knew him or knew *of* him?"

"Knew of him."

She hadn't misinterpreted the conversation the day before. "He came looking for him? He deliberately arranged the showing in Maitland?" And Timothy had deliberately worked his way into her affections. Poor little orphan Jane blindsided because someone paid her some attention.

The tips of his ears turned a painfully unpleasant shade of red. And her temper flared.

Guilty as charged. It was his duplicity that disgusted her. He'd intended right from their first meeting to use her to get closer to Michael and she'd played into his hands.

"Michael's death ruined your plans," she said.

"Not my plans, my father's plans."

That made it even worse. Not even his own underhand plan, simply doing his father's bidding.

"Father had no intention of hurting you. He wanted the answer to a question."

No matter what he said, Jane couldn't get past the fact that he'd used her, courted her—such a funny old-fashioned word, the kind Elizabeth might use. Not because he liked her, but because he wanted something from her. How naive could she be?

"Please let me explain," said Timothy. "I have something more to tell you."

"You have nothing to tell me other than the nature of the business your father had with Michael."

He shrugged and leaned back in the chair, resigned. Did he care how much he had offended her?

And then it hit her. "Do you know a Gertrude Finbright?"

"I've never met her." He swallowed. "My father knows her. She's an old woman, used to be the matron at some orphanage or hospital."

"Where?" she snapped, heart pounding, waiting for the confirmation she knew would come.

"Liverpool."

The Gertrude Finbright Michael had written to, without a doubt. "Brownlow Hill?"

"I'm sorry?"

"Brownlow Hill is the name of the place in Liverpool where Gertrude Finbright worked."

"I don't know."

Or he wasn't telling. All she wanted to do was storm out of the place, but she needed more answers. "What business did your father have with an orphanage in Liverpool?"

"We're trying to trace my mother's sister." The air stilled.

Jane shook her thoughts aside. Assumptions proved nothing. She needed facts, tangible evidence. "You think Michael might have known something about her. Why didn't your father ask him when we met in Sydney, at the National Gallery?"

Silence hung until he shrugged his shoulders. "I've got to be going. I told Father I'd meet him at the Pig and Whistle."

Without another glance Timothy made his way downstairs. The door banged behind him, ending their conversation, and her foolishness.

How long she sat staring at the table, she had no idea, but when she finally stood her leg had gone to sleep. There was a mountain of random facts that had to be logically sorted before she would have a solution. She must not jump to conclusions, and she couldn't take her half-baked theories to Elizabeth. It simply wouldn't be fair. She had to talk to Marigold and find out the full story about her sister. Timothy was no good to her. He'd only regurgitate what his father had told him, and she didn't believe a word of it.

Stuffing her notebook into her pocket, she wandered downstairs and into the auction room. As chance would have it, Marigold had the broken picture laid out on the table, a new piece of timber lined up alongside, the broken stretchers dangling loosely from her fingers.

"Could you spare me a moment or two?" Jane asked.

It wasn't until Marigold lifted her head that Jane regretted her intrusion. A large, purple-tinged bruise marred her cheekbone.

"Oh, I'm sorry, so sorry. Is there anything I can do?"

Marigold pulled a grimace and scuffed her hand across her cheek to brush away the remnants of her tears. "It's nothing." She snapped the broken stretcher and tossed it aside.

"Let me get you something for that bruise. Some witch hazel, a cool towel."

"No, thank you. It'll heal. What can I help you with?"

"Timothy told me that you came to Australia to try and trace your sister."

"Yes, we did. We thought Michael Ó'Cuinn might be able to help us. My husband learned he was the last person to be seen with the young girl we believed might be my sister." The woman's bleached face, the color of old bones, stared back at her. "We'd always thought she was stolen by the gypsies, until we received word that a girl fitting her description had been taken in by the workhouse in Liverpool."

Jane pointed to a painting of a string of covered drays and carts converging on a picture-perfect waterfall.

"Those are the gypsies," Marigold said.

"Of course. We don't see many in Australia."

"They're a nomadic people and tend to return to the same place at the same time every year. This painting is called *Tinkers' Bubble*. The spring flows through the woodlands; it ends in a small waterfall by the road. Bubble is the gypsy name for a waterfall. They camp by the spring every year and graze their horses. Unfortunately, if anything happens while they are in the area, they tend to be blamed—it's always the gypsies.

"They were there when my sister vanished. We searched, searched their camp, called the police. The entire village helped. We never found her." Her words poured out almost faster than the tears tracking her cheeks.

"Every year, when the gypsies returned, Mother would haunt the woods, convinced she'd find her among the children. We even offered a reward. No one came forward." A harsh sobbing laugh, more like a groan, erupted from Marigold's mouth and she pulled a handkerchief from her pocket.

"Did you see them take her?"

She shook her head. "One minute she was sitting under the apple tree in the front garden at home, trying to make herself a princess crown with daisies; the next moment she was gone." Marigold dropped her head into her hands. "I don't remember. Mother said I was sulking upstairs, jealous because there were no marigolds for my princess crown." After a moment she lifted her gaze to one of the paintings on the wall. "I sometimes dream of her walking down the path to the village, holding someone's hand."

"Whose?" Jane snapped the question.

"I don't know. A boy, not a full-grown man—scrawny. I can't remember. I don't know what's the truth and what I've been told. There's the painting; that's my memory." She pointed to the picture next to the one of the gypsy camp. "Mother spoke of nothing else until the day she died. I was never enough. They'd stolen her angel."

"Do you think Michael might have taken her?" The mood of the painting implied nothing menacing.

Marigold shrugged. "My husband had word from the workhouse."

A barrage of questions filled Jane's mind. She opened her mouth to speak, but the look on Marigold's face restrained her. Just one more. "How old was your sister when she went missing?"

"Too long ago . . ."

"How long?" Jane couldn't control the edge in her voice.

"More than fifty years ago."

"Be specific."

"The afternoon of August twenty-eighth, 1862."

"How old was she?"

Marigold lifted her tear-stained face. "Four."

Cold fingers trickled down Jane's back as the facts lined up. "How far is Liverpool from your home?"

"About two hundred miles."

In that instant Jane fully understood. "You believe Michael kidnapped her and took her to Liverpool?"

Marigold gave an embarrassed nod.

Why would Michael travel two hundred miles to kidnap a child?

The calculation didn't add up, no matter how Jane manipulated the facts.

THIRTY-ONE

Good morning, Miss Quinn."

Elizabeth resisted the temptation to groan as Lucy poked her head around the door.

"I've brought you some tea and toast. I thought you might prefer breakfast in bed."

"No, no. I'll get up. What time is it?"

Lucy put the tray down on the bedside table and drew back the curtains with a degree of relish. "Ten thirty, miss."

Ten thirty. How had that happened? She'd slept for over twelve hours, and without any of Lethbridge's magic potion. "Very well, thank you." Not a suspicion of nausea or dizziness either.

Lucy puffed up her pillows and settled the tray on her lap. "That's all."

Relishing the refreshing scent of jasmine, Elizabeth poured a cup of tea and picked up a sliver of toast. Once she was properly awake she'd brave Michael's study—she hadn't set foot in there since he died—and see if she could find anything that Jane might have overlooked. Highly unlikely, the girl had a mind like a rabbit trap.

She topped up the cup and reached for another piece of toast, and there, sitting flat on the tray, was an envelope addressed to Michael Ó'Cuinn. Strange, she hadn't noticed it before. The poorly formed writing on the cheap paper didn't look familiar. Nor did the stamp. On closer inspection she discovered the letter came from England.

She slid the knife under the flap and pulled out the single sheet.

Dear Michael,

    The memory of you has stayed with me for many a long year . . .

For heaven's sake, she couldn't read this. Was this Michael's long-forgotten love she knew nothing of, or worse, some long-remembered love? She flipped the piece of paper over to look at the signature.

Gertrude Finbright

The name was familiar. She sipped her tea. Jane had mentioned it. A decent night's sleep had refreshed her memory.

Gertrude Finbright.

"She worked at Brownlow Hill, the workhouse in Liverpool. He contacted her after he received this telegram from the authorities."

That was it.

Elizabeth pushed away the tray and stared out of the window.

What would Michael want her to do?

She had no idea. A few months earlier, she would have read it without a second thought. Now, she wasn't sure she wanted to know the truth. Ridiculous. They'd lived under the same roof for more years than she cared to count. Been through drought, flood, depression, and good times. Many good times. He would want her to sort this conundrum. Otherwise he would have taken her secret to his grave. She returned to the letter.

Dear Michael,

    The memory of you has stayed with me for many a long year.
Compassion and courage in one so young is rarely seen. I am sure you grew to be a fine man.

A tear trickled down Elizabeth's cheek and she brushed it away. He had. A very fine man.

> Brownlow Hill remains much as you would remember, and I still make the pilgrimage once a year to Lizzie's grave, as I promised. I have often hoped you might one day return and we could share this small remembrance. Would you recognize me? I doubt it, for I am now well past my prime. You, I am certain, have fulfilled your promise.

Oh, for goodness' sake! She reached into the bedside drawer and pulled out another handkerchief. This was worse than the eulogy at Michael's funeral. This woman had known a Michael Elizabeth barely remembered. Michael as a young boy.

> Now, to your query. Of course I remember the little girl you speak of. Lizzie took her under her wing.

The hateful throbbing returned to her temple and she could feel herself slipping. Why couldn't she remember? She gritted her teeth and pushed higher up the bed.

> I well remember the night she arrived, the poor little cherub, freezing cold, wet through, and stinking of fowl manure, deposited on the doorstep by a young boy who knew nothing of her origins. He claimed to have found her outside the railway station.

A tremor ghosted across her shoulders, and she pulled up the counterpane before turning the thin paper over.

And this is where circumstances appear to have come full circle. Some months ago, before I received your letter, a man visited me, a Mr. Langdon-Penter. He had a picture of a young girl who resembled Lizzie's friend. It appears her family has been searching for her for a very long time and he was keen to offer them closure by way of a death certificate.

I explained that the last time anyone saw her was the morning I gave you the dreadful news of Lizzie's passing. I mentioned your name but could offer him no contact details other than the fact I believed you had immigrated to Australia.

Elizabeth dragged the bell from her bedside table and shook it furiously. "Lucy! Find Jane and send her to me this minute. Do you hear me? This minute."

Langdon-Penter. Jane was right. There was something decidedly suspicious about the man, and Elizabeth intended to find out what it was. She scanned the last few lines, constantly ringing the bell.

An advertisement under his name appeared the following week in the paper requesting information regarding a Daisy Dibble. I saw no need to respond, as he had already made contact with me. Sadly, I can offer you no other information.

Michael, I will remember you in my prayers and trust that life has been kind to you and hope we may meet again.

Yours in our Lord,
Gertrude Finbright

"Jane! Where are you? I need you this moment." Elizabeth's voice boomed, surprising her. How long was it since she'd shouted?

"Aunt Elizabeth!" The door flew open. "Are you all right?" Jane stood there, blouse hanging out, hair askew.

She had never been so pleased to see anyone in her life before. "Read this." She handed Jane the letter and threw back the bedcovers. "Turn your back while I dress, and say nothing until I am ready."

Only when she was fully clothed did Elizabeth realize she'd forgotten to put on the ghastly mourning dress. She ran her hands down her navy skirt and finished buttoning her blouse. No matter. Michael would understand. Might even approve. Besides, she had more important matters to attend to.

"I'm ready."

Jane turned, the letter held in both her hands. "You realize what this means . . ."

"Don't say another word. I am well-aware of the implications. We will deal with this one step at a time. I want the Penters here, in the dining room, at one o'clock sharp."

"There is something I have to tell you first."

Why could the girl never do what she was told? "Hurry up."

"I spoke to Marigold, Mrs. Penter, yesterday. She told me her sister disappeared and admitted they had come to Australia in search of Michael. They believed him responsible, that he kidnapped Marigold's sister."

"What rubbish! I will not have his name besmirched."

"Marigold said her sister was seen walking down the path with a scrawny boy, not a full-grown man."

"Exactly where and when was this?"

"Norton-sub-Hamdon, Somerset. Twenty-eighth of August, 1862."

An icy trickle ran across Elizabeth's shoulders. She had to get to the bottom of this. "Michael never made mention of having visited any part of England other than Liverpool, certainly not the West Country. I'd know. Give me that letter, and do not mention a word to anyone."

Jane opened her mouth to speak again, but Elizabeth's glare sent her beetling for the door.

"Bring Michael's papers to me before you go and get the Penters."

———— ≋ ————

"Will you be wanting lunch served?"

"No, I will not, Bessie, so you can wipe that tedious look off your face," said Elizabeth. "When they arrive, I want you to show them in here—you and not that Lucy girl—and I want you to make sure we are not disturbed. I am also expecting the Messrs. Brown."

"What about Jane?"

"Send her to me as soon as she returns."

"She's back."

"Then send her in here now, and ask her to bring a tray with some glasses and water."

"Nothing more?"

"No. Nothing more. This is not a social occasion."

Within moments Jane appeared. "They'll be here in ten minutes."

"Very well. I want you to sit down there." Elizabeth pointed to a chair in the corner of the room. "I don't want you to say a word; however, I want you to make notes of everything that is said. You can manage that, can't you?"

Jane's courses in shorthand and typing had stood them in good stead on many an occasion; she was more than capable of keeping a perfect record of everything that occurred.

"You have your notebook?"

A stubby pencil and a bedraggled handful of papers appeared

from Jane's pocket and she quirked a grin. She must see the girl got some more notebooks; she went through them like barley sugars.

The Penters—all of them, the boy as well—arrived on the dot of one and Bessie showed them in. Dispensing with the niceties, Elizabeth gestured to the chairs at the other end of the table, having chosen her usual place at the head of the table.

"Thank you for being prompt."

"It doesn't appear we have an option." Langdon-Penter pulled out a chair and sprawled into it, giving no thought to his wife.

The boy held a chair for his mother. At least he appeared to have some semblance of civility.

"What's this all about?"

Elizabeth peered down her nose at Langdon-Penter and raised her hand. "I will do the talking, and I would like your responses to be succinct. Jane will be taking notes so there can be no confusion or misinterpretation. I have asked Messrs. Brown and Brown, my solicitors, to join us."

As if on cue, the door opened and Bessie ushered the two men into the room.

"Please take a seat, gentlemen."

One of them raised an eyebrow and chose a chair on her right, the other on the left. They had attended enough meetings she'd chaired to know exactly how matters would proceed; they were there simply to give substance to the proceedings.

"What in the devil's name is going on?" Langdon-Penter rolled his eyes and drummed his fingers on the tabletop.

Refusing to acknowledge his petulance, Elizabeth addressed his wife. "What brought you to Australia, Mrs. Penter?"

"Why, my paintings. The National Gallery bought one some years ago and made an offer on another. I have friends in Melbourne from my days in Paris, and I thought it the perfect opportunity to renew our acquaintance. My mother died recently, and we all needed a change of scenery. She had been ill for a long time." The poor woman's voice hitched.

A pang of remorse shot through Elizabeth. But Michael was more important. This was for him. No one would besmirch his name. Not if she had anything to do with it. The matter of her own identity would have to take second place until this accusation was resolved. "Please continue."

"I fail to understand why this is any of your business," Langdon-Penter interrupted.

"I believe that it is. Mrs. Penter?"

"Mother clung on to life for as long as she could. We held out the hope that one day my sister would be returned to us."

"Returned to you? She didn't pass away?"

"Oh no, that was Mother's difficulty. She believed my sister was taken by the gypsies, was convinced she was still alive. Every year, on the anniversary of her disappearance, she put an advertisement in the local papers. Nothing ever eventuated until last year."

"When did your sister disappear?"

"In the autumn of 1862, not long after her fourth birthday."

That matched Jane's information.

Langdon-Penter pushed his chair back, half stood. "We should not be subjected to this inquisition. I'm not going to—"

"Sit down, sir." The Browns glared across the table at him. Such good fellows. They knew nothing of this but they were in her corner.

"Over fifty years ago and your mother still hadn't accepted her daughter's disappearance?" Elizabeth asked.

"Mother was a little, how should I put it, fey. She believed she would know in her heart if Daisy had died. I believed the same, because of the bond we shared. We were twins, though not identical. Mother used to say we were autumn and spring. Daisy's hair was the color of autumn leaves, mine the color of spring sunshine."

"I would prefer to deal in facts." Elizabeth shot a look at Jane, who raised her head and gave her a nod, assuring her she had everything down. "I have received a letter."

She wouldn't mention it was addressed to Michael. That would complicate matters. She held up the envelope. Langdon-Penter stood to make a grab for it, but she had the little man's measure.

"Later, Mr. Langdon-Penter. I believe you know Gertrude Finbright, one time matron of Brownlow Hill, the workhouse in Liverpool."

"What of it?"

"A simple yes or no will suffice."

"Yes." He rested his elbows on the table and steepled his fingers.

"Could you please explain to me how you came to know her?"

"She answered the advertisement about Marigold's sister, Daisy Dibble."

"Is Liverpool close to where you live? I was under the impression you came from the West Country. Jane, how far is that from Liverpool?"

Jane's scratchings stopped and she lifted her head. "One hundred and seventy-one and a half miles by train, slightly more by road."

"Thank you. You said the advertisements were placed in the local newspapers; one hundred and seventy miles hardly seems local."

Langdon-Penter cleared his throat. "On this occasion we placed advertisements farther afield."

"Was there a reason for this?"

"I'm not putting up with this rubbish. We're leaving . . ."

Shooting him a look of defiance, Marigold shook her head. "My mother's will stipulated that I should only receive half of the estate. The other half was to remain in trust for my sister, should she return home, unless proof of her death could be established."

"I see." Messrs. Brown broke their silence in unison, much as they did everything else.

"We broadened the range of the advertisements in an attempt to reach closure," said Marigold. "I also included drawings of her as she looked when she disappeared and as I thought she might look as a young woman."

"Did Miss Finbright answer this advertisement?"

"She did."

Elizabeth controlled her grin of triumph. "Could you explain to me why Miss Finbright says in this letter: 'Mr. Langdon-Penter approached the workhouse and they sent him to me.'"

Langdon-Penter wiped his hand over his face. "She's mistaken, she's an old woman."

"Her letter doesn't read as one whose rationality is in any way impaired. She also adds: 'An advertisement under his name appeared the following week in the paper requesting information regarding a Daisy Dibble. I saw no need to respond, as he had already made contact with me.'"

The silence hung.

Marigold bent her head toward her husband. "You told me *she* contacted *you*."

"What does it matter?"

"It matters very much. How did you know to approach the workhouse?"

"A lucky guess."

"What a coincidence." Timothy spoke for the first time, and Jane's head came up, displaying more than a glimmer of curiosity.

"How did you know Daisy had been taken to the workhouse in Liverpool?" Marigold articulated each word slowly and clearly, a hint of menace in her tone.

"Everything I have done has been for you. I have your best interests at heart."

"Lying to me about Daisy's whereabouts—how can that be in my best interests? How long have you known? How long? Mother went to her grave brokenhearted."

"Maggie's heart was broken long before Daisy vanished."

"Whatever do you mean?"

The Messrs. Brown cleared their throats. Elizabeth had no intention of curtailing the conversation, as uncomfortable as it had become. Michael was no more involved in the disappearance of this woman's sister than she was. She would see this debacle cleared up if it was the last thing she did.

Langdon-Penter sat back, arms folded, a smug expression on his face. "You know exactly what I am referring to—your mother's indiscretion. And now due to her death I own Langdon Estate."

"Mother owns the Langdon Estate, not you, Father."

Unless Elizabeth was mistaken, the senior Mr. Brown had kicked her under the table. She shot him a look, caught his monstrous ears reddening, and swallowed the reprimand on the tip of her tongue. It would seem she had unwittingly opened the proverbial can of worms.

"In case you've forgotten, boy, I am her husband."

Senior Mr. Brown shot to his feet. "Perhaps I should provide a point of law here. The Married Women's Property Act came into force in 1882."

"I've got no interest in you colonials and your ridiculous notions about women's rights. We're talking about England, where a man's rights stand."

The other Mr. Brown rose and cleared his throat. "The act applies in England, Wales, and Ireland, and has provided the model for similar legislation in other British territories."

"What's that got to do with me? I'm acting on my wife's behalf."

"It allows for all women to own and control their own property." With something resembling tight bows, the Messrs. Brown sat back down.

Langdon-Penter shot to his feet and glared at his son across the table, his face suffused with blood. "Marigold, you better make a decision. Do you want to find out what happened to Daisy or do you want that little upstart"—he waved his finger under his son's nose—"who's never done a decent day's work in his life, to spend his days in the lap of luxury while I relinquish everything I have worked for?"

Jane scrambled to her feet. "Mr. Langdon-Penter, please . . ."

"Sit down." Elizabeth hissed the words at her, gestured with her hand. No need for anyone to say anything. Flotsam always found its way to the surface. "Keep up with your notes."

"You must have known all along Daisy was taken to the workhouse." Marigold's voice held such a note of disappointment and regret, then a long, low moan dribbled between her lips and she buried her head in her arms.

Elizabeth could hardly contain her urge to caress Marigold's clenched, knuckle-white fists. There was more, much more to this than she had anticipated.

Langdon-Penter slammed the palms of his hands down on the table. "For goodness' sake woman, pull yourself together."

"Sit down, Mr. Langdon-Penter." Elizabeth pinned him with a ferocious stare and he subsided into the chair. "I think now might be the moment for a cup of tea. Don't you? Jane, go and have a word with Bessie. Let's all take a moment."

Jane tucked her notebook firmly into her pocket and left the room with a smile on her face. Gertrude's letter had given Elizabeth a new lease of life—that, and the thought Michael's name might be discredited. Between them they would get to the bottom of this nonsense. She fanned Michael's folder, wondering if there was anything she'd missed, and sneezed as the dust flew into the air, bringing with it the scent of the crumpled past. She would solve the rest of this mystery.

"Jane, wait."

Timothy! What in heaven's name did he want? She didn't want to speak to him; it was too difficult. She couldn't decide whose side he was on.

"What do you want?" She stopped and turned around, her hand on the kitchen doorknob.

"To talk to you."

She rounded on him. "How will I know whether you're speaking the truth?"

He had the grace to look a little shame-faced, his eyes dulled and downcast. "Can you spare me a moment?"

Something complex, far more difficult to understand than Sir Isaac Newton's approximation, batted around her insides and her anger dissipated. "After I've arranged the tea. Go and wait on the back veranda, through there." She pointed to the screen door at the end of the hallway before scuttling into the kitchen. "Bessie, Aunt Elizabeth would like tea for seven in the dining room."

"Please."

Taking no notice of Bessie's huffs and puffs, Jane pushed open the screen door and stepped outside to find Timothy propped up against the veranda post.

"I didn't set out to keep anything from you," he said.

Unable to remain still, she paced the length of the veranda searching for any sight of the chickens. Lucy couldn't be trusted to keep them contained, and Jane didn't want anything upsetting Elizabeth, not now, not when she seemed so much more her usual self.

Timothy said nothing more; she could tell from his expression some internal debate was going on. He better get a move on because Bessie would be yelling for her in a moment or two. She wasn't certain he deserved any of her time; he still hadn't made any effort to justify his lies. "I haven't got all day."

"My father's not telling the whole truth."

Didn't she know. Why would his son turn snitch? "About what?"

"About Grandma Maggie's will, the reason we came to Australia."

"I think we all know that, thanks to Gertrude's letter."

"There's more to it than that, a lot more. When Grandma Maggie died, she left half of the estate to Mother and the other half in trust to Mother's sister, Daisy. Her will stipulated that if proof was found confirming Daisy's death then her portion would pass to Mother. If not, then I inherit Daisy's portion on my twenty-first birthday. Grandma Maggie didn't leave anything to Father. In fact, she stipulated that he should have no control whatsoever."

"Why would she do that?"

"Because she remembered him as a boy, always chasing sixpence, wanting something for nothing, she said."

That definitely rang true. Langdon-Penter's inappropriate remark at Michael's wake sprang into her mind. "What made her think your father was only interested in the estate?"

"It's a long story, goes back a few generations. Mother and her sister were"—his face flushed a little—"born out of wedlock. Their father, my grandfather, Oliver Langdon, was the son of the local landowner. All hell broke loose when the twins were born. Oliver was off in India; he promised to marry Grandma Maggie once he returned. Trouble was, he didn't make it home. Great-grandfather Langdon saw Mother and her sister as a stain on the family honor. It wasn't until he died that Great-grandma and Grandma Maggie were reconciled and she and Mother moved into the big house. To cut a long story short, Mother and her sister, if she ever returned, inherited the Langdon estate."

"So you think your father married her hoping he would obtain her share of the estate?"

"It seems that way." His fist clenched. "Father grew up there. His family worked for the Langdons; he did too. As the years passed, Mother spent more and more of her time in Paris, painting and studying, and I was sent to boarding school. Father saw himself as the rightful heir. He had this bond with the place, loved it, more than he loved Mother or me."

That wouldn't be difficult to believe, if the black eye Marigold sported was anything to go by. "He wants the estate in his name."

"Well, that's obvious, isn't it? Reckons he's entitled to it. He's managed it since Great-grandfather Langdon died, thinks of it as his own. Even changed his name. It's just Penter, Tyler Penter, not *Langdon*-Penter. He claims he wants to find out what happened to Mother's sister as much as she does. The truth of the matter is, he wants proof she's dead because that's the only way the other half of the estate can pass to Mother and give him control of it all. He engaged a private detective to track down Ó'Cuinn. Discovered he'd changed his name to Quinn, was a renowned businessman in Maitland, and was involved with the Labor party. That's why we came to Australia."

So Penter had an agenda right from the very beginning when he'd come looking for Michael. Jane had no trouble believing that, and she certainly wouldn't be calling him Mr. Langdon-Penter anymore. "He thought Michael might have proof because he was the last person to be seen with the young girl they believed might be Marigold's sister."

"It's all a bit far-fetched when you put it like that."

"Jane! This tea'll be cold if you don't come and get it."

"That's Bessie. I've got to go."

Timothy's hand came down on her sleeve. "I'm sorry you thought I'd duped you."

"Used me would be more accurate." She shrugged him off and went into the kitchen to collect the tray.

The Penters and the Messrs. Brown made short work of the fruit-cake and sandwiches Bessie served. Jane managed to force down a glass of water but not much else. More than anything, she wanted to go up to her room and sort out the jumble of information bouncing around in her head. However, Elizabeth insisted she stay and keep taking notes, still worried that in some way Michael's name and reputation might be tarnished.

"Aunt Elizabeth, I don't think there's much more to be said, is there?"

"It seems we have become embroiled in some sort of family dispute. I do, however, want it on record that Michael had nothing to do with that poor child's disappearance. I intend to recap the situation and ask Messrs. Brown to draw up some sort of formal agreement. Transcribe your notes and pass them on to Messrs. Brown."

"I have one more question, though, about the exhibition," Jane said. "It's due to open at the weekend. Do you think it should go ahead or should we cancel?"

"Providing Marigold's happy, we'll go ahead. Imagine Mrs. Witherspoon and her friends if we canceled. It doesn't bear thinking about." Elizabeth patted Jane on the arm in an affectionate gesture, then moved to the head of the table.

"Thank you for your time today. I think we have firmly established Michael had nothing to do with your sister's disappearance. As to who is responsible . . ." Elizabeth paused and glared at Penter as though she was in no doubt he knew more than he was letting on. "I will leave that for you to follow up. I've asked Messrs. Brown to draw up a record of our conversation. Jane has taken notes, and I will ensure a copy is delivered to your accommodation. I would appreciate your signature acknowledging it is an accurate record."

"What about the exhibition? We've invested a deal of money in it." Penter's petulant tone echoed in the room.

Marigold sat motionless, a distant expression on her face, her pale hair sweeping her forehead, the planes of her face perfectly symmetrical. She didn't show a flicker of interest in her husband's inquiry; instead, she turned her eyes to Elizabeth and gave a half smile.

"I'm happy for the exhibition to go ahead," Elizabeth said. "You have everything down, Jane?"

"I'm sorry." Jane gazed down at the blank page in front of her. She'd been so far away she hadn't heard a single word of the conversation. "Most of it, yes."

Unfortunately, nothing explained why Elizabeth had become so upset at the technical college, and again at the preview. Unless there was something that linked the two events. Something they'd all missed.

THIRTY-TWO

There is some truth in the saying 'there is no greater cause for melancholy than idleness.' I feel quite my normal self." Elizabeth relaxed back in the chair with what might have been a satisfied smile on her face. "I couldn't bear the thought that Michael's name might be tarnished."

Which was the perfect lead for Jane. "Does the name Daisy mean anything to you?"

"My name is Elizabeth." She turned her vibrant blue eyes up and offered her trademark half smile. "I will always be Elizabeth, and in my heart, I will always be Michael's sister, in the same way as he will always be my brother."

Jane's mind stilled as she stared into Elizabeth's eyes. But for her dark hair caught in a carefully wound chignon, she was looking at a face so similar to Marigold's as to be uncanny. The more she studied Elizabeth, the less ridiculous the idea became. She had been four when she and Michael left for Australia. Surely at four, a child knew her name. Unless for some reason she'd hidden it, forgotten it, or suffered some tremendous shock. What had Lethbridge said? A traumatic event causing amnesia and loss of speech.

"I think I'll ask Lucy to bring us some tea. This rain has chilled me to the bone," said Elizabeth, ringing the small bell on the table.

"No, on second thought, a glass of Michael's whiskey would be appropriate."

Jane didn't answer, too busy searching for a way to prove conclusively Daisy and Elizabeth were one and the same. The prospect of solving such an intricate puzzle left her giddy and a little light-headed.

"I do think that Langdon-Penter man is appalling. I can't get over the fact that he helped himself to Michael's whiskey."

"And another man's name, to boot. His real name is Tyler Penter. Langdon was Timothy's great-grandfather's name."

"Why would he do that?"

"Marigold's family home has always been known as the Langdon estate." Jane glanced down at her notebook and for the umpteenth time wrote the name Daisy. Who had taken her and how had she gotten from Somerset to the workhouse in Liverpool, where she met Michael?

"I guess in his eyes he's the lord of the manor." Elizabeth gave a derogatory toss of her head. "It's archaic. He is a particularly offensive little man. I have no idea how much longer it will take them to give women the vote in England. His attitude is outrageous. Ah! Thank you, Lucy. Put the tray down here. The jug of water was a thoughtful addition; however, I don't believe we'll be needing it."

Throwing Jane a look of pure loathing, Lucy left the room. "Do you remember any of the paintings at the Tost and Rohu exhibition?"

"You aren't expecting me to go back over that debacle, are you?" Elizabeth took a mouthful of whiskey and let out a long sigh.

"Do you remember the paintings?" Jane asked again.

"No, no I don't. If I close my eyes all I can see are swooping birds. Take this and sip it slowly." Elizabeth pushed a cut-glass tumbler into her hand.

As Jane's fingers closed around the glass she inhaled. Michael, his study, all she owed him, and those final words. *"Do this for me. She has to know."*

She brought her lips to the glass, sipped, and choked.

The palm of Elizabeth's hand came down on her back, knocking what little breath was left in her lungs out in a rush. She put the glass down and groped for some air.

"It's an art."

An art Michael and Elizabeth had obviously perfected. It took Jane a good few moments to recapture her breath. "The painting at the technical college exhibition was *The Village Church*. I found your hat under a display case beside it. Do you think the combination of the picture and the taxidermied birds might have triggered your . . ."

"Dilemma."

"Yes. Your *dilemma*. *The Village Church* was also on show at the preview."

"The occasion of my second *dilemma*."

"Indeed." Jane took another sip of the whiskey, held it in her mouth for a moment, then let it trickle down her throat. Warmth blossomed, giving her courage. She'd never reached a satisfactory resolution without a neatly written equation, but this conundrum didn't lend itself to equations. She took another sip. "I have a hypothesis."

"Go ahead."

"Daisy Dibble disappeared on the twenty-eighth of August, 1862, at the age of four. Five days later, on the first of September, a young girl of similar age was found in Liverpool and taken to the workhouse, one hundred seventy-one and a half miles from Daisy's home. Could that girl have been Daisy?"

"How would a four-year-old child travel that far in a matter of days? Someone must have taken her there."

"Correct." Jane took yet another sip. The flavor was almost smoky, pleasant, if it wasn't taken at speed. "On September the seventh, a week later, Michael's sister, Lizzie Ó'Cuinn, died, along with twenty-one others in a fire in the girls' dormitory at Brownlow Hill in Liverpool. The following day Michael set sail for Australia with his sister."

Elizabeth topped up the two glasses. "Impossible. She was dead."

"Correct."

"Are you being a little pedantic? We are well aware I boarded the ship with Michael."

"Just ensuring we haven't jumped to any unproven conclusions. The last person to see the little girl at the workhouse was Gertrude Finbright, when she was talking to Michael the day after the fire, and she gave him the news of Lizzie's passing."

"You think the little girl who boarded the ship with Michael was Marigold's sister, Daisy." Elizabeth downed the contents of the glass, her pale skin instantly infused with color. She sat statue still for a moment, then slowly lowered the glass to the table. "Which would mean I am Daisy Penter."

"Dibble. Daisy Dibble. Marigold's maiden name was Dibble." Jane waited as a play of emotions swept Elizabeth's face.

"I'm not sure I want to be Daisy Dibble. It's a ridiculous name. I prefer Elizabeth Quinn."

Jane smothered a laugh, or perhaps it was a hiccup, and pushed herself to her feet. "That would make the offensive little man your brother-in-law."

Another hiccup managed to escape Jane's lips. Her knees didn't appear capable of supporting her legs. The ceiling of the room merged horribly with the floor and the rose-patterned wallpaper took on a bilious hue.

Elizabeth tucked her arm under Jane's elbow and led her upstairs to her bedroom. "It's an acquired habit. You'll be fine in the morning." Dear, oh dear. The girl's education was seriously lacking.

There was no one to blame but herself. She could well remember the first time Michael handed her a glass of whiskey. It was in the early days of the depression, the day she'd bought the first of the properties at auction, while he was busy trying to find somewhere for the poor owners to stash the remains of their belongings.

Aye! How she missed him. Missed his comforting presence, his rollicking laugh, his overprotectiveness, and, more than anything else, his friendship. She couldn't have asked for a better brother . . . yet he wasn't. It was all a little strange. More peculiar than knowing she wasn't Elizabeth Quinn.

She was. She'd become Elizabeth the moment she'd followed him up the gangplank and taken his hand.

So many people standing on the dockside, shouting and screaming, pushing barrows and heaving packing cases. It was impossible to know where she was going. Knees, hundreds of legs and knees, some patched, some scratched and bleeding, others covered by skirts and petticoats, one set bare, petticoat hitched to waist height as a man leaned against a woman and bumped her into the wall.

All she wanted was to find Michael.

She'd seen him leave the workhouse after he'd spoken to Miss Finbright, his big broad shoulders heaving. She knew he was crying. He'd walked so fast, not looking back, almost running. It wasn't until he'd reached the gangplank that she caught up. As he took a step she recognized the sole of his shoe, covered with ash and dirt. The ash and dirt they'd thrown over Lizzie and the other girls. Dropping them deep into the pit, hiding them from the light. Lizzie didn't like the dark; Daisy didn't either.

Elizabeth's chest heaved and she rushed for the bowl and vomited, vomited all of Michael's best whiskey and a bundle of memories she hadn't known she carried. She swished some water around in the bowl, opened the window, and chucked it out into the rain, hopefully beyond the veranda. She wiped her face and lowered herself onto the bed. She should sleep, but the dark tide of memory refused to abate.

Ebb and flow. Like the magic lantern show she'd once seen with Michael. Flickering images, a darkened path, a sweaty hand dragging, no, hauling her along.

Her feet went from under her, stuck under his stinking armpit like a basket of dirty washing. The slam of the door, the darkness, the stench. Worse, worse, the flapping wings, diving and swooping, brushing her cheeks with their feathers, the strangled shrieks.

She burrowed under the bedcover, arms shielding her head.

Deep breaths, slowly pulling the air into her lungs.

Clickety clack, clickety clack. The smell of burning coal, belching smoke. *Tonk, tonk, tonk.* Grit in her eyes, scratching and sore, and dark, so very, very dark. The plaintive cry of a whistle. Then light. Bright, bright light. A great door creaking open. The reek of stale cabbage and sweat, tutting sounds. *"Hop in here with Lizzie."*

A small body, arms pulling her close, and blessed warmth beneath the rough blankets.

───────※───────

Jane groaned and closed her eyes against the blinding light shafting through the curtains.

"Miss Elizabeth thought you might like a cup of jasmine tea." Lucy's face drifted into focus.

She ran her tongue over her parched lips, struggled into an upright position. "Yes, please." The banging in her head reached a crescendo. "Leave the curtains, Lucy. I'll sort them out when I get up."

"That'll be right now. Miss Quinn's in the dining room waiting on you. She's had her breakfast."

The mere thought of the smell of kedgeree set her stomach roiling. "Tell her I'll be down in a moment."

"She says you're to bring your notebook."

"Thank you, Lucy."

For some reason it took Jane much longer than usual to get downstairs, and when she finally reached the dining room door she realized she'd forgotten her notebook.

"I'll be there in a moment, Aunt Elizabeth." She trooped back upstairs, each footstep reverberating inside her skull. What was wrong with her? She never suffered from headaches, not even at that time of the month she wasn't supposed to mention. With a sigh, she pushed open her bedroom door, collected her notebook, and trotted back downstairs.

Elizabeth eyed her with a half smile. "You look like something the cat dragged in." She pushed a small teapot across the table. "Drink this."

"I've had some."

"This is green tea, and you need to eat that with it." Elizabeth pointed to a blackened piece of something on the small saucer.

"What is it?"

"A dried plum."

Jane popped the shriveled nugget into her mouth and spat it straight back out again.

"Better if you nibble on it while you drink the tea. An excellent cure for overindulgence the morning after."

And how would Elizabeth know that?

"How do you feel?"

"A little strange. Disorientated. Vague." So vague she hadn't noticed Elizabeth was dressed in her hat and coat, and her large black umbrella sat propped against the table. "Are you going out?" It wasn't Sunday, was it? What difference did that make? Elizabeth hadn't set foot inside a church since Michael's funeral; perhaps it was something she'd done to please him, not for any belief of her own.

"I am, and so are you." Elizabeth peered down at her, almost a challenge. "Finish your tea."

"Where are we going?"

"To the auction house." She glanced at the carriage clock on the mantelpiece. "We're meeting Mrs. Penter there in half an hour."

"Marigold? Not Mr. Penter?"

"The message I sent asked her to meet me there at eleven. As you can see, we have fifteen minutes. Hurry up. Lucy has fetched your things. You'll need an umbrella. It's been raining nonstop since last night."

Had it? She hadn't noticed. "We can call a cab."

"No time. A bit of rain never hurt anyone."

"Why do you want to see Mrs. Penter?"

"It occurred to me last night that unless I face my fears I may never know my origins."

Jane finished the rest of the plum and washed it down with some tea.

"We must tell Marigold of our suspicions, share everything with her. If she is my sister, she has a right to know as much as I do. I must face the past. How did I get to the workhouse in Liverpool?"

Elizabeth's question made Jane start. "You've remembered something." No need to ask the question. She could tell by the look on Elizabeth's face.

"Last night I had this . . . I don't know what to call it. It wasn't a dream . . ."

Jane straightened. "A repressed memory surfaced, as Lethbridge said it might."

"Indeed. I was being dragged down a path, struggling. I was thrown into some place, and the birds came. Then I was on a train. I'm certain it was a train. I could smell coal smoke and my eyes were gritty with soot."

"Were you alone?"

"No."

"Who was with you?"

Elizabeth stopped her pacing and picked up her umbrella. "I don't know."

———≈———

By the time they reached the auction house the rain was coming down in sheets.

"Good morning, John."

"Good morning, Miss Quinn." He took Elizabeth's umbrella and held out his hand. "Miss Jane."

She handed over her dripping umbrella. "Good morning, John."

"Mrs. Penter is here. She's waiting in the auction room."

"Very good, thank you. Come along, Jane."

Marigold stood in the middle of the room looking damp and more than a little forlorn. No color tinted her pale face and dark circles shadowed her eyes.

"Mrs. Penter, thank you for coming."

"I expect you've decided you want to cancel my exhibition."

"No, on the contrary, we are expecting it to go ahead. I thought I made that clear yesterday."

THE GIRL IN THE PAINTING

"Circumstances have changed." Marigold took off her hat and gave it a shake. Drops of water scattered across the floor.

"Why don't you take off your coat as well? You're wet through."

She fumbled with the buttons and shrugged out of the sopping garment. "Thank you. It's been pouring all night."

"Surely you didn't spend the night outside?"

"No, but I've been out since early this morning." Her shoulders heaved. "Timothy and I have been searching for my husband. He seems to have vanished."

"He's gone back to Sydney?"

"I have no idea. Timothy is still out looking for him. No one saw him leave our rooms last night. Timothy is checking the railway station."

"I'm sure he will turn up in his own good time."

"I hope so." Marigold's face flushed. "We had an argument last night."

"Why don't you come and sit?" Elizabeth led Marigold to the bench seat in the middle of the room. "Jane, perhaps some tea?"

That was the last thing she wanted to do. "I'll ask John."

"I'm sure you can manage. Milky tea with sugar. John will have some milk, and bring some of those Iced VoVos you've got stashed in the drawer upstairs."

———— ≈ ————

Elizabeth waited until Jane left the room before sitting next to Marigold. "How can I help?"

"I feel so bad I even considered the possibility Michael might be responsible for taking Daisy."

"Think nothing of it. We all jump to conclusions."

"Last night Tyler lost his temper. He'd been drinking and he, well, when he drinks he becomes arrogant, difficult. He accused me of sabotaging his attempts to secure the estate, our future."

"I'm sure it was simply the alcohol talking." Elizabeth offered the platitude even though it didn't ring true. "May I ask a personal question?"

Marigold rummaged in her pocket and brought out a soggy handkerchief, patted the reddened end of her nose, then nodded.

"Your mother's will. Is there provision should Daisy's death not be proven?" Surely the family had received advice from solicitors.

"Indeed there is. If Daisy is not found, then her share of the estate passes to Timothy on his twenty-first birthday, next year."

"I can't imagine that causing any great problem. Surely Timothy would want to keep the estate intact."

"Of course he would. And when I die, as my only son he will inherit my portion as well. However, my husband doesn't see it that way. As you know, he firmly believes he is entitled to all of it."

Elizabeth patted Marigold's hand and stood and edged toward the paintings, waiting for her heart to begin pounding and the birds swooping. Like a fleeting shadow, Lethbridge's words drifted through her mind. *"A repressed memory of a traumatic event . . ."* She boldly fronted the painting of the pair walking along the path hand in hand. "Who are the people in this painting?"

"I don't know. In her later years, my mother suggested that the bond between twins might mean I had, in some way, absorbed Daisy's memories." She lifted her shoulders in defeat. "That painting represents one of many memories that flit in and out of my mind—when I wake, before I fall asleep. You must know what I mean."

Oh yes, she did. The night before she'd possibly experienced a very similar memory, except she hadn't walked happily away; she'd been hauled, screaming and kicking.

"Do you believe that painting relates to Daisy's disappearance?"

"As I said, Mother was convinced it did."

Elizabeth studied the painting. "The little girl doesn't seem to be afraid. She seems to be quite comfortable holding the boy's hand."

And he was a boy, not a man. Small and thin, a smock over a pair of ragged trousers and dirty bare feet. How could she have let the odious Penter man suggest it could have been Michael? He'd been a big strapping bloke, wide shoulders and a grin to match, not cowered and scrawny.

"Where were you when it happened?"

"I don't remember. Mother and I went over this time and time again. When she discovered Daisy was missing, she searched the garden and then we went down to the gypsy camp."

"She took you with her?"

"Of course. After Daisy vanished she never let me out of her sight. She was terrified I'd be taken too."

"If you don't know who took your sister, how can you presume that the girl in the workhouse in Liverpool and Daisy are one and the same?"

"That's the very argument Tyler and I had last night. I can't understand how he knew to go to the workhouse. He is convinced Daisy died in the fire, but how did she get there? A four-year-old couldn't find her own way to Yeovil and onto a train to Liverpool."

"If we could answer that question it would solve both of our . . ." Elizabeth cleared her throat. "Our dilemmas."

Marigold's head came up with a snap.

Elizabeth drew in a deep breath and sat down next to her. She reached out and took one of Marigold's cold hands in her own and chaffed it. Peculiar to think that she might be holding her sister's hand.

"I believe I might be Daisy."

The poor woman let out a mournful wail, which brought Jane skidding into the room, scattering pink biscuits and coconut all over the floor. "Can I do anything?"

"Pick up the biscuits and pour some tea." Elizabeth slipped an arm around Marigold's shoulder.

"I'm sorry." Marigold sniffed. "It's all too much. After all this time."

Jane produced a cup of milky tea laced with sugar. The mere thought of it turned Elizabeth's stomach, but Marigold took it in both hands and sipped. Gradually the color returned to her cheeks.

"I'm not sure I quite understand." Marigold rubbed at her arm and Elizabeth's skin prickled in response.

"It's a very long story, and one I would like to share with you. But first, let's find you some dry clothes. We'll take a hansom cab and return to Church Street."

Marigold started to rise, then sank back down again. "I told Timothy I'd be here. When he finds his father he'll bring him here."

"If he finds . . ."

"I beg your pardon, Jane?"

"Nothing, nothing, Aunt Elizabeth. Why don't I stay here and you and Marigold take a cab home?"

"An excellent idea. Marigold and I are much of the same size. I'll find her some dry clothes and we'll wait for you there. Please make sure you clean up those biscuits."

THIRTY-THREE

Jane picked up two of the cracked biscuits and crammed them both into her mouth. She was starving. She hadn't had any breakfast except for the strange dried plum and tea that smelled of freshly mown grass and something she'd rather not dwell on.

While she chewed she stared at the paintings. In the faded yellow-gray light it was difficult to see the details. Through the window, storm clouds were massing, and as if in answer to her observation, a huge clap of thunder sent her rocketing to the window. It was a good thing Elizabeth and Marigold had decided to take a cab. They'd be drenched if they'd tried to walk. She'd simply have to stay put for a while and survive on Iced VoVos.

The tea in the pot was still warm, so she poured a cup and wandered around looking for the girl in each painting.

A sudden rap made her turn.

Timothy! His face pressed to the glass, hair flattened, rain streaming down his face. She gestured to the door.

He as good as fell through and landed in a heap at her feet. "It's pouring. I've never seen anything like it. Australia doesn't do anything by half, does it?"

"How do you know?" That was a bit brusque, but she still hadn't got over the fact he hadn't been honest with her from the outset. He peeled off his coat and dropped it to the ground, then his jacket, until he was in his shirt sleeves and braces. A great damp patch ran across his shoulders, making his shirt stick to his skin. "I can't find Father. He had a skinful last night and Mother's worried he might make a nuisance of himself. He doesn't do well when he's been drinking."

"I expect he's found somewhere nice and dry."

"Nah! I reckon he took the train back to Sydney. He was in a right mood. I went to the station; they thought a man matching his description might have got the last train. Couldn't be sure, though."

"The last train?"

"Yep. The rails are under about two feet of water and it's rising. Something about some dam that's broken its bank and sent the water rushing over the railway line. No more trains until the water level drops." He shook the rain from his hair. "Does the sun ever shine in Maitland? It's done nothing but pour since we've been here."

"That's a ridiculous exaggeration. It didn't rain for Michael's funeral."

"It was raining the day I arrived with the paintings."

"We're due for some rain."

"Looks like a bit more than rain to me out there. More like a flood. The water's up to the bottom of the bridge."

"It'll go down." There hadn't been a decent flood in Jane's lifetime. The last one had been in 1893. She'd seen the levels marked on some of the older buildings. "Your lips are blue. Would you like a cup of tea? I'll make another pot. There are some biscuits too."

She picked up the tray and led the way past John's empty office and upstairs. He'd probably gone to check the water; his mother lived down near the river.

"Sit." Jane shoveled a whole load of brochures and advertising flyers into a pile and made room at the table. Once she had her back to him, lighting the stove, she summoned up the courage to speak. "I still haven't forgiven you."

"For what?"

"For not telling the truth."

Timothy came and stood alongside her. "I told you the truth." His contrite expression was at least in his favor. "I just didn't mention a few things, and by then it was a bit late."

"It was, wasn't it." She plonked the teacup in front of him, minus saucer, and she wasn't too sure he deserved an Iced VoVo either. "Where else did you look, apart from the railway station?"

"I checked all the pubs, called in at some of the shops, the School of Arts and the technical college. I thought perhaps he'd gone there since they'd offered to have the exhibition in the first place."

Hopefully Mrs. Witherspoon would be more worried about the rain than spreading rumors of Penter's disappearance. Jane pushed the packet of biscuits across the table.

"Thanks." Timothy chewed thoughtfully for a moment. "Do these come ready-made from the shop?" He turned the packaging over and took another.

"Delicious, aren't they? Arnott's biscuits—they make them locally, in Newcastle. Everyone loves their biscuits, meat pies too."

"I'm not surprised."

She wasn't letting him off that easily. "What about this business about Michael being the one who kidnapped Daisy."

He scratched at his head, making his wet hair flop over his forehead. "Father came up with it. I'm not sure when, but he decided that because Michael was the last one to see Daisy alive he must have been the one who took her to the workhouse."

"Ah! So he put four and four together and came up with . . ."

"Something close to fifty-six, now the truth is out."

"Are you upset to find out that he lied to your mother about contacting Gertrude Finbright?"

"It came as a shock, of course it did, but I can't say I was upset about it. I was almost pleased."

"Pleased?" The word ended in a shrill squeak.

"I wouldn't care if I never set eyes on my father again. It's as simple as that. He pushes Mother around, makes her life a misery. When he drinks he belts her. He's about given up on me because I'm bigger than him, but it wasn't always that way."

Jane sneaked a glance at his broad shoulders and the corded muscles in his forearms below his rolled-up sleeves, where drips of rain still clung to the pale hairs. She clenched her fingers, resisting the impulse to reach out and touch his arm.

"I didn't want to come with them on this trip. I wanted to walk away, leave him to his own misguided ambitions. But I couldn't leave Mother."

The image of him standing in front of Marigold in the auction house, protecting her and taunting his father, sprang to her mind. "But he's your father, surely . . ." She couldn't imagine having a family, a real mother and father, and hating either one of them.

"A mother who lived in the shadow of her missing sister and escaped into her art, and a father who was obsessed by money and position. He believes he has some God-given right to be lord of the manor, like old man Langdon. Once Grandma died there was no stopping him. He wants to restore the Langdon estate to its former glory. He didn't want to *find* Daisy. He wanted Mr. Quinn to provide proof she was dead."

"But she may not be." The remains of the Iced VoVo churned in Jane's stomach.

"What do you mean she may not be? Who's keeping secrets now?"

This was a bit tricky. Was it her place to tell Timothy that she be-lieved Elizabeth was more than likely his long-lost aunt?

"Where is Mother, by the way? She said she would be here, some-thing about the exhibition being canceled." He turned and searched the room as though she might jump out from behind a cupboard.

"She and Aunt Elizabeth decided to go home."

"G'woam?"

Why did he have to say it like that? It made Jane shudder. Most of the time she barely noticed his accent.

Timothy propped his elbows on the table, rested his chin on his interlocked fingers, and stared into her eyes. She couldn't hold his gaze.

"I've got the feeling you're not telling me the whole truth," he said. "What's good for the gander . . ."

He had her there.

"You remember Aunt Elizabeth was . . . unwell."

"The turn she had at the preview, you mean."

"Yes, and one prior to that. I'm certain they were caused by re-pressed memories triggered by your mother's paintings."

"I'm not sure I'm following you. What's a repressed memory?"

"Something your brain chooses to forget because of the trauma it induced. Aunt Elizabeth suffers from ornithophobia."

"Is it asking too much to request you speak English?"

Jane smiled. "A fear of birds."

"There aren't any birds in Mother's paintings."

"You're right. That's exactly what I don't understand."

Timothy frowned at her. "There is the dovecot."

"The what?"

"The dovecot. Next to the church." He held out his hand. "Come downstairs and I'll show you."

It seemed perfectly natural to clasp his hand as they clattered down the stairs. Jane's heart lifted. It was so very good to have a friend. Perhaps she had forgiven him.

"It's this one." He stopped in front of *The Village Church*. He dropped her hand and rested his index finger against the canvas. "There. The dovecot."

Jane stared at the painting she'd looked at more times than she could count. "It's a mausoleum. A burial crypt."

"No. It's a dovecot, a pigeon house."

"Why would you keep birds in a graveyard?"

"The building wasn't originally in the church grounds." Timothy sketched an area in the painting with his finger and then pointed to the narrow openings at the top of the building. "The birds fly off every morning through these tiny windows, forage, then come home each night to roost. Their droppings are collected and used on the land. Free, since the birds don't have to be fed, and free eggs and squabs."

"Squabs?"

"The young. They can't fly until after the four-week-old mark. Easy pickings. It dates way back, hundreds of years. You had to have permission from the king to own a dovecot; it was a bit of a status symbol."

"Did the Langdons own it?"

"Until Grandma Maggie sold off a parcel of land about twenty years ago and it was incorporated into the grounds of the church."

Jane's mind cartwheeled . . . If nothing else, it explained Elizabeth's reaction to the picture. "I don't know what I'd do without you. Aunt Elizabeth will be thrilled we've been able to make sense of her reaction to the painting."

She'd delivered the playful punch to his shoulder before she'd given it a second thought. His eyes widened. The air stood still. His palms cupped her cheeks.

Tiny flecks of color danced in his eyes as he leaned in and planted his warm, soft lips on hers.

"Oh!" She reeled back, practically sending them both flying. Was that a kiss? No one had ever kissed her before. She'd read about kissing. Thought there was something slightly unsavory about the entire idea. Perhaps not.

"I'm sorry." He raked his hands through his hair, his face the color of the fruit in Bessie's summer pudding.

Jane's heart thundered fit to bust. What was she supposed to do now? She shuffled her feet. The next thing she knew he was doing it again. Soft, warm. Her eyes closed.

And then he pulled away.

It took her a moment or two to gather her thoughts, then she asked, "Why did you kiss me?"

He looked remarkably pleased with himself. "I've wanted to ever since I found you at the technical college with Mother's painting on the floor and a guilty look on your face."

"I've never been kissed before." She ran her fingers over her buzzing lips; they felt as though they'd been stung. Perhaps they had.

"I'm sure you have," said Timothy.

"No. Never."

"Not even a peck on the cheek, a goodnight kiss?"

"No."

"What about a kiss-it-better kiss?"

"No, not one of those either."

And then he got this sort of pitying look on his face. She wasn't going to have that. Words bypassed her brain and tumbled out of her mouth. "There's a possibility Elizabeth Quinn could be your mother's missing sister."

"I beg your pardon?"

That got his mind off pity and anything else he might be thinking. No one was going to look at her as though she was poor little Nell Trent in *The Old Curiosity Shop*, surrounded by doodads and thingamabobs.

"It can't be proven, but it appears logical. All the facts indicate that Elizabeth Quinn was, in a former life, your aunt Daisy Dibble."

Perhaps the most satisfying fact was that his mouth gaped.

≈

Quite where the rest of the afternoon and evening disappeared to, Jane wasn't certain. She and Timothy talked and talked. There wasn't any more kissing, although they did drift closer, and something other than a fire kept her warm while the rain continued to drum on the iron roof, cocooning them in a world of their own. With a silent apology to Michael and Elizabeth, she told Timothy about the sequence of events that had led her to believe Elizabeth and Daisy were one and the same, and plied him with questions, which he answered willingly. None of them helped her solve the unsurmountable stumbling block.

"Unless we can discover who took Daisy and how she got to the workhouse in Liverpool, I can't see any way to prove your theory," said Timothy. "Wouldn't it be wonderful if there was some way of taking a sample of two people's blood and comparing them? Perhaps phrenology could help match their bone structure."

He gave a lopsided sort of half smile, which suddenly reminded her of Elizabeth.

Elizabeth! "I think we better go."

"It's still pouring."

"I've got an umbrella, and there are some galoshes and oilskins out the back. We should get moving."

THE GIRL IN THE PAINTING

Timothy followed her downstairs. There was still no sign of John, and the auction hall remained as they'd left it. Jane found John's stash of wet-weather gear hanging on the back of the door of his cubbyhole and they bundled themselves into the huge coats. Barely able to see over the collar of the oilskin, Jane opened the back door and stepped outside, straight into a puddle that lapped the top of her boots.

She wrangled the padlock and chain into place, then Timothy tucked her arm through his.

The water sloshed and pushed against them. It had to be over the embankment near Belmore Bridge. They fought through the swirling tide, slithering and sliding, laughing and carrying on like a couple of children. By the time they reached Church Street, rain had soaked right through the oilskin to her clothes.

"We're almost there. I'm surprised Aunt Elizabeth hasn't sent out a search party."

"I wonder what happened to Father." There was a plaintive note in Timothy's voice. Perhaps all his harsh words about his father masked a disappointment, or maybe he still held out hope it was all a misunderstanding. "No matter what he has done he's still my father."

They waded up the front path. One look at the side of the house told her the only way in was through the front door. Jane slammed the knocker hard three times, and before she could draw breath Lucy stood there, the frills on her cap wilting around her damp hair.

"Where have you been? Bessie's been carrying on a treat and we didn't dare send out a search party in this weather."

"At the auction house. Is Aunt Elizabeth home?"

"'Course she is."

"Are you going to let us in?"

Lucy raised her right eyebrow high up her forehead—a trick that had always made Jane jealous. "Who's this?"

"This is Timothy Penter. Mr. and Mrs. Penter's son. You would have seen him at the preview."

"I don't remember you 'anging off his arm like that."

Jane disentangled herself and tried to ignore Timothy's gruff bark of laughter. It was difficult. A grin kept creeping across her face when she least expected it.

"Better take those wet things off and leave 'em out here. I'll tell Miss Quinn you're home. The both of you."

Lucy stomped off, managing to make the paintings in the hallway rattle despite the thick carpet.

They shrugged out of their sopping coats and boots and left them in a pile by the door. "Might be a good idea if we hurry. Lucy's probably spinning some fairy tale."

The sound of laughter drifted along the hallway. Jane led the way, Timothy only a step behind her, making her conscious of the heat of his body. She suspected he'd grasp her hand given half a chance.

When they burst into the sitting room, Elizabeth and Marigold barely noticed their arrival. They were sitting together on the rose-covered sofa, so alike that Jane was left in no doubt about their relationship. Both had their legs crossed at the ankles, their shoulders straight, and they were angled toward each other, the tilt to their heads leaving only a minuscule gap between them.

"Ah! We were wondering . . ." Elizabeth began.

". . . where you'd got to," finished Marigold.

"Have you looked outside?" said Jane. "The river must have breached the embankment. High Street will be flooded by the morning."

"I think that's highly unlikely. It hasn't happened for twenty years or more." Elizabeth turned to Marigold. "Your rooms are on the upper floors, aren't they?"

"Yes, they are." Marigold's eyes lit on Timothy and she lifted her eyebrows in question.

He raised his shoulders. "Last seen at the railway station a good few hours ago. I checked the nearby pubs—no sign, and no one remembered seeing him."

"What have you been doing all this time?"

Timothy's warm hand closed over Jane's and he tugged her to his side.

"I see." Marigold and Elizabeth said in unison, quirking identical half smiles.

Elizabeth turned and flicked aside the curtain. The sound of the rain hammering against the window instantly filled the room. "How did you get home?"

Marigold let out an easy laugh. "That was a silly question. Look at the pair of them. They're both sodden."

"Go and get into some dry clothes, and, Jane, ask Bessie to see what she can find for Timothy."

"I'm perfectly fine."

"Nonsense. We don't want anyone coming down with a chill."

Jane slipped her hand from Timothy's grasp. "Aunt Elizabeth, can you spare me a moment. I have something I'd like to tell you." She could hardly stand still. One more question answered. To know that Elizabeth's reaction to the painting was perfectly logical filled her with such a sense of satisfaction.

"Not now, Jane. Not now. Marigold and I are busy. We have a lot of catching up to do."

This was far more important. "Aunt Elizabeth—"

"Jane, go and get out of your wet clothes and ask Bessie to find something for Timothy."

Incapable of containing her loud huff, she marched out of the room and made her way to the kitchen, where she found John sitting at the table looking like something dredged from the bottom of the Hunter.

He stood up. "Hope you locked up before you left."

"Yes, I did. How bad is it?"

"Not good. Came to tell Bessie here. We'll be needing to get those paintings upstairs if this keeps up. Not much else that'll come to any harm. Got that to be thankful for, even if the river does keep rising."

"So it's going to?"

"No doubt about that. Message came in from Singleton about an hour ago. River's topped forty-seven feet. They're saying everyone in the lower parts of the town should prepare for the worst. It'll take a bit to make its way downstream."

"Not much we can do until it happens," said Bessie. "Ain't no one going to put a stop to that water. Look at you, Miss Jane. Like a drowned rat. Go and get some dry clothes on."

"I'm on my way. Bessie, Aunt Elizabeth asked if you could dig something out for Timothy. We got saturated on our way back from the auction house." She pulled him into the kitchen.

"Oh, did *we* indeed. I expect you'll be wanting something to eat too. Go on, off you go. I'll dig out something for Timothy while his clothes dry. There's mulligatawny on the stove. You can eat in here. Miss Elizabeth and Miss Marigold have already had a bite."

"Bessie, what about you? You may not be able to get home."

"I'll be all right, don't you worry. Worse comes to worse, I'll bunk down with Lucy."

Swallowing a gurgle of laughter at the look on Lucy's face, Jane ran up the stairs.

It bucketed all night. Marigold and Timothy ended up staying at Church Street, and the following morning a bedraggled John appeared with news that the river had risen even more, although no one would ever know by how much because the gauge had washed away sometime during the night.

Jane still hadn't managed to get Elizabeth on her own. Somehow she couldn't bring herself to tell her about the dovecot in front of Marigold. They seemed to be getting on so very well, but Elizabeth was such a private person and Jane had simply no idea how much she had told Marigold.

"They've lost a heap of outhouses and fences," John reported, "and someone said one of the brick houses washed away. It's eight or nine feet deep on the road to the south."

"Do you think it'll reach High Street? Do we need to move the paintings?" Elizabeth asked.

"Not real sure. They've got sandbags at Belmore Bridge and last night's Newcastle train only got as far as Tarro. The line's under."

"I'm so sorry." Elizabeth reached for Marigold's arm. "Last time the waters dropped quickly. I expect everything will be back to normal soon."

Which would be a shame. Jane shot a look at Timothy. On second thought, perhaps it was a good thing. Neither he nor Marigold would be going anywhere for the next few days.

"Timothy?"

"Mother?"

"I'd like you to go back to our rooms and see if your father has returned. If he's not there, go and see what else you can find out. Perhaps John would be kind enough to go with you." Marigold turned to Elizabeth. "Would you mind? I'd prefer he didn't go alone."

"John, would you go with Timothy? You have a much better understanding of the floodwaters, and the locality."

Timothy didn't appear dreadfully keen on the prospect. He finished his tea and pushed back his chair, his mouth stretched taut like a fence line. "Supposing I do find Father, what would you like me to say?"

"Better to inform him that I am here."

His eyes flared. "How much more of his rubbish are you going to take, Mother? Haven't you had enough? Look at you." He pointed to the bruise still shadowing Marigold's cheek. "When are you going to call a halt to it?"

"Timothy, this is neither the time nor the place for this discussion."

"I think it is. The man's done nothing but make your life a misery. You find out he's lied, used you and Grandma Maggie to further his own misguided greed, and you still care about where he is. I'm sorry, Mother, but I am not going to do it."

"Timothy, he's my husband, your father."

"Quite honestly, I hope he's drowned." Timothy slammed out of the room, leaving gaping mouths and a thundercloud to rival Mother Nature.

"I'll go with Timothy." Jane bolted through the door before Elizabeth or Marigold could protest.

She found him on the back veranda, shrugging into a damp oilskin.

"Wait for me." She pulled on her boots and tossed her shoes through the back door. "I know the area better than you do. We'll go back to the station and talk to Mr. Marsh, the stationmaster, and if he thinks your father left on the last train we'll see if he can telegraph ahead."

THIRTY-FOUR

Overnight the waters had risen alarmingly, and the noise from the continuing rain and the river made conversation impossible. All the shops were closed, and a group of men were filling sandbags and carting them up into High Street.

It took ages to reach the station. One look at the tracks confirmed the fact there'd be no trains going anywhere for at least a week. Jane hammered on the window of the ticket office, and eventually Mr. Marsh appeared and waved her to the door.

"What brought you out in this lot?"

"This is Timothy Penter."

"Don't stand there, come in, come in."

They eased through the door and stood dripping in the waiting room.

"We're trying to locate Timothy's father, Mr. Penter. You said yesterday you thought he might have taken the Sydney train."

"No, I didn't."

Timothy opened his mouth to speak, but Jane rested her hand on his arm. "Are you sure you didn't see him?"

"Not right sure. If you mean the rude sod who barged in here throwing his weight around and buggered off without a by your leave, then I might well have."

"You thought he might have taken the last train," Jane prompted.

Mr. Marsh stuck out his chest and glared at Timothy. "*Might* being the operative word. Someone ought to teach that father of yours a few manners. We don't deal with people like that around here."

Jane shot a look at Timothy, who lifted his shoulders before turning to stare out at the water gushing over the gutter and onto the platform.

"Mr. Marsh, could you please tell us what happened? I'm very sorry if Mr. Penter caused a problem. He'd been feeling unwell and—"

"Drunk as a skunk he was, reeked of the stuff. Told him the train was running late. There was water on the lines, but we thought it'd get through. Left him sitting over there. Next thing I knew, there was a big to-do going on and he stormed off. Last I saw of him he was standing at the end of the platform. Might have got the train, might not. To be honest, I don't care very much."

Jane sank down onto the bench seat. "Is there no one who might know? I wondered if we could telegraph ahead and see if anyone saw him getting off the train in Sydney."

"Be like trying to find a tadpole in the ocean."

"Can you remember any of the other people who were in the waiting room?"

"'Course I can. There was Mrs. Pettigrew and her two daughters, Major Witherspoon, the bloke from the Pig and Whistle—he's the one that Penter fellow tried to take on. If it hadn't been for my boy they would have knocked each other senseless."

"Your boy? Hunter."

"Yeah, 'Unter. He was here giving me a hand with the sandbagging."

"Where's Hunter now?"

Mr. Marsh flicked a thumb over his shoulder. "Up at the house moving the furniture upstairs."

"Can we go and have a word with him?"

"Be my guest." He eased open the door. "Off you go, quick smart. Don't want any more wet in here."

Jane and Timothy trudged back out into the rain. "Why didn't he tell me that yesterday?"

"I think maybe your father upset him, and he wasn't overly keen on being helpful."

"Good thing you came with me." Timothy tucked her hand into the crook of his arm and, heads down, they battled the wind to the stationmaster's cottage.

Hunter must have seen them coming because he was hanging out of the upstairs window before they had a chance to knock on the door. "Hey, Jane. What're you doing out in this rubbish?"

"Looking for someone, thought you might be able to help."

"Give us a tick and I'll be down." He pulled the window closed and disappeared.

"Let me do the talking," said Jane.

Timothy nodded and stepped back under the eaves as the door swung open.

"Come in."

"Thank you." Jane stepped inside. "I won't keep you a moment. I'm trying to find out if someone got the last train yesterday. A Mr. Penter."

Hunter shook his head, pulled a bit of a face. "Nope. Not that I know. What's he look like? Thought I knew most people around here."

"Not terribly tall, quite thin, pale eyes."

"Oh, the ratty bloke, three sheets to the wind. Nah! He didn't get on the train. Got fed up waiting, decided he was going to hire a sulky and head for Morpeth. Didn't like his chances. The bridge went under sometime last night, but he wasn't taking no for an answer."

"Any idea where he was going to hire the sulky?"

"Pointed him in the direction of Smythe's. He's the only person who'd hire him a horse in this weather. Do anything for a quid, that bloke."

"Thank you, Hunter." Jane clasped his hand in both of hers, watched his ears turn a horrifying shade of purple, then bolted.

Resisting the temptation to call out to Timothy, she ran down the length of the platform and found him sheltering under the awning.

"Any luck?"

"He went to hire a sulky. Come on." She grabbed his hand and towed him down the road.

When they reached Smythe's, the stable was locked up. Not a body in sight, human or equine.

"Now what?"

"We're going to have to go right to the end of High Street." Thirty soggy minutes later, Jane stopped. "The bridge is down there. Over Wallis Creek." She pointed into a vast expanse of swirling water.

"Right, well, that's not going to do us much good. Is there another way to this Morpeth place?"

She shook her head. "Not without crossing the creek."

"It's clearing up a bit." Timothy pointed up to a small patch of blue between two scudding clouds. "If it stops raining the water will drop."

"Not for two or three days, it won't. Might even rise as it comes downriver."

"So we're cut off? All of Maitland."

"That's about it."

"I can see the edges of the bridge."

"That's the handrail."

"Maybe we could—"

"Don't even think about it. Those waters can carry a house away."

"Let's go and take a look."

Shaking her head, Jane followed Timothy down the road. They didn't get within fifty feet of the bridge. With the water lapping at their knees they watched whole trees and heavy branches, an upturned wagon, fence posts, and what looked remarkably like the bloated remains of a sheep hurtle downstream.

"I get your point. What am I going to tell Mother?"

"We can't do any more than we have." For goodness' sake, Penter was a grown man. If he'd been foolish enough to try and cross the river in full flood it served him right. "We better be getting back. If the waters keep rising we won't be able to reach Church Street."

Jane turned off the road across country. They'd cut the trip in half if they didn't go back along High Street.

"It's not the way we came," said Timothy.

"I know. It's a shortcut. If we're lucky, we'll be able to get through. If not, we'll just backtrack."

"Rain's stopped." Timothy unbuttoned his oilskin and scratched at his hair under his hat. "It's warm." A gust of wind snatched his hat and it flew down the bank toward the river.

"You'll never catch it."

"Not mine. John's." He took off.

Jane stood on the rise, unable to control her smile as Timothy galloped down the bank, arms flailing. A bubble of joy broke in her chest.

So many dreadful things had happened in the past few weeks. But the whole mystery surrounding Elizabeth had fired her with an enthusiasm she hadn't known she lacked. Not only that, Timothy's arrival had turned her life around, making her realize how lonely she'd been. As much as she appreciated Michael's bequest, he had made her realize the narrowness of her life in Maitland. She couldn't wait until she was twenty-one. So much to explore—university, travel, a thousand possibilities.

She lifted her arm and waved.

Standing under a large tree, the wide expanse of water behind him and John's hat nowhere to be seen, Timothy waved his arms around and around his head, high in the air.

"Jane!" His voice drifted up toward her as he beckoned.

She folded her arms and stood watching him. If the hat was gone, it was gone. There would be plenty of others coming through the auction house, and John wasn't the sort of man who'd be upset about an accident.

"Jane! Jane!" The breeze from the river amplified his words and she picked up a tinge of panic.

Without further thought, she bolted down the incline, cursing her damp skirts and the overlong oilskin. It wasn't until she'd almost reached the tree that she spotted the remains of a sulky, no sign of the horse.

"I've found him. Father's here." Timothy's voice quavered. "I think he's dead."

She stared down at the crumpled body propped up against the twisted wheel and dropped to her knees. Gritting her teeth against the overwhelming stench of alcohol and putrid river water, she rested her ear against Penter's chest. Felt for a pulse.

"He's alive. Quick, help me."

They pulled him away from the wheel and Jane slipped behind him, hooked her hands under his armpits, and wrenched them back.

"Stop it! You'll hurt him." Timothy grabbed at her arm, tried to drag her aside.

A jet of foul-smelling river water and vomit spewed from Penter's mouth.

"Go and get help," she said.

"I'll stay. You go."

"No." She dragged in another breath and yanked Penter's arms back again. "First aid. Know what to do. Go."

Timothy stared blindly in the direction of the town.

"Go up the hill until you get to the railway line, half a mile. Then follow it to the station. You'll see Church Street on your right—six hundred paces and you're there. Get John to bring the wagon. Go!"

With one backward glance, Timothy left, loping across the paddock until he faded into the rising mist.

Jane worked on Penter for several more minutes, counting the time between each stretch of his arms, while the foul water spewed from his mouth. When he finally began to splutter, she rolled him onto his side.

There was no sign of Timothy along the bank, so she sat down and drew her knees up, matching her breaths to the rise and fall of Penter's chest. How long would Timothy be? What if Penter died and she was left sitting beside the rising river with a corpse? What rubbish! He was breathing. They'd found him in time. It was hours off sunset, the water level hadn't risen any further, and the rain had eased to a fine drizzle. Timothy could hardly get lost, and if he did, he was quite capable of asking directions to Aileen House.

"A man's job."

Jane crawled closer to Penter.

"See. I did good fer yeh." His lips twisted in a sycophantic grimace. "I did me best."

She crouched to catch his mumbled words. The accent thick and slurred, nothing like the drawling tone she associated with the man in the checked jacket she'd first met at the gallery.

He gave a feeble cough and a stream of fetid water trickled from the corner of his mouth. "I got 'er tucked up. Safe 'n sound. Maggie took t'other. 'Tweren't my fault, Mr. Langdon, sir."

Mr. Langdon? Timothy's great-grandfather?

"Did like yeh said." He struggled to push upright.

Jane tucked her hands under his arms and tried to lift him but his weight was too much.

"Ain't told no one. Not ever. Kept me mouth shut." He lolled to one side and she lost her grip.

"Still got me shiny sovereign." His hand groped for the inside pocket of his jacket, then fell free and his eyelids fluttered closed.

Jane sat, her eyes fixed on his bleached face. After a few moments, the frantic movement of his eyeballs behind his closed lids ceased and his pale eyes flashed open.

What should she do? She rested the palm of her hand against his chest, felt the feeble rise and fall. "Not long now, Mr. Penter. Timothy will be back soon. We'll get you home."

"G'woam." A satisfied smirk settled, as though everything had worked out just the way he'd planned.

Jane felt for his pulse, rested her ear against his chest. A plaintive sigh whisked between his blue lips and his body went limp.

She lurched upright. Penter's sightless eyes gazed at her. No breath, no sign of life. Easing his limp body flat, she choked back a sob. There was little she could do until Timothy returned.

What she wouldn't give to know the thoughts that had left that look on his face. Gently she lowered his lids before sliding her hand into his inside pocket.

Her fingers closed over a round metal disc. A polished coin, still warm.

She swallowed the lump in her throat and angled it to the single ray of sun breaching the clouds.

The head of the young Queen Victoria encircled by the words *Victoria Dei Gratia* and beneath, the date—*1862.*

The year Daisy Dibble vanished.

———— ≈ ————

Jane's face pulsed warm as she tried to make sense of Penter's words. If only Michael were still alive and she could talk to him. She gazed at the growing break in the clouds, far more fanciful than she'd ever admit, hoping Michael was looking down, guiding her.

Perhaps he was. Through the clearing mist, Timothy came running down the hill. She stood up, pushed the wet hair off her face, and walked toward the man she might very well have fallen in love with, to tell him his father was dead.

"Don't say anything. I can tell from the look on your face." Timothy pulled her to him and hugged her tight. His snatched breaths reverberated against her. "Don't tell me he suffered. I didn't mean what I said to Mother. He made me angry. I hated the way he treated her, but I wouldn't wish anyone to die like this."

It was on the tip of Jane's tongue to tell Timothy of his father's words, of the theory that had formed while she sat by Penter's body, but the memory of walking into the house and finding Michael gone restrained her. That hollowed-out feeling, and worse, the fear. The knowledge that no matter what happened from this point in time, life would be inextricably changed.

———— ≈ ————

Darkness had fallen by the time Jane and Timothy reached Church Street. They'd traipsed back through the town behind the wagon, all the way to the mortuary, neither of them speaking. Both immersed in their own thoughts, knowing their return would herald a torrent of emotion.

Jane took Timothy's hand and led him around the back of the house through the sloshing water, hoping they'd be able to slip inside without having to face Bessie and Lucy. The kitchen was in darkness. They peeled away their oilskins and kicked off their boots, leaving them in a miserable heap on the veranda, and made their way toward the sliver of light spilling beneath the sitting room door.

The moment Jane pushed open the door, Marigold leapt to her feet. Timothy took his mother in his arms and led her to the window.

Elizabeth raised one eyebrow.

Jane shook her head in reply. A great torrent of despair washed through her. "I tried, I really tried. I thought I'd saved him, and after Timothy left he seemed to be breathing normally. He started talking as though in his sleep, dreaming perhaps, his eyes moving beneath his lids. Then he smiled and . . ." Tears rolled down her cheeks and she buried her face in her hands.

Elizabeth patted the cushion next to her and Jane sank down on the sofa.

"Shh. It's not your fault. You did your best." She wrapped her arm around Jane's shoulders and pulled her head close, one hand cupping her cheek.

"That's what Penter said. 'I did me best.' I was too late. I couldn't save him."

Elizabeth's face creased in a frown. "This was not *your* fault. I know you did your best. You always do. Now take yourself upstairs, you're exhausted. I'll bring you a cup of tea."

"Bessie and Lucy have gone to bed." Jane wiped the back of her hand under her nose.

"Surprising as it may seem, I am quite capable of making a cup of tea. Now, off you go. I shall see Marigold and Timothy settled and be with you shortly."

Casting one last look at Timothy and Marigold, Jane slipped through the door and made her way up to her attic bedroom. The next day she would have to tell them of Penter's last words; now was not the moment.

Half asleep, comforted by the sliver of moonlight illuminating her bed, Jane was taken by surprise by the knock on her bedroom door. Before she'd managed to get out of bed, Elizabeth had put a tray on the corner of her desk. Waiting for the inevitable complaint about the state of her room, she swung her legs over the edge of the bed and struggled to get up.

"Get back under the covers. I don't want you catching a chill. You spent all day sopping wet." She passed Jane a cup of black tea and poured her own jasmine tea into her favorite cup.

In the moonlight, Elizabeth's hair shone. *"Daisy's hair was the color of autumn leaves."* Marigold's words slipped into her mind as stealthily as the auction house's cat.

"Do you mind if we talk?" Elizabeth settled on the side of the bed as though it were a nightly ritual.

Jane jerked upright, a little of her tea spilling onto the sheet. She brushed it aside, unsure how, or even if, she should respond. The look on Elizabeth's face was one she'd never seen before, unguarded perhaps, and in the low light Jane fancied they could be two friends sharing each other's secrets.

"While you and Timothy were gone, Marigold and I talked. We

talked all morning and afternoon." A look of surprise flashed across her face. "I feel such a connection with her. We have a similar outlook, yet our lives have been so different." Elizabeth sipped her tea and let out a luxurious sigh. "Seeing you with Timothy and sipping jasmine tea makes me realize how much, how very much I've missed Jing."

Every nerve in Jane's body stilled. She didn't even draw breath. She'd never heard mention of Jing.

"I was telling Marigold about him, and explaining to her the way I'd allowed my life to be ruled by Michael. I was trying to make her see that Penter's manipulation was no fault of her own. Despite all our brave words about women's rights, we are products of an earlier age."

Elizabeth ran her finger around the lip of the paper-thin cup, then placed it onto the tray. "She, in turn, recounted her own story—her time in Paris, and the way she and Penter had grown apart, how he'd strived to better himself, moved from nothing more than a peasant pigeon-keeper to the manager of the huge Langdon estate."

"Pigeon-keeper." The word exploded from Jane's mouth.

"Yes, pigeon-keeper. Such a quaint term. I don't think we have them in Australia. Not a job I would relish. All those birds."

"Aunt Elizabeth, stop!" She rocketed out of bed. "I've been trying to tell you this since yesterday. When you and Marigold left the auction house I talked to Timothy."

"You seem to have established quite a rapport with the young fellow."

"This is more important. Listen!"

Elizabeth's eyes flashed. "Continue."

"Marigold's painting of *The Village Church*—I missed something, made a mistake. The building in the foreground is not a mausoleum, as I presumed. It's a dovecot, a pigeon house. It used to be part of the

Langdon estate. It was sold off about twenty years ago and incorporated into the churchyard."

"A pigeon house, you say. Birds. Well, that might perhaps account for my reaction to the painting." Her eyes flickered and she turned her gaze to the window. "There was a pigeon tree in Hill End. I hated it. When the birds came home to roost they'd flock, squawking and flapping in a great cloud. I always avoided it. I was telling Marigold about it. We swapped so many stories of our childhood."

"The dovecot is the one thing that connects everything." Jane's mind spiraled back to the story Timothy had told her about his father growing up on the estate and taking the Langdon name. "Did Marigold say anything about Penter, how she met him, why she married him? They seem so very different."

"They do, don't they. She did say that no matter what he'd done she couldn't fault him for the way he'd worked his way up . . ." Elizabeth's eyes widened. "Oh good heavens . . ."

With a satisfying *clank*, rather like the beads on the abacus, Jane saw the connection become clear to Elizabeth. "Is there anything else you remember?"

As she twirled a flyaway strand of hair around and around her index finger, Elizabeth's cheeks pinked. "I haven't felt I should share the few memories that have surfaced . . ."

Jane's head came up with a snap. "More repressed memories?"

"I have no idea. To be honest, I don't know if they are simply dreams."

"Have you told Dr. Lethbridge?"

"Of course not. One more seal on my doolally status." Jane shifted to the edge of the bed.

"First the birds, obviously swooping, their wings brushing my cheeks, and the smell, an awful smell I can't get from my throat."

Elizabeth's hand rose and her fingers wrapped around her long neck. "I have such a feeling of claustrophobia, as if I was confined in a small space. And trains. I don't like trains." She covered her ears with her hands. "The noise. As if my heart is pounding, about to burst from my chest."

"That's why you won't travel to Sydney."

"I used to, when the steamers still ran up to Morpeth, but no, I haven't left Maitland for many years. I feel safe here."

Elizabeth's cobwebbed memories slipped neatly into the picture forming in Jane's mind. "A train line runs from Yeovil to Liverpool."

"When Michael told me about the fire at the workhouse, I remembered answering to Lizzie's name, but not much more. And Marigold's painting is wrong. I didn't want to go with him. He ran, tucked me under his arm like a squealing pig." Elizabeth dropped her head into her hands, her shoulders heaving as the tears rolled down her cheeks.

"Him? Who is he? Who didn't you want to go with?"

"I don't know. He squashed me under his arm and ran and ran, then threw me into the dark and the birds came." Elizabeth's head came up and her eyes widened. "He put me in the dovecot."

"I think he did, and then he took you on the train to Liverpool and left you at the workhouse."

"Who?"

"I believe it was Penter, the pigeon-keeper."

As the words left Jane's lips, the truth of it settled in her mind. *"I got 'er tucked up safe 'n sound. 'Tweren't my fault, Mr. Langdon, sir. Did like yeh said. Ain't told no one. Not ever."* "I think Timothy's great-grandfather put him up to it."

Elizabeth's face creased into a frown. "Langdon? Why— Why would he?"

"Timothy told me he saw Daisy and Marigold as stains on the

family name. They were born out of wedlock." She bent down to the pile of damp clothes she'd dropped onto the floor and rummaged through the pocket of her skirt. "I believe Langdon paid Penter. Before Penter died he said he'd done as Langdon said and hadn't told anyone. Said he'd kept his mouth shut."

Jane held out the sovereign. "I'm not very proud of this. I took it from Mr. Penter's pocket after he died. I think he'd kept it as some kind of talisman."

Elizabeth took the coin and turned it over in her fingers. "It's dated 1862." Her eyes filled with tears. "I wish Michael was here."

EPILOGUE

MAITLAND TOWN, 1913

Jane cast one last look around the auction room and crossed to Timothy's side. "I think everything is ready."

"It looks perfect, and so do you." He tipped the brim of her new straw boater, smiled, and held out his hands to her. "I had my doubts we'd ever see the day."

It had been a difficult few weeks. Penter's funeral had had to be postponed, and his body had laid in the mortuary until the flood-waters receded, along with a Mr. Egan of Morpeth. He, too, had perished trying to cross the Wallis Creek bridge, the poor man.

The waters had continued to rise after the rain stopped and turned High Street into a river. They had to cart all Marigold's paintings upstairs and delay the exhibition. Jane and Timothy worked alongside the townsfolk, plying High Street in a rowboat, handing out blankets and rations to those trapped in their houses and then helping with the dreadful clean-up. However, the good moments well outweighed the bad.

"Time to open up." Jane peered out into the street at the large crowd who had gathered on the footpath, impatient for the exhibition to open.

"I'll unlock the doors and let them in," said Timothy. "You go and get Mother and Aunt Elizabeth. They said they wouldn't come down until everyone was settled."

Jane clattered up the stairs. At last the time had come to lay all the rumors to rest, and Elizabeth seemed to relish the opportunity. She and Marigold had spent every moment together, talking long into the night and making plans for the future, both firmly convinced Elizabeth was Marigold's long-lost twin sister, Daisy.

Much to Lethbridge's interest, Elizabeth had continued to remember snippets from the past. The color of a cushion, the placement of the rocking chair by the fire, the words of the lullaby Maggie had sung every night.

But it wasn't until the evening Marigold produced her art folio and showed them the picture she had painted of Daisy as she'd imagined her to be at eighteen that the last remaining skerrick of doubt was laid to rest. Sealed by a faded photograph Elizabeth produced, taken in Hill End in 1872, showing an identical young girl.

"Are you ready?" Jane stuck her head around the door.

"Indeed we are," Elizabeth and Marigold replied in unison.

Jane stood behind and waited until they reached the bottom of the stairs. A hush fell as they made their way to the auction table at the front of the room.

With a flourish, Elizabeth brought the gavel down hard on the cedar tabletop. "Ladies and gentlemen, welcome."

She paused while the two-hundred-strong crowd settled. "Before I undertake this momentous occasion, I would like to say a few words. We have not only lived through a monstrous natural disaster, we have lived through a flood of emotion." She reached for Marigold's hand and drew her closer. "You may think you know me; after all, Miss Elizabeth Quinn has been something of a fixture in Maitland Town for more years than I care to remember. I stand here in front of you today to tell you a little more about the woman you think you know."

Not a movement, not a sound. Every one of them captivated by Elizabeth's words. Jane couldn't resist a wry grin as she slid into the spot next to Timothy and took his hand. That alone would give Mrs. Witherspoon and her cronies something to chew over.

"I didn't begin life as Elizabeth Quinn. In fact, I was born Daisy Dibble, and, as many of you rightly ascertained, Michael was *not* my brother. I grew up believing he was, but the fact is, we were not related. I'm not even Irish, as I'd always thought. I was born in Somerset, in a little village not far from Yeovil, one of twins." She paused, turned her head to Marigold, and smiled. "I would like to introduce you to someone dear to my heart, my sister, Marigold Penter."

The silence was palpable, enough fuel to stoke a long-lasting bushfire. Though how anyone had failed to recognize Elizabeth's and Marigold's similarity was now beyond Jane's comprehension. With their hair drawn back in neat chignons, their facial structure was identical. There may never be any tangible proof, but as Elizabeth had assured Jane in a remarkably un-Elizabeth-like comment, their souls knew, and that would suffice. The world would simply have to accept it.

"At the age of four I was deposited on the doorsteps of Brownlow Hill, the Liverpool workhouse," Elizabeth continued. "Michael rescued me from that atrocious place and together we came to Australia and forged a new life, a life that brought us both a great deal of pleasure."

Across a sea of smiling faces, even the gossips remained silent, for now they knew it all. So many people from the town, so many she counted as friends, so many Elizabeth and Michael had helped. There would be nothing to feed their curiosity now.

When the first mutters of conversation began, Elizabeth stilled the crowd again with a raised hand. "Marigold and I intend to travel to England where I shall reacquaint myself with my roots. I will be leaving Quinn Family Auctioneers and Accountants in Jane's and Timothy's capable hands."

Thunderous applause greeted her words.

"Marigold and I will then return to Maitland to free Jane to accept the place she has been offered at the University of Sydney to study mathematics."

Jane hugged her arms tight as the bubble of euphoria threatened to carry her away. With all the events of the past weeks, she'd as good as forgotten sitting the entrance exam, and when the letter arrived it had come as more than a shock. Elizabeth had simply offered her trademark smile and said that she hoped she'd follow in Fanny Hunt's footsteps.

Timothy's reaction had been slightly less enthusiastic, until Jane pointed out that his mother had a career and so had she. There was little difference. Finally he'd embraced her, and the idea, on the condition she would consider his marriage proposal once she graduated.

After a slight pause, and some looks of askance from some members of the audience who likely believed a woman's place was at home, a series of loud claps resounded from the back of the room. Somewhat reluctantly, the assembled crowd joined in offering their congratulations.

"And now," Elizabeth's voice rose, "it is with great pleasure that I open this exhibition of my sister's work. I give you the renowned English artist, Marigold Penter."

Applause broke out once more and Elizabeth stepped back, surveying the packed room. Her face paled. Her lips formed a single word and curved into what may have been a smile, and her arms lifted.

Jane's heart stuttered. Not again, not now, not in front of all of these people. She took two steps toward Elizabeth, ready to support her if she fell. Lethbridge pushed through the crowd to her side, and Jane's gaze came to rest on a lone figure leaning on a cane at the back of the room.

———— ≈ ————

Memory or imagination? More ghosts rearing up from the past? Elizabeth had no idea, but she had every intention of being more than a passive observer. With a silent apology to Michael, she stepped from the raised platform, shunning every one of the well-wishers, intent only on traversing the length of the auction room.

"Miss Elizabeth."

He removed his bowler hat and smiled with such pleasure, she forgot everything and ran into his embrace. And while the stunned audience of Maitland's finest drew an outraged gasp, the scent of incense, jasmine, and never-forgotten love enveloped her.

Finally, Miss Elizabeth Quinn could lay the past to rest.

HISTORICAL NOTE

The Girl in the Painting is a work of fiction, an invented narrative, inspired by imagination yet based around a series of unconnected historical events. I very much hope that if you are reading this you have already read the story—there may be a spoiler or two!

On September 7, 1862, a serious fire broke out at the workhouse in Liverpool, England, destroying the chapel and one of the children's dormitories. Twenty-one children and two nurses burned to death.

Child migration has a long and checkered past and is well documented. The first one hundred children, "vagrants," were dispatched from London to Virginia in the Americas in 1618, while the last nine children were flown to Australia in 1967 under the auspices of Barnardo's. In all, more than one hundred thousand children were sent from Britain to Canada, Australia, and other Commonwealth countries through various child migration schemes. Many came from workhouses or were found destitute and homeless in overcrowded cities and declining rural areas. Each set of embarkation papers recorded the name, religion, and education but not an exact date of birth. Passengers were listed as either an adult (over fourteen years of age) or a child (seven to fourteen, four to seven, and one to four).

On March 12, 1868, at Clontarf, a popular picnicking spot on Sydney Harbor, an Irishman, Henry James O'Farrell, attempted to assassinate Queen Victoria's son, Prince Alfred. Although O'Farrell fired his pistol at close range, the bullet inflicted only a slight wound, thanks to the prince's braces, according to some accounts, and the prince recovered completely. O'Farrell narrowly escaped lynching by the crowd and was immediately arrested. The events that followed included an outpouring of prejudice and racism toward the Irish. The New South Wales government passed the Treason Felony Act, making it an offense to refuse to drink to the queen's health; however, they failed to uncover any conspiracy. O'Farrell was convicted of attempted murder and was hung. A public subscription fund was opened to finance a hospital to commemorate Prince Alfred's safe recovery, known today as the Royal Prince Alfred Hospital, Camperdown.

The history of Hill End in the second half of the nineteenth century is well known and thoroughly documented largely thanks to the Holtermann Collection, one of the world's most unique collections of glass wet-plate negatives. They came to light in 1945 in the back shed of a house in North Sydney. On my most recent visit to Hill End I discovered the Heritage Centre, a brilliant interactive museum that brings the sights and sounds of the past rushing back through a series of recordings, photographs, and artifacts of the European history of the area and also that of the Chinese who were among the earliest gold diggers at Hill End. And of course, tribute is paid to Holtermann and his gold nugget found October 19, 1872, at the Star of Hope Gold Mine.

The Art Gallery of NSW and Maitland Technical College, now Maitland Art Gallery, were both built by Walter Liberty Vernon. In 1890, he was appointed NSW government architect and is responsible for many other buildings that make Sydney the city it is today—the

HISTORICAL NOTE

Mitchell Library, Central Station, Long Bay Gaol, and Customs House to name but a few.

Tost and Rohu, the mother-and-daughter taxidermy artists who ran "the Queerest Shop in Sydney," have featured in my books before. An exhibition of their work, the giant diprotodon and paintings from the National Gallery, were shown in Maitland at the technical college, and reports can be found in the *Maitland Mercury*.

Maitland has suffered a series of floods since the town's establishment in the early nineteenth century. Although longer lasting than many, the 1913 flood caused the least loss, but poor Mr. Egan died attempting to take his sulky across the Wallis Creek bridge. Today the town is protected by a large levy bank.

Norton-sub-Hamdon is a village in the English county of Somerset, five miles west of Yeovil. The manor was granted after the Norman conquest; however, it was broken up and sold in the 1850s (a fact I chose to ignore for the purposes of this story!).

And lastly, the name "the Australian Labour Party" was adopted in 1908, but the spelling was changed to "Labor" in 1912 (right in the middle of the story). For the sake of consistency, I have used the modern spelling throughout.

So, those are the facts I weaved through the story of *The Girl in the Painting*. The major players, the other characters, and the events that shaped their lives are figments of my imagination. My aim was to produce a story that, though fictional, was plausible. I hope I've achieved that aim and you, the reader, have enjoyed following in Michael's and Elizabeth's footsteps.

ACKNOWLEDGMENTS

I would like to acknowledge the Wiradjuri and Wonnarua people as the traditional owners of the land where this story is set and pay my respects to Elders both past and present.

There are so many people I wish to thank: my wonderful publisher, Jo Mackay, and her team at HQ fiction; Annabel Blay and Dianne Blacklock for their assistance in turning my manuscript into a real book; the marvelous designer Darren Holt, who has produced my favorite cover to date; Natika Palka and the HarperCollins sales team, who take my stories out into the world; and James Kellow for providing the very first spark of inspiration for this story. And in the US my thanks to Amanda Bostic, Julie Monroe, and every member of the Thomas Nelson fiction team. It is an ongoing pleasure and privilege to work with you all.

Thanks also to the numerous people who help me with my research: Daphne Shead, researcher and founder of the Hill End Family History group, who allowed me access to some of her amazing files; Ann Campbell of the Maitland Family and Local History Research Group, who read a very early draft of *The Girl in the Painting* to check if I had the flavor of Maitland; and Ray Richards of the Lost Maitland Facebook group, for his help with the history of the steamships. And finally, the State Library of NSW. What a wonderful organization!

As always my thanks to chief historian, Carl Hoipo, and chief researcher #1, Charles, particularly for his help with Jane's outlandish mathematical calculations; and also to Dawn—there's a little bit of you in Jane. Do you still know the train timetable by heart?

To my daughter, Katy, my writing friends, and my Wollombi friends, and most especially my critique partners, Sarah Barrie and Ann Harrison, for braving my dreaded first drafts. Thank you for your support and patience.

And finally, to you, my wonderful readers, thank you for all your support, reviews, emails, encouragement, and enthusiasm. You are the icing on the VoVos!

DISCUSSION QUESTIONS

1. From the opening chapter, Jane defines herself around her orphaned status, sharing her secret dream that Florence Nightingale would one day come claim Jane as her own. How do you think Jane's parentage influences her relationship with the Quinns? Do you think being an orphan helped her see more to Elizabeth's story?

2. How did the Quinns' recognition of Jane's mathematical ability change the course of her life, as both an orphan and a woman in the early 1900s?

3. Jing and Elizabeth forged a relationship during a time when interracial relationships were unwelcome. What did you think of their relationship? How did becoming friends with Elizabeth impact the trajectory of Jing's life? What did their relationship show Elizabeth about the racism experienced by Chinese immigrants in Australia? What do you think of Michael's reaction to their close friendship?

4. Michael made a lot of decisions for Elizabeth without her involvement. What do you think of his decision to pretend Elizabeth was his deceased sister? Do you think he should have attempted to find Elizabeth's birth family sooner or told

her the truth of her identity? How might knowing the truth of her past have mitigated Elizabeth's traumatized response to seeing the painting?

5. Michael finally decides to research Elizabeth's history but still does not tell her he is doing so. He says in chapter 25 that "all he'd ever intended . . . was to keep her safe." Is safety the same thing as love? Knowing the triggering experience Elizabeth has to the painting and the following period of anguish, did Michael succeed? Is safety more important than honesty?

6. Did you suspect the connection between Elizabeth and Marigold? How did the two sisters (Elizabeth/Daisy and Marigold) cope differently with the trauma of Elizabeth's abduction and disappearance?

7. At the end of the book Elizabeth says, "Despite all our brave words about women's rights, we are products of an earlier age." What do you think she means by this? How is this book about women's rights, or lack thereof?

8. What do you think the future holds for Elizabeth and Jing, who the author suggests has returned to Elizabeth in the epilogue? What is the significance of the red thread Jing gave Elizabeth early in the book?

9. Loss of a parent or being orphaned early in life is a shared bond between many of the characters: Jane, Elizabeth, Michael, Jing, and Marigold. On page 176 Jing says, "It is lonely to be without a family." Discuss the significance of family, both biological and created, in the story. What does the word *family* mean to you?

ABOUT THE AUTHOR

Copyright © Katy Clymo

Tea Cooper is an established Australian author of historical fiction. In a past life she was a teacher, a journalist, and a farmer. These days she haunts museums and indulges her passion for storytelling. She is the bestselling author of several novels, including *The Horse Thief*, *The Cedar Cutter*, *The Currency Lass*, and *The Naturalist's Daughter*.

———— ≫ ————

teacooperauthor.com
Instagram: @tea_cooper
Twitter: @TeaCooper1
Facebook: @TeaCooper
Pinterest: @teacooperauthor